Ashes and Understanding

A Pride & Prejudice Variation

Tiffany Thomas

Dedication

For the brave first responders
who run into flame, flood, and fury
to rescue those in need of saving.

Table of Contents

Prologue

Derbyshire, February 1795

Twelve-year-old Fitzwilliam Darcy pinched his lips together, desperately trying to hold back the severe coughing fit that threatened to overwhelm his emaciated frame.

It had been three months since a bout of influenza had laid him low, and though the fever had long since broken, the lingering effects of pneumonia still clung to him like a shadow. Each breath felt like a labor, and every laugh turned into a painful hack that left him weak and trembling.

He adjusted the blanket draped over his legs, willing his body to cooperate. Across from him, George Wickham shuffled a deck of cards with practiced ease, grinning mischievously.

"Come now, Fitz," George said, dealing the next hand. "Surely you cannot let me win every round."

Fitzwilliam smirked faintly, though his voice was hoarse. "You've only won because I have been too generous to point out your blatant cheating."

George pressed a hand to his chest in mock offense. "Cheating? Me? Never."

The two boys dissolved into laughter, but the sound caught in Darcy's throat. He leaned forward, clutching his chest as another violent paroxysm overtook him. George was on his feet in an instant, steadying him and handing him a handkerchief.

"Easy, Fitz. Do not strain yourself," George's tone was unusually gentle.

1

Darcy waved him off weakly, taking small sips until the fit subsided. "I am fine," he rasped, though his voice was hoarse. "Just… do not make me laugh again."

George grinned. "No promises."

Resuming his seat, George began to deal the cards. "I might let you win this one, out of the goodness of my heart, of course. One must have pity on the less fortunate, after all."

Before Fitzwilliam could respond, the door to Fitzwilliam's bedroom swung open. Mr. George Darcy strode in, his presence commanding and his expression as severe as ever. His eyes darkened as his gaze fell on his son, lying in bed in the middle of the day.

"What is this?" Mr. Darcy demanded, his voice sharp. "Still in your nightclothes, even though it has been months since you fell ill? Playing cards, laughing like a fool and wheezing like an invalid? This is *not* how a Darcy behaves."

Fitzwilliam looked down, his hands tightening around the blanket. "I—"

"Spare me your excuses," Mr. Darcy snapped, cutting him off. "You are a disgrace, Fitzwilliam. Weak and pathetic, lying here like an invalid. I had hoped the Darcy blood would prevail, but it seems your mother's influence is stronger than I feared."

Wickham spoke up, his usual easy charm laced with tension. "Sir, if I may—Fitz has been improving. The doctor said laughter can lift the spirits, and he's been doing much better this week."

"Silence," Mr. Darcy snapped, his eyes narrowing. "I will not have you making excuses for him. He is my son and will answer for himself."

Struggling to sit upright, though his weakened frame trembled with the effort. "Father, I—"

"Enough," Mr. Darcy interrupted, his tone cold. "You are a disappointment, Fitzwilliam. Weak, feeble. You lie here wasting away while other boys your age grow strong and capable. I can only hope going to school next year will toughen you."

Fitzwilliam flushed deeply, ashamed that his friend was witnessing— for the first time— Mr. Darcy's berating of his son. In the past, he had always envied the rapport between his father and his friend, especially as George always told Fitzwilliam how he wished his own father was more like Mr. Darcy.

Wickham, his voice steady despite the tension in the air, said in a pleading voice, "Sir, Fitz has been improving. The doctor said he needs rest—"

"And you think I do not know what my son needs?" Mr. Darcy's voice was sharp as a blade. "I know what he lacks. Strength. Discipline." He turned back to Fitzwilliam, his expression cold. "You are your mother's spawn, boy. I suppose it is fitting you bear her family's name."

Darcy flinched, but he did not reply. His father stared at him for a moment longer before turning on his heel and leaving the room. The door closed behind him with a sharp click, leaving an oppressive silence in his wake.

The words stung, and Fitzwilliam looked away, his pale hands clutching the blanket tightly. Wickham's fists clenched at his sides, but he said nothing. Fitzwilliam could see his friend's bewilderment, unsure of how to respond to what to him was quite uncharacteristic behavior.

After a long, tense silence, Mr. Darcy straightened his coat and turned on his heel. "Perhaps school will succeed where I have failed. I can only hope." With that, he left, the door closing behind him with a decisive click.

The room was quiet for a moment before Wickham let out a low whistle. "Well," he said, his tone light but forced, "I would say he's in a particularly foul mood today. Perhaps the valet tied his cravat too tight."

Darcy sighed, sinking back against the pillows. "You needn't defend me, George. It only makes things worse." His words were punctuated by sharp coughs. When the fit finally ended, he said casually, "Besides, it is no different than what he's said to me before. He got worse after Mother died giving birth to Georgiana."

"I have always thought him quite amiable," George said. "But just now... that was not just chastisement— it was cruelty."

"He believes it builds character."

"Character," Wickham repeated, the word laced with disdain. He shook his head, running a hand through his dark hair. "I have always thought your father was stern with you based on what you said, but this... I never imagined."

Darcy offered a wan smile. "He's different with you, George. You are not his son."

The words hung in the air, heavy and undeniable. Wickham frowned, his earlier good humor evaporating. "It does not excuse him," he muttered. "You do not deserve that, Fitz. No one does."

Before Darcy could reply, a soft knock at the door drew their attention. A maid stepped inside, balancing a tray with a teapot and cups. She curtsied, her cheeks tinged pink. "Your tea, Master Fitzwilliam."

A knock at the door interrupted them, and a maid entered, carrying a tray with a teapot and cups. Darcy offered her a faint smile. "Thank you, Emily."

She curtsied, her cheeks pink. "Of course, sir."

George stood and took the tray from her hands with an easy charm. "Allow me."

Emily lingered, her eyes darting toward Wickham. "If you need anything else, Master George, just call." Her voice was soft, almost coquettish.

Fitzwilliam braced himself for one of George's usual flirtatious comments, but instead, his friend hesitated and looked back at him. Something shifted in his eyes, and he gave the maid a polite nod. "Thank you, Emily."

She curtsied again, looking puzzled, then left the room. Wickham set the tray down and poured a cup of tea for Darcy, his movements unusually subdued.

Darcy took the cup with a curious glance. "What happened to the George Wickham who never met a pretty face he could not charm?"

Wickham shrugged, handing him a saucer. "I do not know. These last few months... helping you, being here—it feels different. Better. Not the usual 'sneak into the stables' kind of fun, but real. Like I have done something right for once."

Darcy studied his friend, a small smile tugging at the corners of his lips. "That's what it feels like to do good, George. To help others, to think beyond yourself."

Wickham settled back into his chair, his usual bravado replaced with a quiet introspection. "It is strange, though. I have spent so much time causing trouble, I almost do not know what to do with this... feeling."

"You get used to it," Darcy said simply. "It is why I try to do what is right, even when it is difficult. It is worth it."

Wickham stared at him for a long moment, his usual bravado replaced with something quieter, more introspective. "You are a strange one, Fitz. But maybe you are onto something. I think... I will try it your way. Being good. At least for a little while."

Darcy chuckled softly, though it was punctuated by a brief cough. "A good place to start."

Wickham grinned, though there was a new sincerity behind it. "Then it is settled. I will try to be more like you. Though do not let it go to your head."

Darcy smirked faintly. "Perish the thought."

The two boys lapsed into a companionable silence, the tension of the earlier encounter fading into the warmth of their shared resolve. For the first time in months, Fitzwilliam felt a glimmer of hope—not just for his recovery, but for the bond they had forged through hardship.

Perhaps going to school will not be so terrible after all; not when George is going with me.

Hertfordshire, December 1805

Twelve-year-old Elizabeth Bennet looked down anxiously at her seven-year-old sister, Kitty. *Just keep breathing*, she pleaded.

The household had been struck by an influenza of some kind that had resulted in everyone feeling ill with fevers, body aches, and coughs for a week. Each member of the Bennet family had recovered— save Kitty, who was left with a cough that wracked her thin frame. More than once, Elizabeth had watched in terror as Kitty's lips turned blue, the sight haunting her even in her dreams.

Mrs. Bennet's nerves were shattered, and she retreated to her chambers. The matron claimed she was unable to handle the stress of tending to her second youngest daughter, so the care of the girl was left to Jane, Elizabeth, the nurse, and the occasional visit from Mr. Jones, the apothecary.

But even Mr. Jones had been candid about his limitations.

"I have done all I can," he had admitted after his latest visit, shaking his head as he packed up his case. "The usual remedies are failing her, and I have no knowledge of anything else that might help. I am sorry, but you all may need to prepare yourselves for the worst. She will only decline."

Elizabeth had stood in silence, her chest tight with frustration and fear. As she sat beside Kitty now, dabbing a damp cloth across her sister's forehead, her mind whirled with questions. There had to be something they could do. Someone, somewhere, must know of a remedy.

Her gaze drifted to the window, where the late afternoon light streamed through the curtains. A memory surfaced of her Uncle Gardiner and his tales of far-off places—exotic spices, silks, and herbs brought to London from lands she could scarcely imagine. The thought planted a seed of hope.

"Jane," Elizabeth said softly, looking up at her elder sister. "Do you think Uncle Gardiner might know of something? He imports goods from all over the world, does not he?"

Jane paused in her stitching, her brow furrowing in thought. "He does, though I do not know if he would have knowledge of medicines. Still, it could not hurt to ask."

Elizabeth nodded, determination hardening her features. "I will write to him tonight."

⚹

Two weeks later, Elizabeth sat at the breakfast table with a letter in her hand and a small sachet of dried herbs before her. She had read her uncle's response twice already, her heart lifting with cautious optimism.

Dearest Lizzy,

Your letter touched me deeply, and I am so sorry to hear of poor Kitty's struggles. I have spoken with my managers, who in turn have asked around at the docks. Some of the workers—immigrants from far-off lands—shared knowledge of remedies used in their countries for ailments like the one you described.

Enclosed are some dried herbs one of them recommended, along with instructions for preparing them. Many of their suggestions are for plants that do not grow in England, so I have sent inquiries for many to be brought with my regular imports.

I cannot promise they will work, but I will continue to inquire and send along anything else I discover. Give my love to Kitty and the family. My betrothed, Madeline, likewise sends her regards and begs me to tell you that Kitty is in her prayers.

I think you will like your new aunt, Lizzy.

Yours affectionately,

Edward Gardiner

Elizabeth turned the sachet over in her hands, the faint scent of the herbs unfamiliar yet oddly comforting. "Jane," she said, looking up, "I think we should try this."

Jane glanced at the letter, her expression cautious. "Do you think Mr. Jones will agree?"

Elizabeth's jaw set in quiet resolve. "He must. If we do nothing, Kitty…" She could not bring herself to say the words.

Mr. Jones was sent for, and he warily looked at the small package. "Well, I suppose there is no harm in trying it," he admitted when Elizabeth pressed it into his hands. "Lord knows she will die in any case."

Leaving Jane with Kitty, Elizabeth led the apothecary to the still room, where Mr. Jones carefully prepare the mixture according to Mr. Gardiner's instructions. Together, they steeped the herbs in hot water from the kitchen until the room was filled with their strange, earthy aroma.

ϒ

Hertfordshire, February 1809

The Bennet household was alive with the usual morning bustle. The sound of chairs scraping against the floor, the clink of teacups, and the murmur of conversation filled the breakfast room. Mr. Bennet unfolded his newspaper with a decisive snap, the scent of ink mingling with the aroma of freshly baked bread.

Suddenly, a pair of hands covered Elizabeth's eyes from behind. "Guess who?" said a gruff voice.

Elizabeth sniffed. "Lydia," she declared with certainty.

Lydia pouted and slid into her chair. "It is not fair. Elizabeth always gets it right."

"Because she can *smell* us," Kitty said with a smirk. "Like a dog can."

Elizabeth nearly snorted, part amused and part offended. Mr. Bennet looked up from his newspaper. "Indeed, a most useful trait in a daughter—provided she does not start barking at visitors."

Everyone burst into laughter and resumed their breakfast. Mr. Bennet was halfway through the front page when he abruptly exclaimed, "Well, now, that's quite the disaster."

Elizabeth, now sixteen years of age, looked up sharply. "What is it, Papa? Surely not news of the French?"

"Napoleon?" Mr. Bennet blinked at her with a confused expression. "No, no. He remains where he ought—for now. Though I do appreciate your flair for the dramatic, Lizzy. This, however, concerns matters much closer to home on our own shores."

"What is it, then?" Jane asked softly, her hands resting neatly in her lap.

Mr. Bennet adjusted his spectacles and peered over the paper. "Drury Lane. Burned to the ground last night."

Elizabeth gasped, her hand flying to her mouth. "Drury Lane? Surely not!" Memories of glittering chandeliers, the velvet-covered seats, and the actors' powerful voices filled her mind. "Surely you are jesting?" she pleaded.

"I never jest about such matters, my dear," he replied, holding the newspaper aloft. "It says here the blaze began late last night and consumed the building entirely."

"It was magnificent," Elizabeth murmured sadly, more to herself than anyone else.

Jane's brows knit together. "How terrible. Were the fire brigades unable to extinguish it, then?"

"Apparently not," Mr. Bennet said, his tone dry. "It seems the firemen did not arrive until an hour after the blaze began. And when they did arrive, there was no water to be had."

"No water?" Elizabeth echoed, incredulous. "But they have—*had* those large cisterns on the roof, did they not?"

"Empty," he said with a shrug. "No one knows why, at least not yet. By the time other sources of water were found, the fire had consumed nearly everything."

Jane placed a hand to her heart. "Was anyone hurt?"

"One man killed," Mr. Bennet replied, his tone sober. "A wall collapsed on him during the efforts to extinguish the flames. Beyond that, very little could be saved."

Mary set down her toast, her expression somber. "It is a tragedy that such a cultural institution could be lost to negligence."

Elizabeth nodded, her mind drifting to the performances she had seen there with the Gardiners. "I remember how grand it was," she said wistfully. "The chandeliers sparkling, the actors commanding the stage. Jane, do you recall the evening we saw Twelfth Night?"

Jane's lips curved into a small smile. "I do. You were so taken with Viola's line, 'Make me a willow cabin at your gate.' You repeated it for days afterward."

Elizabeth grinned. "Well, it is a fine line. Shakespeare knew how to turn a phrase."

Mary sighed heavily. "I suppose I shall not attend the theater when I visit the Gardiners after all. I was quite looking forward to my first play."

"Not unless you care to sit among the ashes," Mr. Bennet quipped, earning a giggle from Lydia.

"Perhaps when it is rebuilt before your come-out," Jane said with a gentle smile.

"Rebuilt?" Mr. Bennet scoffed, folding the paper. "With what funds? The theater was already drowning in debt from its recent refurbishments. I will eat my hat if Sheridan will not be in debt for three hundred thousand pounds by the time it is finished, and I doubt insurance will cover a tenth of that."

"Three hundred thousand?" gasped Lydia. "La, I should be an actress with that kind of money!"

Kitty giggled along with her sister, but both fell silent at a quelling look from their father. A thought struck her, and her eyes widened. "Does this mean all of London could burn again, like it did before?"

"Do not be silly," Lydia scoffed. "They are far too clever now to let that happen."

"Are they?" Mrs. Bennet fretted, waving a handkerchief. "Oh, Mr. Bennet, what of my brother and his family? Could they be in danger?"

Mr. Bennet sighed. "Calm yourself, my dear. Your brother lives in Cheapside, which is a great distance from the theaters. London is not the tinderbox it once was."

"Why not?" Kitty asked, her face as anxious as her mother's.

"Well, after the Great Fire of 1666, they rebuilt the city with wider streets and brick buildings to prevent such a calamity from occurring again.

That, coupled with the formation of fire brigades, new building regulations, and tiled roofs should prevent even large fires from wreaking complete destruction."

"But two theaters have burned in a matter of months," Elizabeth pointed out, her tone thoughtful. "First Covent Garden, now Drury Lane. That cannot be a coincidence."

Jane tilted her head, her voice gentle. "Perhaps it is merely unfortunate timing."

"Perhaps," Elizabeth allowed. "But it seems odd. And to think," Elizabeth said, her tone lighter, "that we shall never again hear, 'If music be the food of love, play on,' from such a stage." She glanced at Jane with a wistful smile.

Mr. Bennet shook his head, standing with his customary air of wearied patience. "That is quite enough excitement for one morning. I have spoken more to my children than I care to in a day. I shall retire to my study to recover." He gave them all a grin and bow, then left the room.

The Bennet sisters exchanged smiles, knowing their father to be in jest. Despite the dire news, their father's wit remained as constant as the rising sun.

As Elizabeth looked around the room at her sisters and mother, whose conversation moved to lighter topics, she could not help but feel a pang of unease lingering beneath her outward composure. While Mrs. Bennet and her daughters spoke of casual nothings, —the newest fashions, Lydia's endless fantasies of balls, and Kitty's musings on ribbons—Elizabeth's mind remained tethered to the morning's news.

Two theaters, both pillars of London's culture, reduced to ashes in such a short span of time. It was troubling, to say the least. The thought of those glittering halls, now blackened ruins, struck a melancholy chord. More than that, it unsettled her sense of security, reminding her how fragile even the grandest institutions could be.

Her gaze settled on Jane, whose gentle countenance radiated calm as she sipped her tea. Elizabeth envied her sister's ability to find hope in any situation. Mary, ever serious, was busy jotting notes into her little book— likely some reflection on the moral lesson to be gleaned from the morning's discussion. Kitty and Lydia, meanwhile, were already squabbling over who might wear which color to their next imagined social event.

And then there was her mother, oblivious to the deeper implications, now fretting over the state of Mr. Bennet's waistcoat and whether it needed mending.

Elizabeth sighed inwardly. How easily they all returned to normalcy. Yet the image of flames consuming Drury Lane lingered in her mind. Was it truly just negligence? Or was there something greater at play?

She picked up her teacup and sipped, the porcelain warm against her hands. Whatever the truth, the events of the morning were a stark reminder of how swiftly life could shift. With one spark, a building, a business, even a life could be reduced to nothing but ash.

Chapter 1

London, February 1811

The warmth of White's club was a welcome reprieve from the chill of London's streets as Fitzwilliam Darcy entered, shedding his overcoat and handing it to a waiting manservant. The familiar din of quiet conversation and the occasional clink of glass created a sense of comfortable routine. Near the hearth, Charles Bingley waved him over, his easy smile evident even from across the room.

"Darcy! Over here!" Bingley called, his smile broad.

Darcy made his way to the table, inclining his head as he took the seat opposite his friend. "You look as if the cold has bested you," Bingley laughed. "Here, let me order you a drink."

Nodding his head in gratitude, Darcy removed his gloves and held his hands towards the blazing fire. "Bingley. How are you doing today?"

"I would be much happier if the snow would let up," Bingley waved his glass towards the nearby window, where several inches of snow had risen to cover the glass from the outside. "I am tired of Caroline shouting at the maids about the mud and snow being tracked across the rugs in the foyer."

Darcy smirked faintly. "You could always threaten to buy her a house in Cheapside. Something with fewer maids and less snow, perhaps."

"Do not give her ideas. She already thinks the street name refers to the price of housing and not *ceapan*."

"Your father should have requested his money back from her finishing school," Darcy replied with a sigh.

"It definitely did give her all sorts of... *ideas*."

"That it did," Darcy replied with a shudder. "Perhaps I ought to remove Georgiana from her school and set her up with her own establishment."

"If only I could do so with Caroline. You are lucky, Darcy, that your sister is all that is sweet and good."

Darcy nodded his agreement. A server brought Darcy's glass, and the two men drank their claret in peace for a few moments.

"So, Bingley, what has you occupied these days? Some new business scheme?"

Bingley grinned, setting his glass down. "No schemes, I assure you. In fact," he hesitated, "I am considering purchasing an estate."

Eyebrows raising, Darcy leaned forward and focused all his attention on his friend. "Where at?"

"Oh, I have not chosen one or anything. No, I am not at that stage yet. I have had my man of business send out a few inquiries, but nothing firm."

Relieved, Darcy sat back in his chair, the tension easing from his body. "Perhaps you might wish to consider leasing an estate first, rather than purchasing one."

Bingley tilted his head thoughtfully. "Leasing, you say? I had not considered that."

"It allows for flexibility," Darcy explained, putting his empty drink on the table. "You can determine whether the estate suits your needs without committing your entire capital. It is a wiser course, especially if you are unsure of the area."

"Sound advice, as always," Bingley admitted. "Though I confess, my sisters would balk at the idea of renting. They would think it beneath the Bingley name."

Darcy smirked. "Your sisters do seem to prioritize appearances."

Bingley laughed. "Indeed, though sometimes I wonder what my father would think of how we have all turned out. His fortune was hard-earned, you know. Trade is an unforgiving world, but he thrived in it."

"He built a legacy," Darcy's tone respectful. "And you've been wise to preserve it."

"Well, I try," Bingley said with a modest shrug. "In fact, I have been thinking of ways to grow it further, put it to better use than just sitting in the bank."

Darcy tilted his head, interest piqued. "How so?"

"Have you ever heard of reinsurance?"

Darcy shook his head. "No, the term is unfamiliar to me."

"It is tied to property insurance," Bingley explained. "After the Great Fire, insurance companies began to offer coverage for homes and businesses. But lately, those companies have realized the risks they face. They are making money while things are going well, but if, say, a fire were to devastate an entire area, it could ruin the insurer."

"But do not those companies all insure different buildings in different places?" Darcy asked in confusion.

"Yes, but there are not many insurance companies, and many areas tend to use the same companies. On Mayfair, for example, my neighbors use my insurer— the Sun Fire Office— based on my recommendation."

"As is true for Grosvenor Square; we use the Fire Office."

"Precisely; it is largely on word of mouth. Additionally, the insurance companies are the ones who fund the fire brigades. It is more cost effective for them to have several properties in one area being protected by one fire

Darcy's brow furrowed. "That makes sense."

"But if a large fire were to break out one of those areas and be unable to be contained," Bingley explained, "then the one company would be liable for much more property value than they would have in their coffers."

"Especially since many have just now begun to include more than just the building and land, but also the contents of the building."

"Exactly! More lately, these companies are realizing the risks they take on."

"Naturally," Darcy replied, "but what does reinsurance do, and how does it solve the problem?"

"By spreading the risk and establishing financial backers," Bingley answered. "Essentially, the insurance companies that insure themselves with private investors. Gentlemen such as yourself offer to cover the value of claims higher than a certain amount. In return, you are granted a portion of the monthly insurance payments for that coverage."

"And you are considering investing in this?"

Bingley nodded. "The Royal Exchange Assurance is one of the leaders in this, especially for the warehouses down on the Thames. They are looking for investors to provide capital, and I thought it could be an excellent opportunity. Profitable, but also necessary. These warehouses and docks are the backbone of commerce, after all."

"It is an intriguing idea," Darcy said thoughtfully. But you know the disdain many of the upper class have for ventures tied to trade."

"Yes, which is why they approached me. I am already tied by trade due to my father, but the fortune is larger than many of the upper class. You know, I have never entirely understood why an accident of birth makes some people better than others."

Darcy sighed. "It is a lot of nonsense, when you think about it. But I must say that I do prefer more refined company, and that often is something ingrained in a person since their birth."

Guffawing, Bingley reached over to clap his friend on the back. "When have you ever preferred *any* kind of company, my friend?"

"Touche. I am just concerned for your status, that's all. Investing could definitely improve your wealth, but not necessarily your position. Why are you so eager to strengthen your ties to your father's past? I thought you said he wished for you to put it all behind you and enter the gentry."

"I will not lie, Darcy," Bingley said earnestly. "It is not just about the returns or even the risk. It is the idea of it—the practicality. These warehouses, these businesses, they are the heartbeat of London's economy. Without them, society crumbles."

Darcy regarded him with quiet respect. "You speak with conviction. It is refreshing."

Bingley laughed lightly. "Well, that's a first. Usually, my enthusiasm is dismissed as naivety."

"Not by me. I just hope for the best for you, my friend. There are many benefits for not just yourself, but also for your family, if you become a landowner."

Bingley grimaced. "I know, which is why I am a considering purchasing an estate. I would not have the capital to both purchase and

19

invest. If I heed your advice, however, and simply lease for a year, then the investment can still be made."

"Leaving you with a larger sum of money when you are ready to purchase."

"Precisely, which means a larger estate."

Darcy steepled his hands in front of his chest. "I actually think it quite a brilliant idea, Bingley."

Shoulders relaxing, Bingley beamed in relief. "Excellent! I was planning on attending an informational meeting with them tomorrow; I will share the good news with them then."

"When is this meeting?"

"Tomorrow afternoon, near the docks. Royal Exchange is hosting a tour of their facilities, followed by a discussion."

Darcy's brow furrowed slightly. "The docks are an unconventional venue."

"They want to show potential investors the scale of what is at stake," Bingley explained. "The warehouses, the goods being insured—it is meant to drive home the importance of the venture."

"I suppose there is some wisdom in that approach," Impulsively, Darcy made a decision. "I will join you, if you will allow it. If only to see whether this is as promising as you believe."

Bingley grinned broadly. "I knew you would see the potential. Your insight will be invaluable."

"Let us hope it proves worthy of my attention," Darcy replied, though a faint smile softened the sharpness of his words.

"Darcy, you will find it compelling," Bingley assured him. "And who knows? Perhaps this will be the start of something significant."

"Perhaps," Darcy said, his gaze distant as he considered the implications. "But let us leave the future to unfold as it will. For now, I had best be on my way— I have much business to attend to."

Bingley laughed. "Now that's the Darcy I know."

X

The air near the docks was thick with the scent of salt, damp wood, and the faint tang of smoke. All around, the narrow passageways between stacks of lumber and crates of shipped goods seemed to be alive with the ceaseless movements of commerce. Distant squawking of gulls mingled with the cries of laborers unloading the cargo from ships and the creaking of timber from the wooden walkways above the stinking river water.

Darcy stepped out of the carriage his boots meeting the cobblestones with a solid thud. Beside him, Charles Bingley adjusted his coat, his gaze sweeping over the bustling scene with evident curiosity. Around them, the road appeared to be almost swaying with the backdrop of ships straining against their moorings.

A man in a dark overcoat approached briskly, his polished boots and confident stride distinguishing him from the workers around him. He approached Darcy and Bingley, his face splitting into a wide, practiced smile. "Gentlemen! Welcome."

Bingley extended a hand. "Mr. Cartwright, thank you for the invitation for my friend here. Darcy, might I have the honor of introducing you to Mr. Cartwright?"

Darcy nodded and Cartwright bowed in greeting. "We are honored to have such a distinguished gentleman here today."

Darcy inclined his head slightly. "I am here to learn. It is quite the operation going on down here."

Cartwright beamed. "Indeed, the lifeblood of London's economy. Shall we begin?"

They were ushered into a modest meeting room overlooking the river. Maps and charts lined the walls, and several other prospective investors were already seated, murmuring among themselves. They fell silent as Cartwright gestured for everyone's attention.

Once all eyes were on him, Cartwright began his presentation with practiced ease. "Gentlemen, the docks represent not only the heart of our city's commerce but also its greatest vulnerability. Fires, theft, and natural disasters pose significant risks. That's where our firm steps in—to ensure that merchants, landowners, and the economy itself are protected."

He spoke at length about the history of property insurance and the evolution of reinsurance, emphasizing its importance in spreading risk. Darcy listened with careful attention, his brow furrowing slightly as Cartwright described their reliance on underwriters and fire brigades.

When Cartwright paused for questions, Darcy broke the silence. "You mentioned underwriters. How are they selected, and what is their process for assessing risk?"

Cartwright's confident smile faltered briefly before he answered. "Our underwriters are highly experienced, chosen for their expertise in the field."

"And the inspections?" Darcy asked. "Are they frequent? Comprehensive?"

"Well," Cartwright hedged, "it varies. The industry is still evolving, as you understand. We rely on the reports provided by property owners and occasional follow-ups from our team."

Darcy's expression remained neutral, but his silence spoke volumes. Beside him, Bingley cleared his throat lightly, attempting to ease the tension. "I imagine it is a challenge to inspect every property thoroughly, given the volume you manage."

"Precisely," Cartwright said quickly. "Our focus is on efficiency and trust."

Darcy's expression remained impassive, but he noted the vague answer. "But surely there are *some* standard practices in place?"

"Of course, of course," Cartwright said quickly. "Our methods are rigorous, I assure you."

The tension eased slightly as the presentation concluded, and the group was led outside for a tour of the docks. Cartwright gestured expansively at the bustling scene. "Gentlemen, this is the heart of London's economy. Every barrel, every crate you see here represents livelihoods, commerce, and progress."

Darcy's sharp gaze swept over the area. He had done a study the evening before on the Great London Fire of 1666, including Thomas Vincent's analysis of the non-deistic causes included in his book "God's Terrible Voice in the City." While much of the tome focused on God's punishments, it also included several reasons why the fire burned as long as it did.

As he surveyed the scene with a critical eye, Darcy was dismayed to see much to alarm him. The ramshackle, wooden warehouses were cramped, their wooden structures blackened with soot. Barrels of oil and other flammable materials sat precariously close to stacks of crates, and the passageways between the warehouses themselves were primarily narrow and filled with all sorts of lumber.

"What measures are in place to prevent fires?" Darcy asked, his tone measured but firm.

Cartwright's smile tightened. "We have arrangements with the local fire brigades." He directed the investors' attention towards a dilapidated wagon— *sans wheels*— bearing a water pump. "And as we wait for them, we have items on site that can be used."

"*This* is what you plan to use to put out a fire?" Darcy asked incredulously.

Cartwright hesitated. "Yes, it was purchased from another insurance company when they upgraded their fleet for residential properties in the city."

Darcy's lips thinned. "Secondhand equipment for an area as critical as this? And how far is your nearest brigade?"

Cartwright shifted uncomfortably. "About a quarter of a mile, but they are highly trained."

"Distance and training mean little when fire can consume these warehouses in minutes," Darcy said, his tone sharp. He gestured toward the barrels and timber crates. "These materials are highly flammable, yet they are stored with no regard for containment. One spark, and the fire would spread unchecked. Do you have firebreaks in place?"

"We rely on the fire brigades," Cartwright replied, his voice tightening. "Gentlemen, this is not the time to nitpick operational details. The broader system—"

"The broader system will collapse if you neglect the details," Darcy interrupted. "Your equipment is outdated, your inspections insufficient, and your reliance on proximity to fire brigades assumes a speed they cannot achieve."

The murmurs among the other investors grew louder, and Cartwright's polished demeanor began to crack. "Mr. Darcy, we are here to discuss investment opportunities, not to endure a lecture on logistics."

"And yet," Darcy said, gesturing to a nearby warehouse, "those barrels of oil are positioned next to timber crates. Should one spark occur, the entire building would be consumed before a brigade could arrive."

The other investors murmured among themselves, and Cartwright's demeanor shifted. "Mr. Darcy, these are operational details. The broader picture is what matters—the resilience of the system, the strength of our partnerships."

Bingley, who had been quiet, now stepped forward. "Forgive me, but are not the operational details precisely what ensures that resilience? If one fire could destroy half the docks, would not that undermine the entire system? How can we consider backing this venture without assurances of safety measures?"

Cartwright's expression darkened. "Gentlemen, this meeting was not intended to be an inquisition. "I believe you misunderstand the scope of what we do here. This is not about nitpicking individual flaws. It is about supporting progress."

Darcy's lips pressed into a thin line, the defensiveness grating against his sense of reason. It reminded him too sharply of Wickham's deflections—evasive answers dressed up as charm. "It is not an inquisition to ask how you propose to safeguard the assets you insure." He folded his arms and looked at Bingley. "As they cannot provide satisfactory answers, I see no reason to continue."

Bingley nodded his agreement, and the two men left the group, their footsteps echoing on the cobblestones as they walked away from the docks towards their carriage. Once inside, Bingley exhaled sharply. "Well, that was… less reassuring than I had hoped. What do you think?"

Darcy's face was grim. "Their defensiveness is quite troubling, and I am concerned about their lack of accountability. The way they resorted to evasion rather than substance when the risks were evident for all to see…"

"Well, for *you* to see."

"I did stay up half the night reading Maitland's *History of London*, as well as some folios I found in the library… but even without that knowledge, it should be clear to any Englishman what they are doing bears a repeat of 1666."

"You do not trust them?"

"No," Darcy said flatly. "Their infrastructure is fragile, their plans reactionary. Investing in such a venture would be folly."

Bingley frowned. "I thought perhaps you were being overly cautious at first— you know how much I detest confrontation— but… yes, you are right. It felt wrong. Their priorities seem misplaced, and the way they bristled against your questions does not sit right with me."

"You are right to trust your instincts," Darcy said. "They speak of resilience, yet they neglect the foundation. Without that, the entire structure is vulnerable."

"Then we will not invest."

"No." Darcy shook his head firmly. "We most definitely will not."

As the carriage jolted along the uneven cobblestones, Darcy turned his gaze to the frost-laden window. The city beyond was muted, the bustling energy of the docks replaced by snow-covered streets and the flicker of distant lamplight.

The muffled sounds of the city—calls of street vendors, the distant clip of hooves—created an eerie serenity. Yet, his mind was anything but calm. The images of the cramped docks, the timber warehouses, and the outdated equipment lingered like shadows in his thoughts.

A sense of foreboding crept over him, tightening his chest. All it would take was one spark—one careless act or unforeseen accident—and the docks could become an inferno. The narrow passages, the flammable materials, the woefully inadequate response infrastructure: it was a perfect storm waiting to ignite. Darcy pressed a gloved hand against the glass, his reflection staring back at him.

Commerce, industry, society itself—they all depended on such fragile foundations. And when those foundations burned, the consequences would be catastrophic. His breath fogged the glass as he exhaled, and a single thought echoed in his mind: *They are building their fortunes on kindling.*

Chapter 2

Elizabeth Bennet was about to cry.

The mirror offered no kindness as she stared at her reflection, her lips trembling and her hands clutching the sides of the dress as though it might somehow reshape itself.

She had trusted Madame Dupont's expertise, had even looked forward to this fitting with her usual sense of optimism. Shopping with her fashionable aunt Gardiner in London was always so much more enjoyable than in Meryton with her mother's insistence of more lace and a lower neckline.

Yet now, standing in the modiste's elegant fitting room surrounded by gilt-framed mirrors and the gentle rustle of silk, she could only think one thing: she looked like a squash.

A frilly, feathered squash.

Staring at herself in the full-length mirror in the fitting room, Elizabeth could scarcely believe what she saw. Lace cascaded from the bodice like a frothy waterfall, feathers bristled from the shoulders in an affront to all sense of decorum, and embroidery in garish gold swirls sprawled across the skirt like a map to some imaginary treasure.

The thought of the gown being stolen by a pirate to seek out gold nearly caused Elizabeth to lose control of her last threads of sanity. She pushed back the tears of laughter that had formed in her eyes and turned around to address the other person in the room.

"This," she declared to her aunt, who was perched on a nearby chaise, her lips twitching dangerously, "is not what I ordered."

Mrs. Gardiner coughed delicately into her handkerchief, though it did little to hide her amusement. "I should say not, my dear."

"I am not certain why the waist is so loose." Elizabeth gestured at the drooping fabric. "Surely I do not look as though I require this... extra room."

"And yet the bust and hips are tight," Mrs. Gardiner added, her amusement growing. "The dress seems to have no idea what it wants to be. Unless, of course, you secretly aspire to be a particularly flamboyant bird of paradise."

Elizabeth threw her an incredulous look. "I hardly think even a bird of paradise would wear this."

She turned back to the mirror, grimacing as she attempted to adjust the waistline, which hung awkwardly loose while the bodice strained precariously. The skirt, pooling at her feet in an alarming volume, seemed designed for a woman several inches taller and quite differently proportioned. While Elizabeth's waist was kept trim from her usual ramblings throughout Hertfordshire, her hips and bust had become quite... curvier over the last year or so.

This dress was made for a woman who was built like a twig, not a pear.

Mrs. Gardiner stood, circling her niece with a critical eye. "Perhaps," she said thoughtfully, "the modiste mistook you for a dowager duchess who fancies herself a fashion icon. Or a guest at a masquerade ball—one where peacocks are the theme."

Elizabeth pressed a hand to her mouth, her shoulders shaking. "Or someone who wishes to frighten small children," she said, her voice muffled by laughter. "Truly, Aunt, it is a crime against fabric."

"I must admit," Mrs. Gardiner said, her composure wavering, "the color alone is enough to make one reconsider the merits of sight."

"It would certainly frighten any foxes out of the henhouse. Perhaps I ought to recommend it to Hill for each of the maids?"

Mrs. Gardiner pressed a hand to her lips, her shoulders shaking. "Or perhaps to Jane, in order to ensure no suitor with bad poetry ever dares to call again," she managed, her voice muffled with barely contained laughter.

Elizabeth let out a half-sob, half-laugh, her composure teetering on the edge. "Do you think... do you think Madame Dupont hates me?"

Mrs. Gardiner stepped closer, circling Elizabeth as if examining a particularly curious painting. "I think," she said solemnly, "she may have mistaken you for someone attempting to impersonate a particularly flamboyant canary."

That was too much. Elizabeth clutched the sides of the monstrosity as laughter bubbled out of her, mingling with her earlier despair. "It is awful," she gasped. "It is so awful I do not even know where to begin."

Mrs. Gardiner tilted her head thoughtfully. "Perhaps with the feathers. I am not certain why anyone would think shoulders need plumes."

The sound of their mirth echoed through the small fitting room. Just as Elizabeth was about to attempt an escape from the lace prison, the door swung open, and Madame Dupont herself bustled in.

"Ah, mademoiselle!" the modiste exclaimed, her eyes widening as she took in the sight before her. "Oh, mon Dieu! Non, non, non, this is all wrong!"

Elizabeth turned, still shaking with laughter. "I should say so."

Madame Dupont clasped her hands to her cheeks, the picture of dismay. "Forgive me, please! That dress—it is not yours!"

"Is it not?"

Mrs. Gardiner arched a brow. "I should hope not. My niece has better taste."

"No, no, no! This was for another client—a much taller client! I am mortified, mademoiselle. Please, allow me to help you out of it at once." The modiste flushed but hurried forward, flapping her hands as though she might shoo the dress off Elizabeth. "I tried to dissuade the other customer, truly. I told her the orange—it does not suit her complexion, nor anyone's, but she insisted it was the height of fashion."

Elizabeth stepped out of the gown with relief, her laughter subsiding into a bright smile. "Perhaps she thought it might distract from her other faults."

Madame Dupont chuckled nervously, shaking her head as she hung the offending dress on a nearby stand. "She is... très particular. But you, mademoiselle, shall have the gown you ordered. And this one—" She gestured at the orange creation with a dramatic flourish. "This one, I shall pretend I never saw on you."

Elizabeth exchanged a conspiratorial glance with her aunt. "An excellent idea."

As Madame Dupont disappeared to retrieve the correct gown, Mrs. Gardiner sat back down, her eyes twinkling. "Well, Lizzy, if nothing else, this will make a delightful story."

Elizabeth grinned. "Oh, I fully intend to tell it. The trick, of course, will be deciding whether to include the part about the feathers."

X

As Elizabeth sat down with the Gardiners for dinner that evening, she looked wistfully around the dining room. It had always been a warm, bustling space, but now it felt oddly bare. The shelves that once held polished silver and colorful crockery stood empty, their contents packed away in neat crates lining the far wall. The absence of familiar trinkets and framed prints gave the room an unfamiliar hollowness, and there was a distinct musty smell in the air.

"Although I am excited for you to relocate to Hertfordshire, I must admit that I will miss your home here in town," she said. "It is almost as if this room is saying goodbye before you do."

Madeline Gardiner followed her gaze and sighed. "Yes, it does, does it not? Packing has a way of hollowing out a house, even before you leave it."

"Will you miss being here in London?" Elizabeth asked curiously. "Having lived my entire life in at Longbourn, I cannot imagine moving somewhere else."

"I will miss my friends, and there are quite a lot of conveniences here in town. But I definitely will not miss the terrible air and smells. I look forward to living in the country once again, and I keep reminding myself that Stoke House will soon feel like my own."

Mr. Gardiner looked up from his plate, a glint of humor in his eye as he spoke for the first time after tucking in. "Lizzy, you must not let her talk you into believing she's entirely resigned to the move. She's still mourning the loss of Derbyshire."

Elizabeth grinned. "I suspected as much. But think, Aunt, about how lovely it will be to have you settled so near to us. I look forward to seeing what you do with the estate, both the house and park, as well as the empty tenant farms you purchased. You have a talent for making spaces feel warm and inviting, no matter where they are."

Mrs. Gardiner smiled, her expression softening. "Thank you, my dear. That means a great deal to me. I must confess, though, the drawing room will take some effort. It is a touch smaller than I would like."

Mr. Gardiner chuckled. "It is quite large enough for our purposes, my love. Besides, the children will be too busy exploring the grounds to notice its size."

"What do you children think?" Elizabeth smiled at the four young Gardiner children, who had been wiggling on their seats, eager to be invited to participate in the discussion. "Will you all enjoy being near us in the country, or will you miss the city?"

"I want to see cows!"

"And sheep!" another child added enthusiastically.

The table erupted in laughter, but the children's attention soon turned back to Elizabeth. "Cousin Lizzy," the eldest began, leaning forward eagerly, "can we play the game now?"

Elizabeth tilted her head, feigning confusion. "The game? What game could you possibly mean?"

"The guessing game!" the child exclaimed. "You close your eyes, and we bring you the next course. You have to guess what it is by the smell."

Elizabeth sighed dramatically. "Oh, very well. But only because you've asked so sweetly."

The children cheered, and Mr. Gardiner chuckled as Elizabeth obediently closed her eyes. The clink of plates and hushed whispers signaled the arrival of the next course. Elizabeth inhaled deeply and a smile crept across her lips.

"Roast duck," she declared confidently. "With rosemary."

The children gasped in awe, and the youngest one cried, "She's a magician!"

"Not a magician," Mr. Gardiner said, shaking his head. "Simply a woman with an extraordinary sense of smell. Lizzy, if you ever grow tired of Hertfordshire, I daresay you could make a fortune in the perfume trade."

Elizabeth opened her eyes and laughed. "I will keep that in mind, Uncle. Though I imagine your children would be far less enthusiastic about smelling perfumes than roasted duck."

"Indeed!" one of the children exclaimed, already reaching for another piece of bread.

"You spoil them, Lizzy," said Mrs. Gardiner, a smile softening her words.

"And that is precisely why you decided to relocate closer to Meryton," retorted Elizabeth with a cheeky grin.

Mrs. Gardiner laughed and shook her head, then tucked into the poultry on her plate. As the meal continued, the room filled with laughter and warmth.

It will be wonderful having them so nearby.

Once the meal was completed, Mrs. Gardiner shooed her children towards their nurse. "Time for bed, now, my dear ones."

Elizabeth turned to Mr. Gardiner. "Uncle, do you mind if I retire as well?"

Mr. Gardiner smiled fondly at Elizabeth. "Not in the slightest. We had quite the busy day, and there is still one more week of overseeing the packing until we officially leave. I think an early bedtime is a wise choice for all of us."

"Do not stay up too late reading," she said, nodding at the book that had somehow appeared in his hand once the family had left the table.

"I might say the same to you," he responded with a wink and jovial grin.

Elizabeth smiled in response, then excused herself from the table and made her way up the stairs, not far behind the Gardiner children, their mother, and the nurse. Their playful chatter echoed down the hallway as they continued on to the third floor, while she made her way to the guest room that had been hers to use during her visit.

Once inside, she shut the door gently, taking a moment to breathe in the stillness. As much as she loved the Gardiners and enjoyed spending time with them, one of the difficulties of Gracechurch Street was the lack of solitude. At Longbourn, if her family became too loud and overwhelming, she could retreat to the familiar paths that wound their way through the property and up to Oakham Mount.

No matter, Lizzy. Only one more week, and you will be back to your ramblings again.

Crossing to the vanity, she ignored the bellpull on the side of the wall and began moving the hairpins that held her coiffure in place. Though the Gardiners had a maid who might assist with her toilette, Elizabeth preferred to manage her routine herself unless she was preparing for a formal engagement. No servant could replace her beloved sister Jane's attendance, and tonight especially, Elizabeth welcomed solitude.

As she laid each pin on the small tray before her, Elizabeth's dark curls tumbled free, the weight lifting from her scalp. She reached for her small silver brush— a gift from the Gardiners two Christmases ago— and ran it through her hair in slow, deliberate strokes until the curls shone in the candlelight.

Once the one-hundred strokes her mother insisted upon each night were complete, Elizabeth dipped a soft cloth into a small porcelain bowl of warm water. She gently wiped away the day's dust and faint traces of soot from their excursions in the city. A jar of rosewater infused cream was next, its delicate scent soothing as she massaged it into her skin.

Her face now clean, Elizabeth stood from the small stool and reached behind her to begin unfastening the buttons of her gown. She wore no stays this evening, as the loose day dress she had chosen required none. Had she been wearing a more formal gown, she might have needed assistance unlacing her stays, which would have been a task for the maid. But tonight, the simplicity of her attire allowed her to manage alone.

She slipped into a linen bedgown—a simple garment, soft and flowing, that fell just past her knees. Its design was modest but comfortable, with long sleeves to ward off the night's chill. She pulled her shawl around her shoulders and padded to the small fireplace in the corner of the room. The faint glow of embers remained, and she added a piece of kindling to ensure the room stayed warm through the night.

Finally, Elizabeth knelt by the low bed, clasping her hands in her lap. Her nightly prayers were a private ritual, a moment to reflect on the day and seek guidance for the next. She murmured softly, the words of gratitude and hope rising in the quiet.

Rising, she slipped under the heavy coverlet, sinking into the feather-stuffed mattress with a sigh of contentment. The fire's soft crackling and the distant sounds of the city lulled her into a state of calm, and the last conscious thought she had before drifting off was a simple one.

How wonderful it will be to return to Hertfordshire with all of my family settled near one another. Things truly could not be any better than this.

X

Several hours later, Elizabeth awoke with a start. She sat up in bed, and as she blearily rubbed her eyes, she became aware of a faint, acrid scent that was tickling her nose. She blinked around in the darkness, disoriented and still foggy-headed from slumber.

The moonlight streaming through the window told her that morning was still quite some time away. She laid down again and rolled to her side, pulling the counterpane closer.

But sleep would not come. Instead of drifting off again, Elizabeth's nose wrinkled as the odd smell grew sharper, tugging at her attention.

Her brow furrowed. *Smoke? At this hour of the night?*

Perhaps one of the maids had risen early to stoke the fire in the hearth. It would be a bit unusual, but not unheard of. She listened closely, but the house was as silent as a tomb— no scurrying footsteps, no faint clatter of pots or the hiss of water being warmed.

Elizabeth sat up again, her heart beginning to beat more quickly as all drowsiness vanished entirely. *It could be a candle*, she reasoned, her mind reaching for an explanation. *Perhaps someone lit a candle on the stairs and snuffed it out, leaving behind a tuft of smoke... The nurse fetching something for one of the children?*

She pressed her lips together, her unease growing. There was no reason for anyone to be awake at this hour, and the smell... *It just does not fit.*

Rising from her bed, she reached for her dressing gown and wrapped it tightly around her shoulders. The cool air of the room sent a shiver down her spine as her bare feet touched the wooden floorboards.

Opening the bedroom door cautiously, she peered out into the hallway, which was dim and still. Her pulse raced as the scent grew stronger, though it was still faint enough that she doubted herself. Stepping through, Elizabeth closed the door softly behind her and moved through the shadows, her ears straining for any sound that might alleviate her fears.

The darkened staircase loomed ahead, and she descended it slowly, the air became more frigid with every step. By the time she reached the ground floor, the smoky scent was undeniably sharper, especially given that she was now fully alert. It swirled through her nostrils with each inhale, curling into her lungs like an unseen specter, lingering and oppressive.

Perhaps it is coming from the kitchens? Maybe the fire there was not extinguished properly?

She made her way down the servant's corridor, past the housekeeper's office, and into the cook's domain. To her dismay, she found the hearth cold— no sign of flame, ash, or smoke.

Nothing.

The unease in her chest tightened, and she returned to the main corridor, walking quickly towards the front of the house. *It is possible there is still a fire burning in my uncle's study or another room.*

As she passed the drawing room, a faint orange glow caught her eye. It spilled into the hallway through the window far window, casting long, flickering shadows across the wall. Her breath caught as she pushed her way through the door and look southward out of the glass towards Gracechurch Street and the docks beyond.

Her heart dropped, and she gasped for breath.

Not far in the distance, past Gracechurch Street and down towards the river, the horizon was swallowed up in an inferno.

The flickering light she had prayed was the sunrise was, in fact, the ominous, jagged movement of tremendous flames licking upward. The sky above was streaked with thick, curling smoke that sought to swallow the stars. A thick haze was spreading, made all the more malevolent with the eerie glow of the roaring blaze.

Panic prickled at the edges of her mind, but she fought them back as she turned and bolted up the stairs towards her uncle's room. She began to pound on the door, her voice urgent. "Uncle Gardiner! Please, wake up!"

After a moment, the door opened, and Mr. Gardiner— his hair tousled and his expression groggy— blinked at her in confusion. "Lizzy? What on earth is the matter?"

"Uncle, please, you must come," she urged, tugging at his sleeve. "There is a fire— I saw it from the window. It is down at the docks."

His expression darkened, the last vestiges of sleep falling away as he ran down the stairs after her to the closest window facing the flames. One look was enough to send him into action. "Gather your things, then wake the nurse and the children. They need to dress— quickly! Help them collect what they can, but only what can be carried. Then go to the servants and tell them the same."

Elizabeth nodded and hurried off as Mr. Gardiner disappeared back into his chamber to rouse his wife. Moments later, Elizabeth could hear his voice giving calm but urgent instructions. Elizabeth returned to her room, grabbing her small carpet bag and stuffing it with what little she could think to take— her writing case that was a gift from Jane, a spare gown, and a few other sentimental trinkets.

Pausing for a moment to steady herself, she drew in a sharp breath. There was no time to waste, but she could not help the cold fear that spread through her veins.

Please, God, keep us safe.

Chapter 3

The servants!

Elizabeth bolted from her room, bag in hand, her heart racing as she ran down the hall towards the servants' quarters, which were near the kitchens.

"Wake up! Fire!" She ran from room to room, pounding on the closed doors.

"What on earth?" Mrs. Batson, the housekeeper, sleepily poked her head out of her room, nightcap askew. "Miss Lizzy? What is going on, child?"

"There is no time to delay," Elizabeth said, her voice steady despite the chaos churning in in her mind. "The docks appear to be on fire, and the wind is blowing the flames towards us. We must all leave—immediately!"

Gasps and murmurs rippled through the hallway as other servants began to emerge, their expressions a mix of confusion and alarm.

Elizabeth turned to face the growing group, her tone calm but commanding. "Gather only what you can carry—valuables, warm clothing, and nothing more. The Gardiners and I will be leaving within minutes, but I understand if any of you wish to seek out your loved ones instead. No one will be punished for abandoning their posts."

One of the footmen hesitated, his brow furrowed. "Miss Bennet, my brother is on the night shift at the docks. If the fire started there…"

"I know," Elizabeth interrupted gently, meeting his worried gaze. "You must do what you feel is right. But be careful—these streets will soon be crowded, and it will be much more dangerous for those on their own. If you

43

choose to stay with us, we will do all we can to keep you safe, but I cannot make any promises about anything."

Mrs. Batson straightened her cap, determination lighting her face. "I will come with you, miss. Someone will need to help Nurse keep the little ones calm."

Others nodded, clutching bags or hastily dressing. A few cast lingering looks back toward the servants' stairwell, as though still weighing their decisions. Elizabeth offered each of them a brief, encouraging nod.

"Five minutes," she said firmly. "Be ready, and meet us at the front door."

As the group dispersed, Elizabeth's heart pounded with the weight of the choices being made around her. There was no time for regret, only resolve. With a last glance toward the servants' rooms, she turned and hurried back upstairs to help her family.

She met Mrs. Gardiner coming down from the second floor towards the front, a firm expression on her face and a satchel in her hand. "Put your bag at the door, Elizabeth, then come help me with the children."

Obediently, Elizabeth practically tossed her bag into the entryway before racing up the stairs after her aunt to the third floor. The scent of smoke was now much heavier, and Elizabeth knew that everyone could most likely smell it by now.

Nurse was already quite busy in the children's room, gathering blankets and coaxing the younger children awake. Elizabeth stepped in to help, gently shaking her oldest cousin's shoulder. "Come now, darling, you must wake up. We need to leave."

Eleven-year-old Beth blinked sleepily and yawned, stretching her arms above her head. "What is happening, Cousin Lizzy?"

Elizabeth forced a calm smile, brushing a stray curl from Beth's forehead. "We are going on an adventure, my love... but we must hurry. Can you be a brave girl for me?"

Beth nodded, still too drowsy to grasp the gravity of the situation. Together, Elizabeth, Mrs. Gardiner, and Nurse hastily dressed the children, bundling them in whatever layers were in reach. Although it was summer, the nights could grow chilly with the humidity and wind. Two-year-old baby Alexander whimpered as Elizabeth scooped him up, his small fists clutching at her gown.

"I think that's everything," Mrs. Gardiner said, casting a quick glance around the room. "We should go before the smoke thickens."

With the children in tow and a few bags with them, the two women made their way back down the stairs. The murmur of voices grew louder as they neared the front hall, where Mr. Gardiner was organizing the handful of remaining servants into a small group, lantern in hand.

"Everyone is ready?" he asked briskly, his gaze sweeping over the assembled group.

"Yes," Mrs. Gardiner confirmed, shifting four-year-old Christopher in her arms. "Elizabeth and I have the two youngest children. Nurse, can you manage Jacob? Stay close, Beth."

Nurse nodded and gripped the eight-year-old boy's hand tightly. Mrs. Batson stepped forward. "I can watch Beth."

Mrs. Gardiner gave the housekeeper a grateful nod. "Thank you," she said fervently. Looking around at the group, she turned to her husband. "Shall we go?"

Mr. Gardiner nodded. He raised his voice and addressed the crowd. "Stay close together, everyone, and keep moving. We will head toward the river first, south of the docks, and see if the bridge there is passable. The other side of the water is the only way to guarantee the fire cannot reach us."

Elizabeth tightened her grip on the baby, steeling herself for the chaos awaiting them. As they stepped onto the street, it was like entering another world, one that had been ripped from the pages of Revelation. The orderly rows of houses were shrouded in an eerie glow, the orange light from the docks flickering like some malevolent force.

Now outside, the smell of smoke was overpowering. The air, sharp with ash, scratched at Elizabeth's throat, and she forced back the urge to cough as the group moved cautiously down the steps and out into the street.

"Maybe we should fetch the carriage," a footman yelled above the noise from scores of people running to and fro, their cries of terror echoing off the walls of the closely-built houses lining the roadway.

Mr. Gardiner shook his head firmly. "It is too late for that. The streets are crowded, and the horses will be spooked by the smoke and commotion. We will make better progress on foot."

"But the children—" Mrs. Batson began, clutching Beth's hand tightly.

"We will carry them on our backs if we must," Elizabeth interrupted, grateful her voice held steady. "Mr. Gardiner is correct; we must be able to maneuver easily through the crowds."

"Now, stay close together," Mr. Gardiner's expression was grim but resolute. "Watch your step and each. No one gets left behind, understood?"

Everyone nodded, and the group pressed forward into the hordes of panicked Londoners. They forced their way southwest, towards the river but further from the docks. *Lord, let us reach the bridge quickly*, Elizabeth prayed fervently.

In spite of their progress, the heat in the air grew more oppressive with each passing moment. The distant crackle of flames was becoming a steady roar, punctuated by the occasional crash of collapsing buildings. Elizabeth forced herself to focus on the path head, her throat aching from the smoke as she held Alexander tightly to her chest.

The pandemonium around them increased, with people darting out of alleys, clutching bundles of possessions, some with tears streaming down soot-streaked faces. A man barreled past, nearly knocking over one of the maids, and Elizabeth reached out to steady her.

"Keep moving," she urged, her voice loud enough to carry but calm enough to reassure. "The more distance we put between us and the fire, the safer we will be."

They turned down a narrow alleyway, using a route that normally Elizabeth would never have dared in the daytime, let alone the wee hours of the morning. It significantly decreased the distance between them and the bridge, however, and there were fewer people along that route.

Eventually the alleyway ended, expelling the weary band of refugees onto the main room. They only made it a half-dozen yards when it became clear that there was no way to continue on. The street was jam packed with hundred—if not thousands—of people, shoving their way towards the river.

"What is going on?" Mrs. Gardiner cried to her husband, who just shook his head and looked around in dismay.

Elizabeth spied a stone bench near one of the buildings, and she ran over to step on top of it. Although she was not tall herself, the added height allowed her to see over the heads of the panicking, unruly mob.

Her heart sank.

In front of her, the frantic masses were surging forward towards the bridge. The cries of children and shouts of soldiers who were attempting to maintain the peace blended into one loud cacophony. The bridge looked ahead, its entrance choked with bodies, wagons, and discarded belongings.

There is no escape.

Thinking quickly, she jumped down from the bridge and urgently sprinted back to the Gardiner group, where Mr. Gardiner was looking at her anxiously.

"We cannot get through here," she shouted, trying to be heard above the din. "It is impossible. There are too many people."

"We must," Mr. Gardiner replied, his voice strained. "If we can just reach the other side—"

"We will be trampled before we set foot on the bridge," Elizabeth said sharply. "That, or we will burn to death because the fire will catch up long before it will be our turn."

"But—"

"Look at them!" she shouted, gesturing towards the bottleneck, where the crowd had devolved into shoving and shouting. "We will have to find another way."

She spun around to look behind them, thinking frantically as her mind raced with possibilities. "The parks!" she shouted, pointing northwest. "We can go to Hyde Park. There is open space, and it is far enough away from the docks to be safe."

Mrs. Gardiner glanced nervously toward the glowing sky. "But the fire—if it spreads…"

"It will not," Elizabeth assured with more confidence than she actually felt. "We can take some of the back roads and get there more quickly than we could through this crowd. Uncle, please."

Mr. Gardiner took a deep breath and looked around, assessing the situation before nodding. "Very well. Everyone, follow Elizabeth."

She pulled Alexander tightly against her, and the boy burrowed his face into her neck. They turned away from the river and went back through the same alleyway they had come down.

"That way, miss!" shouted a footman. She glanced behind her and saw him pointing ahead where another alley jutted out to the left. "It is a shortcut I use all the time."

They turned as one and followed along the narrow path. Smoke curled between the buildings, and Elizabeth fought back the panic rising in her chest. *What if the fire catches up to us? What if the buildings collapse? It is so narrow here. Where are we, even?*

But all she could do was press forward; there was no turning back.

At long last, they once again arrived on a main street, and she sighed in relief upon recognizing the main road that would lead them to the wealthier part of town: Mayfair, Hyde Park, and Westminster were always easily found if they just continued straight ahead.

The path westward had fewer people, but it was no less fraught with challenges. Even though it was further from the fires, word had quickly spread through the city, turning it into a type of war zone. The streets were littered with debris—overturned carts, barrels of wares, and even a few horses had been abandoned in haste.

At one point, they passed a group of laborers attempting to haul a water cart toward the docks. The men's faces were streaked with soot, their shouts barely audible over the din. Elizabeth's heart ached for their futile efforts; she knew the docks would be gone long before they reached them.

The two elder Gardiner children stumbled here and there, their small feet catching on the uneven cobblestones, but Nurse and Mrs. Batson held their hands tightly, and Mrs. Gardiner whispered soft, encouraging words to keep them moving along.

Elizabeth's arms were burning from the weight of her cousin in her arms, but she refused to pass him on. The young boy had clamped himself around her and would not be separated, not even for his father. Christopher had become too heavy for Mrs. Gardiner, so he rode now on the back of one of the stronger footmen.

Just when she thought she would not be able to take one more step, she raised her eyes and saw the large trees of Hyde Park in the distance. "We are almost there!" she shouted in relief. "Not much longer till Mayfair, and the park is just beyond that."

"Aye, and the rich toffs will not let their houses burn none, now will they?" said a footman with a wry grin.

"They will do all they can to prevent it," Elizabeth replied, "except extinguish the flames themselves."

The group laughed perhaps a bit too heartily at this small jest, but it served its purpose in raising their spirits. They walked along with more vigor, and Elizabeth became so engrossed in the tales the servants were sharing that she nearly walked into a person who suddenly appeared in front of her.

"Oh, my apologies!" she began, but any further words died on her lips when she saw that the individual she had nearly trampled was a young woman of about sixteen years of age, holding an infant in her arms. Her body trembled with indecision as she stared towards the east, the advancing flames reflecting in her large, vacant eyes.

Without hesitation, Elizabeth shifted Alexander into one arm and extended the other to the girl. "Come with us."

The girl just shook her head. "I… I cannot. He said…"

"Yes, you can," Elizabeth insisted, placing a steady hand on the girl's shoulder and guiding her along. "Follow me. I will carry your baby if it makes it easier."

The girl hesitated, but something in Elizabeth's tone seemed to cut through her panic. She nodded shakily and handed over the infant into Elizabeth's empty arm.

With a child on each side, Elizabeth's steps began to slow. Mrs. Gardiner rushed forward. "Let me take one of them," she insisted.

Elizabeth attempted to hand Alexander to his mother, but he began to wail and fight. "Izzy! Izzy!" he sobbed, clinging to her neck.

The infant had a similar reaction, and Mr. Gardiner said, "We will waste more time trying to fight them than to allow them to remain with Lizzy. We should just keep going."

Fortunately, they had arrived at the edges of Mayfair, and Hyde Park was only about a half mile ahead. By the time they reached the lawn, Elizabeth's legs burned with exertion, and her lungs felt raw from the smoke. Relief washed over her as she saw the open expanse of nature spread out before them. The early morning sun cast long, distorted shadows that flickered as the rays passed through the curling smoke of the fire in the distance.

The park was crowded with others who had had the same idea as Elizabeth. Families seeking refuge huddled together with what little they had managed to carry. Mr. Gardiner led his group to a quiet corner. A few blankets were laid out, and Elizabeth sank gratefully to the ground.

"Come, Alexander, lie down here," she urged. "I will sit right next to you as we take a rest on the grass. There, is that not nice?"

She attempted to hand the babe back to the girl, who shook her head. "Oh, no, miss. It is not mine."

"Excuse me?" she gaped.

"He's my neighbor's, but she left when she saw the flames."

Elizabeth froze at the girl's casual remark. "You mean to tell me this baby does not belong to you? What is your name? How did you come by him?"

"I'm Meg." The girl shrugged into her tattered shawl. "No, miss. Deena—that's my neighbor—she shoved it at me when she saw the flames. Said she'd be back. But she never came, and I didn't see the point in looking for her."

Elizabeth's stomach churned. "But you carried the child all this way. Surely you—"

"Don't get me wrong, miss," Meg interrupted with a tired smirk. "I don't mind a bit of kindness here and there, but I'm no mother. Best to leave the little thing at a workhouse. They'll sort it out."

Elizabeth stared, aghast. "You mean to abandon an innocent baby?"

"Better than dragging it into my life," Meg said with another shrug. "What'd you have me do? Raise it in the gutter? The workhouse is where it'll end up either way."

"But surely the father—?"

Meg shook her head vehemently. "Well, it's not like Deena knew who he was, did she? There've been too many men to count."

As Elizabeth gaped at the girl, she noticed for the first time the inappropriateness of her clothing. Even for nighttime, the low neckline and threadbare hem of her dress seemed out of place. The realization struck Elizabeth like a blow—this girl was no servant or maid.

She is a woman of the night!

Before Elizabeth could say anything, a rough voice called out, cutting through the chaos around them. "Meg! Oi, there you are!"

Elizabeth turned sharply to see a burly man storming toward them, his face smeared with soot and his expression a mixture of anger and relief. Meg stiffened at his approach, but she rose to her feet to meet him.

"What're you doing here?" the man barked, grabbing Meg's arm roughly. "I've been looking all over for you."

"I was trying to find Deena," Meg mumbled, her gaze dropping to the ground.

"Deena?" the man snorted derisively. "She's dead. Saw a beam fall on her myself—snapped her neck clean."

Meg blinked, her expression unmoving. "Oh."

Elizabeth's eyes widened in shock. "She's dead, and that's all you can say?"

The man's eyes flicked to Elizabeth, narrowing. "Who's this, then? Someone nosing where she don't belong?"

"I am someone who believes this young woman does not have to go with you," Elizabeth said firmly, her chin lifting.

Meg turned to Elizabeth with a wry smile. "Don't waste your breath, miss. He's better than being stuck scrubbing pots in some fine house. I'd rather stick with what I know."

"But you could do better," Elizabeth insisted.

Meg shook her head. "Better?" She gave a hollow laugh. "Better don't exist for the likes of us. Come on, Sam."

The man grunted in approval and grabbed Meg's arm again, steering her away. Elizabeth took a step forward, calling after her. "What about the baby?"

Meg paused, looking back with a tired expression. "Not mine, miss, remember? I've done my bit. He's your problem now."

And with that, she was gone, swallowed into the crowd with the man.

Elizabeth stood frozen, the baby cradled in her arms, its small whimpers breaking her stunned silence. Mrs. Gardiner came over, staring at the spot where the two strangers had disappeared. "What on earth happened, Lizzy?"

Shaking her head slowly, Elizabeth peered down at the motherless baby. "I have absolutely no idea. His mother abandoned him to Meg— the girl who followed us— when the fire started." She paused, her voice cracking. "And then Deena—the mother—I think they are both..." her voice dropped to a whisper... "prostitutes."

"Is she coming back?"

"I do not think so." She blinked away a tear. "She went with... the man who owns her, I guess? She did not want to stay, and she told me to take the babe to a workhouse or something."

Mrs. Gardiner's face softened as she reached out to the bundle Elizabeth held. "We will see to him," she said firmly. She pulled back the blanket covering his face and gasped. "Why, this little mite cannot be more than a few months old!"

"How are we going to feed him?" Elizabeth asked, heart sinking.

"We will figure something out," Mrs. Gardiner said firmly. "We will not leave him to fend for himself. Half of babies born die as it is."

Elizabeth glanced down at the infant, her heart aching as his tiny fist curled around her finger. "No," she whispered. "We will not."

Chapter 4

The sounds of muffled yelling jolted Darcy from his repose. *What is going on?*

He quickly sat up in bed and looked around the room, his mind scrambling to make sense of the noise. Another shout revealed the noise to be coming from outside. *Some young fool probably racing horses again.*

In truth, he had not *really* been asleep. As was his habit, he had awoken some time earlier, his mind too accustomed to rising early in the country. His bed was too comfortable to wish to leave it, so he had burrowed deeper in the blankets, allowing himself a rare moment of stillness before the day.

Mornings were his sanctuary, a brief reprieve before the duties of the day pressed upon him. As he had lain somewhere between consciousness and dreamland, his mind wandered to the day ahead. Business meetings correspondence, dinner with Georgiana, perhaps even a quiet evening of reading—his tasks always organized themselves each morning in his mind into a neat schedule that helped lift the burden on his shoulders.

Now, any semblance of peace was shattered.

An urgent knock came on his door from his changing room, followed by the familiar voice of his valet, Bates. "Mr. Darcy, sir! Are you awake?"

"Yes, come in."

Darcy swung his legs over the side of the bed and stood, stretching his stiff muscles. Walking to the window that overlooked the garden on the south side of the house, he frowned at the peculiar color of the morning's fog.

Bates entered, his usual composed demeanor replaced by an anxious expression. He carried a candle, which was unusual for this time of the morning in the middle of the summer. Darcy's sharp eyes immediately caught the tension in his valet's movements as he set the morning tray on the table.

"What is the matter?"

The man hesitated, clutching the edge of the tray. "Sir, I… there is a fire, at the docks. It started in the night and is spreading westward. The winds are carrying it…"

Darcy stiffened, his hand stilling as he reached for the glass of water. "How far?"

"It is not yet near Mayfair," Bates assured him quickly, though his tone lacked conviction. "But the smoke, sir—it is… alarming. And people from that part of town are gathering in Hyde Park to escape."

Darcy's jaw tightened as he remembered the narrow passageways and other unsafe conditions of the docks when he had inspected them only months prior.

"I knew this would happen," he muttered in a low, bitter voice.

Bates blinked, but before he could speak, Darcy waved him off. "Fetch my clothes. I will dress now."

Bates hurried to comply, and within just a few minutes, Darcy was striding down the stairs to the foyer, Bates just a few steps behind him with the abandoned tray carrying toast and tea. A footman hurried to open the front door, and Darcy stepped outside.

The scene before him was nothing short of unprecedented chaos.

People ran in every direction, clutching bundles and leading frightened children. Wagons piled high with belongings creaked noisily as they rolled past, their owners shouting instructions over the din.

And above all, a tremendous cloud of thick, black smoke billowed up from the east, casting an ominous shadow throughout the city as the rising sun struggled to shine through.

For the first time, Darcy realized the enormity of the disaster. He drew in a deep breath, and his lungs immediately protested the foul air's entry into his body. His breath rattled in his chest as he choked. Struggling to regain control, he steadied himself against the doorframe.

"Sir?" the footman asked in alarm.

Darcy waved the man away, then hailed a man who was walking quickly past. "What is happening?" he rasped.

"The bridge is blocked, so everyone is being told to gather to Hyde Park."

Darcy nodded curtly, then retreated back into the house as another bout of coughing overtook him. His chest burned, and his hands shook slightly as he made his way to his study. Collapsing into his large chair behind the desk, he rang the small bell to summon the butler and housekeeper.

The fits left him fighting for air. Between gasps, Darcy issued instructions. "I doubt the fires will actually reach here, but we should prepare just in case. Mr. Harcourt, you shall oversee the arrangements. You know what to do."

Harcourt gave a curt nod. Darcy turned his attention to his housekeeper. "Mrs. Porter, we will provide aid to those who need it. The kitchens are to prepare as much bread and sustenance as possible to distribute in Hyde Park."

"Sir, with the price of flour—" she began.

"I will cover the expense; it will not come from the household budget," Darcy said a reassuring smile. Her relaxed shoulders told him he had guessed her hesitation correctly. "I imagine there will also be a great need for clothing and blankets."

She nodded and stood up straight. "We will do our best, sir."

"Are there any of the staff who needs to check on the welfare of their families?"

Harcourt and Mrs. Porter exchanged a glance. "I can make inquiries, sir," Harcourt finally said. "I am sorry that I do not know right now."

Darcy waved a hand and coughed before speaking. "Let me know if anyone needs to be excused from their duties. If there are several who wish to leave, set them up in rotation schedules so we can still render aid to as many in the Park as necessary."

As the two begin to leave, Darcy called out, "Harcourt? Send footmen to the Park and surrounding streets. I want to know what is being done, who is organizing relief efforts, and where the greatest need lies."

Harcourt bowed his acknowledgment and followed Mrs. Porter from the room. Darcy frowned and turned his attention to his desk, pulling out a sheet of paper. The housekeeper's mention of the rising cost of food due to the war with France and tensions in America had sparked a concern. He quickly penned a note to his uncle, Lord Matlock; the docks burning would have repercussions far beyond London.

As he pressed his signet ring into the hot wax to seal the letter, Georgiana entered with wide eyes. "Brother, what is happening? Is Aunt Catherine coming?"

He gaped at her, prompting another coughing fit. "Why on earth would you think that?"

"Well, the servants are rushing about the house as if the devil were chasing them. It only made sense."

Biting back a chuckle so as not to irritate his lungs further, he reached out a hand and motioned for her to sit. "There is a fire spreading rapidly from the docks. From what I can tell, it will not actually come all this way, but there are hundreds fleeing to Hyde Park."

She gasped. "Oh, those poor people."

"I want you to stay in your rooms with Mrs. Annesley until I personally come to get you."

"Surely it is not so dangerous—"

"It is," he said sharply. She flinched, and he groaned internally, softening his voice. "If the situation does worsen, the house could be overrun by desperate people. I will not risk your safety."

Her face paled, and she nodded reluctantly. "Very well."

"I have assigned footmen to guard your door," he added, "and a maid will attend to anything you need. Stay there, Georgiana. Promise me?"

"I promise," she whispered, leaving the room with a fearful glance towards the smoke-filled windows.

By late morning, Darcy's voice was nearly gone, the smoky air exacerbating his childhood weakness that typically only emerged in the coldest months or when he overexerted himself.

"Sir, please allow me to send for Dr. Thompson," Bates begged.

"Absolutely not," Darcy snapped, though his weakened voice carried little force. "There are many out there who are in need of a doctor's assistance. I can manage until the disaster has passed."

"Then at least let us prepare willow bark tea, sir."

Darcy made to object, but the pleading look on his valet's face caused him to sigh and nod reluctantly. "Very well, Bates; if it will quiet you on the matter."

Bates snapped at a passing maid and issued the order. Knowing it would be a few minutes until it could be prepared, Darcy retreated to a guest room on the upper floor, where the east-facing windows provided are clearer view of the disaster unfolding on the city. He stood for a long while, watching the flames devour the area along the docks and creep towards Mayfair. The distant roar of destruction, combined with the cries of alarm and the urgent shouting of fire brigades, would not be a sound he would soon forget.

As the flames finally began to slow, Darcy maintained his silent vigil, his head bowed in silent prayer. *Lord, forgive me. I should have stopped this. Have mercy on us all.*

※

It took almost an entire day for the fires to be quenched; the amount of smoke in the air was suffocating. It was not until the following morning that Darcy was able to leave his home and personally go to Hyde Park to see what needed to be done. Coughing lightly into his gloved hand, he surveyed the scene before him.

In a scant twenty-four hours, the area had been transformed into a refuge, no longer the pristine retreat of London's upper class, but a sprawling encampment of makeshift tents and huddled groups. Fortunately, he saw evidence of order beginning to take shape amidst the chaos; white canvas shelters had been erected, and soldiers and city officials moved between clusters of displaced families.

The air was thick with smoke, along the stench of unwashed bodies and waste and the dull roar of wearied murmurs mixed with the occasional wail of a suffering child.

Darcy's jaw tightened as he made his way through the crowd, several footmen and maids trailing behind him, handing out baskets of provisions. *At least there is some organization,* he thought, looking at a soldier placing up a barrier. The sheer number of people seeking aid, however, made the relief efforts appear almost insurmountable.

A commotion ahead drew his attention, and he hastened his footsteps to ascertain the cause. Near a grouping of supply carts, a tense argument was unfolding. A soldier, his red coat dulled by soot, stood rigidly before a young woman who held her ground with unwavering defiance.

His breath caught as he approached close enough to take her in. She stood near a grouping of supply carts, the dark fabric of her gown streaked with ash and soot. Strands of chestnut hair had escaped their pins, curling wildly in the damp air, framing a face that was—

Magnificent.

It was not a word he had ever used to describe a woman before, but it was the only one that fit.

The world seemed to narrow around her. She was not simply beautiful—though she was, in a way that struck deep, past logic and reason. No, it was something more. The fire had left devastation in its wake, yet she stood amid it all like a force of nature, steady and unshaken.

And she was arguing.

The woman—who was decidedly not a servant, nor the sort of lady one typically found overseeing relief efforts—stood her ground, her posture rigid with defiance. She had rolled up her sleeves despite the morning chill, and her voice was firm as she looked up into the soldier's face towering above her.

"You cannot expect him to move!" The woman gestured towards a huddled figure on blankets near the carts. "He is severely burned, barely conscious, and in a great deal of pain. Where is your humanity?"

The soldier, his patience visibly fraying, squared his stance. "Miss, we need to clear this area for additional supplies. There is room in the tents—"

"He will not survive being dragged across the park like a sack of grain," the woman countered, her chin lifting. "He needs careful handling, not rough hands and haste."

The soldier's jaw tightened. "Miss, I have orders."

"And I have sense," she shot back.

The corner of Darcy's mouth twitched, despite himself. Her fire was unlike anything he had ever seen. Where most ladies of his acquaintance might shy from confrontation, she stood firm, unwavering. There was a fierceness to her that demanded to be acknowledged.

The soldier, however, was not amused. "This is not your decision."

Before the conversation could escalate, Darcy stepped forward. "I believe the lady is correct."

Both the soldier and the woman turned to look at him. The soldier stiffened upon recognizing the fine cut of Darcy's coat and his air of authority. "Sir?"

Darcy inclined his head toward the injured woman. "If he is as badly burned as Miss..." He glanced briefly at the young woman.

"Bennet," she supplied, her voice crisp.

"Miss Bennet claims," he continued, "then moving him improperly could worsen his condition. Would it not be wiser to summon a physician before making that determination?"

The soldier hesitated, then gave a reluctant nod before stepping back. "I will send for someone."

Darcy barely acknowledged him. His attention was wholly consumed by the woman before him.

She turned to face him fully, and for the first time, he saw the full depth of her eyes—rich and dark, alive with intelligence.

"I had it handled," she said, her voice even.

Darcy let out a short breath that could have been a laugh. "Of that, I have no doubt."

She gave him a long, measuring look, as if assessing whether he was an ally or an obstacle. Then, seeming to decide on the former, she nodded once in acknowledgment. "Thank you."

Darcy inclined his head. "It was only sense."

Before she could reply, a sharp, ragged cough tore through him, doubling him over slightly. He turned away, pressing a fist to his mouth, his chest seizing with the effort.

When he finally straightened, he found Miss Bennet watching him, one brow arched.

"You should not be out here," she observed.

Darcy cleared his throat. "Neither should you."

Her lips quirked, but she did not argue the point. "Is there something you require, Mr.…?"

"Darcy. Fitzwilliam Darcy."

She gave no sign of recognition, merely inclining her head. "Then, Mr. Darcy, can I help you with something?"

Stay here and continue speaking with me until the world rights itself again.

But instead, he said, "On the contrary, I was about to ask if you required anything."

"I thank you, but no. We will be leaving soon for my father's estate. Thank you helping me assist this woman." She turned to walk away.

"Wait, she is not with you?"

Elizabeth shook her head. "No, she stumbled into the park late last night."

"You argued with a soldier—for a stranger?"

She tilted her head, considering him as if the question were strange. "Of course."

Darcy studied her, astonishment flickering through his thoughts. She had argued—boldly, passionately—with a soldier over a woman she did not even know. How many others in her position would have turned away, claiming it was not their concern? He had never seen such conviction in a lady before.

"Why get involved?" he asked, his curiosity overriding his usual reserve.

Her fine eyes met his, unwavering. "Because she could not speak for herself."

The simplicity of her words struck him deeper than he expected. He had heard countless justifications for action in his lifetime—duty, honor, pride—but this was different. No self-righteousness, no need for recognition. Just… an innate, immovable sense of rightness.

The ladies of his acquaintance concerned themselves with embroidery and drawing-room gossip, not standing their ground against uniformed men for the sake of an unknown woman. Even the most charitable among them donated funds and spoke kindly of their efforts—but they did not act.

Yet here stood Miss Bennet, covered in soot, defying orders with no apparent hesitation.

Before he could form another thought, she gave him a polite nod. "Thank you again, Mr. Darcy. Good day."

And just like that, she was gone.

He turned slightly, his eyes following her form as she walked away, moving with sure steps across the field. Her skirts skimmed the trampled grass, and the hem of her stained gown was coated six inches in mud. But as he watched her go, he was unable to shake the feeling that he had just encountered someone singular—someone unlike anyone he had ever met.

Then, she reached a small gathering of people. Without hesitation, she bent and lifted a tiny child—a baby, really, swaddled in a worn but clean blanket—holding him close, murmuring down at him

His stomach clenched.

A child.

His mind leapt to the most obvious conclusion—*her child*. She was married.

Of course she was. A woman like that, a woman of such striking beauty, such command, would not have remained unattached for long.

A strange weight settled on his heart. He did not understand it, nor did he try to. Instead, he forced himself to look away, coughing into his fist as the thick air once again reminded him of the current situation.

It was an absurd reaction—what should it matter to him? And yet, as he stood there, feeling the rasp of smoke in his throat and the distant hum of voices in his ears, all he could focus on was the way she held the child, how naturally she moved among the people who looked to her for guidance.

Of course she was married. A woman like that—strong, resolute, breathtaking—would not be left to navigate the world alone.

She was a remarkable woman.

But she was not for him.

His fingers curled at his sides, and he exhaled slowly, willing away the tightening of his chest.

"Sir?" a voice interrupted his thoughts.

Darcy turned sharply. One of the footmen he had sent out earlier had returned, waiting for instructions.

"Yes," he said, steadying himself. "Find out where the most urgent aid is required and report back."

The man bowed and hurried off, leaving Darcy to cast one last glance in Elizabeth's direction before forcing himself to turn away. There was work to be done, but for the first time in a long while, he did not know what to do with himself.

Chapter 5

Two months later…

Elizabeth pressed a gentle kiss on little Benjamin Bennet's forehead. "Sleep well, dear one."

The tiny baby let out a soft whimper, and Elizabeth's heart clenched. "Maybe I should stay home tonight."

"Nonsense," said Mrs. Bennet firmly. "You must attend the assembly tonight and meet. Ben will be just fine for the evening. It is not as if we are leaving him all alone— he has Nurse here with him."

Nurse, whose real name was Nancy Harold, served as both wet-nurse and caretaker of the child, shooed Elizabeth from the room. "Go on now, Miss Lizzy. You know I will watch him close, and it is only his teeth that are bothering him; he's not ill."

Nancy had been working for the family in London who had all been killed in the fires, not having had enough time to flee their home. Nancy's own child had passed away several years ago shortly after birth, and she had since then worked as a wet-nurse for a variety of families. It had been a miracle when they discovered Nancy at Hyde Park, desperately searching for someone who could feed the crying infant.

"Very well," Elizabeth said reluctantly.

"Even the Gardiners will be attending, and they have more young children to worry about!" Mrs. Bennet took Elizabeth's arm and began pulling her out of the nursery and down the stairs. "Even with all of that business with their house burning down and the issues with the insurance agency not paying yet, they still are making time for fun."

71

"I know you are worried about him, Lizzy," Jane said in a soothing tone as the ladies bundled into the carriage. "He will be quite well, and it is important that you take a rest now and again."

Kitty sniffed. "One would think that he were your own child with the way you fuss over him, instead of being a foundling."

"I still do not see why you need to adopt him, Mama," Lydia said in a sulky tone. "It is not as if he could inherit the estate or anything."

"You are just jealous because Mama has been paying more attention to him than to you lately," Mary smirked.

Lydia scowled at Mary's remark. "I am not jealous!" she huffed. "I simply do not see why we must keep him when the Gardiners offered to take him."

Mrs. Bennet gasped. "Give up my darling boy? Never! From the moment I laid eyes on him, I knew he was meant to be ours." She patted her heart dramatically. "No, no, I could not bear it."

Elizabeth sighed, adjusting the folds of her shawl. "It is not a matter of sentiment alone, Mama. We are looking into what must be done legally."

"Well, he certainly could not remain a foundling forever," Mrs. Bennet declared. "And you certainly take on more than your fair share of mothering, Lizzy. You fret over him as if he were your own babe."

Elizabeth opened her mouth to respond, but Jane laid a gentle hand on her arm. "You love him, Lizzy. That is all Mama means."

Elizabeth nodded, looking out the carriage window at the rolling countryside illuminated by the moon. "Of course I do."

"Well, I think it is all very silly," Lydia grumbled, slumping in her seat. "If he cannot inherit, what is the point?"

"Not everything is about inheritance," Jane said mildly.

Mary, never missing an opportunity, smirked. "Indeed, Lydia, some of us concern ourselves with duty and kindness, rather than who will inherit what."

Lydia narrowed her eyes. "And some of us do not want to end up as old maids."

"Some of us would rather be old maids than foolish wives."

Jane sighed. "Let us not quarrel, please."

Mrs. Bennet waved her handkerchief. "Yes, yes, enough of this nonsense. We are nearly there, and I will not have you ruining my evening. Netherfield has been let at last, and Mr. Bingley and his party will be there tonight! You must all be in your finest spirits."

Elizabeth smiled faintly, though her mind was still half at Longbourn, listening for Benjamin's soft whimpers. *This assembly had better be worth it.*

Upon arriving at the assembly hall, the Bennet ladies were greeted by Sir William, who served as master of ceremonies for the event. After making polite small talk for a few moments, they quickly dispersed throughout the room in search of their favorite companions—or, in Mary's case, a seat in the corner with her book.

Elizabeth had just retrieved a glass of weak punch when she spotted Charlotte Lucas approaching with a knowing smile.

"I must say, Lizzy, I had my doubts that you would come tonight," Charlotte teased.

Elizabeth sighed, shaking her head. "You and everyone else, it seems. I have been told by no fewer than three people that I must not allow myself to become a recluse."

Charlotte chuckled. "And were they wrong?"

"Perhaps not," Elizabeth admitted. "But I do not regret staying home these past weeks. There is nothing quite like the chaos of a baby to keep one occupied."

"I imagine your days are not quite what they used to be."

Elizabeth smiled, thinking of Benjamin's chubby hands reaching for her in the mornings. "No, but I do not mind it."

Charlotte arched a brow. "I always thought you would be the last of us to become so devoted to a baby."

"As did I," Elizabeth said with a laugh. "But Ben is… different."

Charlotte tilted her head. "Because he needed you?"

Elizabeth hesitated, then nodded. "Yes. Because he needed me."

Charlotte gave her a searching look but said nothing, sipping her own punch.

The musicians struck up a lively tune, and Elizabeth glanced around at the crowd beginning to arrange themselves for a dance. "And what of you? Have you enjoyed yourself thus far?"

Charlotte gave a wry smile. "Oh, exceedingly. My father has already assured me, twice, that we are all filled with 'such capital enjoyment.'"

Elizabeth grinned. "And I suppose you agreed wholeheartedly?"

"Naturally."

They both laughed, Charlotte's more reserved than Elizabeth's, before turning to observe the room.

"I hear Mr. Bingley is quite agreeable," Charlotte remarked after a moment. "It will be interesting to see if he truly is as charming as they say."

Elizabeth hummed in agreement. "I suppose we shall find out soon enough."

And as if on cue, the murmur of the crowd shifted, a wave of whispers rippling toward the entrance.

The Netherfield party had arrived.

Craning her neck to see above the crowd, Elizabeth attempted to get a glimpse of the newcomers. The first gentleman to enter was fair-haired and affable, his smile easy and warm as he exchanged greetings with Sir William.

"Sir William," came a bright, cheerful voice from the front of the hall. "It is a pleasure to make your acquaintance. I am Charles Bingley, and may I introduce my sisters, Miss Bingley and Mrs. Hurst? And my brother-in-law, Mr. Hurst."

On Mr. Bingley's arm was his unmarried sister, as evidenced by her lack of cap. She was tall and elegantly dressed, with sharp features and an assessing gaze. Her gown was of the finest silk, cut to perfection, and adorned with enough embellishment to suggest ostentatious. As she looked over the crowd, a flicker of barely concealed disdain passed over her face before she schooled her features into polite indifference.

Behind them came a well-dressed woman on the arm of a sluggish-looking man—*these must be the Hursts*—who seemed far more interested in surveying the refreshments than in the people gathered before him. The lady, in contrast, carried herself with grace and a quiet sort of superiority, her gaze not nearly as cutting as Miss Bingley's but equally distant.

Then, at last, another figure entered.

He was tall—easily the tallest of the group—but Elizabeth could not quite see his face. The movement of the guests had placed her behind a cluster of women whose elaborately feathered hats blocked her view.

"Ah, and this is my good friend, Mr. Darcy," Bingley continued.

Elizabeth barely registered the name as she shifted, standing on her toes in an attempt to see past the towering plumes.

Finally, the crowd adjusted.

And she saw him.

Her breath caught.

It was *him*.

The man from London. The one who had helped her in Hyde Park.

Elizabeth's heart slammed against her ribs as recognition washed over her.

What is he doing here?

⚒

The moment Darcy entered the rooms for the assembly, he knew he had made a mistake.

The atmosphere was thick with the mingling scents of sweat, candles, and far too many bodies crammed into a small space. As he breathed in the heavy air, his lungs—still weak from the London fire—tightened in protest.

He swallowed hard, pinching his lips together to stifle the deep, wracking cough that threatened to escape.

This is intolerable.

The chilly evening air on the drive over had aggravated his condition, along with the stifling carriage ride with Bingley's sisters. Both women had doused themselves in enough perfume to smother a horse, and he had spent the journey struggling to find enough fresh air to give rest to his tired lungs. His chest still ached from his efforts, and now, in this overcrowded hall with barely any space to breathe, panic clawed at the edges of his mind.

I cannot breathe!

His hands curled into fists at his side as he forced himself to focus on anything but the way his lungs refused to cooperate. He could not afford to make a scene. Letting his gaze drift over the room, he barely registered anything in the sea of unfamiliar faces.

And then—

He saw *her*.

Instantly, he truly could not breathe—not from his rebellious lungs this time, but from sheer, unrelenting shock.

For two months, he had tried to forget her. Oh, how he had tried. But the more he attempted to push her from his mind, the more insipid every debutante he had encountered since seemed dull in comparison.

He had spent countless nights convincing himself that his fascination was fleeting— that the fire and the desperation of the moment had heightened his emotions. He told himself he had imagined the way she seemed to command the chaos around her, the way she had defied the soldier without hesitation, the way she looked at him—not with awe, not with flirtation, but with steady, unwavering certainty.

But now, here she was.

Darcy felt rooted to the spot, as if the earth itself had shifted beneath him. She was staring at him, too, her dark eyes wide with something unreadable.

Time slowed.

Then, too soon, someone stepped forward, speaking her name— Elizabeth? —and she turned, allowing herself to be led onto the dance floor.

Darcy blinked, as if waking from a trance.

Elizabeth.

He watched her step into place for the set, her white gown swishing around her feet as she danced in time with the music. A single, incredulous thought struck him: *she is not married.*

She wore the colors of a maiden. No husband stood at her side. Perhaps the child—*the child!* —had not been hers.

Shock pulsed through him, followed swiftly by something else. Something he refused to name.

He exhaled slowly, forcing himself to the side of the room, where he could lean against a column and collect himself. His eyes, however, never left her. She danced with effortless grace, her expression alight with amusement as she exchanged words with her partner, then ended the dance with a curtsy.

It was an unfamiliar sight. He had only known her in the midst of tragedy, her face streaked with ash, her hands steady as she directed others through the chaos. And yet, even here, in this world of lighthearted chatter and polite society, she was just as captivating.

"Darcy!"

Suddenly, Bingley appeared at his elbow, causing him to lose sight of her. "Well?" Bingley grinned. "What do you think? A most delightful assembly, is it not?"

Blast! Bingley's interruption had caused him to lose track of the girl. He reluctantly turned his attention to his friend, answered in clipped words so as not to spark a coughing fit. "It is lively."

Bingley chuckled. "Come now, you must dance. I will not allow you to brood in the corner all evening."

Darcy stiffened, pressing his lips together to keep from coughing. "I have no intention of dancing."

"Allow me to have my partner introduce you to her sister. She is quite pretty, you see, and I understand she's quite the conversationalist as well." Bingley pointed towards someone to the side of him, and Darcy's eyes followed his friend's gesture.

Before he could actually see the figure indicated, however, his control slipped, caused by being forced to speak. The tightness in his chest surged into something sharper, and the fire in his lungs he had been suppressing for hours was fighting to break free. He clenched his jaw, pressing his lips together, willing the attack to subside.

It was no use.

He had mere seconds before he would embarrass himself completely. Without a word, he turned sharply and strode toward the door, forcing himself to keep his back straight even as his lungs burned.

He strode out into the hallway, barely registering Bingley's startled call behind him.

He needed air.

X

Elizabeth gaped at Mr. Darcy's retreating figure, her pulse racing. *Did he really just* cut *me?*

For weeks after the fire, she had thought of him with gratitude—and perhaps even with admiration. He had been decisive and commanding, stepping in when the soldier had refused to hear her pleas for the injured woman.

And now, when she finally saw him again, he looked at her with contempt?

Had she imagined it? The way his eyes had locked with hers, the way time itself had seemed to slow? Surely, she had not been mistaken in recognizing him. He was definitely the man who had aided her in Hyde Park, who had spoken on her behalf, who had looked at her then with such... intensity.

And yet, now he had turned away from her as if she were nothing. The look in his eyes tonight had been different.

Disdain, a voice inside her whispered.

Heat flooded her cheeks, and her heart pounded as confusion swirled within her. *Did I do something to offend him in London? Perhaps he did not truly approve of my assertiveness?*

No, that was impossible; her behavior had been well within the bounds of appropriate conduct, especially in light of the situation. She had been firm, yes, but she also had been civil in her discourse with the soldier.

Had he only helped her out of pity? Had he looked upon her then as a mere curiosity—some half-wild woman commanding order in a disaster—

and now regretted lowering himself to acknowledge her? Had he thought her worthy of respect when she was covered in ash and desperation but found her lacking when placed in a ballroom?

Or perhaps he did not believe a woman *should be the one to interfere.*

Yes, that must be it. Perhaps he believed her to have overstepped her place. Perhaps he thought her too bold, too unfeminine.

Elizabeth's hands clenched into fists at her sides.

How *dare* he?

The more she turned the matter over in her mind, the more her mortification transformed into anger. If he had taken issue with her actions that day, he should have said so then, not pretended she did not exist now, like some arrogant, spoiled aristocrat.

How dare he judge me when he does not even know me?

She took a deep breath, her resolve hardening. She would not allow this insult to go unanswered. If he wished to snub her, then he could at least have the decency to explain *why*.

Her feet carried her swiftly across the room to the beverage table, her irritation fueling every step. She barely registered the music, the chatter, the laughter around her. Lifting her chin, she squared her shoulders and slipped out the doors into the hall.

The cool night air blowing in from an open balcony met her skin, a welcome relief after the oppressive heat of the assembly hall. Scanning the dimly lit corridor, she caught sight of him only a few feet away, leaning heavily against a column.

He was coughing—violently, uncontrollably. His entire frame shuddered with the force of it, his shoulders hunched forward as he braced himself against the stone pillar. His face was flushed, his cravat slightly loosened as if he had tried to ease his constricted breathing. But it was not enough.

Her righteous fury vanished in an instant, replaced by something far more powerful: compassion.

His lips were parted in a desperate attempt to draw in air, yet the illusory vice around his chest would not allow it. His complexion was turning from red to something far more alarming—purple. One gloved hand clutched the wooden paneling beside him as though the force of the attack might bring him to his knees. His head was bowed, his shoulders shaking with each rasping, agonizing breath.

Elizabeth had never heard such terrible coughing before—deep, ragged, and unrelenting. It clawed at his throat, stole his breath, and rattled his entire frame. He was drowning in it, barely able to stand upright.

Was this why he had left so suddenly? Not because of her—but because he could not breathe? This was no mild ailment. This was something deeper, something painful, something that stole the air from his lungs and left him drowning on dry land.

Is he dying?

Panic jolted through her. Was anyone coming to assist him? Had no one noticed him slipping out? She realized neither Bingley nor his sisters had followed him; and now, standing here, watching him, she realized how alone he was.

Elizabeth's heart pounded. She had been ready to confront him with righteous indignation, to demand an explanation for his coldness—but now, all she could think was he needs help.

She took a step forward, then another, her feet moving before her mind had caught up.

"Mr. Darcy—"

He did not seem to hear her. His head was bowed, his body still wracked by the attack.

Without thinking, she ran.

Chapter 6

There was no time to waste. Elizabeth barely registered her movements as she turned on her heel, her skirts brushing against the doorframe as she slipped back into the assembly hall.

Her heart was still racing, but this time it was from panic. The bright, lively noise of the ballroom hit her like a wall. The laughter, the chatter of the guests, the musicians tuning their instruments for the next dance—how could everything be so normal when only a few steps away, someone was struggling for breath?

The drink table had been set up just to left of the doorway and was laden with glasses of weak punch and lemonade. Most of the guests were far too absorbed in changing partners or speaking with friends to notice her movements. She ducked her head, thankful for the distraction provided by the lively reel that had just begun, and crept towards the table as inconspicuously as possible.

Her fingers shook slightly as she reached for a glass of lemonade, her attention divided between the task at hand and the thought of Mr. Darcy waiting outside. Grasping it tightly, she quickly—but carefully—made her way back outside.

Darcy was still leaning against the column, but his coughing fit had seemed to ease somewhat. His chest still heaved with uneven breaths, and a faint sheen of perspiration beaded on his forehead, but at least his face had resumed a more usual color.

"Here," she murmured, pressing the cool glass into his gloved hands.

He hesitated for just a moment before taking it, his fingers brushing against hers. The brief touch sent a tingling sensation up her arm that lingered even after he lifted the drink to his lips. Sipping carefully, some of the tension in his shoulders loosened.

Elizabeth remained at his side, watching him in silence. His attack reminded her of the ones Kitty used to get as she was recovering from her pneumonia as a child. *Poor man, to be so afflicted as an adult.*

After another sip, he lowered the glass and exhaled slowly. "Thank you," he said hoarsely.

"Shall I fetch your friend for you?"

He pressed his lips together and shook his head.

Her stomach tightened. *Is he angry with me again? Did he not wish for my assistance?*

Then she looked into his eyes and saw reflected in them a hint of desperation, not anger. It was the same pained expression he had worn inside earlier, when he had been suppressing his cough.

Understanding dawned. "I think I understand," she said gently. "Speaking makes it worse, does it not?"

He opened his mouth to reply, and she hastily added, "No need to strain yourself. You may nod or shake your head as you like."

After looking at her for a long moment, his expression unreadable, he gave a small incline of his head.

"My sister, Kitty, is the same way. She contracted influenza at a young age, and it left her with a horrible cough. I am so sorry; I remember the pain was quite agonizing at times for her."

He gave a brief nod again. Reaching for the small purse attached to her wrist, Elizabeth unfastened it and withdrew a tiny sachet of powders wrapped in a scrap of muslin. "My uncle, who owned an importing business in London at the time, used his contacts to make inquiries in far-off countries on their local treatments. After much trial and error, we finally found a combination of herbs from the Far East that work well."

Darcy watched her intently as she spoke, his dark eyes fixed on her face. Swallowing, she continued. "Kitty is much better now, but if she exerts herself too much—like dancing—her breathing grows difficult again. I always keep some of these herbs with me."

He remained silent, the weight of his gaze boring into her. She cleared her throat, suddenly self-conscious about her ramblings. "Did you fall ill as a child?"

A brief nod.

"Did the smoke from the London fire make it worse?"

Another nod.

"I suspected as much." Elizabeth sighed. "The air was dreadful for days afterwards." She lifted the sachet slightly. "Usually, I steep this in hot water for Kitty, but lemonade serves just as well in a pinch. Would you like to try it?"

He hesitated, his gaze flickering from her face to the small pouch in her hands. She realized in that moment just how much he was trusting her. To take an unknown remedy from a woman he technically had never been introduced to... especially given their secluded location.

I could easily claim compromise!

But before he could refuse, another cough burst from his lips, shaking his entire frame. She saw his jaw clench in frustration; then, in a rasp barely above a whisper, he said, "Please."

Elizabeth gave a small nod and took the half-filled glass from him. Kneeling on the ground, she unwrapped the powdered herbs and began pouring them in. She swirled the glass to dissolve them as best as she could. "It will taste bitter," she warned. "Even when we prepare it properly, we add honey and milk to make it more palatable. I am afraid you shall have to simply bear the taste."

He gave no response, merely watching her with quiet intensity.

"No sugar, either, I am afraid. We do our best to avoid it."

His brow furrowed slightly, and she let out a nervous giggle. "It is a rather long story, but a few years ago, my father read us an article about the abolitionist movement. There was a call to boycott sugar from the plantations that relied on slavery. Lydia—my youngest sister—was only thirteen years old at the time, and she was so moved by the idea that she insisted we all give it up."

Something shifted in his expression. She bit her lip and swirled the mixture more quickly, her words bubbling forth. "I supposed 'insisted' is too gentle a word. She rather bullied us about it for days. My father protested at first, but it was far easier to concede the point than to endure her lectures on morality."

Something like amusement flickered across Darcy's features. She gave him a small smile, then passed him the glass. "I am afraid I could not get all of it to dissolve—not without a way to stir it properly. I hope it helps."

Darcy took it without a word and lifted it to his lips. He grimaced slightly at the taste but forced himself to drink it entirely.

As soon as he finished the vile concoction, Sir William's voice echoed faintly from the assembly hall. "Ladies and gentlemen, the final dance of the evening will be *La Boulangere*."

Elizabeth exhaled slowly. "I should return before someone sees us out here alone."

Darcy nodded wordlessly and extended the glass to her. She took it, hesitating. "If you find the herbs are helpful, have Mrs. Nicholls—she's the Netherfield housekeeper— send a note to Mrs. Hill at Longbourn."

He looked at her questioningly, and she hastened to assure him. "They are both very discreet, and I can easily have more herbs sent to you through them if you would like."

"Do not want… use all," he rasped.

"Oh! Please do not worry about that. We grow them in our still room now, so we have plenty. I can easily send over what we have stored and dry more if Kitty needs."

He gave her a small bow. "Thank you." His voice was still hoarse.

"My pleasure," she replied. "I will be sure to include a list of their names and properties as well."

Darcy bowed again, and Elizabeth gave him a small smile before turning around and slipping back into the assembly room to watch the final dance of the evening. Her heart and face were both warm from their private *tête-à-tête*, a conversation unlike any she had ever shared with a gentleman before.

She had expected coldness from him, perhaps even further rudeness or even disdain. Instead, she had found a man struggling not with arrogance, but with something far more human—pain, vulnerability, and an affliction he clearly tried to keep hidden. And yet, despite his silence, he had listened to her, trusted her.

As she wove through the crowd, the lively strains of the musicians filled the air, yet the world felt strangely distant, as though she were caught between two realities: the bright, bustling warmth of the assembly and the quiet intimacy of the dimly lit corridor where she had just stood with Mr. Darcy. Even now, she could feel the weight of his gaze lingering on her back, as if he were still watching, still trying to puzzle her out.

Shaking herself, Elizabeth shook off the strange spell of the moment and smoothed the folds of her gown. It was foolish to dwell on it. In the morning, everything would return to normal. And yet, as she found her mother at the edge of the dance floor, she could not quite shake the feeling that something had shifted—something she did not yet have the words to name.

X

Darcy stared at the retreating figure of Elizabeth Bennet—*Miss* Elizabeth! He could scarcely believe his good fortune. Of all the women in all the places in all the country, she was here, and she was unmarried.

The faint scent of lavender lingered in the air long after she had left, a quiet reminder of her presence. His hands dangled at his sides, fists clenching and then opening again in disquiet, the warmth of her kindness settling deep into his chest.

When he first realized she had followed him, he braced himself for at best, embarrassment at being caught in such a state, or, at worse, a tongue-lashing for having walked away from her before being introduced. He had resigned himself to either the wide-eyed horror or simpering concern that women often displayed upon witnessing his coughing fits.

Yet none of that had occurred.

No recoiling, no nervous fidgeting, no forced reassurances that made him feel all the more like an invalid. Instead, she had been calm and practical—just as capable in an emergency as she had been that morning in Hyde Park.

He had not been treated thusly since… *Since Wickham.*

Brushing the thought of his long-lost friend aside, Darcy considered Elizabeth's unique response to him. Other women often turned pale or even had a fit of the vapors at his struggles. Even his aunt, Lady Matlock—who was often spoken of as a woman with considerable fortitude—had pressed a perfumed handkerchief to her nose and fled the room the last time she witnessed a particularly bad fit overtake him.

Do not forget Lady Catherine. He shuddered at the memory of the last time he had been in her presence during an attack. She had lambasted him the way his father often did, decrying him to be a weak, worthless man. The only good thing to come from the experience was that she had declared him to be an unfit husband for her daughter.

But Elizabeth Bennet had done no such thing. She moved *toward* him, not away.

When she first fled, he had resigned himself to having made a fool of himself in her eyes. He could scarce believe it when she actually returned to his side with a cup of lemonade, offering comfort and aide instead of derision and scorn. She had spoken gently to him, understood that he need not force words out, and had produced—*from her own purse, no less*—a possible treatment.

And it seems to be working!

To Darcy's great astonishment, his breath was coming easier. The tightness in his chest, the raw constriction that had been his constant companion since the fire, was noticeably lighter. He had not even realized just how crushing it had been until now.

For the first time in months, he could almost draw a full breath without it catching painfully in his lungs and sparking a round of coughing.

Could it really be the herbs? The foul taste lingered in his mouth, a mix of dirt and lemons, and he laughingly thought that he would never taste lemonade the same way again.

He tried countless treatments since his lungs were damaged in childhood—poultices, tinctures, and even blood-letting—but none had offered more than temporary relief, if that.

But after trying these are herbs, he *felt* better.

He exhaled slowly, his mind turning over this revelation, when Bingley strode through the doors from the assembly hall, followed by his sisters and Hurst. "There you are, Darcy!"

Darcy straightened as his friend approached with his usual easy smile. "We have been looking for you, old chap. I was beginning to think you had entirely abandoned us."

"You never returned to the ballroom, Mr. Darcy," said Miss Bingley with an exaggerated pout. "You left me feeling quite bereft."

"I required fresh air."

Her expression changed into one of sympathetic disapproval. "Oh, yes, I understand. How *intolerable* it was in there. So *crowded,* so *stifling.* I truly cannot imagine how anyone endures such an event." She let out a delicate sign. "But of course, Charles absolutely *insisted* on attending, though I know not why."

Bingley chuckled, unbothered. "I found it delightful. So many pretty ladies—several of them were uncommonly pretty."

Miss Bingley sniffed. "You are far too good-natured, Charles; always insisting on seeing the best in every*one* and every*thing*." She shot Darcy a sidelong glance. "I daresay Mr. Darcy did not enjoy it in the least."

"I found it to be lively." Darcy's tone was emotionless.

Mrs. Hurst lifted her chin. "It was overwhelming. The smell alone was unbearable—sweat, smoke from the tallow candles, and cheap perfume. Ghastly."

"Shall we go?" Bingley asked, attempting to change the conversation.

The group made their way to the front, the driver waiting for them outside. As soon as they all entered the carriage, however, the ladies' chosen topic was once again at the forefront.

"I do so despise attending a public ball," Miss Bingley complained. "They allow *all* sorts in—merchants and tradesmen, even attorneys—to mingle with the local country gentry. Quite savage."

"And the fashion!" Mrs. Hurst shook her head with dismay. "Did you see those gowns? I counted at least three young women wearing styles that were from at least two years ago."

"I counted *five*," Miss Bingley replied smugly.

Mrs. Hurst pressed a hand to her chest as if wounded. "If one cannot dress properly, then one should not attend at all."

"Little wonder poor Mr. Darcy sought fresh air outside." Miss Bingley cloying tones gave Darcy a headache. "To be breathing such thick, plebeian air—had I thought of the idea myself, I should have joined you in the hall."

Darcy shuddered, doing his best to mask his feelings. The very the idea of Miss Bingley being the one to discover him instead of Elizabeth was repugnant.

Mrs. Hurst, who had followed her siblings from the room on her husband's arm sighed. "I do not know why Charles insists on these little excursions into the country. The company is so much better in town, is that not right, my dear?"

Mr. Hurst, barely paying attention, let out a lazy grunt of agreement.

Miss Bingley scoffed. "Naturally! The right people attend private gatherings. But these public assemblies? Anyone may come. And anyone does." She shuddered theatrically. "It was oppressive, really."

Louisa nodded sagely. "And the conversation was even worse."

"Indeed! I had to endure the dullest discussion about farming, of all things! Do they truly have nothing better to speak of?"

Mrs. Hurst made a face. "You think that was dreadful? I was accosted by some old woman who prattled on about pickling for nearly half an hour."

Darcy barely heard them. His thoughts were still back in the corridor, with Elizabeth Bennet offering him an herbal remedy from her own purse.

Miss Bingley prattled on, oblivious. "And do not even speak to me of the gentlemen. Did you see some of those men? Coarse hands, thick accents—ugh! Why, I nearly expected to see one of them attempt a jig in the middle of the ballroom."

Louisa let out a quiet laugh. "Did you see the woman who tripped on the hem of her own gown? She landed directly into her partner's arms. I was mortified on her behalf."

"It was exactly as I feared," Miss Bingley continued with a sigh. "When one allows the lesser classes to mingle freely, one simply must expect such vulgarity."

Bingley rolled his eyes. "Caroline, you enjoyed yourself well enough. I saw you speaking quite pleasantly to Miss Bennet."

Miss Bingley stiffened but quickly recovered. "Oh, well, she is—mildly agreeable. But even she is far too tolerant of her dreadful family. I suppose she's the best that the country can offer, but were I to see her in London, I daresay I would not give her the time of day."

"Precisely, Caroline." Mrs. Hurst nodded emphatically. "At least in town, one may be selective about with whom one associates. It is hardly our fault if the standard of company is lacking."

Miss Bingley turned back to Darcy, her voice shifting to something more honeyed. "You must admit, Mr. Darcy, that an event in town would have been far more enjoyable?"

Darcy let the silence stretch long enough that she began to fidget. Then, in a flat voice, he replied, "I do not much care for dancing, whether in town or in the country."

This set Miss Bingley on a string of assurances that she agreed with him, and how their thoughts were always in perfect harmony. She declared it to be remarkable but understandable, as they were such close friends.

Darcy said nothing. He had neither the patience nor the inclination to argue, nor did he wish to encourage further discussion. But as he followed his party down from the carriage and into Netherfield, his thoughts remained fixed not on Miss Bingley's complaints, but on a woman with warm brown eyes, who had met him at his weakest and had treated him not with pity, but with quiet understanding.

And as he retired to his room, he allowed himself a single, private thought: Elizabeth Bennet had been the most remarkable part of the night.

Because for the first time in months, he could breathe.

And not because she did not take your breath away.

Chapter 7

Longbourn was quiet the following morning; the ladies of the house were having a lie-in to recover from dancing at the assembly until the wee hours. By the time lunch was over, however, the occupants had resumed their various levels of vigor.

With the expected arrival of the Lucases and Gardiners—a tradition dating back several years for the day after an assembly—the drawing room was filled with lively conversation.

Elizabeth was sitting on the settee, baby Benjamin nestled comfortably in her arms. After greeting the others in the room, Mrs. Gardiner made her way over to Elizabeth and sat down on the settee. The two exchanged warm smiles as the Lucases were announced.

Once everyone was settled, Mrs. Bennet—perched at the edge of her chair and fluttering a lace handkerchief—was the first to speak. "Well! I must say, last night was quite the triumph, was it not? You began the evening very well, Charlotte, being Mr. Bingley's first choice."

Charlotte smiled. "Yes, but I do believe he much preferred his second better."

"Oh, yes," beamed Mrs. Bennet. "It was quite the triumph for my dear girl, was it not? I knew from the moment I laid eyes on Mr. Bingley that he would admire her, and lo and behold—two dances! Two!" She turned to her eldest daughter. "Jane, my love, he was quite obviously smitten with you."

Jane turned a becoming shade of pink. "It was very kind of him," she said quietly. "He was very amiable, but it was still only two dances."

Mrs. Gardiner chuckled. "Still, Jane, it is a mark of favor. A gentleman does not request a second set unless he is particularly taken."

"She is quite right," Lady Lucas added. "There were plenty of young ladies who would have been delighted to dance with him, yet he returned to you."

Mrs. Bennet sighed dreamily. "Oh, I have no doubt that he will be calling at Longbourn before the week is out."

"And did you have a nice time, Lizzy?" Mrs. Gardiner asked smoothly, intending to change the topic of conversation.

"I daresay she did not!" scoffed Mrs. Bennet. "First, she is cut by Mr. Darcy, and then she disappeared for the remainder of the evening."

"Someone gave you the cut direct?" gasped Mrs. Gardiner.

"Yes, and he was the most disagreeable man I have ever had the misfortune to meet," sniffed Lady Lucas.

Elizabeth hesitated, her fingers twisting the fringe on Benjamin's blanket. "I actually do not believe he intended to be so rude, Mama."

Charlotte's eyebrows rose high on her head. "I must say, Eliza, I would not expect such forbearance from *you*! Jane, perhaps… but I would expect you to be mocking him just as much as the rest."

"I am not *so* prejudiced as that," Elizabeth protested, "but in this case, I have firsthand knowledge about the situation that I daresay none of you have."

The women all leaned in eagerly, even Jane and Mrs. Gardiner. Mrs. Bennet's eyes were bright. "Yes, my dear?" she asked eagerly.

Elizabeth laughed. "Oh, nothing so dramatic! I simply overheard someone from his party say that he was feeling very unwell with a megrim, but he had come regardless, in support of Mr. Bingley."

All the ladies sat back in their seats, and Kitty let out a disappointed moan. "What a let-down, Lizzy. I thought you might have a good bit of gossip to share," the youngest Bennet girl complained.

"Although it does put his behavior in a different light," Mrs. Gardiner said thoughtfully.

"Indeed," Mrs. Bennet nodded. "What a good friend he must be."

"I suppose I shall have to forgive him for ignoring my friend," Charlotte said with a smirk, "even if that friend did disappear for the second part of the evening."

Elizabeth pushed back her alarm as the ladies once again looked at her with curiosity. "My goodness, Charlotte," she said, forcing a laugh, "you act as though I slipped out for a rendezvous on the terrace. No, simply some cramping that had me concerned my courses might have begun early."

All the women sighed in commiseration. "You are well now, I trust, Lizzy?" Jane asked, concern etched across her lovely face.

"Oh, quite," Elizabeth assured her, waving a hand dismissively. "It was nothing of consequence."

"Speaking of disappearances," said Mrs. Bennet, turning to Mrs. Gardiner, "we were quite disappointed to not see you and your husband last night. I hope everything is alright at home?"

"Yes, I was truly sorry to miss out, but the children had a bit of a fever," Mrs. Gardiner explained, "and Mr. Gardiner was quite exhausted from matters of business."

"How is everything going with your new home?" Lady Lucas asked eagerly. "Have you made many changes yet? The drawing room is not as large as I would like, but at least the attics are not as dreadful as those at Purvis Lodge."

"Stoke Estate is coming along well enough—"

Mrs. Gardiner was cut off by a squeal from Mrs. Bennet. "Stoke Estate—oh, how wonderful that sounds! It is such a comfort, my dear sister, that you are now in possession of your own property. When Mr. Bennet dies," the lady threw a glare in the direction of her husband's study, "any of the unmarried girls and I will be taken care of. Not Jane, of course, as she will be settled at Netherfield as Mrs. Bingley by then. I quite despair over Lizzy and Mary, though…"

Her voice trailed off, and Mrs. Lucas once again asked Mrs. Gardiner about her plans for the estate.

"Unfortunately, we will not be making very many changes as of yet. The plan had been to use the money from leasing our London house. After the fire, we spoke to the insurance company to claim payment, but they have been slow in responding."

"That is unacceptable!" Mrs. Bennet cried indignantly.

"Surely they must know how many families have been affected," Jane said in a soft voice. "Why would they not provide the help that is so desperately needed?"

"They may not have enough money to pay everyone who lost their property," Elizabeth explained.

Mrs. Gardiner nodded. "And now an inspector has written to inform us that he will be coming to Meryton to make inquiries about the fire."

"What kind of inquiries?" Kitty asked.

Mr. Gardiner's mouth twitched. "It seems that some of the servants at Hyde Park mentioned that our group was among the first to arrive. The inspector finds it curious that we left our home before many others had even woken. He finds it…suspicious."

Elizabeth blinked in surprise. "Suspicious?"

"He wants to know how we became aware of the fire so quickly."

Charlotte let out a laugh. "Well, Lizzy, it seems you may have to prove your remarkable sense of smell to an inspector now."

Lady Lucas chuckled. "Indeed! He will have to be made to understand that Lizzy could detect the fire before anyone else had even noticed."

Elizabeth groaned theatrically. "If he wishes to be convinced, he may sit me before a tray of spices, and I shall identify them all with ease."

The room erupted into laughter, but Mary cut it off with a stern admonition. "We must take care not to make light of the trials suffered by our fellow man."

The room fell into an awkward silence for a few moments, and Benjamin began to stir in Elizabeth's arms. "How is this little one doing?" Mrs. Gardiner asked, changing the subject. "Has his birthmark faded at all?"

Elizabeth smiled, adjusting the baby in her arms. "Not in the least. It is still as clear as the day I first saw it."

"Birthmark?" Charlotte echoed curiously.

"Yes," Elizabeth replied. "The first time I changed his nappy, I discovered a heart-shaped birthmark on his thigh—about the size of my thumb."

"Oh, how charming!" Lady Lucas cooed.

Charlotte grinned. "A little mark of love for a little boy so well adored."

Elizabeth pressed a light kiss to Benjamin's forehead. "Indeed. He has captured all of our hearts, has he not?"

Mrs. Bennet sighed. "He was meant to be ours, from the very beginning."

For a few moments, the conversation drifted to lighter topics, filled with shared laughter and memories. It was a moment of peace, a brief respite from the challenges ahead.

But in the back of Elizabeth's mind, she could not help but wonder— what *would* that inspector make of her ability to smell the fire before anyone else?

)(

The following day at Longbourn began pleasantly enough, with the household gathering together for breakfast and discussing the day's plans. That peace, however, vanished the moment Lydia declared her intention of going into Meryton.

"Absolutely not!" shrieked Mrs. Bennet. "Do you not remember what happened to Mrs. Long's eldest niece last week? I told you girls right then that you would not be allowed to go into the village without a footman."

Lydia groaned, flinging herself back in her chair. "Oh, Mama! That is so unfair. We always go alone!"

"Yes, but things are different now," Elizabeth interjected, glancing at her Jane. "With so many displaced people wandering from London, Meryton is not as safe as it was."

"Unhappy as the event must have been for Miss Long, we must remember that loss of virtue in a female is irretrievable," Mary interjected solemnly, peering over her spectacles at the youngest Bennet daughter. "One false step will involve you in endless ruin; you cannot be too guarded in your behavior towards the undeserving of the other sex."

Kitty let out a long-suffering sigh, but Lydia was not so easily subdued.

"Well, that's just ridiculous," she snapped. "Why should I be punished because of some dirty beggars? It is not *my* fault people lost their homes in the fire and have come here! I still have mine, and I want to go to Meryton—without some great, lumbering footman breathing down my neck like a watchdog!"

"Lydia," Elizabeth said sternly, "please see reason. Miss Long is fortunate that the vagrant only made off with her reticule. Had Sir William not happened to be nearby, much worse things could have happened."

"Is there not a way we can help those poor people?" Jane's large blue eyes filled with tears. "They must be in truly desperate straits, to behave in such a way."

"What does it matter?" Lydia burst out. "Nothing would happen to me, for I am quite taller than Miss Long—than any of you! I should be just fine."

"No, Lydia," Mrs. Bennet said angrily. "You will do as you are told."

Lydia stomped her foot hard enough to rattle the dishes on the table, causing Mr. Bennet to lower his morning paper and glower at her over the pages. "Lydia, your shrieking is far less pleasant than usual, and I am rapidly losing my patience. Either lower your voice, or I shall be forced to consider the unthinkable— agreeing with your mother."

Lydia gasped as if she had been struck. "Papa!"

"I do not make idle threats, my dear." He raised his paper once more. "Besides, your mother is right. The roads are unsafe."

Lydia's eyes flashed with fury. "That is ridiculous! The only danger in Meryton is that it might bore me to death."

"Then I suppose we must all prepare for your funeral," Elizabeth quipped with a smirk.

Lydia screeched, turning back to her mother with an expression of utmost betrayal. "Mama, you cannot allow this! I shall be the only girl who is treated like a child!"

Mrs. Bennet dabbed at her eyes with a lace handkerchief. "Oh, Lydia, my love, you are my baby, but you must listen to your father! I could not bear it if something happened to you."

Lydia let out a high-pitched growl of frustration and flung herself onto the nearest settee. "This is so unjust! I might as well be locked away in a convent!"

"I may consider the possibility," Mr. Bennet said dryly.

Elizabeth fought back a laugh as Lydia began to wail.

It was at this precise moment that Mrs. Gardiner arrived. She entered the room just in time to witness Lydia throwing herself backward against the cushion of her chair in an exaggerated show of despair. Her sharp gaze swept over the room, taking in Kitty's sulky expression, Mrs. Bennet's flustered distress, and Mr. Bennet's smirk.

Her brow rose. "A tantrum at the breakfast table, Fanny? This is exactly what I meant the other day. Even Beth is better behaved than this."

Mrs. Bennet let out a heavy sigh, dabbing at her eyes with a lace handkerchief. "I do see it, Maddie, I do… but what am I to do? She gets so upset."

At this, Lydia spun toward them, her face a picture of outrage. "What are you talking about?" she shrieked. "Why are you comparing me to some child? I am practically a grown woman! I was out last year, and Beth is barely eleven!"

Mrs. Gardiner fixed her with a cool stare. "And that is precisely the problem, Lydia. In London, girls are not 'out' in society before seventeen. When they are let out earlier, they are often spoiled, poorly behaved, and far too immature to make wise decisions about courtship and marriage."

Lydia let out a strangled sound, somewhere between a sob and a shriek. "This is cruel—unforgivable—I will NEVER forgive you, Aunt Gardiner! You are SO unkind, and I hate you!"

Mrs. Gardiner gestured toward Lydia's stamping foot and flailing hands. "And this display is only proving my point."

Lydia let out an indignant screech. "You do not know anything! You do not get to tell me what to do! Mama, are you going to let her—"

"Oh, my nerves," Mrs. Bennet whimpered, pressing a trembling hand to her temple. "I cannot bear it when she gets like this!"

Mrs. Gardiner exhaled through her nose. "Fanny, I believe it is time someone took Lydia in hand."

Mrs. Bennet sniffled but gave a tearful nod of permission.

Lydia's eyes widened. "What does that mean?"

"It means you are coming with me."

Before Lydia could react, Mrs. Gardiner seized her firmly by the arm and marched her toward the door.

"MAMA!" Lydia wailed, kicking her feet uselessly as she was dragged along.

Mrs. Bennet whimpered into her handkerchief. Mr. Bennet leaned back in his chair, looking vaguely entertained.

The door swung shut behind them, muffling Lydia's continued protests. The remaining family exchanged glances, waiting to hear what would happen next. It was all Elizabeth could do to keep herself from standing and cheering.

All was still and silent, and then—

SLAP!

A loud, unmistakable crack echoed through the hall.

Kitty's mouth hung open. Jane paled. Mary adjusted her spectacles, as if questioning whether she had imagined the sound.

Mrs. Bennet let out a weak noise and promptly fanned herself.

For a long moment, no one spoke, then Kitty whispered, "Do you think she really…?"

Mr. Bennet cleared his throat. "Well," he mused. "That is one way to handle things."

The door opened, and Mrs. Gardiner re-entered the room alone, her expression entirely composed.

Lydia was nowhere in sight.

Mrs. Gardiner dusted off her hands. "Now then," she said smoothly, as if nothing at all had happened. "If you all have finished eating, shall we adjourn to your drawing room, Fanny?"

Nodding mutely, Mrs. Bennet rose from her seat and lead the way for her family to the drawing room.

"I will fetch Benjamin," Elizabeth said, eager for a moment to collect her thoughts—and perhaps have a private laugh at Lydia's chastisement.

As she stepped into the hall, Hill appeared from the direction of the still room. "Oh, Miss Lizzy, a message arrived just now from Netherfield."

"Ah, from Mrs. Nicholls about Mr. Darcy?"

"Yes, miss," Hill said. "She says he would be grateful for any medicine we can spare... I was not entirely certain what that meant."

Elizabeth's lips parted in surprise. So, he truly had found relief from them. Somehow, she had half-expected him to ignore her suggestion altogether.

"That's my fault, Hill," Elizabeth apologized. "I gave some of Kitty's herbs to Mr. Darcy last night when he was coughing at the assembly and told him we could provide more if he found them effective. I meant to tell you, but I had not found the time."

"I see. Shall I send them, then?"

"Of course. Please see that a proper portion is dried and packaged, and I will write out the list of ingredients." She paused, one foot on the stairs. "And if Mrs. Nicholls asks, assure her that there is plenty more should Mr. Darcy require it."

Hill gave a knowing smile. "Very good, miss."

With that settled, Elizabeth continued upstairs to the nursery, where Nurse sat knitting near the fireplace. "He's just now stirring, Miss Lizzy. It is almost like he knew you were coming."

Benjamin was lying in his cradle, blinking up at the ceiling with wide, curious eyes. The moment he saw her, his tiny arms flailed excitedly, and a soft coo escaped his lips.

"Oh, my love," Elizabeth murmured, scooping him up and pressing a kiss to his plump cheek. "Have you been a good boy?"

Benjamin gurgled in response, snuggling into her embrace. Cradling him close, she returned downstairs to the drawing room, where Mrs. Gardiner was already deep in discussion with Mrs. Bennet.

"—but you must hold firm, Fanny," Mrs. Gardiner was saying as Elizabeth entered and took a seat on the settee. "Lydia's behavior is not just a matter of youthful high spirits. It is a true risk to her future, and to that of your entire family."

Mrs. Bennet sniffed, dabbing at her eyes with her handkerchief. "But she is so young! It is natural for a girl of her age to want some enjoyment—"

"Enjoyment is one thing, recklessness is another," Mrs. Gardiner interrupted. "Fanny, if she is not reined in now, what do you suppose will happen? I tell you plainly—if she is not checked, I will not allow her to stay with us should the worst befall Mr. Bennet."

A stunned silence filled the room.

Even Elizabeth, who had been prepared for a lecture, looked up sharply. "Aunt," she said, her tone caught between shock and reproach.

Mrs. Gardiner did not waver. "And if she is allowed to run wild before then—if she ruins herself and drags your reputations down with her—none of you will be welcome."

A stunned hush fell over the room. Even Kitty, who was usually inclined to defend Lydia, seemed too shocked to speak.

Mrs. Bennet raised a trembling hand to her chest. "Maddie, surely you do not mean—"

"I do," Mrs. Gardiner interrupted. "I love my nieces, but I love my own children more. I will not risk their futures for Lydia's foolishness. You must take her in hand, or you will all suffer the consequences."

Mrs. Bennet burst into fresh tears, while Jane reached for her hand in silent comfort. Elizabeth, meanwhile, swallowed hard and looked down at Benjamin, his tiny fist wrapped around her finger.

But Aunt Gardiner is right. Something must be done, or Lydia could ruin us all.

"Very well, Maddie," Mrs. Bennet whispered. "I will do what I can."

Elizabeth let out a slow breath. *Hopefully it is not too late.*

Chapter 8

Within the week, the ladies of Netherfield paid a call on those at Longbourn, and the visit was about to be returned. Mrs. Gardiner accompanied her sister-by-marriage and her nieces—although Lydia was left at home, still locked in the nursery. The youngest Bennet girl was not adapting to her new circumstances very well, and Elizabeth was relieved that the room was located in a way that Lydia's infuriated shrieking was muffled to the rest of the house.

"I am quite looking forward to finally seeing Netherfield Park," Mrs. Gardiner said as the estate came into view. "I have never been inside."

"It has always been a handsome house, even when I was a girl," Mrs. Bennet replied. "When Lucy and I were girls just coming out, there were several parties hosted by Sir Reginald, the owner. Edward would have been too young to attend, of course, but Lucy and I passed many wonderful evenings in these rooms."

"Of course, it must be in a much different condition now," Elizabeth said. "Having sat empty for so long, I imagine Mr. Bingley must need to do quite a bit for it. It has been empty for so long that I am surprised anyone was even interested in it."

"There were actually quite a number of people who were interested," Mrs. Bennet said, leaning forward and speaking in a hushed voice to add to the intrigue. "Mr. Bingley is just the one who offered the best leasing agreement."

Elizabeth raised an eyebrow. "Indeed?"

Mrs. Bennet nodded furiously. "Oh, yes, I had it from Lucy. Mr. Philips was the one to provide the papers for the contract, and he told her all about it. Apparently, the price was driven up considerably when another gentleman attempted to secure the estate in spite of the deposit being paid."

Elizabeth exchanged an amused glance with her aunt. "How fortunate that he has such deep pockets, then."

"I should hope so," Mrs. Bennet said. "I only wish it had been a sale rather than a lease. That would be a true sign of permanency. But perhaps, once he realizes how much the area has to offer..." She looked meaningfully towards Jane, whose cheeks turned pink.

"The fire certainly had a tremendous effect on Hertfordshire," Mary interjected. "I would not have thought so, given that we are so far from London."

"We are closer to London than many other counties with large estates, and Meryton is along one of the main thoroughfares," Elizabeth replied. "It only makes sense that estates within a half-day's journey of London would be highly sought after."

"I wonder how long he intends to stay," Jane mused softly.

"I should think that depends entirely on whether a certain young lady maintains his interest," Mrs. Gardiner said with a smirk.

Jane blushed deeply, but before Elizabeth could chime in, the carriage came to a halt. "We are here!" Mrs. Bennet squealed, causing Mrs. Gardiner to reach over and pat her hand in an attempt to calm her nerves.

Without ceremony, the part was ushered inside, where they were soon welcome by Miss Bingley and Mrs. Hurst, both impeccably dressed and standing with their noses in the air.

Greetings were exchanged, with Mrs. Bennet introducing Mrs. Gardiner to their hostess, and they were all civilly invited to take their seats. They spoke of the weather and other banal topics until the tea was brought in. After asking each guest how they took theirs, Miss Bingley began to disperse the cups.

"I understand you are new to the area, Mrs. Gardiner?" Miss Bingley's honeyed tones caused the hair on the back of Elizabeth's neck to raise.

"Indeed," Mrs. Gardiner said smoothly, inclining her head.

Miss Bingley's smile was all polite indifference. "How lovely. I do hope you have not found your relocation from Cheapside too... taxing. A change in status can certainly be unnerving."

Elizabeth saw the glint in her aunt's eyes before she spoke. "Not at all, Miss Bingley. Stoke Estate has proved a most charming place, and we are quite pleased to be its new owners." She took a sip of tea, then added, "I trust you are finding your leasing of Netherfield to your satisfaction?"

The words were delivered lightly, but their meaning was clear. The Gardiners owned their estate, while Bingley, for all his wealth, was merely leasing Netherfield.

Miss Bingley's smile tightened ever so slightly.

"How fortunate for you," Mrs. Hurst interjected, forcing a laugh. "Though I cannot imagine leaving London entirely—such a sacrifice!"

"It has its advantages," Mrs. Gardiner said pleasantly. "And with the current state of affairs in London, I believe many have found themselves desiring a quieter life in the country."

"I daresay you must be noticing the stark contrast to town. Your husband was in trade, was he not?"

"He was."

Miss Bingley's nose wrinkled at the polite, yet brusque, answer. "Now, where were you residing before?"

"Our house was in Gracechurch Street."

Mrs. Hurst gave a theatrical gasp. "Oh my, was that not one of the places in Cheapside that burned down with the docks? How fortunate that you were able to afford to relocate with such…advantage."

"My aunt and uncle were already in the process of moving," Elizabeth said testily. "Uncle Gardiner sold his business some six months before the fire; he was quite successful at what he did."

Miss Bingley's teacup paused briefly before reaching her lips. "How… admirable."

"And you, Miss Bingley?" Mrs. Gardiner asked, tilting her head. "Do you and your sister enjoy country life?"

Miss Bingley set her teacup down with a carefully measured smile. "It is… an adjustment."

"Ah, yes," Elizabeth smirked. "I imagine it must be quite different when one is merely visiting rather than settling permanently."

Miss Bingley's lips pressed together.

Mrs. Gardiner patted Elizabeth's hand lightly, her own expression perfectly pleasant. "Yes, indeed. There is something quite different about putting down roots. I imagine you will discover that for yourselves soon enough."

Jane, who had been looking anxiously between the two opposing sides, sought to change the topic by asking Mrs. Hurst about the lace on her gown. This put an end to the one-sided battle of wits, and fashion became of the focus of the remainder of the visit, with Mrs. Bennet and Kitty eagerly sharing their opinions.

Elizabeth sat back and watched as Miss Bingley and Mrs. Hurst launched into a detailed discussion of the latest styles from town, their tones notably lighter now that they were on a subject they could dominate. Mrs. Bennet, ever eager to ingratiate herself, nodded enthusiastically at every remark, while Kitty listened with rapt attention, hanging on every word about flounces, trims, and the superiority of London dressmakers.

Elizabeth, however, was not fooled. She noted the tightness around Miss Bingley's mouth, the way she clutched her teacup just a little too firmly. Despite her attempts at superiority, the woman was rattled.

And that is what happens when you cross swords with my family.

The following morning was cool and damp, with the scent of approaching rain lingering in the air. The ladies of Longbourn had gathered in the drawing room after breaking their fast, and they had just settled in when a footman entered bearing a note for Jane.

"Who is it from?" Mrs. Bennet asked eagerly.

"Miss Bingley is asking me for dinner this evening," Jane replied, her face lighting up.

"Let me see." Mrs. Bennet snatched the paper from Jane's hand and read it over. "Oh, that's disappointing; the gentlemen will be dining out."

"It is very kind of them to extend the invitation," Jane said. "May I have the carriage, Mama?"

Mrs. Bennet pursed her lips and looked out the window. "No, I think it will be needed on the farm today. You shall ride Nellie."

"Go on horseback?" Elizabeth gasped, bouncing Benjamin lightly in her arms. "Mama, she will be soaked through by the time she arrives!"

"Nonsense," Mrs. Bennet declared. "A little rain never hurt anyone! You shall ride on horseback, Jane. It will do your complexion good, and they cannot refuse to keep you at Netherfield overnight should the rain become too heavy."

Jane hesitated. "I do not wish to put them to any trouble—"

Before Mrs. Bennet could insist further, another voice interrupted from the doorway.

"I believe I can offer a solution," Mrs. Gardiner said as she stepped into the room, having just arrived from Stoke Estate. "My carriage is waiting outside. If Jane is to go, she may take it while I visit with you all."

Relief flickered across Jane's features, and she quickly accepted. Within minutes, she was bundled into her cloak and stepping outside to the waiting carriage. Elizabeth followed, still cradling Benjamin, to bid her sister farewell.

"Enjoy your evening," she said warmly.

"I am sure I shall."

A low rumble of thunder echoed in the distance as the carriage set off. Five minutes later, the skies opened, and rain poured down in torrents.

Mrs. Bennet, peering anxiously out the window, sighed in satisfaction. "There now, you see? Had she gone on horseback, she would have been obliged to stay the night!"

Kitty, stretching on the settee, let out a dramatic sigh. "I do wish I had something interesting to do today like Jane does. Perhaps we ought to go into Meryton."

"You do quite enough gallivanting," Mary sniffed, not looking up from her book. "Between the weather and the homeless, the idea of going into the village is ludicrous."

"You should come with us next time, Mary," Kitty said mischievously. "If only to look at the latest fabrics. Perhaps a new gown might suit you."

"Indeed, Mary," Mrs. Bennet agreed, clasping her hands. "You are always dressing so plainly. We must find you something a little more... fashionable."

As Kitty and Mrs. Bennet began discussing ribbons and trims, Elizabeth noticed Mrs. Gardiner shifting in her seat, her expression slightly troubled.

"What is it, Aunt?" she asked quietly, adjusting Benjamin against her shoulder.

Mrs. Gardiner exhaled, shaking her head as though trying to dispel a troublesome thought. "I should not worry you with it, my dear."

Elizabeth arched a brow. "Now you must tell me."

Mrs. Gardiner hesitated, then leaned in slightly. "The inspector coming next week has me feeling a bit uneasy."

Elizabeth frowned. "Why should he? It is ridiculous to think that you or Uncle Gardiner would be under suspicion."

Mrs. Gardiner sighed and folded her hands in her lap. "It is not so much what he has said but what has been implied. When we first received word that an inquiry was being made into the fire, I thought nothing of it—surely it was to determine the extent of damages, perhaps to root out fraud among the insurance claims. But now, Elizabeth..." She hesitated before continuing in a lower voice. "Now, it seems the authorities believe the fire was not an accident."

117

Elizabeth's heart gave an uncomfortable lurch. "What do you mean?"

"They believe it was arson," Mrs. Gardiner admitted grimly, her voice barely above a whisper. "Not carelessness, not misfortune—arson. Deliberate destruction."

A chill ran down Elizabeth's spine, though the drawing room was warm. "That is absurd. Who would do such a thing?"

Mrs. Gardiner shook her head. "That, they do not yet know. But, Elizabeth... we were among the first to flee."

Elizabeth sat up straighter. "Because we knew about the fire first.

"Precisely. The inspector finds it curious that we were able to escape so quickly while so many others perished. He wishes to know how we became aware of the fire before others."

Elizabeth felt a flash of indignation. "We knew because I smelled it! Because I woke up and raised the alarm before it spread too far! Surely that is not suspicious?"

"Perhaps not to those who know you," Mrs. Gardiner allowed. "But to an outsider, to an investigator looking for someone to blame? They might not find it so innocent. They may think we were forewarned."

Elizabeth's stomach twisted. "Forewarned? Do they believe we had something to do with it?"

Mrs. Gardiner lifted a shoulder in an uncertain shrug. "I do not know, my dear. But when men search for answers, they often look first to those who were fortunate when others were not."

"That is absurd," Elizabeth said hotly. "You lost your home! How could anyone believe you had a hand in such a disaster?"

Mrs. Gardiner sighed. "It is not about logic, Lizzy. It is about appearance. And the truth is, we survived and fled early, while others did not. We were seen arriving at Hyde Park before many others had even realized what was happening. We must be prepared for difficult questions."

Elizabeth swallowed, glancing at Benjamin, who was gurgling happily against her shoulder, blissfully unaware of the dark conversation unfolding around him.

"I cannot believe this," she murmured. "To think that instead of mourning the dead, some seek to cast blame where none belongs."

Mrs. Gardiner gave a sad smile. "Human nature is often uglier than we would wish."

Elizabeth exhaled, nodding determinedly. "Well, if this investigator wishes to know why we fled so early, I shall simply tell him the truth: I smelled the fire before anyone else. If he is not satisfied, he is welcome to test me himself."

"He very well might. The investigators are searching for patterns. I cannot shake the feeling that this will not be an easy matter to put behind us."

Elizabeth stared at her aunt, processing the implications. She had always assumed the fire was a tragic accident, a consequence of crowded conditions and misfortune. But if it had been deliberate? If someone had started the fire that had taken so many lives?

For the first time since that awful night, she felt something close to fear.

X

Several hours after Mrs. Gardiner's carriage returned and took her back to Stoke Estate, a note arrived from Netherfield from Jane.

My dear Lizzy,

Do not be alarmed when I do not return to Longbourn tonight, due to some clumsiness on my part. As I was stepping into the carriage Miss Bingley so kindly offered, I lost my footing and took a rather inelegant tumble.

Mr. Bingley and Mr. Darcy had just returned from their dinner in town and were most insistent that I not attempt the journey home with my ankle in such a state. Mr. Bingley called for a maid to assist me upstairs, and Miss Bingley has assured me that I am welcome to remain here until Mr. Jones can examine me in the morning.

Please do not worry—though I am in some discomfort, I am well looked after. Mr. Bingley has been very kind, and Miss Bingley, though somewhat flustered at the unexpected turn of events, has made certain that I have everything I need. I will write again after Mr. Jones has seen me.

Give my love to Mama and the rest of the family, and please assure them that I am in excellent care.

Yours always,

Jane

Elizabeth frowned as she read the letter a second time, concern creeping into her chest. Jane, ever the optimist, was unlikely to complain even if she were in great pain. A twisted ankle could be a minor inconvenience or something far worse.

She folded the note carefully and turned to her mother, who was already fluttering with nervous energy.

"Oh, my poor Jane!" Mrs. Bennet cried, wringing her hands. "What if her ankle is broken? What if she is left with a limp? Oh, how dreadful! She must stay at Netherfield as long as necessary—yes, as long as necessary! I knew sending her in the carriage was the right choice; had she been on horseback, she might have been thrown and suffered far worse!"

Elizabeth pressed her lips together to keep from pointing out that Jane had slipped on the carriage step, not from any treacherous horseback ride.

Kitty and Lydia, meanwhile, were whispering together. "Do you think she will have to stay for days?" Lydia asked with a giggle. "Perhaps Mr. Bingley will be so overcome with concern that he will propose!"

Kitty smirked. "Or at the very least, Miss Bingley will be in fits over the inconvenience."

Elizabeth ignored them, instead turning to her father, who was still reading his newspaper. "Papa, do you think I might walk to Netherfield in the morning to check on Jane?"

Mr. Bennet lowered his paper slightly, peering over the top of it. "You may do as you like, my dear, provided you do not expect me to send the carriage after you if it should rain."

Elizabeth smiled faintly. "I shall take my chances."

Mrs. Bennet, meanwhile, had already begun planning aloud. "Yes, Lizzy, you must go and report back on Jane's condition. And if she must stay longer, well! It can only be to her advantage. She will have the opportunity to further endear herself to Mr. Bingley. Oh! What if he insists on nursing her back to health himself? What a charming romance it would be!"

Elizabeth barely refrained from rolling her eyes. "I hardly think Miss Bingley would allow that."

Mrs. Bennet sniffed. "Miss Bingley may as well resign herself to the inevitable. Mr. Bingley likes Jane—I could see it in his eyes! And now he has the perfect excuse to dote on her. And with one daughter so well situated at Netherfield, we will no longer be in danger of the hedgerows when your father is gone."

"But Mama, the Gardiners have already promised they will be of assistance to us," Elizabeth protested.

"Only if your sisters behave, though." Mrs. Bennet glared at her younger two. Kitty looked abashed, but Lydia frowned spitefully. "With Lydia's lively spirits, I am certain Mr. Gardiner will change his mind. If she does not learn to hold her tongue and behave properly, we may all be turned out into the hedgerows after all!"

Lydia scowled. "I do not see why I must be the one to change. You are all so very dull, sitting around and discussing who should behave this way or that way. If I were at Netherfield, I would bring far more life to the place than Jane ever could."

Elizabeth arched a brow. "Yes, I imagine Miss Bingley would love that."

Lydia tossed her curls over her shoulder. "Well, she is no fun at all! I would be far more entertaining than she is."

"You would be far more something," Mary muttered under her breath.

Mrs. Bennet threw up her hands. "Oh, enough of this! Lydia, you will mind your behavior, or I shall have your aunt take you in hand again."

Lydia shrank back at the warning, and Kitty let out a soft snicker.

Elizabeth, meanwhile, turned back to her mother. "Regardless of Miss Bingley's feelings, Jane would not want to be viewed as an invalid any longer than necessary. I shall go in the morning and see how she fares."

Mrs. Bennet nodded, but her eyes sparkled with excitement. "Yes, and do make note of everything! Tell me how Mr. Bingley looks at her, whether he inquires after her comfort, whether he—"

Elizabeth sighed. "Yes, yes, Mama, I shall do my best to observe everything of importance."

With that settled, Mrs. Bennet finally allowed the subject to drift toward other matters, though Elizabeth suspected she would not hear the end of it until Jane returned home—with or without a proposal in hand.

Chapter 9

Elizabeth glowered down at the mud caked on her hem - it had to be at least six inches deep up her petticoat. With every step along the path to Netherfield, she could feel the damp fabric clinging to her legs, heavy and cold against her skin. Each squelching footfall only deepened her frustration. If Jane had not been injured, she might have been able to laugh at the absurdity of her predicament, but as it was, her concern for her sister dulled any amusement she might have found.

Well, it is a good thing I do not particularly care about what those harpies think of me.

She could already imagine Miss Bingley's disdainful gaze sweeping over her muddy skirts, her lips pursed in that superior way she had perfected. No doubt she would make some cutting remark about country manners or unfashionable resilience.

Let her try, Elizabeth thought with a smirk. *If a bit of mud is enough to scandalize her, I shall have to resist the urge to kick off my boots and make it even worse.*

As she neared Netherfield, a movement in the side garden caught her eye. A tall figure, clad in a dark cloak, was walking along the gravel path, hands clasped behind his back.

Darcy.

He was dressed more casually than she had seen him before, his coat unbuttoned as though he had just returned from a walk. His hair was slightly tousled, and for the first time, she thought he looked less severe, less like the imperious figure from the assembly and more like the man she had met in London—exhausted, yes, but capable, controlled. As she approached, his dark gaze flickered to her hem, then to her face, his expression unreadable.

"Miss Elizabeth." He inclined his head in greeting.

Elizabeth ignored the warmth curling through her at the sound of her name on his lips. "Mr. Darcy. I have come to inquire after my sister. How is she?"

"I confess to being in complete ignorance. I have yet to break my fast, as I wished to take advantage of the fresh air."

"Yes, the morning after a rainfall always makes it easier for Kitty to breathe as well. I believe it is the damp in the air."

He hesitated. "The herbs you have provided seem to have helped as well."

Elizabeth smiled. "I am truly glad to hear it."

"I have already written a letter to inquire about procuring more. I would not wish to continue taking from your household's supply."

She waved a hand dismissively. "Oh, that is entirely unnecessary. We have more than enough stored, and Mrs. Hill has been tending to the plants for some time now. It is no trouble in the least."

Darcy's lips pressed together, though not, she suspected, to suppress a cough this time. "I dislike relying on anyone."

She arched a brow. "That can lead to a very lonely life, Mr. Darcy."

He said nothing for a long moment. His eyes searched hers with such intensity that she almost stepped back—almost. But she stood her ground, heart pattering unexpectedly as his gaze dropped, just briefly, to her mouth. When he looked back up, something unreadable flickered in his expression—a hesitation, a longing, swiftly masked.

Then he gave the barest nod. "So I have come to understand."

Elizabeth swallowed and glanced away, the strange tension between them tightening like a drawn bowstring. She refused to consider what that look meant.

"I must see Jane," she said at last, adjusting her shawl with a briskness that belied the tremor in her fingers.

Elizabeth did not linger on his reaction, nor did she allow herself to dwell on the strange shift in the air between them.

"Please, allow me to escort you inside."

Elizabeth nodded her thanks and took his arm, the contact causing her stomach to fill with butterflies. The warmth of the house was welcome after her muddy journey, though the moment she stepped foot inside the dining, she felt the weight of judgment settle upon her.

Miss Bingley was seated with her sister at the table, and she took in Elizabeth's mud-streaked gown with barely concealed horror. "Miss Elizabeth, my goodness! We were... not expecting you. Did you... *walk* here?"

"Yes, I wished to check on Jane as soon as I could. Tell me, has Mr. Jones arrived yet?"

Miss Bingley's smile was thin. "Not yet, but I did not wish to disturb him if your sister were to have recovered over the night."

Elizabeth frowned. "I beg your pardon?"

Mrs. Hurst gave a delicate shrug. "Well, my dear, you know how some ladies can be." She exchanged a glance with her sister before turning her gaze back to Elizabeth, feigning sympathy. "Do you recall Miss Penrose, Caroline? She fell down the steps last spring and made such a fuss about her ankle, only for the doctor to arrive and declare there was nothing amiss at all?"

"Oh yes," Miss Bingley said with a laugh. "She stayed abed for nearly a week, moaning about her suffering, only to be perfectly fine the moment an invitation to Lady Latham's ball arrived."

Elizabeth stiffened. The insinuation was clear. "I assure you, Jane is not feigning an injury," she said coolly. "If you doubt it, I invite you to come upstairs and see for yourself."

Miss Bingley hesitated, clearly weighing the prospect of entering a sickroom—however minor the ailment—against the opportunity to prove herself correct. At last, she tilted her chin and smoothed the front of her gown. "Very well. Let us see the patient."

Elizabeth led the way up the stairs, her steps brisk with determination. When they reached Jane's room, she pushed the door open to reveal her sister lying in bed, her face pale and her ankle propped on pillows. The moment Miss Bingley stepped inside, her eyes landed on the swollen, bruised skin peeking out from beneath Jane's dressing gown.

The color drained from Miss Bingley's face. "Oh," she breathed, reaching out to grip the bedpost as she wobbled slightly.

"Might we call for Mr. Jones now, Miss Bingley?" Elizabeth crossed her arms.

"I... yes... allow me to send someone for him."

Stupid woman, Elizabeth thought with disgust. *As if Jane would ever behave in such an unladylike manner.*

Mr. Jones arrived in due course and declared Jane's ankle to be badly sprained, though not broken. To Jane's mortification and Miss Bingley's horror, the apothecary insisted she not attempt to return to Longbourn for a week complete. "The jostling of the carriage could cause permanent damage," he explained. "If the pain is not too much, she might be carried downstairs for meals or to enjoy the outdoors, but no more than that."

"Absolutely," Mr. Bingley agreed at once upon hearing the news, attempting to hide his pleasure at these words. "I will personally ensure that she is moved only with the greatest of care."

It was with great reluctance that Miss Bingley also offered for Elizabeth to remain at Netherfield in order to help tend to her sister. Elizabeth gratefully accepted the invitation. *Poor Miss Bingley looks torn between wishing my departure so as not to spar with her, or wishing my presence so her brother's attentions will be lessened.*

Elizabeth spent the remainder of the day at her sister's side, ensuring that her ankle remained elevated getting them both settled into their rooms once their belongings arrived from Longbourn. She was annoyed to discover that their mother had sent dresses more fitting for an assembly rather than day gowns or dinner gowns.

By the time the dinner bell rang, Jane was in a significant amount of discomfort and did not feel equal to the task of dining downstairs. A tray was ordered, and Jane encouraged Elizabeth to join the others. "I already feel like I am being discourteous, Lizzy. I do not wish them to think that I am ungrateful for their kindness. It would be worse if you took a tray as well."

"Very well," Elizabeth sighed dramatically, "but only because I love you, Jane."

As Elizabeth made her way downstairs to the dining room, she mentally braced herself for an evening of forced civility. She suspected

Miss Bingley would find new ways to needle her, and Mrs. Hurst would follow along with idle amusement. Mr. Bingley, of course, would be as gracious as ever, and Darcy...

She hesitated on the final step. *And what of Mr. Darcy?*

Though their interactions had been few, they had been intense. She was still unsettled by the way he had looked at her after she had offered him the herbs. It was not admiration, nor was it disdain. If anything, he had seemed... bewildered.

She shook herself. There was no use in dwelling on it now. If he had any further thoughts about her, he would certainly never voice them.

She entered the dining room to find the gentlemen already present. Mr. Bingley greeted her warmly and insisted that he had just been about to send a footman to fetch her. Darcy stood at the opposite end of the room, near the fire, his usual stoic mask in place. But something flickered in his gaze when he looked at her, and she flushed slightly.

Miss Bingley, seated beside her brother, gave Elizabeth a tight smile. "I trust your sister is comfortable?"

"She is, though she is in some pain," Elizabeth replied as she took her seat. "She sends her apologies for not joining you all tonight."

"Oh, no apologies are necessary," Mr. Bingley assured her. "Her health is far more important."

Miss Bingley pursed her lips. "Indeed, it is such a pity."

Elizabeth merely smiled, and the dinner proceeded with general conversation. Mr. Bingley inquired after Longbourn, speaking particularly to Elizabeth about her younger sisters. She spoke of Kitty and Mary but neglected to mention Lydia, suspecting Miss Bingley would take pleasure in any foolishness her youngest sister had displayed.

As the courses progressed, the conversation turned toward London and the devastation of the fire. Mr. Hurst, who had barely engaged in the discussion thus far, suddenly perked up.

"I say, did you hear about the rumors?" he asked, reaching for his wine glass. "There are whispers that the fire was not an accident. Some say it was arson."

Elizabeth, who had just taken a sip of her own wine, nearly choked.

Miss Bingley gasped dramatically. "Arson? Surely not!"

"Oh, surely so," Mr. Hurst countered, waving his fork. "The docks, the warehouses—it was too widespread, too coordinated. A single spark could not have spread so rapidly."

Elizabeth felt the hairs on the back of her neck rise. She flicked a glance at Darcy, who was watching the exchange with an unreadable expression.

"Who would commit such a crime?" Bingley asked, frowning.

"Rivals, perhaps? Foreign interests? Or perhaps some disgruntled employees," Mr. Hurst speculated.

"Or simple mischief," Darcy said at last, his voice calm but firm. "A tragedy does not always require a grand conspiracy."

Elizabeth exhaled, grateful for his interjection.

Mr. Hurst shrugged and returned to his food, losing interest now that he had imparted his gossip. But Elizabeth could not shake the unease curling in her stomach.

She had not forgotten what Mrs. Gardiner had told her about the inspector's suspicions. Could they truly believe that someone intended for the fire to happen? That it was planned?

And if so—who would they blame?

Pushing her thoughts aside, Elizabeth focused on her meal. There was nothing she could do about it now. And yet, as she felt Darcy's eyes on her once more, she could not shake the feeling that the conversation that evening had been anything but idle.

X

The separation of the sexes was brief, and Elizabeth spent the majority of that time being ignored by the two superior ladies. *Superior only in their own heads, at least.*

When the gentlemen came into the room, Elizabeth quickly made her excuses and went upstairs. Upon seeing that Jane was sleeping soundly, thanks to a draught provided by Mr. Jones, she retired to her bed and quickly fell asleep, thoroughly exhausted physically and emotionally.

Upon awaking the next morning, Elizabeth felt a sense of calm. The first night at Netherfield had been endured without major incident—aside from the troubling conversation about the fire—and Jane had slept well. She rose and dressed quickly, eager to check on her sister before breakfast.

After determining that Jane was still asleep, Elizabeth made her way down the stairs to breakfast. To her surprise, she discovered both Darcy and Bingley sitting at the table.

"Miss Elizabeth!" Bingley's delighted smile prompted her own. "Please, come join us. How is your sister?"

His question was rushed, immediately on the heels of his invitation. She grinned broadly at him and began to make her selection from the sideboard. "She is resting comfortably."

"Excellent... excellent."

He nodded solemnly, though something in the lift of his brow suggested amusement. Swallowing quickly, he asked, "And yourself, Miss Bennet? How are you feeling?"

He held her gaze a moment too long. A prickle of heat crept up Ellizabeth's neck at the unexpectedly intense attention. Gentlemen did not ask personal questions of young ladies in poliite society. "I am doing well, sir," she stammered at last, taking a bite of toast to cover her sudden—and wholly unexpected—nerves.

"Darcy!" Bingley cried in mock horror.

And then she saw it—the faintest twitch at the corner of Darcy's mouth. It was not a full smile, but it warmed his face in a way that made her breath catch.

She laughed, bright and unrestrained. "You tease, sir! I would never have imagined it."

Bingley chuckled, looking between them with open amusement. "Indeed, Darcy! You had us both quite fooled for a moment."

Darcy inclined his head, his gaze not leaving hers. "I suppose I could not resist."

Elizabeth shook her head, still smiling. Her fingers absently smoothed the edge of her napkin as she said, "Well, I am pleased to see that your humor has improved along with your health."

"Oh? Were you feeling unwell, Darcy?"

Her smile faltered, eyes widening slightly. She turned from Bingley's expression of innocent concern to Darcy's—his was unreadable, though she thought she saw the shadow of something more vulnerable flicker across it before he shuttered his features again.

He closed his eyes briefly and said, "Merely a cough, Bingley. The air at the assembly was… bothersome."

Elizabeth's heart ached at the word. That night flashed briefly in her memory—his breathless struggle, the heat of his skin beneath her hand.

Bingley's expression softened. "The sea air of Ramsgate did not cure you, then?"

"I am afraid it proved to be less therapeutic than I had wished."

As Darcy spoke, his eyes shifted once more to hers. There was nothing teasing now in his expression—only gratitude, and something quieter. Something that made her throat go dry.

She quickly looked down at her plate, but her pulse still danced in her wrist, and her fingers itched to brush his hand where it rested near the teacup.

The moment was interrupted when Miss Bingley entered the room, her sharp gaze immediately homing in on Elizabeth's presence. "Why, Miss Eliza," she drawled, taking her seat beside her brother. "How devoted you are to your sister, rising so early to care for her."

Elizabeth merely smiled. "It is no trouble for me, as we are quite used to country hours here. In any case, Jane would do the same for me."

"Indeed," Miss Bingley murmured, her gaze flicking toward Darcy. "Such… devotion is most commendable."

"Speaking of Miss Bennet, will she be joining us today, do you think?" Bingley's eager face looked so much like that of a puppy, Elizabeth had to stifle a giggle.

"Oh, certainly not!" cried Miss Bingley before Elizabeth could answer. "I cannot even imagine a true lady of refinement would be able to rise from her bed the day after such a terrible injury!"

Elizabeth bristled. "Jane will most likely remain in bed today, as Mr. Jones has recommended. Once he allows her to be carried about, however, I am certain she will be happy to come down to enjoy the company of her new friends."

"But once she is well enough to be carried down, will she not be returning home?" Miss Bingley's eyes were wide with a faux innocence that Elizabeth found infuriating.

"I daresay being carried down the stairs is far less damaging than the jostling of a carriage for several miles!" Bingley protested. "In fact, in order to safeguard Miss Bennet's ankle, I shall carry her about myself to ensure it is done properly."

Miss Bingley's fork clattered against her plate. "You, Charles?" she sputtered, her usually poised expression slipping.

Bingley, seemingly unaware of the scandalized look on his sister's face, nodded enthusiastically. "Of course! A footman may not take the same care. I shall be most careful, and I dare say Miss Bennet will find the arrangement preferable to being stuck in her chambers for days on end."

Elizabeth pressed her lips together to suppress a smile. She had no doubt that Jane would be flustered beyond measure at such attentions, but she could not deny that Bingley's enthusiasm was... endearing.

Miss Bingley, regaining some of her composure, sniffed and turned to Darcy. "Surely you agree, Mr. Darcy? A lady of true refinement would not wish to be seen in such a state. No doubt Miss Bennet would prefer to remain upstairs rather than endure such... humiliations."

Darcy set down his cup and regarded her with a steady gaze. "I think Miss Bennet's preference is for Miss Bennet to decide," he said coolly.

Elizabeth nearly choked on her tea.

Miss Bingley's mouth pressed into a thin line, but before she could respond, Bingley beamed at Darcy. "Exactly, my friend! And I am quite certain Miss Bennet will be grateful for the chance to join us in the drawing room when she is able."

Miss Bingley, clearly realizing she had lost this particular battle, exhaled through her nose and picked up her fork once more. "Well," she said, forcing a smile, "I am sure we will all do our utmost to ensure Miss Bennet's recovery is swift and pleasant."

Elizabeth tilted her head. "Indeed, Miss Bingley. I am sure she will be most grateful for your concern."

A slight twitch appeared at the corner of Darcy's mouth, and Elizabeth found herself struggling to hold back a grin.

Oh yes, this was going to be an amusing stay indeed.

❋

A few hours later, after having returned to her sister and assured herself of Jane's comfort, Elizabeth wandered into the Netherfield library, in search of something to read. She browsed the sparsely-populated shelves, lamenting the fact that she had not thought to ask for a few books when a servant went to fetch their things.

"I am afraid you will not find very much."

Startled, Elizabeth jumped slightly and whirled around to face Darcy standing only a few feet behind her.

"Good heavens!" she cried, raising one hand to her chest to cover her beating heart. "I had not known anyone else was in here."

"I apologize for startling you," he said. "It was not my intention."

"I suppose I am just used to my noisy sisters," she said a bit breathlessly.

He inclined his head. "I have always walked rather quietly—my sister often says I ought to tie a bell to my shoes so as not to startle people."

Elizabeth let out a startled laugh, the tension of her surprise completely melting away. "That sounds like something Kitty might say. I suppose I must apologize, then, for not having sharper ears. You might have said something, though."

"I do not speak often unless necessary."

"Well, we make quite the contrast, then!" Elizabeth laughed again. "My mother is always telling me that I talk too much. It seems, Mr. Darcy, that we are destined to be either the best of friends or the worst of enemies."

A hint of amusement flickered across Darcy's face. "I hope, for the sake of everyone at Netherfield, that it is the former."

Elizabeth arched a brow playfully. "A declaration of friendship, Mr. Darcy? Are you feeling quite well?"

"I do not believe my health has much bearing on the matter," he returned dryly. "Though I assure you, my speaking little is no sign of rudeness. Prolonged conversation often aggravates my cough."

Her amusement softened into understanding. "Then I shall endeavor to do the speaking for both of us."

Darcy let out a quiet huff that might have been a laugh. "A most generous offer."

Elizabeth grinned. "Though, in fairness, if we are to be the worst of enemies, I should think you would be required to speak more often, if only to engage in verbal battles with me."

Darcy exhaled lightly, the closest thing to a chuckle she had yet heard from him. "Then I suppose I am fortunate that my silence makes such a battle impossible. You would win too easily."

Elizabeth tilted her head, eyes twinkling. "A wise man knows when he cannot win, I suppose."

"Or when to choose his battles wisely."

They stood there for a moment, the air between them oddly charged, before Darcy abruptly turned toward the shelves. "If you are looking for something to read, I might be able to offer you better options than what Bingley keeps here. His collection is… lacking."

Elizabeth turned back toward the shelves, brushing her fingers along the spines of the books. "You say there is not much of a selection?"

"Unfortunately, no. Bingley had Netherfield let in something of a rush and had little time to stock the library to his satisfaction."

"A pity," Elizabeth mused. "A house without books is a dreadful thing."

"Indeed," Darcy agreed. He hesitated for a brief moment before adding, "However, I do have a book in my own collection that might interest you."

Elizabeth turned back to him, curiosity lighting her features. "Do you?"

He nodded and moved toward the corner of the room, where a small table held a few volumes. Selecting one, he returned and held it out to her.

She took it carefully, her fingers brushing his as she examined the title. "*The Minstrel* by James Beattie." She glanced up at him, surprised. "I have read some of this before."

"If you do not mind annotations, I have made a few notes in the margins. It is a favorite of mine."

Elizabeth took the book with curiosity, running her fingers along the cover. It was well-worn but well-loved, and the weight of the gesture was not lost on her. "I shall take great care with it," she promised.

"I do not doubt it."

Their eyes met again, and Elizabeth's stomach gave an odd little flip. She quickly glanced down at the book and clasped it a little tighter. "Well," she said lightly, "I shall leave you to your silence, then, and take myself off to read."

He inclined his head. "Enjoy it, Miss Elizabeth."

She smirked. "As I would any treasured friend."

With that, she turned and left the library, making her way upstairs with the book tucked close. Yet as she went, she could not stop herself from dwelling on the encounter.

For the rest of the afternoon, her mind was full of Mr. Darcy.

Chapter 10

The following day passed in much the same way as the one before, with Elizabeth doing her best to entertain Jane and alleviate her boredom. Miss Bingley and Mrs. Hurst joined them for a time in the afternoon, and Elizabeth almost began to like them when she saw how much affection and solicitude they showed Jane.

The two ladies were in possession of considerable powers of conversation, and they endeavored to make themselves agreeable to the bed-ridden Miss Bennet. Elizabeth was surprised at how well they could describe an entertainment with accuracy and relate an anecdote with humor and laughter.

When the dinner bell rang, Jane begged to be allowed to come downstairs after the meal. Upon promising faithfully that she would keep her injured ankle elevated in the parlor and not attempt to walk, she was given reluctant permission.

"We shall send a footman to carry you down," Miss Bingley promised.

Elizabeth, remembering Bingley's avowal to be the one to carry Jane, simply bit her lip, resolving to hint at the matter when the gentleman was present at dinner.

The opportunity arrived upon completion of the meal. As Elizabeth rose from her seat, she turned to her hostess. "Miss Bingley, Jane is still desirous of coming downstairs for the evening. Could you please assign a footman to attend her?"

Before Miss Bingley could respond, Bingley's head snapped up, his easygoing demeanor sharpening into resolve. "A footman? Nonsense! I will go myself."

Miss Bingley let out a dramatic gasp. "Charles, you cannot be serious! You cannot mean to enter her bedchamber—"

Bingley waved off her protest. "Miss Bennet's sister will go with her, as will you and Louisa, if you would like. There could be no impropriety in assisting an injured friend, especially to ensure that she receives only the most careful of conveyance."

Elizabeth bit back a smile as Miss Bingley's mouth snapped shut in frustration. Mrs. Hurst merely sighed and exchanged a look with her sister, but neither argued further.

Darcy, who had been silent throughout the exchange, lifted his wineglass to his lips. Elizabeth's eyes flicked to him, expecting to find some disapproving expression, but instead, his gaze was unreadable—though she thought she caught the faintest twitch of amusement.

Miss Bingley, clearly realizing that further protest would be futile, pursed her lips. "Well, if you insist, brother," she said with a haughty sniff. "Do try to be careful."

Bingley grinned and clapped his hands together. "Excellent! I shall collect Miss Bennet at once." With that, he strode from the room, his enthusiasm evident.

Elizabeth followed at a more measured pace, but as she stepped into the hall, she allowed herself a small, satisfied smirk. Bingley's devotion to Jane was becoming more and more apparent, much to Miss Bingley's frustration.

And, she could not deny, it pleased her greatly.

Jane's face was a becoming shade of pink as Bingley carried her down to the stairs and into the drawing room. He gently placed her on a settee near the fire, then courteously stepped back and averted his eyes as she arranged her skirts to cover her elevated ankle and foot.

"Are you in need of anything, Miss Bennet?" he asked eagerly, bouncing a bit on his feet "A pillow, perhaps, or a rug?"

"I am quite well, Mr. Bingley, thank you." Jane's voice was soft and slightly breathless.

Bingley dragged a chair over from another part of the room and sat at Jane's side, engaging her in quiet, earnest conversation.

The remainder of the party, all of whom had followed Bingley upstairs to fetch Jane, trailed into the room after them. Elizabeth sat on a comfortable chair where she could observe the goings-on, while Darcy took a seat at a writing desk. Hurst stretched out on a sofa and quickly fell asleep, and Miss Bingley and Mrs. Hurst sat together near the tea tray, their faces pinched in identical expressions of pique.

Elizabeth took up some needlework, though her eyes strayed more often to her sister and Mr. Bingley than to her stitches. It was impossible not to be pleased at how attentively he listened to Jane, how he seemed to hang onto her every word as though nothing in the world could be of greater importance.

Miss Bingley, meanwhile, stirred her tea with increasing agitation. At last, she could hold her tongue no longer. "It is such a shame that you must endure such an injury, Miss Bennet," she said with saccharine sympathy. "Had I known how treacherous our steps were, I would have warned you before you left."

Jane, ever gracious, smiled. "You are too kind, Miss Bingley. It was entirely my own misstep."

Bingley, however, frowned. "The steps are not treacherous at all. We have had no trouble with them before."

Miss Bingley shot her brother an exasperated look before returning her attention to Jane. "Perhaps the damp weather made them more slippery than usual. One can never be too careful."

"Indeed," Elizabeth murmured, arching a brow. "And yet, I cannot recall hearing you offer the same warning to anyone else who has come or gone these past two days."

Darcy, who had been engrossed in his writing, glanced up briefly at Elizabeth's words. There was an unmistakable flicker of amusement in his dark eyes before he returned his attention to his correspondence.

Miss Bingley's lips pressed together in irritation. "Regardless," she said stiffly, "I am sure you will be most relieved when you are finally able to return home, Miss Bennet."

Bingley, startled, turned sharply toward his sister. "Miss Bennet shall not go before she is fully recovered! She must not risk further injury."

Jane looked at him with wide, luminous eyes. "You are very kind, Mr. Bingley."

Elizabeth bit her lip to keep from laughing. Miss Bingley's expression was nothing short of murderous.

Mrs. Hurst, clearly sensing the need for intervention, cleared her throat. "It is a fortunate thing that the gentlemen returned when they did last night," she remarked, her gaze sliding toward Darcy. "I do not think Miss Bennet could have been persuaded to remain otherwise."

Darcy, though still writing, nodded slightly. "I daresay Bingley would not have allowed her to leave, regardless."

Bingley grinned. "Of course not!"

Miss Bingley gave an exaggerated sigh. "Oh, Charles, you are far too obliging."

Elizabeth smirked. "I, for one, find it quite admirable."

Miss Bingley, desperate for a change in conversation, looked frantically around the room, and her eyes latched on to the paper on which Darcy wrote.

"And what, pray tell, are you writing so secretly, Mr. Darcy?" she purred, rising from her seat and crossing the room to stand at his shoulder.

"It is no secret. I am writing a letter."

"A letter? Oh, I do hope it is not another tedious matter of estate business—how dreadfully dull those must be."

Darcy glanced at her briefly before responding. "No, this is to my sister."

At this, Miss Bingley's entire demeanor shifted into one of affected warmth. "Oh, dear Georgiana! How I long to see her again. I do hope she is well?"

"She is," Darcy replied simply.

"And how did she enjoy your summer together at Ramsgate?" Elizabeth did her best to hide a smile at Miss Bingley's clearly unwelcome perseverance.

"We both enjoyed it."

Miss Bingley clapped her hands together. "Oh, what a delightful holiday that must have been! I daresay nothing compares to the seaside in the summer."

"It was pleasant enough," Darcy allowed, though his expression remained unreadable.

"And how is she enjoying her masters in town?"

Goodness, how oblivious can one woman be? Elizabeth thought with exasperation.

"She is at Pemberley. With the current state of London, I thought it best for her to return to the country."

Elizabeth tilted her head. "Because of the fire?" she asked, entering the conversation for the first time.

Miss Bingley's face grew even more sour when Darcy's eyes finally rose from his letter to focus on Elizabeth instead of herself.

"In part," he responded, "but even more so because of the aftermath. Many have lost their homes and livelihoods. There are too many wandering the streets without work, without shelter. Crime is on the rise."

Elizabeth frowned. "Yes... my uncle has mentioned as much. And the insurance companies have been slow to provide compensation."

"Precisely," Darcy agreed. "It is not a safe place for a young lady, nor is it an easy time for many."

Miss Bingley pursed her lips. "How unfortunate," she murmured, though it was evident that she had little true concern for the plight of the displaced. "But surely, with your wealth and influence, you could ensure her safety in town?"

Darcy's mouth pressed into a firm line. "There are some risks I am unwilling to take."

Miss Bingley tittered, laying a hand lightly on his arm. "You are quite right, of course. And how devoted you are as a brother! Georgiana is very fortunate indeed."

Darcy shifted slightly, smoothly reclaiming his arm as he reached for his letter. "If you will excuse me, I must see this sent off."

With a nod to the group, he strode from the room, leaving Miss Bingley pouting and Elizabeth struggling to conceal her amusement.

The following afternoon, all four ladies were in the drawing room when a footman appeared at the open door. "Mrs. Bennet and Mrs. Gardiner," he announced, standing to the side and allowing the two guests two enter.

Miss Bingley's face tightened, and she turned to a maid who had been waiting quietly in the corner. "You there, fetch some tea and send for the gentlemen." Rising to her feet, Miss Bingley then greeted her guests with a polite smile

Elizabeth had also risen to her feet, setting aside the embroidery she had been painfully working on. *If I poke my finger one more time, I swear I am tossing the dratted thing into the fire!*

Her bloodstained needlework was quickly forgotten, however, when she saw her aunt. Mrs. Gardiner's face was pale, her composed expression lined with fatigue.

"My dear Jane, Elizabeth!" Mrs. Bennet trilled, sweeping into the room with a flourish. "How charming you both look—though Jane, my dear, I must say you are still far too pale. How your poor ankle must be paining you!"

"I am improving, Mama," Jane said from her place on the settee, where she reclined with her ankle elevated on several pillows. "My friends are taking excellent care of me."

"Of course, of course!" Mrs. Bennet sank onto an overstuffed chair. "It is so very good of you to be caring for my dear girl."

This last bit was directed towards Bingley, who entered the room with Darcy and Mr. Hurst behind him. "It is my absolute pleasure to ensure Miss Bennet heals properly," the host of Netherfield said.

Mrs. Bennet beamed, then looked around at everyone. "Oh! This room is quite lovely, is it not? A very pretty chamber, though I daresay a bit outdated." Mrs. Bennet turned a shrewd eye to Miss Bingley. "Netherfield will be much improved when it has a proper mistress."

Miss Bingley stiffened. "Netherfield does have a mistress, Mrs. Bennet— myself."

"Oh, but a sister can never care for a house in quite the same way as a wife." She cast a meaningful glance toward Jane, who flushed and lowered her gaze.

Miss Bingley's expression soured, though she managed to keep her tone civil. "I assure you, Mrs. Bennet, my brother is perfectly content with the way Netherfield is kept."

Mrs. Bennet fluttered her handkerchief. "Oh, I have no doubt you do your best, Miss Bingley. But a house of this size—well! It requires a lady of the house, not just a sister, to see to all the details." She turned to Bingley with an indulgent smile. "A wife would naturally take greater care, ensuring everything is maintained properly—especially when she has a vested interest in its future."

Bingley coughed into his fist and darted an uncertain glance toward Jane, whose cheeks were now a delicate shade of pink.

Miss Bingley, on the other hand, looked positively murderous. "I believe Netherfield is kept to a standard that is more than acceptable, Mrs. Bennet."

Mrs. Bennet nodded agreeably. "Oh, certainly, my dear. But there is always room for improvement, is there not?" She sighed, her eyes taking on a dreamy cast. "And how delightful it will be to see the improvements made by the right mistress, once she is installed."

Miss Bingley opened her mouth, no doubt to offer a scathing retort. Elizabeth, who had been distracted by how worn Mrs. Gardiner looked, now joined in the conversation in an attempt to change the topic.

"We have been more than comfortable here, Miss Bingley. You are a gracious hostess in caring for my sister. Speaking of sisters—Mama, how is everyone at Longbourn?"

"Oh, who cares about Longbourn?" Mrs. Bennet snapped, annoyed at having been denied her favorite pastime of forwarding Jane to handsome gentlemen.

"And Stoke House?" Elizabeth asked Mrs. Gardiner hastily. "Are you quite well, Aunt?"

Mrs. Gardiner, who had thus far been silent, let out a slow breath, as if only now realizing how tense she had become. "I am well, Lizzy. Merely… fatigued."

Elizabeth frowned. "Has something happened?"

Mrs. Gardiner hesitated, her eyes flickering toward the assembled company before she replied in a measured voice, "The insurance adjuster arrived earlier than expected."

Elizabeth sat up straighter. "So soon?"

"Yes. And he has been taking very detailed notes. More detailed than I anticipated."

"What is this?" Miss Bingley's face, eager for gossip and scandal, reminded Elizabeth a bit of her father's favorite bloodhound.

"Our house in London burned down during the fire," Mrs. Gardiner explained, "and insurance has been slow in approving our claim."

"That is to be expected, given the magnitude of destruction."

Elizabeth looked around at Darcy, startled at his joining the conversation. Mrs. Gardiner nodded but did not seem reassured. "He nearly insisted on accompanying me here. I refused, of course, but he was quite determined to speak with you, Lizzy."

Elizabeth's stomach twisted.

"Why would he wish to speak with you, Miss Eliza?" Miss Bingley's eyes were wide with anticipation, her voice smug.

Before Elizabeth could explain, the footman returned and cleared his throat. "Mr. Smithson."

Miss Bingley blinked in confusion. "Mr. Smithson?"

Mrs. Gardiner inhaled sharply. "It would seem he did not take my refusal well—he must have followed us here."

Elizabeth turned just as a tall, thin man entered the drawing room. His eyes were sharp, his gaze sweeping across the assembled party. "Forgive my intrusion," he said, though his tone betrayed no real remorse. "I am here to speak with Miss Elizabeth Bennet."

Raising an eyebrow and refusing to be intimidated, Elizabeth said, "I believe my aunt said I was unavailable right now?"

The adjuster, however, seemed wholly unrepentant. "My apologies, madam, but I am on a tight schedule." He nodded toward Elizabeth. "Miss Bennet, if I could trouble you for a few moments of your time? I have some questions regarding your recollections of the fire."

A thick silence fell over the room.

Bingley, ever the polite host, glanced hesitantly at Elizabeth, then at the adjuster. "Surely, sir, this can wait until after our guests have had tea?"

Mr. Smithson offered a thin smile. "I do not mean to impose, but my business is rather pressing."

"I have nothing to hide, Aunt," Elizabeth said. "I do not mind speaking to Mr. Smithson about what occurred in London during the fire."

Mrs. Gardiner sighed in resignation. "Very well. Miss Bingley, might we be troubled for a private room?"

As she rose to stand, Mr. Smithson shook his head. "Your presence is not required, Mrs. Gardiner. I will speak with Miss Elizabeth alone."

A ripple of protest went through the room.

"Alone?" Mrs. Gardiner's eyes flashed. "Sir, that is most inappropriate!"

"I quite agree," Darcy said suddenly, his voice cold and unwavering. "Miss Bennet is a lady and will not be subjected to such a discussion without proper company."

"I cannot have her account of the incident being influenced by a person who was also present in the house at the time."

Darcy's voice cut through the tension like a blade. "If Miss Bennet is to be questioned, then I will be present."

Elizabeth's head snapped toward him in surprise.

Mrs. Gardiner exhaled in clear relief. "I would have expected nothing less from Lady Anne's son," she murmured.

Darcy's brows lifted slightly, and he gave Mrs. Gardiner a searching look. After a beat, he inclined his head. "I would like to speak more with you at another time," he said, stifling a cough.

Mrs. Gardiner's lips twitched, but she simply nodded.

Elizabeth, thrown by the turn of events, hesitated only a moment before nodding. "Very well. Let us get this over with."

As she rose to follow Mr. Smithson from the room, she could feel Darcy's steady presence beside her. Despite herself, she was grateful for it.

※

Darcy did his best to keep his eyes from watching Elizabeth's hips sway as she walked in front of him down the hall at Netherfield to the music room.

It was growing more dangerous by the day—this attraction to her. What had started as reluctant admiration had deepened into something far more. Every moment in her presence sheared away the carefully constructed walls he had spent years erecting.

She was unlike any woman of his acquaintance—quick-witted, warm-hearted, and completely unintimidated by him.

He had spent the last five years being treated with deference—or, at the very least, with cautious respect. But this mere slip of a woman did not seem to think of him as someone to be feared or flattered.

No, she simply treated him as a man.

And *that* was the most dangerous part of all.

He reluctantly tore his eyes away, searching desperately for something else to occupy his thoughts. As he did so, he stifled a cough.

But even thoughts of his health pulled him back to her.

His cough had improved significantly since the night of the assembly—something that had surprised him more than he cared to admit. The herbs she had given him had worked better than any remedy he had tried before. The tickling pressure in his lungs, once a near-constant affliction, had been reduced to a mere annoyance at night or upon exertion. He could speak more easily, breathe more freely.

For that, he owed her a debt.

And it was one he could repay, in part, by protecting her from this stranger.

Mr. Smithson.

Something about the man sat ill with him. Insurance adjusters were not uncommon in the wake of such devastation, but this one… He was too precise, too shrewd. His eyes were calculating, not merely assessing damages but *searching* for something.

Or someone.

Darcy's instincts had been honed over years of navigating both business and society. He had encountered enough men of questionable intentions to recognize when one was standing in front of him.

And now, this man had insisted on speaking with Elizabeth alone.

Darcy's jaw tightened.

That would not happen.

He had no illusions that Elizabeth required his protection—she had more than demonstrated her ability to take care of herself. But that did not mean he would allow her to be subjected to unjust scrutiny without an advocate present.

His mother had once told him that a gentleman's duty was not only to act with honor but to ensure that others were treated honorably in his presence.

Lady Anne Darcy would not have stood idly by while a woman of integrity was questioned alone by a man who did not deserve such trust.

And neither shall I.

Darcy followed Elizabeth into the music room, bracing himself for the battle ahead.

Chapter 11

Elizabeth took her seat in the music room, smoothing her skirts as Mr. Smithson removed a small notebook and pencil from his jacket. His movements were deliberate, methodical—everything about him struck her as coldly efficient, which seemed at odds with his type of employment.

I had expected someone more… rough; coarse, even.

Darcy sat across from her, his back rigid, his gaze locked onto the insurance agent with a barely concealed disdain radiating from his tense posture.

Smithson flipped to the middle of his book and poised his pencil above it. "Miss Elizabeth, I would like you to tell me—in as much detail as possible—about how you became aware of the fire for the first time. I understand it was the middle of the night?"

Elizabeth met his gaze steadily. "Yes, something woke me up during the night, and I could smell the faintest aroma of smoke, so I decided to investigate."

"What caused you to awaken?"

"I have not the slightest idea."

He raised his eyebrows. "Really? Then you just… awoke and smelled smoke before anyone else in the household?"

She bristled at the disbelief in his voice. "Yes, really."

"You are quite certain?"

"Of course."

"Why do you believe that is?"

She resisted the urge to sigh. "Because I am particularly sensitive to scents. It is something of a family joke, in fact. My younger cousins and I play a game where I attempt to identify our dinner courses by smell alone before they reach the table. I can show you if you would like."

To her surprise, Smithson did not ask her to prove it. He barely acknowledged the statement at all. Instead, he simply nodded and continued writing.

Elizabeth tilted her head. *How very odd.* Most people, upon learning of her peculiar ability, expressed either curiosity or disbelief—and almost uniformly requested her to display her talent. Yet this man was utterly uninterested.

"After you smelled the smoke, what did you do next?"

"I walked around the house to see if a candle had been left burning, or if a fireplace had been left to smoke. I discovered nothing, so I began to return to my room. Then I looked out the upstairs window and saw the flames in the distance."

"And then?"

"Then I woke my uncle and showed him. He told me to wake the servants while he collected my aunt and our various belongings."

Smithson made a small noise and scribbled something down. "And from there?"

"We attempted to cross the bridge, but the sheer number of people had made it impassable. It was a bottleneck, with people fighting to get through. We turned back and headed toward Hyde Park, believing it to be a safer option."

And left them all to die.

The sentiment went unspoken, but the heaviness of the loss of life hung in the air. Smithson cleared his throat. "It seems like it was the sensible thing to do. Between the smoke, the flames, and the crowds, hundreds died."

"I know—I… I read the news articles afterwards."

Her voice broke slightly, remembering the chaos of that night—the screams, the suffocating heat, the press of bodies desperate to escape. Even now, she could recall the acrid scent of burning timber and the eerie glow of the flames consuming everything in their path.

And yet we survived. Instead of relief, Elizabeth felt nothing but guilt. *Why were we so blessed? What made us so special?*

Smithson, however, seemed utterly unaffected. He simply nodded, his pencil scratching across the paper. "Did you encounter anyone on your way to the park?"

Elizabeth took a steadying breath. "Many people. The streets were crowded with those attempting to flee."

"But did you speak to anyone in particular?"

She frowned. "There was a young woman. She had a baby with her."

Smithson's pencil stopped moving. He slowly lifted his head, his gaze pinning her with an intensity that sent a flicker of unease down her spine.

"A woman with a baby," he repeated. "Tell me everything about her."

Elizabeth hesitated, glancing at Darcy. He had been silent throughout most of the interview, but now he sat upright, watching the agent closely.

Her cheeks warmed. "Her name was Meg. She was... she was a lady of the night."

Smithson showed no reaction, but she could feel his attention sharpen.

"Describe her."

"She was young. Perhaps no older than I. I did not quite realize what her profession was until later... she was simply standing in the middle of the street, a dazed expression on her face, a baby crying in her arms. She was in shock."

"And her baby? Describe her baby."

Elizabeth's brow furrowed. "He was very small, perhaps only a few months old. Dark hair, pale skin. He was dressed in a simple gown, nothing particularly fine, but clean. But he was not her baby... that is, she said she was watching him for her neighbor, who had run away."

Smithson's pencil moved rapidly over the page. "Who was his mother, then? How did the woman get him?"

She frowned. *Why is he so interested? What does this have to do with my uncle's house burning?*

"I took the baby from her and told her to come with us. She followed us to the park, and then a man came. I think..." Her cheeks grew hot. "I think he was her... protector."

"But the baby? Who was the mother?"

"If you would let me finish." Her words were clipped and angry. "Meg told the man—she called him Sam—that she was trying to find Deena to give her the baby back, but Sam said that Deena was dead."

"Deena? You are certain?" Smithson was now scribbling furiously in his notebook. "What happened to her?"

"I do not understand," Elizabeth said in annoyance. "I was under the impression that you would be asking me questions about the fire and how we knew to leave early. What do these women and the baby have to do with anything? How is it relevant?"

Smithson glowered at her down his long nose. "I will be the one to judge whether or not information is pertinent to our investigation, Miss Elizabeth—not you. Now, what became of the baby?"

Elizabeth hesitated. Smithson's expression sharpened and he repeated, "What became of the child, Miss Elizabeth?"

Her lips parted. "My aunt and uncle offered to care for the baby—"

"I think that is enough."

Darcy's voice cut through the room, low and firm.

Elizabeth turned to him in surprise. He was watching Smithson with narrowed eyes, his body taut with tension.

Smithson's own expression hardened. "Everything is important. I need to know exactly—"

"Other than Miss Elizabeth's initial discovery of a fire, anything else that occurred is, quite frankly, none of your business," Darcy said coolly.

The agent's lips thinned. "That is not for you to decide, Mr. Darcy."

Darcy's eyes darkened. "On the contrary. I am well acquainted with most of the major insurance companies and their underwriters, having contemplated investing in reinsurance. I am also the nephew of the Earl of Matlock, who has considerable influence in such matters." He leaned forward slightly. "Perhaps you might inform me, sir, under which company's authority you are conducting this investigation?"

Smithson stiffened. "That is not your concern."

"It is precisely my concern."

Darcy's voice was low, even—but it rang with a kind of authority that seemed to echo off the walls. Elizabeth had never heard him speak quite like that before, with such quiet, formidable control. There was no bluster, no raised tone. And yet the very air in the room seemed to still in deference to it.

A charged silence followed. Smithson's fingers whitened around his notebook, his jaw tight. But he did not challenge the assertion. After a long, simmering moment, he snapped the book shut and stood abruptly.

"I believe I have everything I need," he said stiffly.

Without a backward glance, he turned and strode from the room, his boots clicking sharply against the floorboards.

Elizabeth let out the breath she had not realized she was holding, her spine softening against the back of her chair. Her heart, which had been thudding uncomfortably, now raced for an entirely different reason.

She turned to Darcy. He had not moved. He stood tall, shoulders set, eyes fixed on the empty doorway with such intensity that she wondered if he was willing the man to return so he could strike him down with words alone.

Her voice came out quieter than she expected. "What was that all about?"

He exhaled slowly, his jaw still taut. "That," he said grimly, "is precisely what I intend to find out."

Elizabeth stared at him, the warmth still rushing through her limbs. She was not sure what unsettled her more—the momentary confrontation or the deep, unfamiliar flutter in her chest that followed in its wake. There was something deeply arresting about the way he had spoken, the way he had shielded her without so much as touching her. Something in her stirred, low and electric.

She glanced away, fingers tightening on her skirts. Best not to dwell on it. And yet… her skin tingled where his presence lingered close beside her.

Once back in the drawing room, Darcy's thoughts were still occupied with the unsettling interrogation that had just occurred. Smithson's sharp questioning, his fixation on the baby, and his immediate withdrawal when pressed about his employer left an uneasy feeling lodged in Darcy's chest.

Unfortunately, that additional pressure was aggravating his lungs.

Mrs. Gardiner looked up at their entrance, her sharp gaze sweeping over them. "Well?" she asked, setting down her teacup. "How did it go? And where is Mr. Smithson?"

Elizabeth took her seat beside her aunt with a sigh. "He left rather abruptly after Mr. Darcy pressed him for the contact information of the company he represents."

Mrs. Gardiner's brows lifted, and she turned to Darcy. "Oh?"

Darcy merely inclined his head, knowing that any attempt to speak it would provoke a coughing fit.

You are weak, his father's voice echoed in his head. *A disgrace to the Darcy line.*

Elizabeth must have sensed his predicament, taking it upon herself to explain further. "He refused to discuss his employer, which—given his line of questioning—seems quite suspicious."

Mrs. Gardiner blinked in confusion. "What do you mean, his line of questioning?"

"Well, based on what you said, I had expected him to be interested in how we knew to flee so early. I was prepared to defend myself and provide evidence of how I could have smelled the smoke sooner than many others."

"But he was not?"

Elizabeth shook her head. "No, he barely asked me any questions about that. Instead, he became fixated on Meg and Benjamin. He demanded to know everything—what he looked like, where his mother was, and where he is now."

"That is unsettling." Mrs. Gardiner's lips pressed together in a thin line. "Well, at least he is not staying at Stoke Estate."

"Why would he stay with you?"

Darcy, Elizabeth, and Mrs. Gardiner turned startled eyes towards the questioner. Miss Bingley had apparently been listening closely to the discussion.

No doubt attempting to glean scandalous gossip of some sort, Darcy thought cynically.

He stifled a chuckle when he saw Elizabeth's eyebrows fly high up on her head. To his surprise, it was Mrs. Bennet who responded to the question.

"Perhaps you are not yet acquainted with the customs of estate owners, as your brother is merely leasing an estate," she said, "but it is quite common landed members of the gentry to offer lodging to travelers, particularly when business is involved."

Miss Bingley bristled at the insinuation, and Darcy struggled to contain his mirth at the vulgar Mrs. Bennet lecturing the more socially refined young lady about propriety.

"Precisely," Mrs. Gardiner said, nodding her head. "I remember my father being prevailed upon many times for housing while I was growing up on his estate. However, Mr. Smithson—" she hesitated, choosing her words carefully, "—did not strike me as the sort of man I wished to extend such hospitality to."

Miss Bingley opened her mouth as if to argue, then thought better of it and pressed her lips together.

Mrs. Gardiner turned back to Elizabeth, her expression softening. "I do not wish to dwell on unpleasant topics. We will be hosting a small card party tomorrow evening, and I should be delighted if you would all attend."

Elizabeth's face lit up at the invitation but then hesitated. "I would love to, Aunt, but Jane—"

"Oh, Miss Bennet shall be quite well looked after," Miss Bingley cut in smoothly, clearly eager for any excuse to avoid an evening in Meryton. "I shall be happy to remain with her."

Darcy nearly gaped as Miss Bingley fluttered her eyelashes at him. The idea of spending an evening alone at Netherfield nearly made him gag. "I shall accompany you, Miss Elizabeth, to your aunt's card party if you would like."

Elizabeth's head snapped toward him, her eyes wide. "You shall?"

He inclined his head. "Yes. I find myself with a vested interest in speaking further with your aunt and uncle." He turned to Mrs. Gardiner. "I should like to learn more about your connection to my mother."

Mrs. Gardiner gave him a long, searching look, then nodded. "I should be happy to tell you what I know."

Miss Bingley looked aghast at this development, but there was nothing she could do about the situation now, having already committed to

163

remaining home. To change her mind at this point would make her look much too forward.

Bingley, who had been listening with increasing interest, suddenly looked thoughtful. "If Miss Bennet should need anything, it might be best if I stay behind as well." He turned to Miss Bingley. "That way, you would not be alone in keeping her company."

Mrs. Gardiner rose to her feet, preparing to take her leave. "Then it is settled. We shall expect Elizabeth and Mr. Darcy tomorrow, along with the Hursts, if they should like to attend."

Mrs. Hurst looked peevish, but Mr. Hurst spoke up. "We would be delighted, thank you." He fixed his wife with a severe look, and she eventually nodded her acquiescence.

Mrs. Gardiner rose to her feet, preparing to take her leave. "Then it is settled. We shall expect you all tomorrow evening."

Darcy stood as well, watching as Mrs. Bennet fluttered over Jane one last time before finally departing with Mrs. Gardiner.

As soon as they were gone, Miss Bingley turned to Darcy with an incredulous laugh. "You surprise me, sir. A card party in Meryton? That is hardly your usual preference."

Darcy met her gaze evenly. "A man cannot always be predictable, Miss Bingley."

She opened her mouth as if to argue, but he had already turned away, his mind returning to the disconcerting interview with Mr. Smithson. Something about the man sat ill with him, and Darcy had no intention of letting the matter rest.

X

The remainder of the day passed smoothly. Mr. Jones called the following morning to check on Jane's ankle, which he declared to be healing satisfactorily. "I daresay only a few more days before it is well enough for you to return to Longbourn," he pronounced before wrapping the swollen limb with fresh bandages.

"Mr. Bingley has been kind enough to provide ice," Jane said with a faint blush, "and I have been keeping it elevated on pillows."

"Excellent. Continue to do so, and you will be as good as new in no time."

Elizabeth had been feeling guilty about planning to attend her aunt's card party that evening, but Mr. Jones's visit eased her mind considerably.

When the time arrived, she piled into Bingley's carriage with the Hursts and Darcy, with the men on one bench and the women across them on the opposite. Darcy's long legs brushed up against hers as the carriage lumbered through the Hertfordshire roads.

She did her best to focus on the conversation between the Hursts, but each time Darcy's knee rubbed against hers, she completely lost focus. She stole a glance at him, but his expression was as impassive as ever, his gaze fixed on some unseen point beyond the window. Yet, the rigid set of his jaw and the way his gloved hands rested stiffly on his thighs suggested that he was not as unaffected as he appeared.

The Hursts, oblivious to any undercurrents between their companions, spoke of their plans to return to London before Christmas. "Netherfield is pleasant enough," Mrs. Hurst was saying, "but there is no society here. At least in town, one can always expect some form of amusement."

Elizabeth's lips twitched. She suspected Mrs. Hurst's definition of "amusement" involved very little beyond card tables and idle gossip, but she refrained from commenting.

"I suppose you will travel to Pemberley this winter, Mr. Darcy?" Mr. Hurst asked lazily.

Darcy hesitated for a fraction of a second. "I have not yet decided."

Elizabeth noted his reluctance with interest. Was he debating a return to London, despite its current dangers? Or was there something else keeping him here in Hertfordshire longer than he had originally intended?

The carriage soon pulled into the drive of Stoke Estate, the warm glow of candlelight spilling from the windows. As a footman opened the door, Elizabeth stepped down eagerly, glad to escape the close quarters.

The party quickly entered the house, eager to be out of the frigid November air. After greetings had been exchanged, Elizabeth found herself at a card table with Mrs. Gardiner, Kitty, and Darcy. *This is certainly an interesting group*, she thought with amusement. *Poor Kitty looks absolutely terrified to be sitting down next to such a somber man!*

Mrs. Gardiner shuffled the deck and smiled at Darcy as she dealt the cards. "I appreciate you joining us this evening, Mr. Darcy. It gives Elizabeth an opportunity to get out and socialize as opposed to staying at Jane's side."

"It is no trouble at all to tend to my sister," Elizabeth protested.

"Miss Elizabeth has done an admirable job with her sister's care," Darcy said. "Miss Bennet is fortunate indeed to have such a caring sibling."

Elizabeth blinked, startled. She glanced at him sharply, but his face was composed, his tone perfectly neutral—as if he had not just offered her the most sincere compliment she had ever received from him.

Mrs. Gardiner, clearly amused, gave her niece a sidelong smile as she passed out the final card. "You've not changed much, Lizzy. Always pretending to bristle at praise while secretly storing it away."

Elizabeth gave a huff of laughter. "And you, Aunt, are far too knowing. Let us focus on the cards instead of sketching my character, shall we?"

As the game commenced, Mrs. Gardiner made a casual remark about her childhood, prompting Darcy to inquire further.

"My father owned an estate in Derbyshire," she explained as she placed a card on the table. "It was not nearly so grand as Pemberley, but it was home. Unfortunately, he passed when I was twelve, and the estate was entailed away to my uncle—his much younger brother. You perhaps know him, Mr. Darcy—the master of Crescent Hill."

Darcy looked up sharply. "You mean Mr. Baldwin? He is your *uncle*?"

Mrs. Gardiner nodded. "Indeed. He was quite newly married at the time, with no children. My mother and I were, of course, forced to leave. I was sent to a finishing school in London, and it was there that I met my husband."

"I do know Baldwin, though not well," Darcy admitted. "He has always kept much to himself."

Mrs. Gardiner let out a soft, wry laugh. "Yes, that sounds like him. A reserved man, but not unkind. He simply had little interest in family matters that did not concern his direct household."

Elizabeth, sensing Darcy was uncertain how to respond to such an open display of private information, was eager to change the focus of conversation. "I believe, Aunt, that you mentioned knowing Mr. Darcy's late mother?"

"Yes, I met her a few times."

Darcy leaned forward eagerly as Mrs. Gardiner continued. "She was a lovely woman—so gracious and kind. A delicate lady, to be sure, but she cared deeply for those around her. She used what strength she had to see to the well-being of her tenants and the poor. I recall one winter when an entire family nearly perished from exposure—she personally ensured they were housed and cared for."

Darcy, uncharacteristically quiet, merely nodded. Elizabeth watched him carefully. There was something in his expression—something softer, more vulnerable.

Before she could say anything more, a sudden commotion from the hallway disrupted the moment. The murmur of conversation stilled as a footman entered, his face pale. He moved swiftly to Mr. Gardiner's side and whispered something in his ear.

Mr. Gardiner's face paled instantly. Rising to his feet, he crossed quickly to his wife and murmured something too low for Elizabeth to hear.

Mrs. Gardiner gasped and immediately stood as well. "The nursery?"

Elizabeth's heart leapt into her throat. "The children—what happened?"

Mr. Gardiner's jaw tightened. "An intruder was caught trying to force his way into the nursery."

Elizabeth was already halfway out of her seat before he finished. "I am coming."

"And I," said Darcy, rising as well.

They followed the Gardiners swiftly into the hall, where two burly footmen were holding a struggling man between them. Elizabeth recognized him at once.

"Mr. Smithson!" she gasped.

The man's face was twisted in fury, his coat torn at the shoulder. He did not speak—only thrashed and kicked against his captors.

"What were you doing near the nursery?" Mr. Gardiner demanded.

Smithson glared. "None of your business."

"It most certainly is my business!" Gardiner snapped. "That's my family's private quarters! You were not invited to this house—nor were you permitted upstairs!"

Mrs. Gardiner looked like she might faint.

Darcy stepped forward, his voice low and dangerous. "Why were you here?"

Still Smithson said nothing.

"I am sending for the constable," Mr. Gardiner said. "You will answer for this attempt to harm my children."

"Sir William is the magistrate, and he is here tonight," Elizabeth reminded her uncle. "We should have him join us as well."

At that, Smithson gave a violent jerk and broke free. One of the footmen slipped on the polished floor, and in the next instant, Smithson was bolting for the door. Guests in the corridor cried out in alarm, but he was gone before anyone could react.

"Get after him!" Mr. Gardiner bellowed, but it was already too late.

Everyone stood frozen in stunned silence. Mrs. Gardiner clutched her husband's arm, white-faced. Kitty peeked nervously from the doorway.

Mr. Gardiner clenched his fists. "That man will pay for this."

Chapter 12

The chaos naturally caused the card party to end early. Darcy could tell Elizabeth wished to remain at Stoke House with her aunt and uncle, but Mr. Gardiner insisted that she return to Netherfield.

"It is much too dangerous for you here, Lizzy. I need to know you are safe with your friends."

"But what about my aunt and the children?" she protested.

Darcy cleared his throat. "If I may be so bold, sir, I should like to offer the use of a few footmen and stable hands from Netherfield. I shall send them over in the carriage as soon as we arrive."

Mr. Gardiner's shoulders sagged in relief. "Normally I would tell you not to wake them at this hour, but I value my family's safety too much to refuse. We still have not finished fully staffing the property, and our servants are spread a bit thin."

"We shall leave immediately, then, so they may come as quickly as possible."

With that, Darcy escorted Elizabeth to the carriage, where the Hursts were already waiting on one of the benches. As soon as the door closed behind him, Darcy tapped the roof with his cane. "Quickly, please," he called out.

Along the way, Mrs. Hurst fretted and whimpered, while her husband patted her hand in an attempt to keep her calm. Darcy looked down at Elizabeth, who sat next to him on the seat. A small part of him thrilled at their close proximity, but he tampered down the feeling and asked her, "Are you quite all right, Miss Elizabeth?"

Looking up at him with wide, solemn eyes, she whispered, "I simply do not understand what Mr. Smithson would want with my cousins. They are quite young and unable to give him any information about the fire or what occurred. And to attempt to enter the nursery in the middle of the night! There was no need—"

She froze, her words cutting abruptly off as she went pale. "What if he was not after them?"

"What do you mean?" he frowned. "It is not as if the man accidentally went there instead of, say, your uncle's study. Everyone knows that children of an estate are usually kept in the upstairs rooms."

"No, not the wrong room; the wrong *children*. What if he were looking for Benjamin?"

The pieces clicked together in Darcy's brain. "The baby you found in London? But is he not staying at Longbourn?"

"Yes, but what if Mr. Smithson did not know that? In our conversation the other day, he asked where Benjamin was. I told him that the Gardiners had offered to take him, but before I could explain that he was at Longbourn instead, I was interrupted."

Darcy thought furtively back to the interrogation he had witnessed. "I do believe you are right."

Elizabeth spoke quickly, her voice excited with the discovery. "And all of his questions were about Benjamin, not the fire. Remember? He seemed overly eager to learn about his origins. What if he is after him?"

"But why?"

Elizabeth seemed to deflate, her shoulders sagging as she sank back onto the carriage cushions. "As to that, I have no idea. Benjamin is an orphan, or at least partially. His mother died in the fire, and Meg—the woman who had him—was a…" she blushed, her words trailing off. "Well, I simply got the impression that his mother was unmarried and would not know who the father was. So why would he be important?"

Darcy was silent for a moment, his brows drawn in thought. Elizabeth could feel the weight of his attention, but she kept her gaze fixed on the passing countryside beyond the darkened window.

"Even so," he said at last, "there must be something more to it. If Benjamin were merely an abandoned child with no connections, why go to such lengths to find him? Why break into a nursery at night?"

Elizabeth shook her head slowly. "Unless…" Her breath caught. "Unless someone is looking for him. Not out of malice, perhaps, but for some claim. But then why send a man like Smithson?"

Darcy did not answer, and Elizabeth did not press him. Her mind was spinning too quickly to form another question. She glanced across the carriage. Mrs. Hurst had finally gone quiet, though her face was still drawn with worry. Mr. Hurst snored softly, chin resting on his chest.

The gentle rumble of the carriage wheels on the road did little to soothe Elizabeth's frayed nerves. Her thoughts were with Longbourn now—was Benjamin truly safe? Did Smithson know where he was? Would he try again?

She glanced up at Darcy. He sat with his arms crossed, his profile etched sharply in the dim carriage lantern light, eyes narrowed in deep concentration.

"Do you think," she asked quietly, "that someone like Mr. Smithson is acting alone?"

Darcy's jaw flexed. "No. A man like that works for someone. Someone who has money. And secrets."

Elizabeth nodded grimly. "Then it is not just Benjamin's future in danger. It is ours, too, if we continue to ask questions."

The carriage slowed as they approached Netherfield. Before the wheels had even fully stilled, Darcy rapped twice on the roof and called for the driver to ready the stables immediately. "Two footmen and three stable hands need to go to Stoke House immediately," he ordered as they stepped out. "Send them armed and have them report to Mr. Gardiner. I will inform Mr. Bingley."

Elizabeth turned to him in surprise. "You think it might come to that?"

"I do not wish it to," Darcy said tightly. "But I would rather be prepared than caught unawares. Your aunt and uncle have had one close call already."

Elizabeth swallowed hard, her throat dry with nerves and exhaustion. As they stepped into the house and Darcy handed her off to the waiting housekeeper, she turned once more.

"Thank you," she said simply. "For everything tonight."

He inclined his head, but something in his eyes—something dark and urgent—held hers. "Get some rest, Miss Elizabeth. Tomorrow... we will begin to find out who Mr. Smithson truly is."

X

The following morning, Darcy was enjoying a quiet breakfast when a footman appeared at the door.

"Sir, there is a gentleman—Mr. Bennet of Longbourn—requesting an audience. He's already in the drawing room."

Darcy sighed. He was not surprised that Elizabeth's father had arrived so early, given the events of the previous night.

Rising from the table, he placed his napkin beside his plate and gave a curt nod. "Tell him I shall be there directly, and send someone to fetch Mr. Bingley."

By the time he arrived downstairs, he found Bingley already there, an uncharacteristic frown on his face. Mr. Bennet stood with his hands clasped behind his back, staring out the window with an expression far more severe than Darcy had ever seen on him.

"Good morning, Mr. Bennet," Darcy said with a bow.

"Good morning, sir," Mr. Bennet replied, turning. "Forgive the hour, but I am here for my daughters. I would like them returned to Longbourn without delay."

Bingley's frown deepened. "Once again, sir, I must protest. Surely Miss Bennet's ankle needs further time to recover! Mr. Jones said she must not—"

"She will be carried, or laid out in the carriage with every cushion we can manage." Mr. Bennet's tone was clipped, unyielding. "I want all of my family under my roof with my protection. After what occurred at the Gardiner's home last night, I no longer feel comfortable having them scattered across the county."

Darcy studied him. This was not the indolent, ironic patriarch he had come to expect. There was no hint of teasing in his voice—only a tight, simmering dread poorly masked with civility.

Bingley looked wounded. "I assure you, Mr. Bennet, that I would protect Miss Bennet—"

"Better lame than dead," Mr. Bennet said flatly.

Darcy winced at the bluntness, and so did Bingley, whose jaw visibly tensed. Before his friend could respond, Darcy stepped forward. "I understand completely, Mr. Bennet."

Bingley whirled on his friend, betrayal on his face. "You do?"

Without breaking eye contact with Mr. Bennet, who was giving him a measuring look, Darcy replied, "I do. If it were Georgiana—my younger sister, sir—I would be making the same decision."

Mr. Bennet gave him a short, appreciative nod. "Thank you."

Darcy's thoughts were already racing ahead. If Smithson had been after the baby, as Elizabeth suspected… then Longbourn was now the most vulnerable point in the whole arrangement. And if Mr. Bennet wanted his family together so he could protect them personally—well, Darcy could hardly argue.

Still, it left a sour taste in his mouth to imagine Elizabeth gone from Netherfield. Gone from his immediate presence. No more conversations in the drawing room. No more catching her eye across the breakfast table. No more walking alongside her in the shrubbery, watching the sun catch in her curls as she teased him about his lack of conversational ease.

"I will see that the ladies are readied immediately," Bingley said sullenly.

"Thank you," Mr. Bennet said again. "You've both been hospitable— more than I expected. I am grateful."

Bingley murmured something in acknowledgment, his brows still furrowed.

Darcy took his leave then, but not to supervise packing. Instead, he went straight to his study and called for writing paper.

There were letters to write—important ones. And this time, they would not go unanswered.

Once the Bennet ladies had departed, the house fell oddly still. Bingley lingered near the window, visibly deflated, while Darcy retreated to the study and summoned paper and ink.

He penned his first letter to Mr. Reimont, his solicitor:

I require urgent inquiries into the man known as Mr. Smithson, who claims to represent an insurance company. His behavior and intentions are suspect, and I fear he may be involved in criminal activities under the guise of an official investigator. Please send word if there are any known affiliations, aliases, or related claims to this name or identity.

Also, advise whether it is possible to engage a Bow Street Runner to attend to the matter discreetly in Hertfordshire.

Satisfied, he sealed it with his signet.

The next letter was more difficult— addressed to Lord Matlock, his uncle. He hesitated before beginning. The earl had grown distant of late, and his silence in response to Darcy's earlier missives about the fire was… troubling.

My lord,

Forgive the urgency of this letter, but I must implore your attention to a matter that grows more concerning with each passing day...

He once again detailed the events surrounding the fire, only this time, he went into what he learned about Elizabeth's early awareness, the abandoned baby, the interrogation, and now Smithson's attempted entry into the nursery. No detail was omitted.

I beg of you to look into this situation. If you hear nothing of this Smithson through your contacts, I fear something far more sinister is at play than an insurance company wishing to avoid payout. It may be tied to the child. If there is anything you know—anything at all—I beg you to share it without delay.

His hand hovered over the paper before he signed it, sealed it, and wrote the direction on the outside.

Darcy then turned his attention towards the final—and perhaps most important—letter. This one would be to his cousin, Colonel Richard Fitzwilliam, who was currently stationed in London in order to help maintain order in the city after the fire.

Colonel Fitzwilliam,

I know you are in London, and no doubt you are drowning in chaos and duties. But I must ask you for a favor of the kind I suspect you are uniquely able to provide...

This one was more candid, layered with concern and unspoken trust. Last year, when the colonel had returned home from another tour of duty on the Continent, he showed up unannounced at Darcy House, where he proceeded to become thoroughly drunk. Amidst his ramblings of the horrors he had witnessed, he had muttered something about having contacts with the Home Office.

The following morning, the colonel had been alarmed upon hearing of his inebriated state the night before. He had demanded to know what all had been spoken, showing relief upon hearing that it was a bunch of nonsense. He swore Darcy to never speak of it, and since that night, the colonel had refused to drink alcohol in any form or quantity.

Darcy had kept that promise—until now.

I am hopeful that a few of your contacts may be able to help with a strange situation I have encountered here in Hertfordshire. There is a man named Smithson who is claiming to be an agent for an insurance company. The questions he has asked, however, have nothing to do with the destruction of property. Instead, he seems to be uniquely fixated on a baby who was found in Cheapside during the fire itself. The man went so far as to break into a gentleman's home last night in an attempt to reach the children of the household, mistakenly believing the infant was there. He has since disappeared, but I suspect we have not heard the last of him.

There is something strange to all of this. I have not yet received a response from your father with regards to my last letter suggesting that the fire was set deliberately by France. I normally do not involve myself with such affairs of state and politics, but there is now too much at stake for me stand idly by.

Please make inquiries—discreet ones. I have made the same request of your father, and I plan to send for a Bow Street Runner to begin investigations here.

Darcy leaned back in his chair, pressing his fingertips together. Three letters, three directions. He only hoped that something would break before another attempt was made on the Gardiners—or on Benjamin.

Or Elizabeth.

He would not allow that.

⋊

Elizabeth was quite disappointed to have been called back to Longbourn with Jane, but her father's unusual severity did not leave room for question or debate. Watching Netherfield Park fade from view, Elizabeth privately admitted that she would miss the enigma of Darcy most of all.

179

Poor Jane had been forced to endure an extremely painful carriage ride over the three miles of poorly paved road, her ankle jostling at every rut and ditch in spite of the large quantities of pillows, cushions, and blankets being used to stabilize the limb.

Upon arriving at Longbourn, Jane was carried upstairs to her room by Mr. Hill, where she gratefully accepted a cup of laudanum-laced tea. She was soon fast asleep, leaving Elizabeth free to seek out Benjamin, whom she had not seen in several days.

The young lad grinned and reached for her when she stepped into the nursery. Mrs. Gardiner and Mrs. Bennet both agreed that he was now about six months of age, and Elizabeth did not think she had ever seen such a handsome child. His light blue eyes and dark hair …gave him a striking appearance, and though his cheeks were still a touch too thin, he had begun to fill out from regular feedings and proper care. He babbled when he saw her, pudgy arms flapping with delight, and Elizabeth felt some of the heaviness in her heart ease.

Cradling him close, she sat by the nursery window and let him tug at the ribbon of her sleeve while she hummed a nonsense tune. Her time in the nursery flew by, offering her solace and consolation from the disturbing recent events. She took her lunch and dinner on trays, and soon it was time to retire for the night.

"Good night, beautiful boy," she whispered as she kissed a sleeping Benjamin on the head.

As she left the nursery, Elizabeth could scarcely hold back her tears. *Please, Lord, keep him safe. Keep all of us safe.*

X

The following morning, Elizabeth descended to the breakfast room feeling weary in both body and spirit. She had slept poorly; every creak and groan of the house woke her with a racing heart, terrified that Smithson had broken in to take Benjamin.

She entered the breakfast room to find everyone else already at the table, even Mr. Bennet, who was perusing the morning post.

"Good morning," she said, fetching a plate of eggs and ham from the sideboard.

The ladies in the room responded to her greeting with their own, but Mr. Bennet did not reply. He was staring blankly down at one of the letters, the black edging around the paper unmistakable in its meaning.

Elizabeth's stomach turned. "Papa? Who?" She gestured towards the missive, unable to put her thoughts into words.

He looked up at her with a grim expression. "My cousin, Mr. Collins, is dead."

"The heir?" gasped Jane.

He nodded. "Apparently, he was in London when the fire struck. Had just completed his studies and was preparing to take orders. They say he fled in the wrong direction—toward the blaze rather than away from it. He died from smoke inhalation."

Jane's hand fluttered to her chest. "How dreadful."

"They were only able to identify him from the initials on his pocket watch," Mr. Bennet continued. "His schoolmates recognized a sketch in the newspaper and confirmed it. The solicitor was listed as an emergency contact, and he managed to trace us here thanks to Mr. Collins's… frequent boasting about inheriting Longbourn."

"Oh, thank the Lord!" Everyone turned to stare at Mrs. Bennet, whose hands were raised above her head as if in praise. "We are saved!"

But Mrs. Bennet was already rushing forward, her face lit with sudden joy. "If Mr. Collins is dead, then the entail—why, Jane could be the heir! Or even Lydia! Oh, what fortune!"

"We know nothing of the sort," Mr. Bennet said firmly. "The solicitor made it very clear that they would not be handling the matter. The entail must be consulted— Phillips' predecessor drew it up. I will go into Meryton to speak with him."

"And I shall come with you!" Mrs. Bennet declared. "I must tell my sister immediately. This is news worth sharing!"

Mr. Bennet sighed. "Yes, I thought as much."

At the prospect of a trip into town, Kitty and Lydia perked up at once.

"Oh, Papa, please let us come!" Lydia pleaded. "There are soldiers in Meryton, and it is ever so dull here!"

"With so many officers about, we will be perfectly safe," Kitty added.

"Very well," Mr. Bennet said heavily. "But you are to stay with your mother and remain out of trouble."

Lydia gave a squeal of delight and darted off to prepare, dragging Kitty behind her.

Elizabeth caught her father's eye as he stood, and he gave her a small, tired smile.

"I will find out what I can, Lizzy," he said quietly. "And if it truly is the end of the entail… we shall see what comes next."

She nodded, unable to find the words to respond, unease settling deep within her chest. The news of Mr. Collins's death had stunned them all— but somewhere deep inside, Elizabeth could not help but wonder if the fire was done with them yet.

"Lizzy, come!"

Elizabeth looked up, startled. Mrs. Bennet was standing with her hands on her hips, staring down at her. "You had best get dressed and come to the village with us to meet the officers. Lord knows there is nothing for you here at Longbourn."

"But Benjamin—"

"Now, Elizabeth."

Mrs. Bennet's tone brooked no room for refusal. Elizabeth sighed and rose from her chair. *I just hope we do not see Mr. Smithson while there.*

Chapter 13

Elizabeth stepped down from the Bennets' carriage and looked around with some unease. Meryton, though never what one would call sleepy, was usually a neat and orderly little town—a market square with tidy shops and a few elegant homes, its modest bustle constrained by its size and genteel rhythm.

But now, the town was completely different.

It was crowded, almost claustrophobically so. The market square teemed with movement—not just shopkeepers and customers, but ragged strangers leaning against buildings, children darting between carts, and more red-coated soldiers than Elizabeth had ever seen assembled in one place.

"I had not expected such a… crowd," she murmured, eyes scanning the square. A ragged man sat slumped on the steps of the butcher's, his boots worn through, while a woman with a wrapped infant bargained rather too loudly for a loaf of bread.

"It is all the people from London," Kitty whispered, catching her arm. "Aunt Phillips said many came here when the fires started."

Elizabeth nodded slowly, but she could not shake the feeling that the crowd was not merely full—it was frayed. Edges rubbed raw. People muttered, soldiers shouted orders, and the energy in the air was tightly wound, like a storm that had not yet broken.

"I do not like this," she said under her breath, glancing at Lydia, who was peering eagerly across the street at the haberdashery.

"There are officers," Lydia said excitedly. "Look! Over there—four of them!"

"Yes, and more behind them," Kitty chimed in. "Do you suppose the colonel is with them?"

Mr. and Mrs. Bennet had already disappeared into the Philips' front door, so Elizabeth sighed and gestured toward the shop. "Fine. But only the haberdashery, and only for a moment. We will be back here before Papa returns."

The three of them made their way across the street, carefully navigating between wagons and carts. But just as they reached the center of the lane, a cry went up from a driver trying to steady a panicked horse.

"Watch out!"

A crate flew from the back of a wagon with a loud crash, and the startled horse reared. Lydia, caught mid-step, froze like a frightened rabbit in the road.

A flash of red surged into view—an officer's coat—and before Elizabeth could react, the man had swept forward and pushed Lydia out of the way. The crate landed inches from where she had been standing, scattering its contents across the muddy street.

"Lydia!" Elizabeth and Kitty rushed forward, helping her up from the cobbles. She was unhurt, though visibly shaken.

"I—I am all right," she gasped, brushing dust from her skirts.

"Are you certain?" the officer asked, steadying her by the elbow. He had a warm voice and a firm grip, and when Elizabeth turned to thank him, she paused. He was handsome—impossibly so. With a trim figure, a charming smile, and eyes the exact shade of autumn honey, he looked like the sort of man right out of the gothic novels Lydia and Kitty insisted on reading aloud in the evenings.

"I—I think so," Lydia stammered, blinking rapidly and flushing at his attention.

Forcing her eyes away from the man's face, Elizabeth examined Lydia to ensure nothing was twisted or broken.

"She's fine," she declared with relief, then turned her attention to the man who had saved her sister. "Thank you, sir. Truly."

The officer smiled. "It was fortunate I was close by."

"Fortunate indeed," Elizabeth said with feeling. "Who are you?"

"I hope you will forgive the impertinence in introducing myself," he said with a dazzling grin. "In cases such as these, I am certain propriety can be waived. My name is Lieutenant Wickham, newly attached to the Hertfordshire regiment."

Elizabeth introduced herself and her sisters, watching with quiet amusement as her two younger sisters blushed furiously.

"I have only just arrived in Meryton," Wickham said with an easy smile. "The country air is quite a change after the last few weeks."

"Were you in London?" Elizabeth asked, her curiosity piqued.

He nodded. "For a time. It is... not what it was."

"Nor is Meryton," Elizabeth said, looking around. "There are never this many people—soldiers or otherwise."

Wickham gave a small, crooked smile. "Yes, well—when London empties, places like this tend to swell. With so many seeking housing and food, the regiments are receiving a surge of enlistments."

"I think it is wonderful—so many officers in one place!" Lydia enthused.

At that, Wickham chuckled, though his voice held a note of caution. "Yes, well. Uniforms may look the same, but not all men wear them the same way, especially when there is no time to properly inspect qualifications or letters of reference."

Elizabeth glanced sideways at Lydia, who was now openly staring at another young soldier leaning against a post. "I imagine the red coat can be… misleading."

He met her eyes, and for the briefest moment, the charm dropped—just enough for her to glimpse a flicker of something more guarded. "Precisely."

Before the conversation could go further, the sound of approaching hooves clattering over the cobblestones drew their attention. She turned to see Darcy and Bingley

Bingley reined in his horse first, beaming down at the small group. "Miss Elizabeth! Miss Kitty—Miss Lydia! What a surprise to find you in Meryton this morning. We were just on our way to Longbourn to inquire after Miss Bennet."

Elizabeth smiled up at him. "Good morning, Mr. Bingley. We have accompanied our parents to visit with our aunt and uncle Philips. Jane and Mary are at home."

"And how is Miss Bennet?" he asked eagerly.

"Sleeping, sir," Kitty chimed in helpfully. "Mary is watching her."

"Ah, I am glad to hear she's resting."

Darcy came to a halt beside his friend, his expression unreadable beneath the brim of his hat. Elizabeth's eyes flicked to his face, noting the slight pinch around his eyes, the pale hue to his skin, and the telltale tension in his jaw. He was pressing his lips tightly together—too tightly. Her heart stirred with concern, but she said nothing. She knew that look now. He was fighting off a cough and did not want it remarked upon.

At that moment, Wickham stepped forward, the sun catching on the gleam of his uniform buttons.

"Darcy," he said warmly. "Well, this is a surprise."

Darcy's eyes flicked to him, but his expression did not change. He gave the faintest inclination of his head, his lips still tightly sealed, and then, without a word, turned his horse and began to ride away at a steady pace.

The silence that followed was palpable.

Wickham blinked. His easy smile faltered, replaced by a flash of something more complex— surprise, perhaps, and something suspiciously like hurt. He masked it a moment later with a chuckle and a shrug. "Well. That's Darcy, I suppose. Some things never change."

"I do apologize," Bingley said, looking back at his departing friend. "I hope to see you all later."

In an instant, they were gone, leaving Wickham and the three Bennet girls standing in the road.

"La, what was wrong with Mr. Darcy?" exclaimed Lydia. "That was quite rude of him to cut you like that, Mr. Wickham."

Shrugging his shoulders, Wickham gave a little laugh. "Mr. Darcy and I have known one another since our childhood. He probably suddenly remembered the time I caught more fish than him and could not bear the reminder of his humiliation at my hands."

Elizabeth bit her lip, torn between keeping Darcy's affairs private or alleviating Wickham's wounded feelings. Before she could decide, however, she heard her name being called. Turning, she saw her parents standing at their carriage outside of the Philips' residence—and Mr. Bennet did not look pleased.

"Thank you again, Lieutenant," she said, dipping a small curtsy before grasping Lydia and Kitty by their arms. "It is time for us to leave now, as our parents have finished their business."

"It was my pleasure," he said. "Allow me to escort you across to them safely."

She hesitated, noting the deepening glower on her father's face. The crowded street gave her pause, however, and she reluctantly acquiesced.

Wickham offered his arm with practiced ease, and Lydia, undeterred by the warning in her father's scowl, eagerly took it before Elizabeth could protest. Kitty giggled and trotted after them, and Elizabeth found herself trailing behind as they crossed the road.

Mr. Bennet's brows were drawn together, and he tapped his walking stick impatiently against the step. "I thought you were only to visit the haberdashery?"

"That was our intention, Papa, but—"

"Lydia was almost killed!" Kitty burst out in excitement, unable to keep herself from interrupting. "A box fell from a cart, and it would have landed on her if Lieutenant Wickham had not pushed her out of the way!"

Mrs. Bennet clutched her gloved hand to her heart. "La! My poor girl! You might have been trampled or worse!" She turned to Wickham with bright eyes. "Lieutenant, we are most indebted to you. Such gallantry!"

Wickham offered a polite bow. "I am relieved to have been of help, ma'am. I only did what any gentleman would."

"Not every gentleman would bother," Mr. Bennet said dryly, giving the young man a more measured look. "But I thank you, sir. I suppose I should be grateful someone had eyes on the child, even if I did not."

Lydia made a sour face at being referred to in such a way, but then she beamed at Wickham and squeezed his arm. "It was ever so brave of him."

"Indeed, it was!" cried Mrs. Philips, who had been standing at the doorway unnoticed. "To express my gratitude, I would like to personally invite you to my card party tomorrow evening. An invitation has already been sent to Colonel Forster, but you shall be my special guest, in honor of your heroics."

Chuckling, Wickham said with a bow, "I would be delighted, madam."

"Well, girls, we must be going." Mr. Bennet ushered his family towards the carriage door. Before entering himself, he turned and said, "My thanks again, sir."

As the carriage drove away, Elizabeth looked back through the window at the handsome figure of Lieutenant Wickham, who had joined a small group of officers in conversation.

Things certainly have been changing in Meryton. What will happen next? she wondered.

ℵ

The drawing room at her aunt Philips's house was more crowded than usual the following evening. The usual card tables were set up, but now they were flanked by a number of officers in uniform, laughing boisterously and speaking too loudly. Elizabeth, who had grown up attending these parties, blinked at the difference a few red coats made.

A glance at Colonel Forster showed the man smiling tightly, his hands clasped behind his back as though he hoped decorum might return if he simply wished it hard enough. Usually, she would enjoy being in such a large crowd, but not one that was more raucous than festive.

Elizabeth, deciding she had no desire to try her luck at the card tables, especially after overhearing two officers discuss the value of their fish tokens in actual currency, wandered toward the fire. She took a seat near the hearth, grateful for the warmth and distance from the bustle of the room.

She watched with a small smirk as several of the local young ladies— Lydia and Kitty included—vied for the attention of the red-coated men. Lieutenant Wickham appeared to be the most popular, no doubt due to his good looks. She vaguely recognized a few other soldiers that she had been introduced to since the militia had come into the county, such as Lieutenants Denny and Pratt, as well as Captains Carter and Chamberlayne.

Her attention was pulled away by an uproar at one of the card tables. One of the officers shouted in anger, while another gleefully swept the fish into a large pile in front of him. She bit her lip and looked around at her aunt Philips, who was watching the soldiers anxiously. Fortunately, Captain Carter went to the group and was able to quiet them down a bit.

"May I join you, Miss Bennet?"

She looked up and found Lieutenant Wickham standing nearby, his hat tucked neatly under one arm. His expression was open and charming, and she felt her cheeks warm at his attention.

"Of course," she said, gesturing to the empty chair beside her. "Do you not care for card games?"

He smiled as he sat down, the firelight catching in the gold of his uniform buttons. "I like them a little too much, I am afraid."

Her brow rose. "Indeed?"

Wickham gave a rueful chuckle. "When I was at Cambridge, I played far too often. Accumulated more debt than was wise and made something of a name for myself, I fear. Mr. Darcy warned me often enough to stop, but I was too proud to listen."

Elizabeth blinked. "You and Mr. Darcy were at university together?"

"Oh, long before that. We have known each other since we were children." He leaned back slightly, stretching one arm along the back of his chair. "We were often thrown together when we were young—my father was old Mr. Darcy's steward, you see. We were quite good friends, even if I did tease him quite mercilessly at times for his priggishness."

"But no longer?"

His shoulders slumped slightly, and an expression of remorse crossed his face. "No, I am afraid not. We parted ways during our university years. I supposed I did not always make the wisest choices, and Darcy... well, I imagine he grew tired of having to clean up my messes."

"I am sorry," she said, for lack of anything else to say, but he seemed to not hear her. His gaze faced the fire, but he did not seem to even be aware of the flames.

"It is my own fault, really. I have not seen him in several years—not since his father's funeral and the reading of the will. Old Mr. Darcy was my godfather, and he left me a valuable living when he died."

"You were intended for the church?"

Smiling wryly, he said, "Yes, but both Darcy and I knew I would never suit. I was given a sum in lieu of the living and studied law instead. The practice where I worked burned down during the fire, and I used the last of my savings to purchase this commission until the barrister I clerked for is able to reestablish his business."

"I supposed seeing Mr. Darcy was quite a shock, then."

He laughed. "Yes, it most certainly was! Of all the hamlets in all the kingdom, and we both come to this one. I dare say it was more unpleasant for him than for me. How he must still despise me; but then, he has always been one to say that his good opinion once lost is lost forever."

Elizabeth bit her lip, debating. *Should I tell him? He looks so…forlorn.* Making up her mind and praying she was not doing the wrong thing, she said softly, "I do not think his reaction had anything to do with you personally."

His eyebrows lifted. "No?"

"I think…I think he was trying very hard not to cough. The ride into town with the harsh wind must have worn him down."

Wickham blinked, genuinely surprised. "Still the same? But it has been years since his pneumonia! I would have thought he had long since recovered." He peered at her more closely. "I had not realized you and he were on such intimate terms so as to know his past in such personal detail. Certainly not so soon after arriving in the neighborhood."

"He did not exactly confide," Elizabeth said, a little self-consciously. "I stumbled upon him during a rather severe fit. I suppose he did not have the strength to push me away, although I have kept his condition in confidence, of course. I only tell you this so you know the slight may not have been because of you personally."

For a long moment, Wickham just looked at her, something unreadable in his expression. Then he smiled again, softer this time. "Well. I am glad it was you who found him."

Elizabeth felt the warmth of the fire seep into her cheeks.

"I do not know what has truly passed between the two of you," she said, "but I must admit, I have never seen a man try so hard to suppress a cough in all my life. It cannot be easy for him to appear aloof and composed when he is fighting to breathe."

"He was always proud." Wickham looked away for a moment, his smile fading just slightly. "Even as a child. But it does not mean he's unfeeling. Still waters and all that. You are probably one of the few people who can boast of such an encounter with him."

"Boasting would be in poor taste," she said wryly. "He could scarcely breathe."

"And yet," Wickham murmured, looking back toward the card tables, "you seem to understand him more than most. It is more than I can say for myself these days."

Elizabeth did not respond right away. The warmth of the fire flickered across his face, the lines of regret and nostalgia made deeper with the shadows.

"Perhaps you might send him a note or pay a call on him at Netherfield," she suggested. "Being an old friend, he may appreciate knowing the changes you have made in your life."

"Perhaps I shall," he murmured.

𝕏

195

Later that evening, Elizabeth sat at her small writing table in her room, the glow of a single candle casting long shadows across the walls. She had changed into her nightdress, but sleep still felt distant. Her thoughts were too unsettled.

The card party had ended earlier than expected after one of Mrs. Philips's prized vases was shattered—sacrificed to a rather unsteady display of soldierly high spirits. Elizabeth still winced remembering the crash, the awkward silence that followed, and the red-faced apologies delivered between hiccups and laughter. Colonel Forster, clearly mortified, had wasted no time in ordering his officers to return to their quarters.

It had been just in time.

She recalled the way two of the more inebriated young men had looked at her younger sisters—Kitty and Lydia entirely oblivious to the danger, giggling and twirling curls and batting lashes as though it were all a delightful game.

Elizabeth had felt ill at ease. *They are too young to know the danger of it. And too foolish to care even if they did.*

Tomorrow, she resolved, she would speak to her father. He must see how precarious the situation had become…before something regrettable happened.

But not all of them behaved poorly, she thought. As they were leaving, Captain Carter stopped to bid farewell to the party. "I apologize for my fellow officers' behavior tonight, Mrs. Philips," he had said, his lips pressed together tightly. "I can assure you that those under my command will be feeling the consequences of their behavior during drills in the morning."

Lieutenant Wickham had echoed his colleague's words, gratifying Mrs. Philips. The party quickly returned to their various entertainments after the officers had left, and harmony was restored.

Elizabeth's thoughts now wandered to the handsome officer and the story he had shared. *What a coincidence for the two men to end up in the same small town at the same time!*

She was glad for the opportunity to meet them both. Darcy intrigued her. Wickham charmed her. Both compelling in such different ways.

What a study in contrasts they were—one so guarded, so proud, yet capable of astonishing gentleness in moments of weakness; the other charming and open, almost too easy to talk to, yet carrying the weight of regret behind his easy smile.

Wickham was handsome and sociable, with little but his good looks and military commission to recommend him. Darcy, by contrast, had wealth, status—and walls so high it was a miracle she had glimpsed behind them at all.

She had learned far more about Darcy than she ever expected—his illness, his restraint, his startling flashes of dry humor. *And those few rare smiles, how rare they are… and how hard-won.*

And yet…

She shook her head, laughing softly at herself. Neither man had offered her anything beyond a few shared conversations. *Here I am, spinning romantic nonsense in my own mind like Mama planning wedding breakfasts before the couple has even met twice.*

She leaned forward and blew out the candle.

Time enough for dreams.

Chapter 14

Darcy sat alone in the study at Netherfield, the morning sunrise light filtering weakly through the tall windows. A small stack of letters rested on the desk before him, newly delivered and still bearing a fine coating of frost from their journey. He reached for the one addressed in Georgiana's flowing, youthful hand and carefully broke the seal.

Dear Brother,

It is so dreadfully cold at Pemberley now. I told Mrs. Annesley this morning that I felt like one of those little frosted hedgerow birds, chirping despite the chill and quite determined to be brave. I wish I were still in town—well, not town exactly, for I know how dangerous it has become, but I do miss the bustle. Mostly, I miss Ramsgate. The air was so mild and salty, and I still dream of the sound of the waves. Do you remember how the wind tangled my hair every morning, and you pretended not to mind when I borrowed your books and never returned them?"

He smiled at her cheerful tone. Their time in Ramsgate had brought them closer together, making their bond more one of siblings than caregiver and ward. His little sister was certainly growing into a charming, confident young woman, in spite of her childhood timidity.

Mrs. Annesley and Mrs. Reynolds are determined that I shall learn every part of running an estate before I turn twenty. I do wish you had warned me how dull some of the accounting is, Fitz. But I feel quite useful—Mrs. Annesley even let me plan how we will distribute firewood this winter, and I toured the still room yesterday.

I like Mrs. Annesley much better than Mrs. Younge. It is just as well she fled during the fire, though I still cannot believe she left me like that. At the time, I thought we were going to die. Perhaps that's what she thought, too. But I suppose that's what fear does to people—it causes them to react and reveal their true natures. In hindsight, I am rather glad to be rid of her.

He read that line twice, frowning. Mrs. Younge had come highly recommended, but after she abandoned her charge when news of the fire came, he had investigated her further, discovering that her letters of recommendation were forgeries. *I can only thank God that she had such a limited time to influence my sister.* That was one of the few blessings that came from the fire. That, and seeing Elizabeth for the first time.

Elizabeth.

He leaned back and closed his eyes, picturing her fine eyes and light, pleasing figure. She was more than her appearance, however; with her razor wit, her quiet bravery, and her maddening ability to take root in his mind and permeate his every thought.

He saw her still as she had looked that first day in Hyde Park, Hands on her hips, brow furrowed with concern. He had never seen someone so at ease amidst chaos.

She unsettled him. She made him want—things he had never allowed himself to want. Love. Companionship.

Enough! He shook his head. He had no business thinking of her as often as he did. He knew it. Her connections were modest at best, her family often appalling.

Forcing himself back to the present, he turned his focus back to finishing Georgiana's letter.

Now, are you minding your health? I know you. You are probably doing far too much and ignoring your cough again. Just because you can breathe without wheezing, does not mean you are invincible. Please rest. And remember that it is nothing to be ashamed of if you have to cough in public. Honestly, you act like it is akin to fainting at Almack's!

Write soon and tell me everything. And do not work too hard. And for heaven's sake, try not to terrify the local populace with your silent glowers. They are only trying to be kind.

Your ever affectionate,

Georgiana

Darcy huffed out a small breath of amusement, his lips twitching at the corner. Georgiana had grown more confident—more herself—since the fire. He only wished she could have remained near him. But London was no place for her now. He folded the letter with care and reached for the next.

The seal of the Earl of Matlock stared up at him, the wax a deep crimson. Finally.

But his anticipation dissolved as he read.

Nephew,

I understand your concerns regarding this Mr. Smithson fellow, but I would not be overly troubled. Insurance men, by their nature, are an obstinate breed—prone to dramatics and well-versed in avoidance. Likely, he is no more than a penny-pinching functionary hoping to delay a claim.

As for this business about the baby and the fire's origin, I am certain it is nothing. Surely you misunderstood the man's questioning. It will all come to nothing, as these matters often do.

I urge you to take things in stride. I know your sense of justice is great, but not every oddity is a threat. If you like, I shall make a few inquiries, though I doubt it will amount to much.

Yours, etc.

Matlock

Darcy's fingers tightened on the page.

Useless. His uncle had dismissed everything—Elizabeth's interrogation, the attempted break-in, the flight of Smithson—as if it were a mere billing dispute.

He let out a quiet, irritated sigh and tossed the letter aside. *This is how he writes to Georgiana, he thought bitterly. Not to me. Platitudes and reassurance, as if I were some child alarmed by shadows.*

Still no word from his solicitor. Still no sign of the Bow Street Runner he had requested. He pushed back from the desk and stood, pacing the length of the study. Something was not right. And it was not just the fire.

⚹

There are too many things that do not add up. Elizabeth in London, then here. Mr. Smithson's interest in the baby. And now Wickham's arrival.

Wickham.

Of all the improbable turns in recent days, seeing him again in Meryton had been the most startling. He had not seen Wickham in over two years. And then, just like that, there he was—in the middle of Meryton, looking older, thinner, but with the same careless smile, the same easy charm.

But he knew all too well the immorality and vice behind the mask. Some might say to forgive and forget—to move on—but Darcy could not forget.

He leaned back in his chair and closed his eyes, and just like that, he was eighteen again. Two boys arriving at Cambridge, their eyes bright with the promise of independence. Wickham had been giddy with freedom, full of jokes and plans and schemes. Darcy, more reserved, had tried to keep up, tried to believe they could still be what they had been at Pemberley.

But Wickham's vices had bloomed quickly in that fertile ground. Gambling houses. Women of questionable character. Late nights and mounting debts. Darcy had warned him, more than once.

"You must stop. One day, this will catch up to you."

"You sound just like the parson," Wickham laughed, tossing his cards on the table. "So blasted moral. I will be fine, Fitz. I always am."

"This is not who you want to be. I know you, George!"

Wickham scoffed. "Is it not? And what do you know of it, Fitz? You, who have always had everything handed to you. The name, the estate, the future, all neatly wrapped with a ribbon. I have had to scrape for every opportunity I have ever had. You are just uncomfortable because—here, outside Pemberley—for once, it is me that people seek. Me they follow."

Darcy shook his head, feeling the frustration coil tight in his chest and forcing a cough. "They follow your charm, not your character. And that only lasts so long."

Wickham's mouth twisted. "Better to be loved for charm than tolerated for principles."

Darcy said nothing; there was nothing more to say. And when Wickham turned away with a half-smirk and gathered his winnings, Darcy felt the final, irrevocable crack in what had once been friendship.

But that was not the last time he would see Wickham—no, the attorney had sent Wickham a notice to appear for the disposition of any bequests. He had still been reeling from the loss of his father; although the man had berated his son for his weaknesses, he also spent a considerable amount of time teaching him to run the estate. Georgiana, being at such a tender age, was crying herself to sleep at night, mourning the loss of the man who had treated her so well.

And Darcy was all alone, about to face the friend who had abandoned him for debauchery and sin.

Wickham sauntered through the door with his usual confidence, but for once, his face was solemn and his voice was low—it seemed as though his father's godson was not entirely untouched by genuine grief.

"I am sorry, Fitz," said Wickham. "He could be...demanding, but he was a good man. Fair. Better than most."

"Yes," Darcy replied stiffly.

A silence stretched between them—not the companionable kind they once knew, but brittle, taut with all the things unsaid. Wickham shifted his weight, then leaned an elbow on the back of a nearby chair.

"So," he said at last, breaking the silence, "why am I here?"

"It seems my father has left you the living at Kymptom." Darcy reached into the desk drawer and retrieved a sealed envelope. "Along with a bequest of a thousand pounds."

Wickham gaped, then uttered a sharp, incredulous laugh. "A living? Fitz, you must be joking. You know I would never make a good clergyman. The whole parish would be scandalized before the end of my first sermon."

"Then what do you propose?" Darcy had asked, his tone even.

"The law, I think. It is respectable enough, and I have always had a good mind for argument." Wickham paused, his smile fading just slightly. "But studying the law, well—it is not exactly inexpensive."

Darcy folded his arms. "Not the military?"

Wickham scoffed. "Please. You know I have never had the stomach for rough sleeping and battlefield horrors. No, I am better suited to something. ..more civilized."

I knew it, *Darcy thought to himself. There it was. That subtle manipulation—Wickham's old talent for turning a request into a favor owed, a failing into a charm.*

"Five thousand pounds should set me up for the schooling and lodging in London."

"Three," Darcy said promptly, having already been prepared, "in addition to the one thousand in the bequest. Four total."

"Done."

Darcy handed over the envelope, and Wickham opened it. Upon seeing the bank note already made out for four thousand pounds, he smirked. "Well, Fitz, it seems you know me better than I know myself."

As he exited the room, Wickham turned back to Darcy, his face solemn. "You may not believe it, Fitz, but I promise I am going to prove myself."

X

A knock at the door interrupted Darcy's memories. "Enter," he called, leaning forward once more and retrieving his pen to sign the final letter.

"Pardon the interruption, sir," said a maid, "but there is a caller for you."

"This early in the morning?" Darcy asked in surprise. "Who is it?"

"He did not leave a name, sir, but he's waiting in the front parlor. Said you would know him."

Darcy stood, frowning, but he set aside the letters, straightened his waistcoat, and made his way down the main staircase.

The door to the front parlor stood ajar, and as he stepped inside, his suspicions were confirmed. George Wickham stood at the hearth, glancing over a portrait on the wall with an air of easy familiarity.

Darcy exhaled slowly through his nose. "Of course."

Wickham turned with a grin. "Fitz. It has been a long time. How have you been? How is Georgiana?"

Pinching the bridge of his nose, Darcy sighed. "It is too early for social niceties. How much do you want?"

Wickham's smile faded, replaced by something quieter. "Nothing. That is, I do not need any money."

Darcy blinked. "No money?"

"No money."

Flummoxed, Darcy asked, "Then what—why the uniform? Why are you in the uncivilized militia rather than studying law as you once claimed?"

"Ah." Wickham rubbed the back of his neck. "I suppose I can see why you thought I must be here in search of funds. I am making a mess of this already…May I sit? To explain?"

Darcy gestured towards a chair, and the two sat facing one another. It was silent for several moments before Wickham said, "I know I have earned your distrust, Fitz. At Cambridge, I was a disaster. Cards, women, brandy—I chased every indulgence and ignored every warning. Especially yours."

Darcy did not respond at once. He could still see the boyish grin across a stack of cards, the careless shrug when debts were called in.

"I did study the law," Wickham went on. "After I received the money from your father's will, I completed schooling in London. Upon completion, I found a post in a barrister's office in London. Clerk work, mostly, but I was working to support myself and allowing your father's funds to grow in interest. Until the fire."

Darcy's arms dropped to his sides, his expression unreadable. "The fire?"

"It destroyed the building. The office. Files, clients—all gone. The firm's older clerks were taken in elsewhere, but I—well, I am not exactly a shining prospect. With so many displaced men seeking work, there was little left for me. So, I joined the militia. Not for glory or uniform—just for stability. A roof, meals, a purpose."

Darcy stared at him for a long moment, then slowly nodded. "I see."

"I do not blame you for doubting me, But I have changed. Those reckless days—what once felt thrilling now just started feeling empty shortly after we left Cambridge. I remembered how it felt to be needed...like when you were ill as a boy. I liked being the one to help. I wanted to be someone I could respect."

Another silence as Darcy gazed steadily at his old friend, searching his face for signs of deceit.

There was a pause, the weight of years settling between them. "Speaking of your being ill, how are you?" Wickham asked softly. "Miss Elizabeth told me the fire aggravated your lungs."

Darcy stiffened. "Did she?" His voice was tight. "I did not think she was so little to be trusted."

"She was not gossiping," Wickham said quickly. "It was after…after you rode away in town. I was hurt. I thought—I feared your good opinion of me was gone forever. I told her about our childhood. She told me perhaps it was not personal. That you might have simply been trying not to cough."

Darcy looked away, lips pressed into a tight line.

"She said she found you mid-fit once," Wickham added. "That she kept your secret. I was… surprised. You never used to let anyone see you in that state."

"I still do not," Darcy murmured. "Miss Elizabeth happened upon me in a time of weakness, that's all."

Wickham studied him for another moment before saying quietly, "She sees more than you think."

Darcy did not respond at once. His fingers curled into a loose fist at his side. "Perhaps she does."

Wickham smiled faintly. "She's remarkable."

Darcy gave the smallest nod, his throat too tight to reply.

Wickham picked up his hat. "I should go. I have duties to attend to."

Darcy inclined his head. "Thank you—for explaining. I hope you are able to continue on the path you say you've begun."

At the doorway, Wickham hesitated. "Showing weakness does not make you weak, Fitz. I had to learn that the hard way. I do not drink anymore, and I have not touched a deck of cards in over a year. Some things are harder to resist than others, and when I could admit to myself that I struggled with self-control, it actually made it easier to change."

With that, Wickham let himself out, leaving Darcy alone with the silence and the gentle ticking of the clock to ponder the strange turnaround of his old friend.

Perhaps people could change. Perhaps some things once broken could yet be repaired.

But could *he* forgive?

It was, after all, the mark of a true Christian to do good to those who would harm you, so surely forgiving a penitent man would be even more important.

But at what cost? Could he risk it?

He did not know. Not yet.

Darcy stood still for several long moments, the air in the room thick with the past. The memories, the hurt, the sense of betrayal—they all clung to him like damp fog on a chilly morning. And yet, there had been something honest in Wickham's face. Something weary, but not false.

A knock came at the doorframe. "Darcy?" Bingley's cheerful voice cut through the haze. "Fancy a ride? The sun's out at last, and I have been itching to take Titan out before the roads turn to muck again."

Darcy turned, glancing out the window. The morning light was pale but promising, catching the edge of a frostbitten field and the glint of dew on the hedgerows. He felt the familiar ache in his chest, a dull tightness that spoke of stiff lungs and unvoiced worries. And yet—he wanted to ride. He wanted to breathe sharp air and feel the wind bite his skin.

He paused with one hand on the edge of the door. A dozen times in the past, he had refused to participate in such things with others. *What if I have a coughing fit? What if Bingley sees?*

And then, quite suddenly, he remembered Wickham's parting words: *Showing weakness does not make you weak.*

He looked at Bingley's open, earnest face—the friend who had never judged him, who had only ever looked up to him, even when he had not deserved it. For once, he let the inner voice of his father fall silent, the voice that had always said a Darcy must never falter, never show vulnerability, never let anyone see.

Darcy took a breath—not entirely easy, but freer than it had been in some time.

"Yes," he said, stepping into the hall. "A ride is perfect."

And as he did, a strange sensation unfurled inside him. It was not joy exactly, or peace, or even certainty. But it was something like hope.

And for now, that was enough.

Chapter 15

Elizabeth awoke with a start, her cheeks warm and her heart beating far too quickly for the peaceful quiet of the morning.

Good heavens, what sort of dream was that?

She pressed a hand to her temple, willing her thoughts to still. It had not been improper—*not truly*—but it had been... intimate. The feel of a hand clasping hers, a gaze so intense it seemed to strip her bare, lips pressing gently on hers in a kiss—tender and tentative, and so real that her lips still tingled with the memory of it in the morning light.

"I must be losing my mind," she muttered aloud, flinging back the covers and stepping down onto the rug. "It was only a dream."

The fact that the man in question was someone she actually knew—Fitzwilliam Darcy, of all people—was enough to send her fleeing from the house altogether.

She dressed quickly and quietly, glad Jane was still asleep and no one was yet bustling about the halls. The air in the house felt heavy after the uneasy events of the previous night, and Elizabeth needed space. Air. Clarity.

A brisk walk to the top of Oakham Mount should do it.

She donned her boots and a warm cloak and slipped outside without troubling Hill or any of the other servants. The November air was sharp against her skin, but welcome, too—it scoured away some of the heat still burning on her cheeks. Her steps carried her quickly past the edge of the village, up the well-trodden path she had climbed a hundred times.

With each step up the incline, her breathing evened, and the chaos of her thoughts began to find shape.

Darcy...

It was impossible not to think of him. He had surprised her so many times, like in London during the fire—without hesitation, when the soldier had shouted at her. He had stood beside her when no one else had, had protected her dignity in a moment when she had barely thought to guard it herself.

Then at the Meryton assembly, when she had thought him proud and above his company. But then minutes later, he had taken her herbs with such a quiet, vulnerable gratitude that it had struck her breathless. And later, instead of asking for more—indeed, he had needed to be convinced— so as not to take what her sister might need.

What kind of man tries so hard not to burden others that he practically collapses before asking for aid? What could have made him this way?

How odd that a man who seemed so guarded could still be capable of such simple, honest thanks. And how telling, too, that he had been hesitant to accept any help at all. It was clear, painfully so, that he had no one to lean on. No one he trusted with his weakness.

He noticed the simple things, like when he had lent her a book when she was stuck at Netherfield. And then, in a repeat of London, he had shielded her from Mr. Smithson's overreaching questions without hesitation. Both times, he had seen she was uncomfortable and acted.

That is not nothing.

The thought of Mr. Smithson caused her to shudder. Darcy had spoken with such authority to Mr. Smithson, with the weight of his name and his uncle's title behind it. But what could he truly do? Could he protect the Gardiners? Or Benjamin?

Could he protect *her*?

And would he even want to? He was so far above her in wealth and station, and he could do much better than a simple country miss.

She knew she should not hope, but she could not help herself. An image of him from the Gardiner's card party came to mind, and a flutter rose unbidden in her chest. She could still feel the echo of his voice, the storm in his eyes, the firm line of his jaw as he had stood against that odious man. As though it had cost him nothing to do so, even though he scarcely knew the Gardiners.

That, too, was not nothing. Did he do it for her? Or because he was simply a gentleman?

Her boots crunched on the path as she reached the top of the mount, the wind tugging at her shawl. Below her, the whole of Hertfordshire spread out in winter colors—bare trees, pale skies, golden stubbled fields.

Elizabeth folded her arms tightly across her chest and stared down at two men on horseback in the field below, a strange heaviness pressing against her heart. For what seemed like an eternity, she was lost in the freedom the riders represented—galloping fast and far, unconstrained by duty or doubt or fear.

If only I could ride like that. If only I could outrun all of this.

Another gust of wind bit through her shawl, and she shivered, acknowledging her foolishness in climbing to such a high elevation this late in the autumn. The bracing air had done little to clear her thoughts. If anything, the silence only sharpened them. Reluctantly, she turned from the view she adored and began to make her way back down the path.

As she did so, memories of the card party at Stoke House came to her mind. The sight of Mr. Smithson thrashing against the footmen's grip, his eyes wild and unrepentant, made her stomach twist anew. That he had broken into the Gardiners' home—into the *nursery*—was beyond terrifying. He had been seeking something. Or someone.

Does it have something to do with Benjamin? she wondered again, her steps growing slower. *He's just a baby. An unknown orphan of dubious birth, abandoned by his mother's friend in the middle of the fire. Why on earth would he be of interest to a man investigating an insurance claim?*

She was no stranger to the ways of the world. For all the adoration her family gave the baby, it did not make him a legitimate member of the Bennet family.

But those were problems for the future. For now, there were more pressing concerns. What if Smithson truly believed the Gardiners were somehow involved in starting the fire in London?

What if my waking early has made them suspects?

A lump rose in her throat. The thought of her aunt or uncle facing accusations—worse, arrest—because *she* had roused the house so quickly, because *she* had urged them to flee—it was unbearable.

She had always imagined scandal might touch her family through Lydia or Kitty—some flirtation gone too far, some indiscretion in a shop or a dance hall. Never her honorable uncle. Never the most level-headed man she knew.

And if there is scandal—if whispers begin to circulate about the Gardiners or Benjamin—what then? What of the estate? What of their children? What if they lose everything?

Elizabeth pressed a hand to her stomach, trying to quell the sick fluttering there. A week ago, she would have laughed at the idea of her ordinary little family being caught up in a web of mystery and danger. Now, she could not laugh.

At the bottom of the path, the wind picked up again, swirling around her ankles. She pulled her shawl tighter and quickened her pace.mar

A sudden sound—low and wet—reached her ears.

Elizabeth froze.

There it was again. A soft groan, followed by the unmistakable crunch of footsteps on the damp leaves littering the path.

She turned, heart thudding. Nothing but trees behind her, their bare branches scratching against the sky. Still, the hairs at the back of her neck prickled.

Do not be silly, she scolded herself. *It is probably a tradesman, or a tenant cutting through on his way to Meryton.*

But Wickham's warning came back to her with vivid clarity. "Not all of them are gentlemen. Best not to assume red coats always mean safe company."

The revelry from the card party—the laughter, the shouting, the sound of that vase shattering—flashed through her mind. The way one soldier had leered at Kitty. The way another had tried to pull Lydia into a dance that was not proper in any drawing room, let alone their aunt's parlor.

Elizabeth quickened her pace again, causing the toe of her boot caught on a tree root. She stumbled but kept her footing, heart racing now. She was on the main path to Longbourn, surely close enough that someone would hear if she cried out.

Then the sound shifted.

The footsteps were ahead of her.

Not behind. Ahead.

She stopped short, every muscle taut. *No,* she thought. *No, no, no—how did they get ahead of me?*

Panic surged in her chest. Her breathing came faster as she took a cautious step forward, the trees narrowing around her with every pace. She rounded a bend in the trail, her eyes wide and searching—

—and collided into something solid.

She gasped and recoiled with a cry.

The man before her staggered backward, moaning. His coat was soaked through with blood, his face deathly pale, his eyes glassy.

Smithson.

Elizabeth screamed.

She stumbled away, her hands raised instinctively in defense—but he did not lunge. He did not speak. He just stood there for a moment, swaying where he stood… then collapsed forward onto the ground.

His hands, slick with blood, pressed weakly against his stomach. He tried to speak, but it came out as a choked, rattling gasp. "H-help me…"

Elizabeth stood frozen, breath ragged and chest heaving, every instinct screaming at her to run.

But if I leave him, he will die. And what sort of person would that make me?

Still trembling, she forced herself forward. "Do not move," she whispered, falling to her knees beside him. "Do not try to move, just—just let me see."

Blood oozed between his fingers. His shirt was torn open at the waist, and beneath it, the wound was deep—too deep.

"Oh Lord," she whispered. "Oh Lord, oh Lord…"

She tore frantically at the buttons of her pelisse, scarcely noticing the blood that had transferred from Smithson to herself when they ran into one another. She yanked up her skirt and reached for the layers beneath. Her fingers found the hem of her petticoat, and she ripped it free with a violence that surprised her.

She pressed the wadded fabric hard against the wound, her fingers becoming slick as the blood oozed around the makeshift bandage. Smithson groaned, his whole-body shuddering.

"Stay with me," she begged. "Please, stay with me!"

His hand grasped weakly at hers. "Tell… raven…" he gasped. "Tell… the raven… it was the crow…"

"What?" she said, leaning in. "What are you talking about? What does that mean?"

But his eyes rolled back in his head.

"NO!" Elizabeth shouted, pressing harder against the wound. "You mustn't—do you hear me? You must stay awake!"

His body sagged.

She looked around wildly. There was no one. Not a soul in sight. Her own breathing was ragged, almost loud enough to drown out the growing chorus of birdsong in the trees.

Then she did the only thing she could.

She screamed.

"HELP!" her voice cracked. "HELP! PLEASE—SOMEONE, HELP!"

She screamed again, and again, until her throat ached with the effort, until her voice echoed through the bare woods like a cry in a nightmare.

And then she listened, breath heaving, heart racing, hands soaked in blood.

Waiting for an answer.

Waiting for help.

※

Darcy had not realized how much he needed the ride until they were well into it.

The brisk air stung his cheeks, the late autumn sun casting long shadows over the gently sloping fields. He let his horse stretch into a steady canter, the rhythmic pounding of hooves under him stirring something long dormant in his chest. His lungs burned—but not with pain. It was a clean ache, one of exertion, not desperation.

Remarkable, he thought. *The herbs truly* are *helping.* Since his own supply had arrived from London, he had been taking them more regularly—though not as religiously as Elizabeth would likely have prescribed.

Elizabeth.

The name echoed in his mind as he crested the next hill beside Bingley. His eyes drifted upward toward the ridge in the near distance, and a fond, wry smile tugged at the corner of his mouth.

Oakham Mount, they called it.

Darcy chuckled softly. "Mount," indeed. It was a pleasant hill at best—not even worth the name compared to the jagged heights of Derbyshire.

But his amusement faded as his eyes fixed on a small figure at the top of the incline, silhouetted against the pale sky. A woman, shawl wrapped tight against the wind, her posture unmistakable.

He knew who it was. He knew without needing to see the curve of her brow or the color of her eyes. No other woman in Hertfordshire—or perhaps in England—would be so bold as to climb Oakham Mount alone at this hour, with the wind cutting and the ground damp with last night's frost.

Elizabeth.

Bingley noticed his gaze and followed it. "It appears we are not far from Longbourn. We ought to pay a call, do not you think?"

Darcy gave him a sidelong glance, his tone mild. "Ah. You are desirous of seeing Miss Lydia's latest bonnet?"

"What? No—"

"Then it must be Mrs. Bennet. Eager to hear the latest gossip, are you?"

"Certainly not—I only meant—" Bingley stammered.

"Not either of them? Then perhaps you are hoping for a game of chess with Mr. Bennet? Or a spirited discussion of Fordyce's Sermons with Miss Mary?"

Bingley spluttered, tugging his reins a little too sharply. "What? No—of course not! I only—Darcy!"

But then he caught sight of Darcy's expression—amused, faintly smug—and let out a breath of laughter. "You are *teasing* me. *You are actually teasing me.*"

Darcy merely raised a brow, but the corner of his mouth twitched upward. "It seems I am."

"Well," Bingley said, grinning as he shook his head, "You've been far less grim of late. I daresay I prefer you this way."

Darcy was about to reply when the air split with a scream.

Both men froze, listening, but there was nothing save an ominous echo that died away.

Darcy's blood turned to ice. He knew that voice. Even distorted by wind and distance, he knew it.

Elizabeth.

Without another word, both men spurred their horses forward, tearing across the field toward the trees.

The scream had come from the wooded paths that wound between Longbourn and Oakham Mount. As they reached the treeline, three paths branched ahead of them. They reined in sharply, breathing hard, horses stamping.

"Which one?" Bingley asked. "The one that goes towards Meryton is the most traveled—it would be more likely."

Darcy's eyes scanned the narrowing trails, his heart hammering. *If it truly was Elizabeth, then she would have taken the least-worn path up the mountain. But the middle path also veers that direction.*

Indecision haunted him—the wrong choice, leading them further away from the person in distress, could mean the difference between life and death.

The wind rustled the trees, and for a breathless moment, there was only silence. Even the birds had gone still. The seconds ticked by as Darcy furiously attempted to make up his mind.

Then another cry came: "Help! Help! Please—someone help!"

Darcy turned his horse toward the narrowest path without waiting for agreement. "This way!"

They plunged into the underbrush, branches whipping past them, hooves thundering on the damp earth.

And Darcy's only thought—burning hotter than the cold air in his lungs—was, *Let me be right. Let me find her. Let her be safe.*

)(

The pounding of hooves struck the path like thunder, rising from the trees ahead.

Elizabeth turned sharply, still pressing against the sticky, blood-soaked fabric beneath her hands. Her heart surged with wild hope. Someone had heard. Someone was coming.

Please, please—

Two horses burst through the underbrush, their riders silhouetted in the pale morning light. Relief hit her like a wave as she saw two riders galloping down the path toward her.

Darcy.

And Bingley, just behind him.

Relief flooded her so swiftly it almost stole her strength. She sagged forward, but forced herself upright again.

Her breath caught in her throat, and for the first time since the horror had begun, she let herself believe everything might be all right.

Darcy saw her, and his expression—half panic, half fury—was almost more than she could bear.

"Elizabeth!" he called, vaulting off his horse before it had fully stopped. "Are you hurt?"

She shook her head, voice ragged. "No—no, not me—him. Smithson. He's—he's—"

Bingley had dismounted more slowly and stood frozen, staring at the crumpled, bloody figure on the ground.

Darcy did not pause. "Bingley, ride to Longbourn. Fetch Mr. Bennet, and as many footmen as they can spare. Then go for Mr. Jones—the apothecary. Quickly."

That snapped Bingley from his trance. He gave a sharp nod, mounted again, and tore off down the path.

Darcy turned back and dropped to his knees beside her.

Elizabeth could feel him studying her, trying to assess her condition— his breath visible in the cold air, his chest heaving from the ride.

"Are you certain you are unhurt?" he asked, quieter now.

"You are not coughing," she said in wonder.

He gave a sharp bark of surprised laughter. "No, thanks to you and your magic herbs. Leave it to you to think of someone else at a time like this. Are you hurt?"

"I am fine," she managed, "but he's still bleeding."

Darcy reached for her hands.

"No! He—he's still bleeding. I cannot move my hands."

"Let me help," he said.

She turned her face toward him, eyes wild, voice frayed with panic. "If I let go, he will die. I cannot stop!"

He paused, drawing back slightly, not in retreat but in recognition. Then, gently, with a slowness that made her want to weep, he shifted forward and knelt close—closer than propriety would ever allow under ordinary circumstances.

"I will not take your place," he murmured. "But I can help."

He reached down and covered her hands with his own, pressing with her, grounding her. The warmth of his grip was immediate, steadying, powerful.

"I have got you," he said, his voice low, urgent. "You are not alone, Elizabeth. I am here. You do not have to do this alone."

She did not answer, but she did not fight him either. His hands stayed with hers, steadying them both, his presence anchoring her in the storm.

Their heads were bent together over the wound, breath misting in the cold air, hands slick with blood but unmoving. Time passed—seconds, years, she could not tell. Her arms trembled, her knees ached from the cold earth, her mind drifted.

Time blurred.

Then—the sound of rattling wheels.

Bingley's voice called through the trees, and she looked up in a daze to see a cart rolling toward them, flanked by footmen and Mr. Bennet, pale and panting. The footmen jumped down, carrying a board and blankets, and Mr. Bennet rushed to her side.

"Lizzy!" he cried, crouching down. "You've done more than enough. Let us take over now."

Her hands were pulled away as others replaced them. She staggered to her feet, dizzy, the blood on her fingers no longer warm. Everything felt distant, muffled—like looking through glass.

Her knees buckled slightly, but her eyes did not focus.

"Elizabeth?" Mr. Bennet exclaimed in alarm.

She turned toward the sound, tried to respond—but the world tilted, the trees swayed, and everything went black.

And then there was nothing.

Chapter 16

The world returned to Elizabeth slowly.

Her eyelids fluttered, and she felt as if she were rising from the depths of a dream. It was confusing, filled with blood and shouting and desperation.

But there had also been safety… a voice speaking low in her ear, steady hands pressing down on hers, warmth and strength wrapped around her…

"Lizzy?"

She blinked, attempting to make the blurred images come into focus. Mrs. Gardiner sat beside her bed leaning forward with concern on her face. Beside her, Mary of all people was perched with a book closed in her lap, her forehead wrinkled.

"You are awake," Mrs. Gardiner breathed out, reaching forward to touch her hand. "You certainly gave everyone quite a fright."

Elizabeth swallowed. "What… what happened?" Her voice was raspy, and Mary quickly poured a cup of water from a pitcher by the washbasin.

"You fainted," Mary said matter-of-factly. "Mr. Darcy carried you back to the house. He looked quite pale when he did so, I might add."

Elizabeth blinked again, trying to make sense of it. "Carried me…?"

"You've been unconscious for several hours," said Mrs. Gardiner gently. "I was paying a call when Mr. Bingley came tearing into the house, shouting for your father. When Mr. Darcy arrived with you, we sent for Mr. Jones. He told us you were merely in shock and to call him again if you did not wake soon—or if you were in any pain."

225

"I am not hurt," Elizabeth murmured, propping herself up on her elbows slowly. "Truly, I am quite well."

She glanced down—and froze. Her gown was stiff with dried blood, the sleeves and bodice soaked through in a pattern too familiar to mistake. Her heart began to pound.

"Smithson," she whispered, breath catching. "He was—he was dying—and I—"

"It is alright, Lizzy." Mrs. Gardiner leaned closer. "Sir William is here now and wishes to speak with you, but there is no rush."

Memories slammed into her: Smithson's weight against her knees, his blood coating her hands, the eerie intensity in his voice as he rasped those cryptic words—*Tell the raven it was the crow.*

Her chest began to heave. She pressed a hand to her face, the tremors starting deep in her stomach and traveling to her fingers. "I did not know what to do—I thought if I let go, he would die—I could not let him die—"

"Lizzy," Mrs. Gardiner said gently, calling her name again. "Lizzy. Breathe."

She did, shallowly, until the tremors began to ebb. Mary set the water on the side table with a surprising gentleness.

"You do not have to do anything today," Mrs. Gardiner said. "We can delay the interview. Sir William will understand. Mr. Bennet is downstairs, and so are both of your uncles. Mr. Darcy and Mr. Bingley stayed as well."

Elizabeth looked up, heart still pounding, but steadier now. "No," she said after a moment. "I want to get it over with."

She swung her legs over the side of the bed, wincing as the dried blood pulled against her skin. She tried not to think about it. "I need to change, at least."

"You will need to speak to them as you are," Mary said. "I told them they should not ask questions until you had awakened and had a bath, but they want you in the same condition as you were found. For... credibility, I suppose."

Elizabeth grimaced. "Then let's get this over with."

Flanked by Mary and Mrs. Gardiner, Elizabeth went down the stairs to the drawing room. The men rose to their feet upon her entrance, and she was momentarily struck by the tableau they made—Sir William Lucas fidgeting anxiously beside a tea table and Mr. Gardiner near the hearth, arms crossed, brow creased in concern.

Bingley sat to the left of Mr. Bennet, his customary grin was missing from his face. Darcy stood at the window and turned around at her entrance. His expression was unreadable—except for his eyes, which were sharp and steady as they assessed her form. They traveled the length of her with a quiet intensity, lingering just a heartbeat too long below her neck before flicking back to her face.

"Lizzy," her father said hoarsely, moving to her side in two long strides. He embraced her tightly, then drew back to look her over. "You gave us quite a scare."

"I am sorry to have worried you, Papa," she said, her voice low.

Darcy did not move forward, but there was something in the way he inclined his head that told her he had stayed for her. His hands were clasped tightly behind his back, as if keeping himself in check. The tension in his shoulders had not eased.

Elizabeth's gaze flicked back to his for only a moment—but the warmth there, barely veiled beneath his usual reserve, made her breath catch.

Sir William cleared his throat and gave her a clumsy bow. "Miss Bennet—may I say how very grateful we are that you were not harmed further in such a horrifying ordeal. How are you feeling?"

"As well as can be expected," she replied, steadying herself as she lowered into the nearest armchair. She dared another glance at Darcy. He still had not spoken. But he watched her as though nothing else in the room mattered—and for just an instant, she wished they were alone.

Sir William looked at Mary and Mrs. Gardiner and shifted awkwardly. "Er, I must ask—I hope it will not be thought unkind, but I believe it may be best if the room be cleared. At least for the time being. It is important that Miss Bennet speak without influence."

Mary stiffened. "Influence? She's not a criminal, Sir William."

"No, of course not," he said quickly, "but official business must—"

Mr. Bennet's voice cut through, dry but steady. "My daughter has more than enough allies in this room to face any inquiry without fear." His eyes flicked towards Darcy, then back again to the ladies. "I believe she will be in good hands."

Mrs. Gardiner looked torn but finally nodded and pressed Elizabeth's hand. "We will be just outside if we are needed."

"Thank you, Aunt," Elizabeth said.

When the door shut behind them, Sir William turned to Elizabeth with an expression of genuine regret. "Miss Bennet, I must ask you to recount what happened from the beginning. Anything you can remember—no matter how small—may be of help."

Elizabeth folded her hands tightly in her lap and began. Her voice trembled at first, but steadied as she recounted the sound of groaning on the path, the terror of the moment she turned and saw Smithson, the instinctive way she had thrown herself to the ground to keep him alive.

"Did he say anything? Perhaps tell you who did it, or even just give you his real name?" Mr. Gardiner asked.

She shook her head. "No, nothing like that. He said very little—he was gasping for breath. But just before he lost consciousness, he said…" She hesitated, feeling foolish even as the words passed her lips. "He said, 'Tell the raven it was the crow.'"

There was a long pause. Every man in the room looked utterly baffled.

"Raven?" Mr. Bingley echoed, frowning.

Darcy, however, had gone perfectly still.

"Sounds like the sort of nonsense one might say delirious with pain," Sir William said, tugging at his collar.

"It sounded deliberate," Elizabeth said, shaking her head again. "Urgent."

Sir William opened his mouth to look as if he might argue, then seemed to think better of it. Mr. Bennet cleared his throat. "I am proud of you, my Lizzy," he said in a rough voice. "I wish to heaven you had not gone through such a terrible thing, but I could not be more proud."

The other gentlemen nodded and murmured their agreements. Mr. Bennet then gave a weak smile and added, "Your mother always said those long walks of yours were nothing but trouble. I just never imagined this sort. Of all my girls to prove Mrs. Bennet right…"

Chuckles filled the room, lightening the atmosphere. Even Darcy's lips twitched slightly at Mr. Bennet's wry humor.

But the levity faded when he then turned to Sir William. "Am I to understand, sir, that Miss Elizabeth is not a suspect?"

Sir William blanched. "Of course not! No—heavens, no. She's a witness, not a—well, certainly not."

"Then who is?" Darcy asked quietly. "Are there suspects?"

Sir William hesitated, then glanced at Mr. Gardiner. "There… there is some speculation," he admitted reluctantly. "It is only natural to question everyone who had dealings with the deceased."

Mr. Gardiner sighed and stepped forward. "I understand. He was sent to investigate me and my family. And he died here. You would be remiss not to consider me."

"That is completely ridiculous!" Elizabeth burst out, rising to her feet. "Uncle, no one with sense would ever suspect—"

Sir William raised his hands. "Miss Bennet, I assure you, I take no pleasure in this. But I must follow protocol… although with friends and neighbors involved…" The usually jovial man's words trailed off, and he shifted in his chair, clearly ill at ease.

"My late father was magistrate for a time," Darcy said, watching to ensure Elizabeth resumed her seat. "I know it was always difficult when landowners and members of the upper class were involved."

"Indeed," Sir William replied gloomily.

Darcy hesitated, then said, "Would it be of use, sir, if I were to hire a Bow Street Runner or another official to assist in the investigation? That way, there would be an impartial voice, and you would not need to handle this alone."

Sir William looked at him in astonishment. "Would you do that?"

Darcy gave a short nod. "I admit that murder is well outside of my area of expertise, and I assume the same is true for you as well."

Sir William exhaled in obvious relief. "Thank you, Mr. Darcy. I would be most obliged."

Elizabeth sank further into her chair, exhaustion settling into her bones. But somewhere beneath it, under the blood and the shock and the fear, was something else.

Gratitude.

Not just to her family, who believed her. Not only to her uncle, who bore suspicion with such grace.

But to Mr. Darcy, who had not flinched. Not from the sight of her, bloodied and dazed. Not from the weight of responsibility. And not from her.

When others might have looked away, his eyes had remained fixed on hers—steady, grounding, and unexpectedly tender.

She looked up, met his gaze again, and gave him the smallest nod of thanks.

His answering nod was slight, almost imperceptible—but his eyes softened. Just for her.

And for a single moment, despite the heaviness of the room, something warm and unspoken passed between them.

)(

The ride back to Netherfield was silent at first; both Darcy and Bingley were lost in their own thoughts. The rhythmic cadence of their horses' hooves against the damp earth seemed to echo the disquiet that had settled between them. Bingley finally broke the quiet with a disbelieving shake of his head.

"A murder," he murmured, then spoke louder when Darcy asked him to repeat himself. "A murder, Darcy. In Meryton, of all places. This is a peaceful place, even if it is a little busy. Who could have imagined such a thing?"

"The village has been quite busy as of late, at least from what I understand," Darcy replied. "A surfeit of homeless dock workers in search of a way to earn their bread appears to be the main cause."

"It must be one of them, or even one of the new militia men. Certainly Mr. Gardiner is far too respectable a man to be entangled in something so... so nefarious."

Darcy gave a curt nod. "Agreed. Whatever Smithson was involved in, it was not of Mr. Gardiner's making."

Bingley sighed, running a gloved hand through his disheveled hair. "And Miss Elizabeth... to have stumbled upon such a ghastly scene. The horror she must have felt." He paused, his brow furrowing deeper. "At least she has a fair amount of spirit. I shudder to think of poor Miss Bennet in such a situation. It must be difficult for her, right now, to be unable of comfort her dear sister because of her ankle."

Darcy made a noncommittal noise. Bingley continued talking, but his voice became little more than background murmur. Something Elizabeth had said earlier was tugging at Darcy's memory—something important—and it urged him forward to Netherfield so he could put pen to paper.

Upon reaching the estate, the sun had begun its descent towards the horizon. Darcy and Bingley dismounted quickly at the stable yard, handing the reins to a waiting groom. The lad looked anxious, fairly bouncing on his heels as he looked around the fields.

Word of the murder must have already spread through the servants' news network, Darcy thought. *I wonder if any of them have a clue as to who could have done this.*

Bingley looked up at the manor house and grimaced. "Caroline will be curious about our tardiness. We will only barely have time to change for dinner."

Darcy gave a tired sigh. "Indeed."

Upon entering the grand foyer, the familiar scent of polished wood and faint traces of honeysuckle greeted them. Descending the sweeping staircase was Miss Bingley, her gown a cascade of the finest silk, every movement calculated for grace.

"Mr. Darcy," she purred, her eyes alight with a mixture of relief and something more possessive. "You have been out for quite some time. Such... stamina you must have! But you really must be cautious not to overtax yourself in helping my poor brother understand matters of estate. Do not let him drag you all over the property."

"We were not touring the property the entire time, Caroline," Bingley said. "We went as far as Longbourn."

Her expression soured, lips pinching in annoyance. "Longbourn? You called there and are only just now returning? At this hour? Charles, really."

"It is not as if we intended to make a social call," Bingley protested defensively. "But that is neither here nor there. Caroline, might we sit down a moment?"

She blinked. "Sit down? What on earth for?"

"There has been an incident," Bingley said carefully.

Darcy watched as Caroline's face paled ever so slightly. "You are alarming me. What sort of incident? Louisa? Hurst?"

"No, no," Bingley said quickly. "No one in this house is harmed."

"Then why do you look so grave?" she demanded. "Have we had word from London? Mr. Darcy, is dear Georgiana alright?"

"No. It is not about Miss Darcy, Caroline. It happened near Longbourn. A man was stabbed—murdered."

Miss Bingley looked between the two men, her face draining of color. "Murdered?"

Bingley nodded, guiding her toward a nearby chair in the hall. "Caroline, sit. Please. And—" He glanced toward a footman. "Bring Miss Bingley a small glass of wine."

She allowed herself to be seated, albeit stiffly. "What happened? Who is dead?"

"A Mr. Smithson—you might remember him from when he came to speak with Miss Elizabeth here at Netherfield."

"The rude man who came without an invitation?" She sniffed in disdain, then paled further. "Did... did someone from Longbourn kill him?"

"What? Good Lord, no!" Bingley startled. "Miss Elizabeth found him while on a walk. No one knows who actually committed the crime."

"No one knows? You mean, there is a murderer on the loose here in Meryton? That's it, I am finished with this savage place! We must leave for London at once!"

She stood and began to head up the stairs, calling for her maid. Bingley frowned and spoke in a firm tone, halting her progress. "We cannot leave, Caroline. Travel is often restricted following such events. Sir William will likely request that all potential witnesses and suspects remain until the investigation concludes."

"*Suspects*?" she shrieked. "That is completely ludicrous! None of us would dare involve ourselves in something so heinous! And we are not witnesses, are we? You said Miss Elizabeth was the one to find him, and certainly *she* has nothing to do with *us*."

Darcy's voice, calm yet authoritative, cut through the tension. "It would be prudent for everyone to stay until the magistrate provides further instructions."

Miss Bingley pressed her thin lips together so tightly, they practically disappeared from her face, leaving her looking like a ghostly snake. She seemed poised to argue but apparently thought better of it, offering a terse nod instead.

Darcy inclined his head slightly. "If you will excuse me, I have pressing correspondence to attend to."

As he ascended the stairs, he could hear her shrieking, demanding Bingley cut all contact with Longbourn so their reputations would not be tainted by association. He shook his head as Bingley's calm tones quickly turned arguing.

Upon closing the door to his room, the sounds were sufficiently muffled for him to think. The memory of Smithson's dying words fluttered through his mind, ominous and persistent. He reached for his pen and a fresh sheet of paper and began to write.

Fitzwilliam,

I know you have not yet responded to my last letter, but this is urgent.

The man I spoke of before, the insurance investigator named Smithson, was discovered stabbed this afternoon by Miss Elizabeth. He succumbed to his injuries as she held pressure on his wound while calling for help. Fortunately, Bingley and I were nearby and were able to come to her aide.

During the magistrate's interview, Miss Elizabeth shared the man's final words: "Tell the raven it was the crow"...or perhaps it was falcon or vulture. I cannot quite remember. Odd, is it not? It put me to mind of the summer you became obsessed with ravens, claiming they were the most cunning of all the birds. Perhaps the knowledge you gained that summer could be of use in interpreting what the man was attempting to say?

Given the gravity of the situation, I am sending this letter via express courier in the hope that it reaches you with all due haste.

Yours sincerely,

Darcy

Sealing the letter with his personal crest, Darcy rang for Bates. "Send this posthaste with the fastest rider we have. It needs to be delivered to Colonel Fitzwilliam tonight."

"Very well, sir."

As Bates began to leave through the dressing room, he paused. "Sir... is it true... was someone actually found murdered?"

Darcy closed his eyes. "Yes, Bates, I am afraid it is true."

"And no one knows who did it?"

"That is correct."

"The servants are nervous, sir," Bates said. "What shall I tell them?"

"Tell them everything is being done to apprehend the culprit."

"Very well, sir."

"And Bates?"

The valet paused again. "Yes, sir?"

"If you hear anything of use, anything at all, do not hesitate to tell me about it. If someone feels too afraid to speak with me, assure them of my discretion and generosity."

"Of course, sir."

The door closed behind Bates, and Darcy let out a sigh of relief. *Alone at last. What a terrible day this has been.*

He leaned against the windowsill, the chill of the windowpane brushing against his back. The dying light outside cast long shadows across the room, and for a moment, he let himself close his eyes.

He could still hear her scream.

It had sliced through the quiet like a knife. For that brief, horrible moment, he had feared the very worst—that she was lost, that she had been attacked, that he had been too slow to help.

Then they found her, kneeling in the dirt, dress soaked with blood. Her face had been pale and drawn, her voice hoarse from her cries for help.

She had said that she was unharmed, but when she had fainted, he became terrified that some of the blood was hers after all, that she, too was wounded and dying.

He could still feel the shape of her in his arms as he carried her back to Longbourn, the world blurring around them, every step sharpened by the dread that she would not wake.

He had imagined her gone. It was not a thought he had ever consciously allowed before—never dared to entertain—but in those harrowing minutes, he could not stop himself from seeing a world without her in it.

It was unbearable.

That absence, even imagined, had torn something open in him. Even now, he felt an ache in his chest at the danger she had been in.

He pressed a fist to his mouth, trying to contain the rise of emotion, but the questions came flooding through his mind.

What if Bingley and I had not gone riding?

What if we had taken the more worn path?

What if we had been minutes later?

The relief he had felt when Mr. Jones had come down from examining her and pronouncing her unharmed—it was only then that he had allowed himself to breathe.

And later—later she had spoken with clarity and calm before the magistrate, recounting everything she had seen. No hysterics, no dramatics. Just the truth, clear and composed. Brave.

He had always known Elizabeth Bennet was different. But now he understood something more profound: she was the kind of person who ran toward the fire. Who pressed her hands to a dying man's wound. Who stayed.

And what do I offer her?

George Darcy's voice came into his mind: *Nothing. You offer her nothing. You are weak. What could a pathetic man like you possibly have to offer such a strong, courageous woman?*

He curled his hands into fists, fighting off his father's harsh admonishments that would echo in the empty halls of Pemberley every time his son succumbed to a coughing fit.

No, I am not. I can *help her.*

She had been brave today.

It was time he matched her courage.

Tomorrow, he would begin. He would uncover the truth—whatever it cost—and protect her, no matter the risk to himself.

For now, he crossed the room and doused the lamp. The fire burned low, casting flickering gold across the desk and the unspoken vows left lingering in the air.

He could not say the words aloud.

Not yet.

But in the quiet of his heart, Fitzwilliam Darcy knew one thing with certainty.

He would keep Elizabeth Bennet safe.

Whatever it took.

Chapter 17

Darcy ran.

The smoke was thick—black, choking, and acrid. Each breath seared his lungs, each step a struggle. He stumbled through streets he half-recognized: Gracechurch Street twisted into some nightmarish corridor of fire and shadow. Every building burned. Every window shattered and rained glass down onto him. The streets ran with ash and water and panic.

Somewhere ahead, she was crying out.

"Help! Please, help!"

Elizabeth.

Darcy pushed forward, the weight of his own body unbearable. His coat felt like lead. He tried to yell, to tell her he was coming—but the moment he opened his mouth, a violent fit of coughing seized him. His knees buckled.

He fell, wheezing against the ground, his vision spinning.

"Help me!"

Her voice was closer now—so close, in fact, that when he looked up, he could see her through the smoke just in front of him. He could hear the child's sobbing…but there was something wrong. It was too low. Guttural.

Did the smoke damage the babe's lungs?

"Help me," she begged him, reaching out to him.

He tried to rise, to take a step, but he was again brought to the ground, coughing so violently he could sense the copper metallic taste of blood.

"You are useless," she told him angrily. "If you were a real man, you would be able to do this. Why are you so weak?"

"No, Eliz—" His protests were lost once more as his lungs betrayed him.

She turned her back on him, and the blanket fell away from the baby, revealing its face. He recoiled in horror as—instead of the round, delicate features of a newborn—the sharp, pointed visage of Mr. Smithson appeared.

The hideous creature gave him a malicious smirk, then somehow, impossibly, its tiny hands revealed a knife. There was a flash as flame reflected on silver, which turned red as the blade buried itself in Elizabeth's back again and again.

She gasped, then staggered and fell.

He tried to shout her name, to reach out to her—but again, the coughing. It ripped through him like a storm. He gagged, doubled over, unable to get air.

And then she turned those wide, pained eyes back to him. Her lips moved, barely audible:

"Why did you not save me?"

He could not scream.

He could not breathe.

Elizabeth!

X

Darcy woke with a violent start, sitting bolt upright in bed. His breath came in ragged, rasping gulps, his heart pounding in his chest.

The fire was gone.

The baby was gone.

Elizabeth was—

Alive.

He clutched a hand to his chest, trying to steady his breathing. The room was cold, the sheets soaked beneath him. Sweat clung to his skin, and a tremor shook his limbs.

It was just a dream. It was just a dream.

But the images lingered like smoke: the knife, her voice, that terrible moment when she looked at him and found him lacking.

"Bates," he croaked hoarsely, reaching for the bell-pull.

Moments later, his valet appeared, alert despite the early hour. "Sir?"

"Herbs," he rasped, fighting back a cough, "Stronger… than usual."

"At once, sir." Bates rushed from the room, concern for his master apparent in his uncustomary haste.

As the door clicked shut behind him, Darcy swung his legs over the side of the bed, planting his feet on the rug. He pressed the heels of his palms into his eyes.

It was only a dream. A grotesque, twisted dream—but not real.

Still, the echo of her voice—*Why are you so weak?*— left a bitter taste.

He sat in silence until the tea arrived, inhaling the steam with careful, measured breaths. The scent of thyme and licorice root filled the room. He took it slowly, the double-strength infusion burning a little as it went down.

After several minutes, the tightness in his chest eased—just enough.

He debated dressing for a ride, but a glance at the frost-furred windows and the low groan of wind through the eaves changed his mind. Not today. His lungs would not thank him.

Instead, he rose to his feet and, with Bates's help, began to dress for the day, all the while replaying his vision from the night before.

It was completely absurd - Elizabeth attempting to save an infant, but then was in danger from a monster with Mr. Smithson's face… and yet, was it truly so far from reality? After all, she had held a man's life in her hands yesterday, watching him slowly bleed to death in front of her. Her cries of help, while they had been answered, were not enough to fight off inevitable.

And when Darcy had found her, she had been covered in blood. When she collapsed against him, he had never known fear like that in all his life.

Not when his father died, nor even when his mother passed when he was but a youth.

In that moment, when he had thought she was lost, he realized—with a clarity sharper than any blade—that there could be no world in which he would survive her loss.

She mattered too much to him now.

He made his way down the stairs to the breakfast room in a daze. Pouring himself a cup of coffee and taking a plate of ham, eggs, and toast from the sideboard, he sat down at the table, his movements slow and stiff.

He ate without much thought, trying to shake the remnants of the dream.

Elizabeth's face lingered anyway.

She had been brave. Braver than he. Holding pressure on Smithson's wound with her bare hands, refusing to let go even when he begged her to stop.

What kind of man sees a woman like that and walks away?

What kind of man sees a woman like that and does nothing?

Not I.

He was just finishing the last of his meal when the door creaked open and a footman stepped inside, clearing his throat.

"Begging your pardon, sir, but there is a caller for you."

Darcy lowered his cup slowly. "At this hour?"

The footman hesitated. "He would not give his name, sir. But he insisted the matter was urgent."

Darcy's brow furrowed. He set his cup down with care and stood.

"Very well," he said, brushing his coat smooth. "Show him into the front parlor and remain with him. I will be there shortly."

He took his time crossing the hall, understandably wary of uninvited guests. His steps were measured, shoulders tense. But when he pushed open the parlor door, he stopped short at the sight of a man in a red coat casually warming up by the fireplace.

Colonel Fitzwilliam looked up with a broad grin. "Darcy! Excellent— you are already awake. Though I expected you to be brooding in your study, not skulking about in the front hall like a common butler."

Darcy blinked. "Fitzwilliam?"

"No, the other cousin that comes to scold you," the colonel replied cheerfully. "Yes, it is me."

"What on earth are you doing here?"

"What? Am I not allowed to pay a visit to my favorite cousin?" he said innocently.

Darcy raised an eyebrow. "Then I suppose you've taken a wrong turn on your way to Rosings Park. Anne will be devastated."

The colonel barked out a laugh. "Careful, or I will send you to Kent myself to keep her company. Perhaps she will make you read her sermons over breakfast."

Darcy gave him a dry look. "Then you did not come merely to visit."

The colonel's smile faltered slightly. "Ah… well, let's say I was already in the neighborhood. Soldiers do like to keep an ear to the ground for strange happenings in the kingdom."

Darcy folded his arms. "I take it this means you received my express, then?"

Fitzwilliam's eyes twitched, and he glanced briefly toward the footman, still hovering near the doorway. "Perhaps we should sit. Something hot to drink would not go amiss either. The wind is cutting today."

Darcy did not move. "Fitzwilliam," he said warningly.

The sighed and waved a hand. "Yes, yes, I received your blasted letter. And yes, I rode half the night. I would like breakfast and a bed, in that order."

"I do not believe you were given an invitation," Darcy said. "Perhaps Bingley does not want to put up with you."

The colonel gave Darcy a dubious look. "Bingley puts up with everyone—even you. And his sister will be thrilled to play hostess to any family member of yours, especially if said family member is also the son of an earl."

"Fair point. But before I summon the housekeeper, I insist upon knowing: is this in relation to Mr. Smithson's murder?"

The colonel glanced at the door, then back to Darcy. "You must promise me what I say remains between us. At least for now. No word to your steward, your tenants—or your lady friend with the sharp eyes and sharper mind."

Darcy narrowed his gaze. "You mean Miss Elizabeth."

"Whatever her name is." The colonel waved an errant hand. "Oh, do not look so scandalized. It is clear you care for her."

"Stop trying to change the subject, Fitzwilliam. Why are you here?"

"Then promise me."

Darcy hesitated, then gave a reluctant nod. "Very well, you have my word."

The colonel leaned forward, all levity gone now. "Good. Because what I am about to tell you is not just confidential—it could be dangerous."

)(

Elizabeth awoke with a jolt, her heart hammering in her chest, the echo of a cry still ringing in her ears.

The image from her nightmare clung to her mind like fog—Benjamin in her arms, bleeding, and no matter how hard she pressed her hands to the wound, the blood kept pouring. His little cries had echoed like Smithson's last gasp, and her hands were slick and red and useless.

She pressed her palms to her eyes. It was a dream. Only a dream. But it felt as if she had lived it again, as if the weight of yesterday had not fully left her body.

By the time she had bathed and dressed, it was well past breakfast. The sun was higher in the sky than it should have been, and the house was quiet, save for the occasional creak of floorboards above.

In the kitchen, the cook looked up in surprise. "Miss Elizabeth! You gave us all a fright yesterday." She quickly wrapped a muffin in a cloth and passed it over. "I am glad to see you up and about."

"Thank you." Elizabeth accepted it gratefully.

The cook hesitated. "Will you be walking today?" Then her eyes widened, and she flushed. "Oh—begging your pardon, miss, I did not mean—"

Elizabeth gave her a tired smile. "It is quite all right. Nothing short of murder could keep me from walking."

The joke fell like a stone.

She left before the silence became too heavy, retreating to the back staircase and eating the muffin slowly as she walked.

The idea of going for a walk filled her with unexpected dread. Her mind flashed to the path through the trees, the sound of branches cracking, her own screams. She closed her eyes and inhaled deeply.

You've walked these hills a hundred times. More. You've never feared them before.

But still—perhaps not today. There was a murderer who had not been caught yet, and even she knew better than to tempt fate again.

Instead, she went upstairs and retrieved Benjamin from the nursery. The baby was cooing in his cradle, his dark hair curling over one ear, his cheeks flushed with sleep.

"Oh, you dear little thing," she murmured, lifting him into her arms. His head lolled briefly against her shoulder before he looked up at her and grinned.

The warmth of him in her arms, the soft weight of him nestled close—it was more healing than anything she had felt since yesterday. His snuggles, his gummy kisses against her cheek—it reminded her of life, of gentleness, of hope.

She carried him downstairs into the parlor. A maid informed her that Mrs. Bennet had taken Lydia and Kitty into Meryton to "pay calls"—which Elizabeth could only interpret as sharing the tale of her daughter's trauma in as many drawing rooms as possible. Mary was tucked away in the music room, practicing a particularly moody section of Beethoven.

Elizabeth did not mind the solitude. The quiet allowed her to breathe.

She was bouncing Benjamin gently on her lap when Mr. Hill entered the room carrying Jane in his arms. Her sister's smile wavered as soon as she saw Elizabeth.

"Oh, Lizzy." Jane held out her arms as soon as she was seated, and Elizabeth went to her at once, carefully shifting Benjamin to one hip so she could lean into the embrace.

"I am all right," Elizabeth whispered.

"I did not know what to think. I heard only bits and pieces before they brought me down." Jane's eyes filled with tears. "To think that you—oh, Lizzy, someone was murdered."

Elizabeth's jaw clenched. "I know."

Jane shook her head slowly. "I cannot fathom it. Surely no person in their right mind could do such a thing. Perhaps—perhaps it was an accident. A scuffle that went too far. And they ran, in fear and shock."

Elizabeth said nothing. She returned to her seat, holding Benjamin closer and kissing the top of his dark curls. Smithson's words swirled in her mind: *Tell the raven… it was the crow.*

She would not worry Jane with them. Not yet. After all, they made no sense.

Footsteps echoed in the entry hall, followed by the murmur of voices.

"Mr. Bingley, Mr. Darcy, and Colonel Fitzwilliam," Hill announced from the doorway.

Elizabeth turned, startled. Darcy entered first, followed by a man with a warm smile and easy gait—Colonel Fitzwilliam, she presumed. He bore a striking resemblance to Darcy, but his manner was far more jovial.

"My mother is out," Elizabeth said as she rose, "but you are most welcome."

Darcy bowed. "Miss Elizabeth, allow me to introduce my cousin, Colonel Richard Fitzwilliam."

The colonel bowed over her hand with practiced ease. "It is a pleasure to meet the heroine I have heard so much about."

Jane, from her seat, smiled brightly. "Do sit down. I will ring for some tea."

Bingley was already beside her, asking in hushed tones how she was faring and adjusting her cushions.

Elizabeth led the gentlemen to the settee, settling Benjamin in her lap once more. Darcy and Colonel Fitzwilliam took the seats beside her, and for a moment, there was a comfortable hush in the room.

And then Colonel Fitzwilliam turned to her, still smiling—but with a new kind of sharpness in his eyes.

"Miss Elizabeth," he said lightly, "tell me about this delightful child in your arms. A nephew, perhaps?"

Elizabeth raised her chin, adopting a haughty pose, and adjusted Benjamin slightly so he was in a sitting position. "Allow me to introduce you properly, Colonel. This is Mr. Benjamin Bennet, resident philosopher, connoisseur of soft blankets, and our current ruler by popular acclamation."

She gave a small bow of her head. "Benjamin, this is Colonel Fitzwilliam."

The colonel chuckled. "A charming introduction. Please to meet your acquaintance, young Master Bennet. With his surname, is he perhaps your…brother?"

"No." Elizabeth's tone was light, but her grip on Benjamin tightened slightly. "He's been adopted into the family since the fire in London. We had to call him something."

Colonel Fitzwilliam's brows lifted. "Adopted? So… his parents—?"

Elizabeth's expression sobered. "We found him just after the fire. There was a girl—Meg—" she paused, then corrected herself, "—a woman of the night. She had the baby with her and said she was watching him for her neighbor. That neighbor had left him alone in the apartment at one point."

"She left the child alone?" he said with a low whistle. "What kind of—?" He stopped himself.

"She did not come back," Elizabeth continued. "I carried him to Hyde Park, and Meg followed until she was found by a man. She said she was still trying to find Deena to return the baby, but the man—her keeper, I suppose?— said Deena had perished in the fire."

"Deena." Colonel Fitzwilliam repeated the name slowly, and for just a fraction of a second, something flickered in his eyes—sharp, knowing, grim. Then it was gone, replaced by an expression of idle curiosity.

Elizabeth's eyes narrowed. "Do you recognize the name?"

"No," the colonel said quickly. "No, I do not believe so. I have been stationed here and there these past few years, and when in London, I rarely spend time on that side of town."

He leaned forward slightly, eyes on Benjamin again. "Still, it is possible the child has family somewhere. One hears stories, after all—lost heirs, long-lost children identified by a mole or scar…"

Elizabeth stiffened. "Yes, there is a birthmark. However, I do not see how that is any of your concern, Colonel Fitzwilliam—unless you intend to claim him as your own? In that case, you would know its shape and location, would you not?"

The words hung in the room like ice.

Fitzwilliam's eyebrows shot up. "My dear Miss Bennet, that is not… I mean…"

"Forgive me," she said coolly, "but you've taken rather a keen interest in a child you've only just met."

The colonel stood and moved toward the window. "Only admiring the view," he said over his shoulder. "The hills here are quite different from the southern coast."

Elizabeth frowned. *He is too interested in Benjamin. Just like Smithson was. I do not trust him.* She turned to Darcy and gave him a severe glare.

"Do not be afraid, Miss Elizabeth." Darcy's voice was intense. "This is my cousin; I have known him all my life. He is completely honorable."

She turned her face away. "So was Smithson, once, I imagine. He wore a gentleman's coat and used a gentleman's voice. That did not stop him from breaking into my uncle's home and trying to enter the nursery." Her voice dropped. "I tried to save his life, Mr. Darcy. I held his blood in my hands. I screamed myself hoarse for help."

Darcy's expression folded with grief. "I know."

"I am not sure I know anything anymore," she whispered. "And as for you—how long have I known you, truly? A month? Less? Why should I trust your judgment any more than my own?"

That struck something in him. She saw it in the twitch of his brow, the subtle pull of pain at the corner of his mouth.

She looked away, ashamed. "I am sorry. That was unfair."

"No," he said quietly. "It was honest."

"I do not know what your cousin is hiding," Elizabeth said. "But until I do, I think it is best he does not visit again. And that Benjamin not be present if he does."

She rose slowly, her back straight, her arms curled tightly around the boy in her lap. Benjamin whimpered and buried his face against her shoulder.

"I am taking him upstairs." Her voice was final.

Darcy stood as she passed, but he did not speak. The tension hung between them like fog, thick and heavy, clouding all certainty.

And for the first time since the fire, Elizabeth wondered whether anyone could truly be trusted with what—and whom—she had to protect.

Chapter 18

As the door closed behind Elizabeth, Darcy ran a hand over his face and slowly crossed to the window where Colonel Fitzwilliam stood.

The view beyond was unremarkable—just a haze of winter-dulled fields and hedgerows—but Darcy did not even stop to spare it a first glance.

Instead, he hissed in a low voice, "What the devil was that?"

The colonel's arms were crossed as he leaned against the windowsill, eyes still watching the horizon. "Not quite the outcome I was aiming for," he murmured.

"I warned you," Darcy said, barely restraining himself. "Miss Elizabeth is no empty-headed debutante, eager to be flattered by a red coat and vague assurances. She sees through more than most."

The colonel turned, brow raised. "That much is clear. She's sharp as a tack—and fiercely protective. I can see why you admire her."

Darcy glared at him. "Then you also see that you will not be able to learn anything or make any progress into your investigation unless you tell her the truth."

The colonel pressed his lips together tightly. "My superiors would have me hung for treason. It was difficult enough for me to confide in you, and I have known you my entire life. You've known her for… what, a month?"

"That's long enough for me to know she is one of the most honorable, trustworthy young ladies with whom I am acquainted."

There was a pause before the colonel said more softly, "You care for her."

Darcy did not deny it. "I do."

"And what do you intend to do about it?"

"I do not know," Darcy admitted, his voice nearly a whisper. "You saw her face. That distrust was not only for you."

The colonel sighed and ran a hand through his hair. "I do not know, Fitz. You know what is at stake. I cannot afford to take risks."

"Yes, but you also cannot make any progress forward if you do not have the information you need, and she has it."

"There are other ways. I am sure she's confided in others, like friends."

Darcy looked at his cousin with a hint of disdain. "And how long will that take, to establish those relationships and ask questions without raising suspicion? Weeks? Months? You said yourself yesterday that time is of the essence."

The colonel sighed quietly, and Darcy pressed on. "Miss Elizabeth is well liked here. If she distrusts you, she will not hesitate to make it known to her friends. That will significantly hinder your progress as well."

"If I tell her," the colonel said slowly, "and it's the wrong move, it could end everything."

"And if you do not," Darcy said, voice hardening, "you will lose any chance of finding out the truth—about Smithson, about Benjamin, all of it. And I—" He stopped, jaw tightening.

"You will lose her," the colonel finished.

Darcy nodded once. "Please, Fitzwilliam, just tell her."

A long pause followed, the air between them thick with unspoken tension. At last, the colonel exhaled slowly. "All right. When she comes back down, the three of us will go for a walk—where we cannot be overheard."

Darcy gave a curt nod. "Do not make a mess of this. If you do, you will not only lose me her good opinion—" his voice dropped, dangerously low "—you will cost us the only chance we have of finding out the truth."

A voice cut through the quiet behind them.

"What truth?"

Both men turned sharply. Elizabeth stood just inside the room, her eyes dark and unreadable.

⚹

After her confrontation with Darcy, Elizabeth took Benjamin to the nursery, her hands shaking slightly as she ascended the stairs. The baby was already drifting off, his small face pressed against her shoulder, one hand fisted into the collar of her gown.

What is so special about you, Benjamin, that has so many strangers interested in you?

In the nursery, she passed him gently to the nurse, who accepted him with practiced hands and a quiet smile.

But Elizabeth did not smile back.

"I want him watched at all times," she said, her voice low but firm. "No one—no maid, no footman, no relative—is to remove him from this room unless I give permission. Not even my parents or sisters."

The nurse blinked, her brows rising, but the seriousness in Elizabeth's expression left no room for argument. "Yes, miss," she said, nodding. "With what has happened, I understand."

Elizabeth hovered at the doorway for a moment longer, watching the woman settle Benjamin into the cradle. The child's breathing was already even and slow. He looked so peaceful, untouched by the chaos and fear that clung to her like a second skin.

If only I could be that untroubled.

She turned away, closing the nursery door with care, and descended the stairs slowly. Doubt churned inside her. She had trusted Darcy instinctively—had trusted him from the moment he defended her from Mr. Smithson, from the way he had held her in the firelight, supported her when she had almost fainted with shock. And yet now…

Why is his cousin so very interested in Benjamin?

Elizabeth paused at the threshold of the drawing room, her hand resting on the doorframe. What had passed between the two men after she left? Had Darcy tried to defend her—or was he as entangled in this web of secrets as Colonel Fitzwilliam clearly was?

She stepped in, unnoticed, just in time to hear Darcy's low, urgent voice: "Do not make a mess of this. If you do, you will not only lose me her good opinion—you will cost us the only chance we have of finding out the truth."

"What truth?" she asked, her voice cutting through the room like a blade.

Both men whirled around. Their expressions—equal parts shock and guilt—told her enough.

Colonel Fitzwilliam stepped forward first, his manner suddenly all charming affability again. "Miss Elizabeth," he said, "might we trouble you for a walk? The air is fine and brisk, and I find fresh air clears the head for serious discussions."

Elizabeth's eyes flicked to the window. The weather was, at best, inhospitable—cold, gray, and blustery. She raised an eyebrow. "I believe I would prefer to remain indoors," she said coolly. Her gaze shifted deliberately to Bingley and Jane, who were still seated near the hearth, engrossed in conversation.

Darcy and the colonel followed her line of sight—and looked appropriately chastened to realize they had forgotten they were not alone.

Colonel Fitzwilliam's smile slipped. "Miss Elizabeth, this is no small matter. I am prepared to tell you more than I have ever told anyone outside my orders. But it cannot be overheard."

Elizabeth crossed her arms. "There is a murderer on the loose, Colonel. For all I know, you arrived at Netherfield just this morning to invent an alibi. It's possible you arrived earlier but are only now making your presence known." Her voice was even, but the tension behind it made Darcy flinch.

The colonel's eyes darkened, but before he could speak, Darcy stepped forward. "A compromise, then," he said carefully. "We shall walk, but within sight of the drawing room windows. A maid may sit with Bingley and Miss Bennet to observe us at all times."

Elizabeth bit her lip, uncertain. Finally, she said, "I would also like a footman stationed outside within earshot should I call out."

"Within shouting distance," Colonel Fitzwilliam muttered, visibly irritated. "But not close enough to overhear our conversation."

She folded her arms and glared at him. "Why should I?"

Darcy stepped forward and leaned to whisper, "Because Mr. Smithson was not who he pretended to be."

Elizabeth gave him a sharp look but did not argue further. She rang the bell and gave the necessary instructions to the maid and footman, issuing them with a general's clarity and tone. Then she turned and fetched her boots and overcoat from the hall.

As she bundled herself in a thick pelisse and wrapped a scarf around her throat, she could feel both men watching her—waiting, perhaps hoping for something gentler in her expression.

They received none.

The three stepped out into the wind together. Behind them, the window curtains fluttered slightly, and Elizabeth could see the maid watching, as ordered.

"Well?" Her tone was sharp, biting, and it caused Darcy to flinch.

The two men looked at one another, then Colonel Fitzwilliam sighed. "It is a long story, Miss Elizabeth. I am struggling to know just where to begin."

"Perhaps at the beginning," she responded pertly. "I will inform you of any questions I have along the way."

The wind gusted again, sharp and damp, and Elizabeth drew her pelisse more tightly around her. The three of them walked along the edge of the gravel path.

Colonel Fitzwilliam walked with his hands clasped behind his back, his brow furrowed as though sorting through a number of possible beginnings. At last, he said quietly, "I work for the Home Office, Miss Elizabeth. My regiment was merely a cover. I am an agent of the Crown."

Elizabeth stopped walking. "You are a spy?"

He offered a wry smile. "Yes. I suppose that's the common word for it."

She arched a skeptical brow. "This sounds like something from one of my younger sisters' ridiculous romance novels."

Colonel Fitzwilliam laughed once, short and without mirth. "Well, this particular tale does have some romance in it, I admit—but its ending is far more tragic than any of your sisters' novels, I suspect."

Still unconvinced, Elizabeth folded her arms. "And I supposed you mean to tell me that Mr. Smithson was a spy as well?"

The colonel's eyebrows rose high on his head. "Yes, he was. Very clever of you to make that deduction so quickly."

"Did he work for you?"

He nodded, inhaling deeply. "But before we discuss Smithson, you need to understand some of the history. What do you know of the war with France?"

"I know that hostilities resumed in 1803 after the Peace of Amiens collapsed," Elizabeth said, with a hint of pride in her voice. "Napoleon crowned himself Emperor in 1804. There were naval battles—Trafalgar was in 1805, I believe—and of course, the fighting in Spain these past years, particularly since 1808."

The colonel cast a glance at Darcy, who nodded slightly in approval. "Impressive."

"I have read the *Gazette*, and the *Times*," Elizabeth said sharply. "I may be a woman, Colonel, but I am not an ignorant one."

Colonel Fitzwilliam held up his hands in surrender. "I did not mean to imply otherwise. In fact, I am rather impressed. Most young ladies I meet only know which colors the regiments wear, not why the regiments march."

Elizabeth tilted her chin. "I prefer substance to uniforms."

Darcy, beside her, did not speak, but she saw it—the tiniest quirk at the corner of his mouth, gone as soon as it came. Whatever warmth might've followed was instantly doused by the tension still hanging between them.

Colonel Fitzwilliam regarded her steadily. "Then here is the substance. While the official war rages abroad—in Spain, in Portugal, in the Baltic and beyond—there is another war being fought within our own borders. One of information. Of secrets. And occasionally… of betrayal."

"And this is somehow connected to the fire in London." Her voice was calm, but inside, her thoughts twisted. I knew it. *I knew something was not right.*

He hesitated, then nodded once. "Yes. Very much so. You see, we need to go back to before 1803—before Napoleon crowned himself Emperor, before Trafalgar. Back to the revolution itself."

Elizabeth said nothing, but inwardly, her skepticism only deepened. *Is this truly what they had led me outside to say?* Still, she gestured lightly for him to continue.

"At the end of the last century, when the French Revolution swept across France, the people did not just depose their king. They destroyed an entire class. Nobles, aristocrats—whole families were slaughtered. Even children. The very idea of royal blood was seen as a threat. If you were born into a noble house, that was enough to condemn you."

"I know," Elizabeth said quietly. "The Reign of Terror."

She could not help the flicker of pride in her voice. It was not often she got to display the contents of her mind in mixed company. She expected surprise, perhaps condescension, but Darcy only nodded in quiet approval, and the colonel's eyebrows rose in apparent surprise.

"Exactly," the colonel said. "Some managed to escape, of course. Many came to England. But not all. Some went into hiding in France itself. One such family was related to the Bourbon line—distant cousins of the king. They vanished during the purges, and it was assumed the entire line had been extinguished."

"But it was not?" she prompted, her heart beginning to thud uneasily.

His mouth twisted slightly. "No. Earlier this year, word reached certain French revolutionaries that one child survived. A boy—the son of a nobleman whose bloodline tied him—however distantly—to the old crown."

"And they went after him, I assume," Elizabeth said.

"You assume correctly. By this point, the lad was now a man. He had married, and his wife had recently given birth to their own son. A band of militants formed together and tracked the family down."

Elizabeth's breath caught, and she pressed a hand to her mouth.

"Among their number was a young woman name Denisse. Her parents were farmers who had participated in the initial revolution, and she was raised with the same fire in her blood." The wind ruffled the colonel's coat, and for a moment, he looked truly troubled. "As her compatriots ravaged the home and slaughtered the inhabitants, she made her way to the nursery, following the sounds of crying."

Elizabeth's breath caught. She pressed a hand to her chest, a chill sweeping through her that had nothing to do with the weather. "And?" she urged when the colonel remained silent. *What are you getting at, Colonel? What happened?*

"For a brief moment, Denisse was exactly what the revolution had made her: an assassin poised to wipe away a bloodline. But then..." His voice softened. "…then the baby opened his eyes and looked at her, and she was a girl once again. Her heart opened, and she saw him for what he was—a baby only a few days old. Innocent. Helpless."

Elizabeth swallowed hard, her eyes stinging. For the first time, she truly pictured it—some poor girl, barely more than a child herself, standing in a smoke-filled nursery with the blood of a noble house on her hands and a baby in her arms.

She brushed the tears that had begun to stream down her cheeks. Darcy reached into his pocket and removed a handkerchief, which he offered to her. "Here."

Accepting it wordlessly, she turned her gaze back to the colonel, her eyes pleading with him to continue.

"She took him. Ran with him. She knew her companions would have killed him had they known. So, she pretended to carry out the act, but instead… she fled. Headed west, toward Spain."

Darcy added quietly, "Colonel Fitzwilliam was stationed on the Spanish-French border. On orders from a general at Cadiz."

"I found Denisse nearly dead," the colonel said. "Starving, terrified, carrying a crying bundle she had wrapped in rags and hidden beneath her coat. She thought I would shoot her, but when she learned I was English… she told me the truth. Told me who he was."

Elizabeth's mind reeled. "And you believed her?"

"She had proof," he said simply. "Letters. A locket. Things I recognized from briefings I had received. I took her in. Helped her reach London and set her up in a discreet flat, away from the eyes of the public."

"She was Meg's neighbor," Elizabeth whispered. "Deena was an alias for Denisse, then."

He nodded. "When news of the fire's location reached me, I made my way through the burned streets of Cheapside until I found where I had hidden her. The building was burned to the ground, and I found her body a few streets away, but no sign of the infant."

"Because Meg had rescued him."

"Precisely, but it took quite some time to figure it out. As you can imagine, gathering information is difficult in the best of circumstances. When you add in the chaos of the fire, it took months to even discover that Meg was the one who had taken him, and even longer to discover that she had given him to a young woman from Hertfordshire."

Elizabeth turned accusing eyes to Darcy. "And that is when you chose to come with your friend to reside at Netherfield? Did you remember me from Hyde Park, see me with Benjamin, and make the connection? Is your friendship with me nothing more than a façade to reach him yourself?"

Darcy stared at her, speechless.

She thinks...?

His mind struggled to make sense of it. That he had orchestrated this— come to Hertfordshire, befriended Bingley, inserted himself into her life— all with the intent of retrieving a royal infant?

The very notion was absurd. And yet... as her eyes narrowed in suspicion, he felt a sharp stab of something dangerously close to pain.

Does she truly believe me so calculating?

But the moment passed. Logic, ever his companion, surged forward to temper the sting. Of course she did. From her perspective, every detail lined up in dreadful precision: his sudden appearance, his interest in her family, his strange connection to the man who had terrified her. It all added up to incriminate him.

Only it was not true.

"I had no idea," he said at last, his voice firm with conviction. "I swear to you, Miss Elizabeth—I knew nothing of any of this until this very morning. My presence here… it was entirely coincidental."

She gave a skeptical scoff, crossing her arms again. "How convenient."

"It is the truth," he said desperately. "Disguise—deception in *any* form—is abhorrent to me."

That, at least, made her blink.

Behind him, his cousin let out a laugh, loud and unguarded. "It is true," he said with a grin. "Darcy could not lie to save his life. When we were children, if he so much as broke a wood paneling in the stables, he would march straight into the house and confess—without anyone asking! Took the punishment like a martyr. I remember once—he cut down the willow switch himself before my father ever got there."

Darcy groaned softly. "Fitzwilliam—"

"No, let me finish. The point is: subtlety has never been my cousin's strength. If he had known about the situation, you would have seen his deception the moment you met him."

Elizabeth's expression faltered. Her brow furrowed as she looked at Darcy, uncertainty replacing suspicion. He held her gaze.

"You did see through Smithson, after all," the colonel added, "and he was a trained professional."

"Colonel Fitzwilliam only told me everything this morning," Darcy said, his tone softer now. "And when he did, I told him you needed to know as well."

Her eyes flicked to the colonel in confirmation, then back to Darcy. Her shoulders relaxed just slightly.

But it was all that he needed to know that she once again trusted him, and that filled him with hope.

"I let my cousin speak first only because he was the one entrusted with the matter. And—" he cast a glance at the colonel "—because he did not believe me when I said you would see straight through him."

"Clearly," the colonel muttered. "I fell flat on my face."

Darcy's lips twitched, but his gaze did not leave Elizabeth's. "To be fair, it is not entirely my cousin's fault. This does involve national security, and my cousin has sworn a vow to his country. There were legitimate concerns about how much to reveal. But once I understood the situation, I knew you would only be an asset with the full truth, and I insisted you be told."

Both men watched breathlessly as Elizabeth pondered the issue. It was all Darcy could to not to sigh in relief when she nodded and said, "Very well, then, gentlemen. What happens now?"

Chapter 19

Colonel Fitzwilliam nodded gravely. "The first matter of business is verifying the boy's identity."

Her arms instinctively crossed. "You think we might be mistaken? That the child Meg rescued--"

"Not mistaken," he said gently. "But confirmation is necessary. Has the boy any birthmarks?"

She hesitated only a second. "Yes. On his left thigh. A small mark, heart-shaped."

She could see the change in the colonel's countenance the instant she said it. His shoulders, which had been held with the rigid alertness of a soldier on duty, dropped just slightly. A slow breath left his lips. For the first time since she had met him, Colonel Fitzwilliam looked less like a man accustomed to carrying secrets, and more like one unburdened—for the moment.

"That is him," he said quietly. "Without a doubt."

Elizabeth did not speak right away. The implications of that certainty bloomed in her chest like a cold ache.

"And what will happen to him now?" she asked. "Will you be taking him away?"

The colonel's eyes widened, and Darcy stepped forward almost at once, shaking his head.

"No," the colonel said firmly. "There is no plan for that. There is nowhere safe—no court or crown prepared to acknowledge him. And we do not yet know how deeply the French have infiltrated our channels. He is safer here, as he is."

Elizabeth's arms dropped to her sides. A measure of relief stirred within her—but not enough to quell the lingering fear. "What is his name? His real name, I mean."

"He had not been christened," the colonel replied. "He was only a day or two old when Denisse took him. There is no official record of a name, though we know his father's bloodline."

"Then what was his father's name?" she pressed.

But the colonel shook his head. "For now, he is safest being known as Benjamin Bennet, a foundling orphan. To change his name will bring speculation that would prove to be unsafe."

He looked at her closely, waiting until she had nodded in understanding before continuing. "But what concerns my superiors now is this: a Crown agent was murdered in broad daylight, not far from where the child was hidden. The question is whether the French have discovered the child's location—or whether Mr. Gardiner knew more than he let on, and committed the act to protect his family."

The cold inside Elizabeth was no longer from the wind.

"How dare you—" she began, her voice trembling with anger. "My uncle would never—"

Darcy raised a calming hand. "Miss Elizabeth, please. I agree with you—it is highly unlikely Mr. Gardiner would ever stoop to such an act. But my cousin is doing his duty. He must consider all possibilities."

It took a great deal of restraint to not fire back—but his voice, calm and certain, gave her pause. After a moment, she nodded stiffly.

"Well," she said at last, "if we are speaking of possibilities, then perhaps we should also consider Lieutenant Wickham's warning—that many new militia recruits are less than reputable. Desperate men, with unclear pasts."

The colonel frowned slightly. "Wickham? As in, George Wickham? Your father's godson?"

Darcy gave a short nod. "Yes, he has taken a lieutenancy in the local militia."

"But did he not say he was going to study the law? Or at least that's what he said when he took the money from you in exchange for the living you gave my brother." The frown on the colonel's face deepened as he considered the matter.

"Apparently, he did, but the fire ruined the business where he was clerking," Darcy explained. "He took a position in the regiment for the same reason many others have: to earn a living. He did not wish to live on the principal of my father's bequest."

"That is certainly quite the coincidence," the colonel said. "He was in London when the fire began, and now he's here where the baby is."

"Surely you cannot think—" Darcy began to protest.

His cousin cut him off. "As you just told Miss Elizabeth, it is my job to consider every possibility."

"He was dissolute at school, yes, but so were many others," Darcy countered. "It is quite the leap from carousing to treason. Besides, he paid a call on me at Netherfield to apologize for the past and assure me that he was attempting to reform himself."

Turning to Elizabeth, Darcy's expression softened. "And I understand I have you to thank for that, Miss Elizabeth."

271

Elizabeth flushed. "I did not do anything other than betray your confidence," she said quietly. "I was worried you would be upset with me. It was not my place to speak of your health, but he already seemed to know about it. And he seemed…genuinely remorseful."

Darcy's eyes never left hers. "You did exactly the right thing."

Their gazes held, the chill wind momentarily forgotten. Her heart fluttered with something tender—something dangerously close to hope.

A wheezing bark from deep in Darcy's chest broke the moment. The colonel, who had been pretending to examine the path's edge, gave them both a sardonic glance. "If we are finished making eyes at one another," he said with mock impatience, "we do have a murder to solve."

Elizabeth cleared her throat and folded her arms again, though not without the trace of a smile. "Indeed. And how do you propose we do that?"

"We start with a list of suspects," the colonel said. "We look at who had motive and opportunity. My batman can help—he's well-acquainted with the sort of talk that floats through servants' quarters. They see and hear more than we ever do."

Elizabeth arched a brow. "I could collect drawing-room gossip from my mother and Aunt Philips. They, along with Lady Lucas, know more about the goings-in in Hertfordshire than anyone."

"You could also provide introductions and smooth the way for us," Darcy added. "With your friendship, others will feel more at ease in confiding their secrets without being aware of it."

She sighed dramatically. "With your taciturn nature, Mr. Darcy, I have never been more in doubt of a successful operation."

Darcy threw his back and laughed, causing Colonel Fitzwilliam to stare in astonishment. The wind whipped around the three of them again, and Elizabeth shivered and looked towards the house. Behind the chimney, dark clouds were gathering in the distance and moving in their direction.

"My mother will be returning shortly," she said, "and I do believe we have left my sister and Mr. Bingley on their own for much longer than is proper. We had best end this conversation now, especially before the storm arrives."

"May we call again tomorrow?" Darcy asked.

She nodded. "Yes, I think you should. We can use that time to plan a proper strategy."

Without another word, she turned and walked briskly toward the house, leaving the men to follow. The footman gave a small sigh of relief at being able to return to the warm foyer. As they crossed the threshold, they could hear the faint sound of carriage wheels against cobblestones, signaling the arrival of Mrs. Bennet and the two youngest Bennet girls.

In the drawing room, the maid left her post at the window. Elizabeth gave her a smile of thanks, then turned her attention towards Jane and Bingley near the fireplace.

The elder girl was seated demurely on the settee, her cheeks rosy, her expression aglow with quiet joy. As Elizabeth watched, Bingley leaned close to Jane and whispered something in her ear. Jane's eyes widened for a moment, then she nodded, her blush deepening. Bingley rose at once, clearing his throat.

"I… I hope you will excuse me," he said, glancing between the others. "I must speak with Mr. Bennet. It is—an urgent matter."

Elizabeth nearly clapped her hands together. She caught herself just in time, but her face could not conceal her delight. Darcy, beside her, seemed frozen in place, still staring at the door through which his friend had just exited.

"Well," the colonel said, with perfect timing and cheerful gallantry, "it appears Mr. Bingley is about to be the happiest man in Hertfordshire."

Jane laughed softly, tucking a curl behind her ear. "He has merely requested permission to begin a courtship," she said, her voice gentle and almost apologetic. "I… I am honored."

The colonel bowed. "Then allow me to congratulate you, Miss Bennet. I cannot imagine any gentleman more fortunate than one who has gained the good opinion of the fairest lady in the kingdom."

Jane blushed deeper, and Elizabeth gave the colonel a sidelong glance. For all his secrets, he had charm to spare.

The door opened again, and in swept Mrs. Bennet, flanked by Kitty and Lydia. Mary trailed behind, her expression thunderous.

"Oh, my nerves!" Mrs. Bennet cried, fanning herself with her bonnet. "That wind is enough to bring on a chill! I do hope dinner is not delayed, for I am famished from calling all through Meryton."

Kitty and Lydia collapsed into giggles at her heels, each peeking toward the gentlemen.

The colonel politely stepped forward as Mrs. Bennet was introduced. The moment his title was mentioned—son of an earl—Mrs. Bennet nearly dropped her gloves in excitement.

"Your lordship—oh! I mean—Colonel! Such an honor! And you must be so pleased to find yourself in such good company with the officers stationed nearby!"

"I serve with the regulars, madam," he said politely, though his tone carried a note of correction. "Not the militia."

"Oh! Yes, yes, of course. Quite a difference, I am sure."

"A great difference," he said mildly. "Though I will admit I was surprised by some of the behavior I witnessed among certain militia officers as I rode through the village. Not all seem to hold to gentlemanly standards, apparently."

Elizabeth caught the faint narrowing of her mother's eyes and seized the moment to assist. "Indeed, Mama," she said evenly, "do you not recall what occurred at Aunt Philips's card party?"

She briefly summarized the event to the colonel, who shook his head in disgust. "Disgraceful! I am afraid I have seen too many situations where more than one young lady was taken in by the charm of a red coat, only to discover—too late—that it masked intentions that were less than honorable." He raised an eyebrow and glanced meaningfully at one side of the room.

Mrs. Bennet followed his gaze towards her two youngest daughters, who were giggling together as they batted their eyes and cast coy looks in the colonel's direction. Her brow furrowed, and genuine concern crossed her face.

Perhaps she will listen to the son of an earl, Elizabeth thought hopefully.

The moment passed, however, as Mrs. Bennet—not one to ponder too deeply for too long—looked around the room. "But where is Mr. Bingley? Did he not accompany you?"

Jane's expression flickered with nervous anticipation. "He is with Papa."

"With your father?" Mrs. Bennet's voice leaped an octave. "Oh—oh my! Do you think—? Could it be—?"

Before she could gather herself into full effusion, the door opened again and Mr. Bennet entered the room, Bingley just behind him, cheeks slightly flushed but smiling.

Mr. Bennet raised an eyebrow at the assembled company. "Well, I have news that should surprise no one: Mr. Bingley has requested my permission to court Jane, and I have given it."

The room erupted.

Kitty squealed, Lydia shrieked something unintelligible, and Mrs. Bennet let out a delighted cry. "Oh! My dear Jane, how wonderful! I knew all along he would fall in love with you as soon as he saw your beauty."

Jane looked ready to sink through the floor, her eyes wide and cheeks positively crimson. Elizabeth could not help but grin broadly at her sister's mortified joy.

The colonel gaped a little before turning to Darcy, who was still staring at the scene as though thunderstruck. "Well," the colonel murmured, "your friend does not waste time."

Darcy, still recovering, gave a small shake of his head and the faintest smile. "No," he said softly, "he knows what he wants."

Elizabeth caught the look Darcy gave her as he spoke—quick, searching, and filled with meaning—and felt her own cheeks warm.

Outside, the wind howled and the gray clouds thickened. But inside the drawing room, it was all warmth and laughter and love beginning to take root.

And for a brief, precious moment, Elizabeth allowed herself to forget her fears, basking in the joy of family.

That evening, as the Bennet women withdrew from dinner to the parlor to discuss Jane's courtship yet again, Elizabeth took advantage of the free time and went upstairs to check on Benjamin.

The nursery was quiet save for the gentle crackle of the fire and the rhythmic ticking of the mantel clock. The nurse, seated in the corner with her mending, looked up and smiled as Elizabeth entered. Benjamin was sleeping soundly in the cradle near the hearth, his tiny hand curled against his cheek, the blanket rising and falling with each soft breath.

Elizabeth exhaled slowly, the tension in her shoulders easing as she stepped closer. She knelt beside the cradle, brushing a curl from his forehead, and let herself simply exist there for a moment, still and watchful.

So much had changed. So quickly.

A day ago, he had simply been Benjamin—an abandoned babe, a tragic casualty of the fire, folded lovingly into the Gardiner family without question. Now, he was something else. A symbol. A survivor. Possibly a target.

What does that make me? she wondered bitterly. *A governess? A guardian? A pawn?*

She looked at his sleeping face and knew one thing with absolute certainty: *Whatever else he is to the world, he is my responsibility for the moment.*

Her fingers curled against the edge of the cradle. *What if there are more men like Smithson? What if someone else tries to take him?*

Her heart gave a thud of panic before she tamped it down.

No. He is safe here. With us. With me.

In the stillness of the nursery, she could hear the faint hum of female voices rising and falling from the parlor. She knew, without needing to be present, that Mrs. Bennet would be alternating between exclaiming over Jane's good fortune in securing a courtship and lamenting that Bingley had not asked for an engagement.

"We are saved, Jane!" she could just imagine her mother exclaiming. "Saved from the hedgerows!"

She frowned at that, suddenly remembering that her father's unknown cousin, Mr. Collins, had died in the London fire. *Who is the new heir now?*

The question lodged itself in her chest with a weight that surprised her.

It was not as though she mourned Mr. Collins—she had, in fact, never met the man. But her parents often spoke of the late man's father, also deceased, who was miserly and disdainful. She could only help but feel a bit of relief that no one from that line would inherit Longbourn.

But what if the new heir is worse?

A stranger. A man they had never met. A man who might not feel even the feeble pull of duty Mr. Collins might have pretended to observe, for at least her father had met him in person once.

Would he evict them the moment their father passed? Raise rents on the tenants? Sell the land altogether?

Her fingers tightened against the windowsill.

She had been so consumed by the revelation of Benjamin's identity, by Colonel Fitzwilliam's secrets, by Smithson's dying words and the danger that hovered in every corner... she had entirely forgotten the practical, very real uncertainty that had shadowed their lives since her girlhood.

Perhaps she had thought that Mr. Gardiner's fortune might shield them. But now even that felt precarious—subject to suspicion, investigation, scandal.

And what of her father? He had received the letter, had spoken with her uncle Philips in Meryton, but since then...nothing.

She needed to speak to him.

Tonight.

Before the relief of Jane's courtship lulled him into complacency. Before Mrs. Bennet began planning wedding breakfasts and floral arrangements and forgot altogether that their future was still uncertain.

Before another secret could drop from the sky like a spark and set the world alight again.

Elizabeth rose to her feet, one hand brushing absently over the back of the cradle as she moved toward the door and closed it softly behind her. The corridor was dim, lit only by a single candle flickering near the stairwell. Elizabeth descended slowly, her slippers making no sound on the worn steps.

She knew her father would be in his study; he always retired there after dinner, under the pretense of answering correspondence and attending to estate matters, but often with a glass of port, a good book, and a stack of old correspondence he never answered.

Knocking softly on the door, she waited until she heard him say, "Come in" in muffled but alert voice.

Pushing open the door, she stepped inside. The familiar comforting scent of tobacco and paper eased some of her tension. Mr. Bennet looked up from behind his desk, his spectacles perched low on his nose.

"Well, Lizzy," he said, setting aside a volume of Pope's essays. "Have you come to scold me for not weeping with joy over your sister's courtship?"

She smiled faintly but shook her head. "Not tonight, Papa."

He gestured to the armchair opposite his. "Then sit, my dear. Let us be grim and serious together."

Elizabeth crossed the room and took the seat, smoothing her skirt over her knees. She hesitated, then said quietly, "I wanted to ask you about Mr. Collins."

Mr. Bennet blinked. "Ah."

There was a long pause. He leaned back in his chair, folding his hands over his stomach. "Yes. That was rather a shock, was it not?"

"I suppose," Elizabeth said. "But it is not just his death that troubles me—it is what it means. The entail. Longbourn."

Her father gave a noncommittal grunt. "Indeed."

"Do we know who the new heir is?"

He reached into a drawer and drew out a folded paper. "Mr. Phillips is looking into it. The original entail was drawn up by his predecessor. Apparently, it is... quite old. There may be distant cousins, though none we have ever met."

"And if there is no male heir?"

Mr. Bennet tilted his head, studying her with a trace of amusement. "Then perhaps your mother is right, and Jane will save us all."

Elizabeth gave him a reproving look, but he only sighed.

"You know me, Lizzy; I have never much liked dwelling on unpleasant certainties. But you are correct to ask. The truth is that I simply do not know. If there is no male heir, then either the estate will revert to the Crown, or I will be allowed to leave it to whomever I deem fit."

Her eyes widened. "One of us?"

"Or perhaps one of your husbands or sons who is willing to take the Bennet name," he said. "There have been Bennets at Longbourn for over two hundred years; I would hate to be the last one."

She looked down at her hands. "What will happen, Papa, if—if you are not here and we have no place to go?"

"Then I hope," he said gently, "that you will be married by then. Or at least strong enough to help guide your mother and sisters through the storm."

She looked up, and his eyes met hers with surprising clarity.

"I may joke, Lizzy," he said, "but I am not blind. I see the way the world shifts around us. And I trust you to hold your ground, no matter who inherits the land beneath your feet."

Elizabeth swallowed hard, unsure what emotion was rising in her throat—grief or pride or fear. She nodded.

"Thank you," she said softly.

He offered a small smile and returned to his port. "Now, go upstairs and remind your mother that a courtship is not yet a wedding. We must still budget for ribbons."

Elizabeth rose, lingering for a moment at the door.

She had come seeking answers, and in their place, she found resolve.

Whatever storm might come—over Benjamin, over Longbourn, over secrets and fires and traitors—she would be ready.

Chapter 20

Darcy stood at the hearth in Bingley's study at Netherfield, one hand braced on the mantel, the other loosely holding a glass of brandy he had yet to taste. He and Colonel Fitzwilliam had sought refuge there after returning from Longbourn to Miss Bingley histrionics at the news of her brother's courtship.

"Courtship?" she had repeated, her voice rising so sharply it could have shattered the decanter. "With Jane Bennet? But Charles, you hardly know her! We have only just arrived! You cannot be serious—this is absurd—utterly absurd!"

Bingley, to his credit, had stood his ground, even as Caroline had fluttered and wailed, demanded and wheedled. When that failed, she had turned her gaze on Darcy, appealing to him with wide, desperate eyes.

"You must speak with him—reason with him! He cannot mean to entangle himself so irrevocably with that family. Her mother is intolerable, and her youngest sisters are barely out of the schoolroom! And as for Jane—yes, she is pretty, I grant you—but that is hardly the foundation for marriage. Surely you agree!"

Darcy had not answered. He had simply raised a brow and glanced at the colonel. That, more than anything, had seemed to rob her of further breath. By the time he had excused himself from the room, Darcy was left with a pounding headache and a renewed appreciation for Longbourn's chaos over Netherfield's civility.

"Do you think she will send for smelling salts next?" the colonel had whispered with a smirk on their way to the study.

The woman's shrieks had finally died away, and the only sound was the fire crackling behind him. The day's ride and outdoor conversation had once again inflamed his lungs, and the warmth of the blaze was insufficient to thaw the cold that had coiled tight in his chest.

He stared at the flames, but his mind was on Elizabeth. She deserved answers. She deserved peace. She deserved a life untouched by foreign assassins and burnt-out nurseries and men with too many secrets. And yet, what had he offered her? Suspicion. Danger. A dying man's blood soaking through her dress. The memory of her trembling, fingers slick with red, refusing to let go.

He squeezed the glass in his hand, jaw tightening.

"Your Miss Elizabeth really is quite remarkable," the colonel said from behind him, voice low, contemplative.

Darcy did not turn. "She is."

For a long moment, there was only the sound of the fire and the soft clink of Fitzwilliam setting down his glass. Then: "You love her."

It was not a question.

Darcy closed his eyes.

He had tried to deny it—to reason it away as admiration, as concern for a woman caught in an unfortunate circumstance. But every time she walked into a room, his breath caught. Every time she spoke with fire or wit or stubbornness, his chest tightened—but not in the way it used to when his lungs failed him. This was different. This was... *devastating*.

And still, he said nothing.

"You do," the colonel murmured. "God help you."

Darcy turned then, one corner of his mouth twitching. "It is far too late for divine intervention."

Fitzwilliam huffed a dry laugh. "Does she know?"

"I imagine she suspects something."

He looked back at the fire, then added under his breath, "Though I may have lost any chance I had, after today."

"You have not." The certainty in the colonel's voice surprised him. "If you had, she would not have listened as long as she did. And she certainly would not have let you walk beside her."

Darcy ran a hand through his hair. "You saw how angry she was—how fiercely she defended her uncle, how mistrustful she became."

"Because she *cares*." The colonel stepped beside him, folding his arms. "You are not a stranger, Darcy. You matter to her. That's why it hurt."

Darcy set the glass down on the mantel with more force than necessary. "Enough. We have more important matters to tend to then gossiping like women about my feelings."

Colonel Fitzwilliam did not flinch. "Right, then. Murder." He moved to the writing desk, pulling out a fresh sheet of paper and uncapping a small pot of ink. "Let's begin."

Darcy joined him, pacing slowly as his mind turned. "We start with the obvious—who would want Smithson dead?"

The colonel nodded. "The first suspect, naturally, is Mr. Gardiner. He had motive—the boy was in his home. Means—he was in Meryton. And opportunity."

"I dislike it," Darcy muttered. "Everything I have seen of the man suggests intelligence, calm judgment, a good head for business. Not the sort to resort to violence."

"If we are to conduct a proper investigation, he must be on the list."

"Very well," said Darcy reluctantly. "I supposed we must also have Wickham on there, then."

The colonel crossed his arms. "He was in London during the fire and here for the murder."

"As were half the people currently in Meryton, including the regiment."

"We cannot dismiss him out of hand." The colonel added Wickham's name beneath Mr. Gardiner's.

Frowning, Darcy said, "I suppose the biggest problem we have is not that there are too many suspects, but too many possible motives. Was Smithson killed because of his facade as an insurance agent or due to his real occupation?"

The colonel looked up sharply. "You think a French agent did it?"

Darcy nodded. "Smithson was the only link between Denisse and your office. If Napoleon's men discovered he was investigating the fire, or if they learned he had found the boy…"

His cousin was already writing. "Unknown French operative. Potentially a revolutionary loyalist—someone who would recognize Denisse or her mission."

"It may not have been a foreigner," Darcy added. "There are enough desperate men flooding into the militia—unvetted, displaced. Wickham himself said as much."

"Then we add another category," the colonel said grimly, dipping his pen. "Militia member—possibly a traitor, or an opportunist."

Darcy exhaled. "We know Smithson bled heavily. He was injured on the path near Longbourn. Elizabeth found him barely alive."

"Meaning the killer did not finish the job—or did not have time," the colonel sat back. "Which could imply it was done in haste. A crime of opportunity or desperation. Not premeditated."

Darcy's expression darkened. "Or it could mean someone was watching. And ran before they could be seen."

There was a long silence between them.

At last, the colonel tapped the quill against the desk. "So. We have four categories: Mr. Gardiner, Wickham, a foreign agent, or a disreputable militia man."

He frowned. "This is far too vague."

Fitzwilliam did not argue. "It is the best I could do on a first pass. We do not even know who was in the area that afternoon, and with the militia swelling from the influx of displaced men, half the new officers barely have names that can be verified."

Darcy pinched the bridge of his nose. "This will not do. There are too many unknowns—and we cannot go about interrogating everyone in Meryton."

"No," the colonel agreed, "but with your lady love's help—"

"*Miss Elizabeth,*" Darcy corrected quietly, though without heat.

Fitzwilliam raised a brow, then smirked faintly. "Miss Elizabeth's help, we may begin to eliminate some names. Servants hear things. Gentlemen confide too freely when ladies are present. I have seen more plots unraveled by drawing room gossip than through official channels."

Darcy folded the list and placed it on the desk. "Tomorrow, Bingley and I can introduce you to Sir William Lucas and Colonel Forster. If you are to investigate discreetly, you will need their blessing. Then we will return to Longbourn to update Miss Elizabeth and come up with a more concrete plan."

Fitzwilliam stood and refilled his glass. "And our charming hostess?"

Darcy stared into the fire. "She may rail all she likes. Bingley has made his intentions clear, and as for me—I am too weary to indulge her dramatics."

Just then, a sharp knock at the study door drew their attention.

"Enter," Darcy called.

It was a footman. "Miss Bingley requests the honor of your company in the drawing room, sir. She has prepared a whist table."

Darcy's lips thinned. "Tell Miss Bingley that I regret I am occupied with affairs of great import."

The servant looked as though he had been sentenced to the guillotine. "Very good, sir."

As the poor man withdrew, Fitzwilliam let out a bark of laughter. "You are going to be in her black books for a week."

Darcy ignored him. "My valet can question the servants quietly. Your batman can listen among the grooms and stable hands, and you can also speak to the soldiers. Miss Elizabeth and I can keep to the drawing rooms."

The colonel gave him a sidelong glance. "You certainly picked a capable partner, Darcy."

Darcy looked away, toward the window where the last threads of daylight faded behind the trees. "She did not choose me. Not yet."

※

Elizabeth lay curled beneath her quilt, the fire in the grate nearly out, its glow reduced to soft embers that pulsed dimly across her ceiling. The house had quieted at last, but sleep would not come.

Her limbs ached with weariness, her bones heavy with the strain of a day that had offered both joy and dread in equal measure. And yet it was not the murder or the mystery that filled her thoughts—it was Mr. Darcy.

She could still feel his gaze on her when he had told her she was one of the most intelligent women of his acquaintance. Still hear the quiet assurance in his voice as he had said she had done exactly the right thing. Still feel the weight of his hand covering hers as they pressed against the dying man's wound—how warm, how steady he had been in the chaos.

Did he care for her? Truly? Or was it only gratitude? Admiration for her composure? She hardly knew how to trust her own thoughts where he was concerned. That man—so cold and aloof when first they met—had become someone else entirely in her estimation. Someone strong. Quiet. Principled. Someone who listened. Someone who cared.

And yet... how could she allow herself to feel anything, when her world had tilted so sharply?

Her eyes drifted closed at last, her head sinking deeper into the pillow. But peace was not to be found.

The memory of Smithson came unbidden—the terrible, wet rasp of his voice, the blood pooling beneath him, the weight of his body as it slumped in her arms.

Tell the raven it was the crow.

289

The words echoed in her ears again, and her eyes flew open.

She had meant to ask. She had meant to ask the colonel what it meant—what he thought the message could be. But with all the talk of espionage, of Benjamin, of suspects and schemes and shifting loyalties, the words had slipped from her mind.

She sat up slightly, heart pounding. *Tell the raven it was the crow.*

They meant something. They *had* to. A message from the last breath of a man who knew he was dying was no empty poetry. Who or what was the raven? The crow? Were they names? Code names? Enemies? Allies?

She shivered and lay back down, drawing the blankets up tightly beneath her chin. The fire was nearly dead now, and the chill had crept into the room, but it was not the cold that made her tremble.

She would ask. Tomorrow. First thing.

She closed her eyes once more, but sleep came slowly, and her dreams were tangled with wings and smoke.

※

It was early still, the pale autumn light filtering weakly through mist-hung trees as Darcy and Colonel Fitzwilliam rode through the quiet lanes toward the militia encampment. Frost clung to the hedgerows, and the breath of their horses rose in white plumes as they trotted along the rutted path.

"Charming countryside," the colonel remarked, adjusting his reins with gloved fingers. "Peaceful. One would never guess a murder and an international scandal are quietly brewing beneath all this pastoral calm."

Darcy did not reply. His gaze was fixed ahead, jaw tense, his mind already on the task before them.

The encampment lay just outside Meryton, still partially shrouded in morning fog. They found Colonel Forster near the officers' tents, in the midst of directing the day's drills. The moment he spotted them, his stern expression shifted to one of polite curiosity.

"Mr. Darcy!" he said in surprise. "What brings you here so early? You are not joining the militia, I trust?" His smile widened in jest, but then his eyes shifted to the colonel, noting the scarlet of his coat, the bar of rank at his collar, the composed military air—but with no spark of recognition.

Darcy dismounted and handed his reins to a waiting lad. "Colonel Forster, may I introduce Colonel Richard Fitzwilliam of the Regulars—currently attached to the Home Office. He is also my cousin, and he has requested an introduction."

Colonel Forster blinked, then gave a hasty salute. "Begging your pardon, Colonel. I did not—well, I did not realize." He straightened his posture at once and added with a hint of flustered pride, "It is an honor, sir, to meet a man whose reputation so precedes him."

The colonel returned the salute with ease, his tone cordial but businesslike. "Thank you, Colonel. I am afraid this is not a social call. We had hoped for a few minutes of your time in confidence."

"Of course," Colonel Forster said at once. "Come with me, please."

He gave a few orders to a nearby officer, then motioned the gentlemen to follow him into a large nearby tent. Once inside, he brushed off a thin layer of chalk dust from the edge of a rough-hewn table and gestured for them to sit. "You will forgive the disarray—we are preparing to receive more men. There is a great influx lately. Half of them without even proper references, I am afraid."

Darcy exchanged a glance with the colonel. "We will not take long," Darcy added. "We have reason to believe that recent events in the area—

particularly the incident involving Mr. Smithson—may not be entirely disconnected from certain... more sensitive matters."

Colonel Forster's brow rose. "Indeed? I had wondered about that business. The magistrate has been quiet about it, which I suppose is no surprise. The man was an insurance investigator, yes?"

"That was the impression," Darcy said carefully. "But there may be more to it than that."

The colonel stepped in, his tone easy but edged with intent. "I serve with the Crown—unofficially, you understand. There is a possibility Smithson was acting in a capacity far more delicate than insurance."

Colonel Forster blinked. "Good Lord. Do you suspect espionage?"

"We do not know yet. But we are gathering what information we can, as quietly as possible. To that end, I hoped to gain your permission to observe and inquire discreetly among the officers. Nothing official. Just a few quiet conversations and a bit of listening."

To his credit, Colonel Forster did not balk. He looked between the two men, then nodded. "I do not like the thought of spies—or murderers—in my regiment. You may speak with whom you need, but be subtle about it. And let me know if you find anything concerning."

"Thank you for your understanding," the colonel said graciously. "Not every officer is willing to doubt the men under their command."

Colonel Forster straightened his shoulders and puffed out his chest at the compliment. "My loyalties are to my country first. Although to be entirely honest, before the London Fire, I would have balked at the request. But with so many new soldiers who behave as less than gentlemen...."

"Precisely," Darcy chimed in. "With the growth of militia members, it makes security difficult."

"That it does." Colonel Forster's mouth tightened. "They send me a list of names, and I do what I can, but the paperwork is patchy—especially after the fire. A number of men lost their documentation. There is no time to investigate every one of them thoroughly. Most are just trying to get work. Some... I wonder about."

The colonel inclined his head. "But remember," he said sternly, "this is to be kept in the strictest of confidence."

"Absolutely," Colonel Forster said. "What explanation should we give the men?"

"Perhaps we tell people that my cousin has been asked to look into the matter as a matter of routine," Darcy suggested. "As London is still in disarray and the military has been asked to restore order, the murder of an insurance agent could fall under that purview."

"Very good," Colonel Forster said. "I may even hint at how nice it must be to be the son of an earl and able to stay at a manor for the investigation. That will make it seem as even less important."

"Excellent plan, so long as the men are ordered to cooperate," the colonel replied. "Additionally, if you could spare a reliable sergeant or lieutenant—someone discrete and absolutely trustworthy—I would like to use him to perform introductions and report on any suspicious movements among the men. Nothing formal, just... observations."

Colonel Forster nodded. "I have a man in mind. Loyal as the day is long. He will say nothing to anyone, and he's been with me long enough to know who talks too much and drinks too hard."

"Perfect," Fitzwilliam said, rising.

Colonel Forster walked them to the door, his expression grave. "If this truly is a matter of espionage, Colonel, then you have my full cooperation."

Darcy extended a hand. "Thank you, Colonel. We will speak again soon."

"And remember, Colonel, that this is of the utmost secrecy," Colonel Fitzwilliam added. "There are only three men in Meryton who are aware: myself, my cousin, and now you. If word of this gets out, I will know its source."

Darcy gave Colonel Fitzwilliam a confused look but remained silent as Colonel Forster offered his assurances of discretion. After taking their leave, he waited until they were alone before saying, "Only three, Colonel? I believe you forgot a person who knows about the situation."

"I said *men*," Colonel Fitzwilliam replied, mounting his horse with deliberate nonchalance. "Miss Elizabeth Bennet is not a man. And I very much doubt she would let me forget it."

Darcy stared at him for a moment, then gave a short, dry laugh. "You've a dangerous habit of dissembling."

"Dangerous is one word for it." The colonel glanced sideways at his cousin. "One man down."

"Now for the second," Darcy said. "And a far more talkative one. You had best give him the same story that Colonel Forster will be putting out. I am a bit surprised you trusted him, to be honest."

"I have my reasons," the colonel said mysteriously. "I will follow your lead for the magistrate, though."

The remainder of the ride to Lucas Lodge was made in silence. When they were shown into Sir William's study, the garrulous man rose to his feet with pompous ceremony. "Mr. Darcy! What an honor, what an honor, to be one of the first to be introduced to your friend. And a colonel, no less!" He bowed deeply. "Allow me to welcome you to Meryton, sir. And may I say, you have the bearing of a man accustomed to command!"

The colonel, with practiced grace, returned the bow and offered a genial smile. "You do me too much credit, Sir William."

"Allow me to present my cousin, Colonel Fitzwilliam," Darcy said dryly. "He is here to assist you in your investigation of the death of Mr. Smithson."

"Ah, capital!" This exclamation was accompanied by the slight dimming of Sir William's smile as he was reminded of the sordid event. "The whole town is abuzz about the matter; having the presence of an officer to investigate—particularly one with such connections—will cause quite a stir."

Darcy shared a look with his cousin, the corner of his mouth twitching ever so slightly. Sir William, oblivious to the undercurrents, gestured grandly for them to sit.

"I see what you mean," the colonel murmured under his breath as they moved towards the chairs. "This will require a different sort of handling than Colonel Forster."

Darcy leaned close, his voice wry. "You are about to learn that information flows two ways in Meryton—so be careful what you stir."

With Sir William Lucas beaming before them and the scent of tea and pipe smoke thick in the air, Darcy settled in, bracing himself for the next round of diplomacy in waistcoats and smiles.

The real work, after all, was only just beginning.

Chapter 21

The morning at Longbourn passed in relative peace—until Bingley arrived to call on Jane.

Elizabeth had been seated beside her elder sister in the drawing room, helping her to mend a torn hem, when he was announced by Hill. Mrs. Bennet immediately fluttered forward with cries of welcome, while Kitty and Lydia scrambled up from the floor where they had been playing a child's clapping game with discarded ribbons.

Bingley greeted Jane with a bow and a smile so fond, Elizabeth had to glance down at her lap to hide her grin. He sat himself next to her, and the two began to converse in quiet whispers. Mrs. Bennet prattled on with Kitty and Lydia, who had resumed their places on the floor in spite of their guest, leading Elizabeth to flush slightly at their poor behavior.

Her choice of companion having been commandeered, Elizabeth did her best to tune out the room and focus on her mending, but her mind raced. *Where are Mr. Darcy and his cousin? They said they would call again this morning to continue our discussion.*

At a pause in their exchange, she quickly spoke up. "Are Colonel Fitzwilliam and Mr. Darcy not with you today? I trust everyone at Netherfield is well."

Bingley looked up, startled— as if he had entirely forgotten anyone else was in the room. Elizabeth bit back a smile at his besotted behavior as he stammered his response. "I... I believe they were to make one or two calls before coming to join me here, but they left before I did. But yes, everyone is... well at Netherfield, thank you."

He immediately turned his focus back to Jane. *Well, if I did not already believe he was in love with Jane, this bit of inattention to me certainly would prove it!* Elizabeth thought humorously.

Her cheer dimmed somewhat as she remembered why she was so eager to speak with Darcy and the colonel. *If only they were here! I need to tell them about what Mr. Smithson—or whatever his name is—said right before he died. It may be important.*

Lost in her recollections, Elizabeth was oblivious to the rest of the room until a high-pitched squeal interrupted her thoughts.

"Oh, a ball!" Lydia clapped her hands and bounced on the floor. "How delightful!"

"I do love dancing," Kitty added, practically hopping like a frog in delight. "Especially with the officers."

Mary, seated stiffly at the far end of the room with her book of moral essays open before her, gave a disapproving sniff. "Frivolity in excess dulls the mind."

Lydia ignored her entirely. "Perhaps one of the officers will steal me away into the garden for a kiss!" she whispered too loudly to Kitty, who dissolved into giggles.

The effect was instantaneous. Jane's color deepened with embarrassment. Mr. Bingley's amiable smile faltered, his brow creasing in discomfort.

Elizabeth stiffened, debating whether or not it was worth risking her mother's ire to rebuke the younger two. She sought out Mrs. Bennet to gauge her temper, and was astonished by what she found.

Mrs. Bennet had frozen mid-flutter. One hand hovered uncertainly near her bosom, the other gripped the arm of her chair. Her usual simpering smile had vanished, and in its place... Elizabeth saw something far rarer: clarity. Embarrassment warred with alarm in her mother's eyes, and for a moment, the full weight of their guests' discomfort—and what it might cost Jane—seemed to settle visibly upon her shoulders.

It was like watching a mask crack. Elizabeth, so used to seeing her mother as frivolous and exasperating, was struck by how human she looked in that instant. Flushed. Disbelieving. Almost ashamed.

And then something hardened in Mrs. Bennet's expression.

"That will do," she said sharply.

The room fell still.

Lydia blinked. "What—?"

"I said that will do," Mrs. Bennet repeated. "Since you cannot behave like the gentlewomen you are, you will not attend the ball."

Kitty's mouth dropped open. "But Mama—"

"I will not have you throwing yourselves at officers like some common tavern girl," Mrs. Bennet snapped. "Clearly, your aunt Gardiner was right—you are not yet old enough for society. I have turned a blind eye to your behavior in the past, but I shall do so no longer. My eyes are opened at last."

Lydia looked around the room as if expecting someone to intervene. No one did.

"I will not go?" she repeated, in growing outrage. "You cannot be serious! That is not fair! I am not—Mama, please—"

But Mrs. Bennet stood firm. "No balls. No assemblies. No visiting officers. I should have done it weeks ago."

At that moment, Mr. Bennet strolled into the drawing room, no doubt having been drawn by the sudden silence—so rare in a household of five daughters.

"What is this?" he asked mildly. "Is someone dying?"

"No," Mrs. Bennet said tartly. "Just my patience."

Mr. Bennet gaped at this bit of wit from his typically flighty wife. "I beg your pardon?"

"I have decided that you are correct, Mr. Bennet. Your two youngest are some of the silliest girls in England, and as such, they are banned from social gatherings until they can learn some manners."

Elizabeth looked at her father, half expecting him to overturn the ruling with a sarcastic comment. But instead, he looked at his wife with surprise—and then something like admiration.

"Well done, my dear," he said. "I quite agree."

Lydia let out a noise somewhere between a shriek and a sob and burst from the room, Kitty scrambling after her in distress.

For a long moment, no one spoke.

Then Mr. Bingley cleared his throat. "Er—perhaps I ought to wait before sending out the invitations? Unless you have any suggestions for a date?"

"No need to delay on our account," Mrs. Bennet said primly. "I apologize for my daughters' behavior. Rest assured, Mr. Bingley, my husband and I will be very glad to attend your ball with our three eldest daughters at any time you see fit to hold it. But you must give me enough time to take the girls shopping. I daresay Jane's ball gown requires new lace…"

Elizabeth sat frozen, astonishment rippling through her. Never in all her years had she seen her mother so composed, so… decisive. It left her feeling oddly off-balance, as though the ground beneath Longbourn had shifted ever so slightly. She exchanged a glance with Jane, who blinked, equally stunned, though a glimmer of pride danced in her eyes.

Change had come to the Bennet household, it seemed—unexpected and uninvited, but not entirely unwelcome.

And yet even as Elizabeth smiled faintly at Mr. Bingley's cheerful scramble to recover the conversation, a shadow tugged at her thoughts. Smithson's final words echoed in her mind like a half-remembered song.

Tell the raven… it was the crow.

"Why are they not here yet?" she muttered to herself in annoyance— although as she did so, a small part of her was relieved they had missed out on the scene caused by Kitty and Lydia.

Just as she was about to excuse herself from the room in search a way to expend her restlessness, the sound of horses announced that another guest had arrived. Bingley looked towards the window and exclaimed, "Ah, excellent—there are Darcy and Fitzwilliam now."

Within minutes, the two gentlemen were announced. After greeting their hostess, they took seats near Elizabeth, intent on communicating with her. Elizabeth glanced at the window and, upon seeing the weather was not favorable for a walk, raised her eyebrows and said meaningfully, "I am sorry, gentlemen, that we are unable to continue our tour of the gardens today. Perhaps arrangements can be made to finish yesterday's plans at another time."

The colonel nodded sharply and moved to sit near Mrs. Bennet. As he settled beside her mother, she watched with amazement. With no more than a well-placed compliment and a request that she tell him more about where he was visiting, Mrs. Bennet was soon gushing about every detail of the neighborhood.

"Oh, we are very fortunate here in Hertfordshire—we dine with twenty-four families," the matron beamed. "And my brother, Mr. Gardiner, has just purchased Stoke Estate, which includes the great house and all the tenant farms. A sound investment, though it would be better if the drawing rooms were larger. But no matter, for Lady Lucas was telling me that at Purvis Lodge…"

Elizabeth restrained a smile as she watched her mother chatter, with the colonel murmuring at the appropriate places while subtly redirecting her conversation towards each of the families in the area. It was quite clever, really— distracting her with praise while extracting every scrap of information she possessed.

A sniff from the corner of the room reminded Elizabeth that there were other observers in the room. Turning, she saw Mary had taken refuge in said corner with a thick tome. A glance around revealed that Mr. Bennet had vanished altogether—likely into his library the moment Mrs. Bennet uttered the words "shopping" and "lace"—and Jane and Bingley were absorbed in quiet conversation on the settee.

For all intents and purposes, she and Darcy were alone.

She leaned slightly toward Darcy and spoke in a low voice. "Did you and Colonel Fitzwilliam make any progress in making a list of the suspects?"

"Yes and no," he replied, moving his head closer to hers. "Only two are named—your uncle and Lieutenant Wickham—"

Elizabeth bristled as she cut him off. "My uncle would have been at home with my aunt that morning. At least, he arrived with her when she came to tend to me. The servants can confirm it."

"Good," Darcy said, his voice quiet but warm. "The colonel's batman is skilled at such things—he will ask the questions discreetly. That should remove your uncle from suspicion."

"But Mr. Wickham is on the list? I had thought the two of you had reconciled?"

"It is more for the odd circumstances of the situation; he was in London during the fire and here for the murder."

"As were most members of the militia," she pointed out.

"Precisely, which is why my cousin has arranged to speak with each member of the militia. Colonel Forster is cooperating, and he is aware of my cousin's current role in service. It was necessary to reveal it to him in order to gain his willing participation."

She gave a small sigh. "Which is why you said only some progress had been made. All members of the militia and all newcomers to Meryton makes for quite a long list."

"Which is why we also paid a visit to Sir William this morning as well."

"Surely you did not trust *him* with such sensitive information!" *What on earth were they thinking?*

He shook his head vehemently. "No, we told him the colonel was sent in place of a Bow Street Runner, which are conveniently all too involved with maintaining order in London."

Elizabeth quirked an eyebrow and looked over at where Fitzwilliam was still engaging her mother in conversation about the neighborhood. "That was clever. It will allow him to move in society and ask questions without raising suspicion." She laughed softly. "I daresay my mother will not know whether to revere him as the son of an earl or revile him if he does not immediately declare Mr. Gardiner innocent."

That earned a soft chuckle from Darcy, and Elizabeth turned back to glance at him, only to find his gaze boring into her. The intensity in his eyes sent a flutter through her stomach, and she felt her cheeks warm.

"Forgive me," she said quickly to mask her reaction to him, "I have not even inquired after your health. How is your cough? Has it improved at all?"

"Considerably," Darcy replied. "The herbs you and your cousin provided have worked wonders. No more tightness in my chest, save for the occasional twinge. It is the best I have felt since the fire."

"I am glad to hear it."

"I owe it entirely to you," he added, his voice lower now, more earnest. "To your dedication to your sister all those years ago, and your kindness in offering it to me now after you accidentally stumbled across me at the assembly."

Now her face felt as though it were burning, though some of it was due to mortification. "It was no trouble at all... although I am ashamed to admit, it was not entirely an accident that I found you in that corridor. I... I followed you from the assembly."

His face froze in a blank mask, and his voice was stern as he asked, "You *followed* me from the room? Why?"

"I was intending to challenge you for cutting me."

Darcy blinked. "Cutting you?"

She recounted the scene in brief from her perspective—how she had overheard Bingley encouraging him to dance, how Darcy had looked her way, met her gaze, and promptly turned his back and walked away without so much as a word.

"I thought perhaps you were rejecting me, my appearance or my status. It was at such odds with how I remembered you from Hyde Park, and I thought perhaps you remembered me and were put off by my unladylike behavior back then. I was hurt at first, but then I was angry—angry enough to want to confront you."

Darcy looked mortified. "I had no idea at all. I could barely breathe with the heavy air and the perfume. I intended no slight."

"I know," she said, laughing softly. "I realized it the moment I saw your face. You looked utterly miserable."

He shook his head, still looking pained. "I am truly sorry. I would never—"

"There is no need," she said gently. "I forgave you long ago."

He hesitated. Then, in almost a whisper, he said, "Perhaps I might make amends… by reserving the next dance? Should there be another occasion?"

Her heart stopped. *He does not know about the ball. I cannot allow him to make such a request when his honor may bind him to it without all the facts. He could merely be paying lip-service.*

"You should be careful before say such things, as you may be held to them," she lightly teased, attempting to give him a way out. "Shortly before you arrived, Mr. Bingley spoke of holding a ball soon at Netherfield."

She held her breath, waiting for his reply, not daring to hope…

"Then allow me to ask you formally." His voice was soft as he leaned forward, his breath caressing her ear. "Miss Elizabeth Bennet, may I have the honor of the first set?"

She could only stare at him for a moment, searching his face. The sincerity of his gaze broke through the last wall she had erected.

"You may," she said softly. "If your health allows."

"For you," he said, "it would be worth the risk."

The moment held—charged, fragile, and full of something unspoken.

Then a crash sounded from the upper floor, followed by a familiar, indignant wail. Elizabeth flinched, looking around frantically to make sure none in the room had witnessed their proximity.

"Lydia," she groaned as another shriek sounded from above.

Mrs. Bennet hastily rose to her feet. "Those girls will be the death of me! Come, Mary, I shall most likely require your assistance. Excuse me, gentlemen."

As her mother swept from the room, leaving the door just slightly ajar, Elizabeth breathed a sigh of relief that no one had seemed to notice the tender moment she and Darcy had shared. Jane and Bingley were clearly in their own world, already having resumed their conversation.

The colonel chuckled as he rejoined the group, casting a glance toward the doorway through which Mrs. Bennet had just departed. "Your mother possesses an intelligence network that would put some of His Majesty's finest agents to shame," he remarked with a wry smile. "Her knowledge of the neighborhood is both vast and impressively detailed."

Elizabeth could not help but smile at the colonel's observation. "Indeed," she replied, "my mother has a talent for gathering and disseminating information that rivals any formal intelligence operation. Although I doubt that her penchant for neighborhood gossip has any strategic value."

He chuckled. "Strategic, perhaps not. But comprehensive? Absolutely. Her knowledge of the local families, their histories, and their connections is nothing short of impressive. If ever I needed a dossier on the residents of Meryton, I would know precisely whom to consult."

Elizabeth laughed softly. "Be careful, Colonel. Flatter her too much, and she might draft you into her social campaigns."

He grinned. "A fate I shall endeavor to avoid."

Darcy cleared his throat. "Perhaps we should take advantage of this time to speak of more pressing matters."

A bit surprised at his severe tone, Elizabeth turned her full attention towards the man at her side. There was something in his expression—a tension not quite concealed behind the calm exterior—that made her pulse quicken.

Is he...jealous?

The thought flashed through her mind, and she pushed it to the side to contemplate later. Darcy was correct: they needed to use this time together wisely.

"I agree," she said slowly, her tone shifting. "In fact, there is something I have been meaning to mention since yesterday."

She glanced between the two men. The colonel's brows lifted slightly, attentive. Darcy leaned forward almost imperceptibly, as if bracing himself.

"When I found Mr. Smithson," she said quietly, "he spoke to me. Just before he lost consciousness. I did not think to mention it at the time—I was too shaken—but it has been haunting me since."

"I had forgotten," Darcy said, "but I wrote to you about it, Fitzwilliam. His words reminded me of our childhood.

The colonel straightened. "Yes, that was actually part of what spurred me here so quickly. Miss Elizabeth, can you tell me exactly what he said?"

Elizabeth hesitated, remembering the rasp of the dying man's voice. "He said— 'Tell the raven it was the crow.'"

A silence fell over the room. Darcy's jaw tightened. The colonel, frowning, drew a slow breath.

"I thought perhaps it was nonsense," Elizabeth added, "some fevered delusion. But the phrasing was so deliberate. And now that I know more of what was at stake—of who he truly was—I thought it might mean something."

Darcy's eyes were fixed on the colonel now. "Does it?"

The colonel did not answer at once. His gaze drifted past them, unfocused, as though seeing something far beyond the drawing room—as if somewhere far away a memory played itself out in shadows and smoke. His fingers, which had been casually tapping the armrest, stilled.

Elizabeth exchanged a glance with Darcy, her chest tightening at the sudden shift in the colonel's manner, but neither dared interrupt the stillness that had fallen.

When the colonel finally spoke, his voice was quiet—hollow with memory.

"Yes," he said. "It means everything."

And then, without another word, he rose from his seat and walked to the window, staring out into the darkened fields beyond.

"For you to truly understand, we… we must go back. Back to when everything changed."

Elizabeth sat upright, her attention wholly fixed on the colonel. She and Darcy waited for what seemed an eternity in silence. The only sounds were the crackle of the fire in the hearth and the soft murmur of quiet conversation from Bingley and Jane.

Back to what? she thought. *To the fire? To the death of that poor woman—Deena? To France?*

But she dare not speak.

At last, the colonel drew a deep breath and began his chilling narrative.

Chapter 22

It started in Spain.

Colonel Fitzwilliam had been stationed at a windswept garrison near the Pyrenees, on the fractured border between order and chaos. Officially, he was part of a diplomatic liaison, shuttling intelligence to British commanders from partisan informants.

Unofficially, he was one of a growing number of shadow agents operating for the Home Office—men who moved without uniform or rank, who knew how to listen more than speak, who could follow a whisper as though it were a map.

The war was not only one of uniforms and artillery—it was one of whispers. One of shadows.

Napoleon's forces were everywhere and nowhere at once, and British agents were dispatched with more questions than answers, always one step behind some vanishing trail of paper and blood.

Fitzwilliam had already proven himself—first in Cadiz, then in Lisbon. Clever, composed, and fluent in several languages, he was offered a position under General Wellesley's auxiliary command. But it was not tactics they needed from him—it was secrets.

He had chosen his codename quickly, without hesitation.

"Raven," he had said.

The official had raised a brow. "Why?"

"If they are good enough for Odin to choose to be his scouts...." His voice trailed off, and the official shook his head.

"Whatever you want."

He did not realize at the time just how apt the moniker would become—nor how quickly his reputation would grow.

By the time the colonel's first tour on the Continent was complete, rumors about the fabled Raven had spread across Europe in the form of hushed, fearful whispers in dark alleys. And by the time his second round of assignments had commenced, his notoriety was that of legends.

But along with fame came enemies.

The first whisper of Le Corbeau *came not from England, but from a terrified courier in Madrid, who claimed that a French agent—a ghost—was executing royalist sympathizers.*

Cleanly. Quietly.

Always alone.

Always unseen.

And always with a significant amount of sophisticated torture.

No one knew his real name or his face, but he left a calling card each time: a single black crow's feather on the victim's chest or the edge of the scene.

Like an artist signing his painting, Le Corbeau made it clear just who was responsible for each political assassination. The victims were always enemies of Napoleon, and the method of death always reflected a certain level of sadism.

At first, Colonel Fitzwilliam dismissed all of the reports of Le Corbeau as mere stories that grew as they were told, like a small flame being introduced to more air and dry timber.

But then the victims began to change, and a pattern began to emerge.

The banker in Paris. The translator in Brussels. A former general's widow in Marseille. A shipping magnate with ties to émigré movements in Bordeaux. All murdered without clear cause. All of them people Fitzwilliam had been scheduled to contact—or had just missed by hours.

The worst was Bruges. He had arrived at a safe house under rain-slicked clouds, the window still cracked from a hasty exit. The fire was still warm. On the sill, as if placed deliberately, lay a single crow's feather, heavy with moisture.

It had been left for him.

That was the first time it felt personal.

From then on, it became a game. One with high stakes and invisible pieces. He would uncover a lead; it would vanish. He would secure a name; the person would disappear or die. Every time he came close, Le Corbeau slipped away like smoke through fingers. Brilliant. Invisible. Unrelenting.

In the dark hours of sleepless nights, Colonel Fitzwilliam wondered: was it luck? Or was he being tested?

*They began leaving things for each other. Clues. Warnings. A knife with a Latin inscription left at an abandoned checkpoint. A coded note folded into a false bottom of a diplomatic valise. Once, in Prague, Fitzwilliam found a page torn from a children's fable—*The Raven and the Fox—*with a blood-red X over the raven's eyes.*

He had burned it.

It was no longer a pursuit—it was a rivalry.

A battle of wills and wits across half a continent.

Only one would win.

And then, in a tumbled-down town, west of Rouen, Fitzwilliam finally stumbled across a breakthrough. Two decades before, during the great Reign of Terror, there had been a survivor.

A noble child—born to a cousin of the Bourbon line—had been spirited away to grow up in hiding. Raised as the son of a farmer, the young man had grown up, married, and was about to father a child.

Colonel Fitzwilliam was elated. At last, he *would be the one to arrive first.*

But someone betrayed them. He arrived too late. The house was ash and rubble, and everyone inside was slaughtered.

A single crow's feather lay across the mouth of the young man, lying gutted next to his even younger wife—who was astonishingly not *with child.*

Desperately, Colonel Fitzwilliam followed the trail to the edge of the Spanish border, expecting at every moment to encounter the most gruesome of discoveries: a murdered infant.

But instead, he found her: Denisse.

She was barely standing. Her coat torn, her arms scraped from briars, her face hollow with fear and desperation. But she clutched the child like something sacred. When she learned Fitzwilliam was English, she wept— not with grief, but with hope.

She told him everything. The massacre. Her change of heart. Her flight. And the shadow behind her.

Even then, she knew who followed.

Le Corbeau.

Colonel Fitzwilliam brought them to London. Gave them a new name, a new home. He thought—hoped—it would be enough. She had provided details of the man who had incited their group to arms, details that he prayed would be enough to help him finally identify the man he had spent nearly a decade trying to outwit.

But then came the fire.

And when he arrived at the scorched edge of Cheapside, all that remained of Denisse was a body pulled from the street and a building burned to the ground.

The baby was gone.

And in the soot near what had once been the nursery, lying in the cradle, there was a black crow's feather.

Le Corbeau had followed them to England and nearly burned down half of London, killing hundreds, all to finish his assignment: to eliminate the remaining line of Bourbon.

The message was clear: I am still ahead of you.

The colonel had scoured the city for weeks, tearing through records, bribing informants, risking exposure. But the trail had gone cold. He never found out who had taken the child—or if the child had even survived.

He returned to the Home Office with nothing but charred hands and a mind tormented by failure.

Until Darcy's first letter came, and there was a mention of a girl who had rescued a baby during the fire.

An investigator was dispatched...and then murdered.

But his final words: Tell the raven it was the crow.

Le Corbeau—or, in English, The Crow—was in Hertfordshire.

The war had come to Meryton.

Darcy sat frozen. He already knew some of what his cousin had shared, but not to this extent. He knew there was a foreign spy hunting the baby and that Smithson worked for the colonel and England.

But he had not known the full scale of Colonel Fitzwilliam's service in name of king and country.

The things he has seen… what he has been through…

He could not speak—could barely breathe, though it had little to do with the persistent ache in his chest. The room, the fire, the faint ticking of the clock on the mantel—all seemed to fade to some distant hum. Across from him, Colonel Fitzwilliam leaned forward, elbows braced on his knees, his voice still echoing in the space they shared.

Le Corbeau.

The Crow.

The scope of it—espionage, assassination, traitors in the militia, the near-destruction of London itself—it defied imagination. And yet Darcy knew the colonel too well to doubt him. His cousin had always been clever, yes. Witty, charming, quick with a joke and quicker still to rescue Darcy from any awkward moment in society.

But this… this was something else entirely.

Darcy had known Colonel Fitzwilliam served in Spain. He had seen the hardened edge that wartime left in a man. But he had not known this.

How many dinners had they sat through at Matlock House, his aunt complaining about the state of the Empire's trade while the colonel merely sipped his wine and nodded? How many assemblies had they attended where the colonel flirted and danced and laughed, never revealing that he had once chased a ghost across the breadth of Europe?

Darcy felt the hair at the back of his neck prickle. He had always thought of himself as the more serious of the two, the more responsible. But now he realized—perhaps Fitzwilliam had simply been the better actor.

He turned slightly, just enough to glance at Elizabeth.

She was leaning forward towards the colonel, her face unreadable in the firelight. But her eyes—those eyes he had come to study with such devotion—were dark with something deeper than fear. Her hands were folded tightly in her lap, white-knuckled. She was not merely shocked. She was absorbing every word, just as he had.

And something in her expression... something told him that she understood the weight of what had just been placed in her lap. She did not look away. She had not flinched. He felt the swell of pride for her—pride and something fiercer still.

When the colonel finally leaned back and exhaled, it was with the weariness of a man who had dragged a mountain behind him.

Darcy cleared his throat. It was a moment before he could speak. "And all this time..." His voice came out quieter than he intended. "You let me believe you were merely drinking brandy with generals and writing reports."

The colonel gave a tired smile. "I was drinking brandy with generals. And writing reports. Just... occasionally under fire."

Darcy let out a breath and shook his head slowly. "You are the Raven."

The colonel shrugged. "The name suited."

It did. And Darcy saw now just how well. The cunning. The patience. The careful observation masked by charm. He had never fully seen it before. And now he did.

The fire popped in the grate, breaking the quiet.

Darcy looked to Elizabeth again. Her brow furrowed slightly, lips parted as though still considering what to say.

"What does it mean now?" she asked softly. "If Le Corbeau is in Hertfordshire—what happens next?"

The colonel's eyes met hers. "It means the baby is still vulnerable, and there is far less time than we thought."

Darcy's jaw clenched. Elizabeth was in danger.

※

Elizabeth was in shock, unable to do anything more than sit in stunned silence.

The fire flickered and popped in the hearth, but its warmth barely touched the chill that had taken hold of her. The colonel's tale had unfurled like something from the pages of a gothic novel—mystery and murder, spies and shadows, a decades-long hunt that had spanned nations.

And she had sat through it all without interrupting, breath caught tight in her chest, heart hammering behind her stays.

Tell the raven it was the crow.

Tell the *Raven* it was the *Crow*.

An assassin. A ghost. A legend.

And now he was in Meryton.

In her mind, she pictured Benjamin asleep in his cradle just up the stairs in the nursery—innocent, unaware. Her arms suddenly ached to hold him tight against her, to keep him safe from the evil that had intruded into their lives.

She had thought she was saving a baby from a life of misery—or even death in an orphanage.

But no—she was saving the last hope of a noble line, one related to French royalty. A symbol of everything the revolutionaries had sought to erase.

*It was only a simple act of compassion. That's all—it was never meant to be....*this.

Her actions the night of the fire were nothing more than acting on an impulse in the chaos of the moment. She had done what anyone with a heart would have done.

And yet, because of that moment—because of that mercy—everything had changed.

A baby with royal blood—albeit distant—had been saved.

Then Darcy had come across her in Hyde Park, assisting her in her altercation with the soldier...only to show up again in Meryton several months later.

And he just happened to be the cousin of the only man in the kingdom who knew who Benjamin was.

It was all too incredible to believe.

She looked over at Darcy, who was watching his cousin with concern, the lines of worry and resolve carved deep into his features.

How strange it was to imagine that just a short time ago, she had believed him to be proud and cold. Yet here was evidence that still waters truly did run deep. She had believed him when he swore that he had no idea who Benjamin was when he had come to Meryton.

His attempts to get to know her, the friendship they had developed. It was because he *wanted* to, not because he was on assignment from his cousin.

And the colonel—the Raven. His story should have terrified her—should have sent her running for the nursery and bolting the doors.

But instead, she found herself breathless with awe.

All of it—every step—had led to this moment.

It was all too precise, too intricate in its coincidence.

Which means it is not a coincidence. It is Providence.

Somehow, for some reason, she had been placed at the center of this storm—not by calculation or design, but by something greater than any of them could understand.

Her skin prickled. The fear was still there—yes, how could it not be? There was a French assassin hunting her—or rather, the child she protected. There was a war not of soldiers but of shadows. And she, Elizabeth Bennet of Longbourn, was now part of it.

She did not know why she had been chosen. She was not the strongest or the cleverest or the most important. She was merely a young woman who had done what she thought was right.

But if that choice had brought her here, to this moment—if she had been placed in the path of a newborn child who now carried the hopes of a lineage long thought lost—then she would not falter.

The fear gave way for something else: resolve.

She *would* see it through.

She *would* do her part.

For Benjamin.

For her country.

For herself. For Darcy.

Slowly, she lifted her chin and looked between the two men. Her words, when they came, were quiet but sure.

"We cannot let him win."

☓

Darcy stared at her, stunned.

She was pale—he could see the strain on her face, the tight line of her jaw, the faint tremble of her fingers where they rested against the arm of the chair. And yet her eyes burned like twin embers, fierce and determined.

In all his life, he had never seen anyone so brave.

Elizabeth Bennet, with nothing but her courage and wit, had stepped into the center of a secret war and declared she would stand her ground. That she would not falter. That she would protect that child—completely unrelated to her—even if it cost her everything.

It took his breath away.

321

I love her.

The thought struck him like lightning, burning through every wall he had carefully built. Fitzwilliam had pointed it out a smithson prior, but Darcy had not acknowledged to himself.

There was no use denying it now—he was hopelessly, irrevocably in love with her. Every sharp word, every clever retort, every laugh, every fierce loyalty—he loved all of it.

Loved her.

Then marry her.

His mind spun—could he do it? Could he marry the woman that he loved?

You are weak, Fitzwilliam.

The words he had heard time and again from his father and, later on, his aunt echoed in his ears. His weakness, his frailty, was what caused Lady Catherine to change her mind about uniting her daughter with him. While that had been fortuitous, the hateful words she had flung at him had cut deep.

Even his aunt Lady Matlock had looked at him with a mixture of pity and disgust the last time he had been seized by a coughing fit in her presence.

But Elizabeth did not shy away; she had helped him.

Just as she had the elderly man in Hyde Park. Just as she had the baby.

It was who she was, and she was glorious.

No matter what came. No matter what danger lay ahead, he would marry her, or he would never be whole again.

"Then we cannot let him win," she had said, with fire in her voice.

No, they could not.

The colonel nodded solemnly. "We need to smoke him out. But we must be careful—we may not find him directly. We may have to fool him into thinking he's won. Perhaps if we push a false suspect forward—make the Crow believe we are looking in the wrong direction—he will grow careless."

Darcy frowned. "A false suspect?"

"Someone close to the child. Someone plausible." The colonel gave Elizabeth a hesitant glance. "Perhaps... your uncle."

"No," she said at once, her voice sharp as flint. "Absolutely not. My family is already in danger. We have had our home invaded, our safety threatened, and I will not subject my uncle to more scrutiny—especially not when the town is already watching us closely. It would be too much. Too risky."

The colonel raised a hand. "All right. Then who?"

Darcy drew a slow breath, already knowing the answer. "Wickham."

Elizabeth's eyes flicked to him. The colonel straightened slightly. "Wickham?"

"It could work," Darcy said. "He was in London for the fire and here for the murder. We could put it about that Wickham had been overheard arguing with Mr. Smithson about insurance matters. Then if everyone thinks he's the suspect, Le Corbeau might relax his guard and make a mistake."

"We would have to tell Wickham the truth," the colonel said warily. "It adds yet another person who could inadvertently let confidential information slip."

"Not the whole truth," Elizabeth replied. "Only that we are trying to trap the real murderer. That we want to make it appear that he's the primary suspect—to draw the actual killer into a mistake."

The colonel leaned back. "Are you sure it was not Wickham? It is entirely possible that Smithson was not killed for being a spy, but for his faux role as insurance agent. After all, Wickham does have motive; he lost his employment due to the extreme delays of unmonitored insurance companies."

Darcy shook his head. "No. It was not him. I know him too well. He's impulsive at times, certainly, but he has never been evil or malicious, even at his worst."

Elizabeth nodded. "There was truth in his eyes when he spoke to me about his regrets for his poor behavior in the past."

There was a pause as the three of them considered the plan.

"Then we act quickly," the colonel said. "Darcy and I will speak with Wickham and make the arrangements."

"You may also wish to let Colonel Forster know as well," Elizabeth interjected.

The colonel nodded. "We will also begin interviewing the soldiers and servants to confirm alibis, all under the guise of attempting to be fair in the investigation. Miss Elizabeth—your role will be vital. Keep the child under tight guard, but not hidden. You can also assist in spreading the whispers of Wickham's guilt."

"Many people saw us speaking at my aunt's card party. I can spread word that he confided in me that Mr. Darcy has a vendetta against him from a childhood grievance. It will lend credence to the idea that you are targeting Wickham on purpose."

"Excellent," the colonel said. "We can also spread rumors among the officers of debts in London and a grudge against the insurance company for causing the loss of his employment there."

Darcy and Elizabeth only had a moment to agree before the door flung wide open to admit Mrs. Bennet.

"Oh, my poor nerves," she declared as she collapsed onto the settee, oblivious to startled looks she received from the room's occupants. "I do believe Lydia has locked herself in the upstairs linen closet, and Kitty is weeping into her pillow. And as for Mary—well, she is quoting Ecclesiastes at them both, which is hardly helpful!"

Colonel Fitzwilliam straightened, already rising to offer some gallant remark, and Elizabeth tucked a stray curl behind her ear, her composure smoothing into something more practiced.

But Darcy could not look away from her, resolve forming in his mind.

I am going to marry her.

Chapter 23

The following day, Darcy and Colonel Fitzwilliam sent a note to Colonel Forster, requesting that Lieutenant Wickham pay a covert call to Netherfield—preferably in a manner that would avoid attracting the attention of Miss Bingley, the servants, or the increasingly nosy Hursts.

Darcy stood with his arms folded near the hearth in one of Netherfield's smaller drawing rooms, watching as the colonel paced in long, measured strides.

"I still say we should have chosen to meet in the stables," the colonel muttered. "Fewer rugs at risk from all your pacing."

Darcy raised an eyebrow. "I should like to conduct exactly one clandestine meeting in my life that does not smell of horses."

Before the colonel could reply, a soft tap tap-tap came at the window.

They both turned as the glass wobbled slightly in its frame.

A moment later, the sash inched upward, groaning in protest, and Wickham clambered inside with considerably less grace than expected. One boot caught on the sill; he stumbled forward with a muttered curse and landed with a thump against the wainscoting.

"Not quite as easy as it looks in novels," he grumbled, straightening his coat and brushing off his breeches.

The colonel gave a dry look. "And yet, you managed to make an entrance worthy of theater."

Darcy, arms still folded, said only, "You are late. And why are you not using the door?"

Wickham smirked. "Had to convince a chambermaid I was sneaking out, not in. You would be surprised how quickly panic sets in when you are seen climbing over hedges. And we are supposed to be feuding, remember?"

"Lieutenant," the colonel said sternly, "you were not asked to come here in order to provide us with entertainment."

"I gathered as much from the death glares. I would not have thought you to be so sensitive, Colonel, as to still hate me for the time I bested you in poker when we were fifteen." Wickham's easy smile faded as he took in their solemn expressions. "Well, I can see that this is not a social call, although I should have surmised as much when you asked to meet clandestinely. What, precisely, am I here for, then? Am I being arrested?"

"Have you done something that merits an arrest, Georgie-boy?" The colonel's teeth gleamed in a feral grin.

"No," Darcy said shortly. "We need your help."

Wickham's amusement faded. "Go on."

Fitzwilliam stepped forward, voice calm but firm. "We believe the man who killed Mr. Smithson is still in the area—and that he may strike again. Your presence here, your history, and your argument with the victim all make you...convenient."

Wickham blinked. "You suspect me?"

"No," said Darcy quickly, then added more carefully, "but others might. And that's what we want to use."

"You want me to be your scapegoat?"

The colonel crossed his arms. "We want you to be our distraction. If the real killer believes you are under suspicion, he may drop his guard."

Wickham tilted his head, thoughtful. "What about Colonel Forster? What if I am arrested?"

"He has been made aware of the situation," the colonel said. "You will be protected, but you must also play your part convincingly."

There was a long pause, then Wickham slowly exhaled as he dropped into a chair. "Very well, I will do it."

"You will?"

The look of consternation on the colonel's face was so comical, Darcy could not help but smirk. "I told you, Colonel—he says he has changed, and I believe him."

"Now I am not saint, mind you," Wickham protested in mock outrage, "but murder? And of a man who was attempting to harm children? That is worth the discomfort and rejection I will encounter here."

"Darcy has offered to compensate you for your troubles," the colonel replied, ignoring Darcy's surprise.

"I have?"

"You have?"

Darcy and Wickham spoke in unison, then snickered at each other in a way that made Fitzwilliam shake his head and mutter. "Thick as thieves, just like before. But yes, Darcy has. Think of it as a charitable donation to the cause of national security.

Darcy gave him a flat look. "You are very free with my purse."

"I learned from the best," the colonel quipped. "My father is much the same way."

Wickham leaned back, arms crossed behind his head. "Well, then—I expect at least enough to cover the cost of a new coat. If I am to be the tragic villain, I ought to look the part."

"Villainy suits you," the colonel said, deadpan.

"I will take that as a compliment."

Darcy shook his head but could not suppress the ghost of a smile. "You will need to be cautious, though. The real killer is out there."

Wickham's smile faded. "I will, Darcy. Thank you."

"For what?"

"For trusting me. For putting your faith in me. For allowing me to prove myself."

Speechless, Darcy could only nod in reply.

"Now, now, enough sentiment, else you will have me weeping." Fitzwilliam pretended to wipe a tear from his eye, and Darcy scoffed. "We are all in agreement. You, Wickham, will continue as you are—but allow yourself to be seen with a troubled conscience. A few pointed conversations, a little brooding, some remarks overheard by the right ears."

"And you lot?" Wickham asked.

Darcy folded his arms again. "We will handle the rest."

There was a beat of silence, broken only by the faint crackle of the fire.

"Well," Wickham said at last, rising to his feet, "if I am to be your sacrificial lamb, I had best go practice looking guilty."

"Try not to use the window this time," the colonel muttered.

"No promises." Wickham gave them a jaunty salute and slipped through the side door with theatrical stealth.

Darcy waited until the door closed before turning to his cousin. "Do you think it will work?"

Fitzwilliam's face was solemn. "It had better."

ℋ

As soon as a note arrived from Netherfield informing Elizabeth that Wickham had consented to be a false suspect, Elizabeth began her part in the process. As she paid the usual calls with her mother, she dropped little tidbits of information meant to throw suspicion on Wickham. She could only hope that when everything was resolved, the neighborhood would forgive him.

"Lieutenant Wickham seemed quite unsettled at the card party," she remarked to Lady Lucas. "He said Mr. Darcy's and his cousin has long harbored resentment toward him. Some childhood grievance, I believe."

To Mrs. Long, she added in a quiet aside, "It is odd, is it not? Mr. Smithson said he was here about insurance, and Mr. Wickham told me that the reason he had to take a position in the militia was because the property insurance company was delaying repayment at his place of employee. I wonder if there is a connection…" Her voice trailed off and she gave the elder woman a knowing look.

And when Mrs. Goulding tutted over rumors of misbehavior among the officers, Elizabeth nodded solemnly. "It is all so unsettling. I suppose we must take care whom we trust—charming men in red coats are not always what they seem. Mr. Wickham, for example, is almost too good to be true."

At home, she made sure that Benjamin was never left unattended. If he was not in her arms, he was with the nurse and an additional maid. She spoke with the servants and told them that between the murder and the increase in strangers from London, she was worried about all of their safety and asked them to increase their vigilance. She also asked them to be in pairs at all times; no one was to be left alone.

And always, Elizabeth listened—at the milliner's, at the butcher's, in the drawing room when the ladies gathered for tea. She took every scrap of gossip, every whispered tale of debts and odd behavior, and filed it away for Darcy and Colonel Fitzwilliam.

Ж

As Elizabeth sowed her seeds of doubt, the colonel began the painstaking process of interviewing each soldier under the guise of assisting the magistrate. He wore his uniform for these visits—neat, unadorned, and unmistakably authoritative. It granted him instant deference, and even the most unruly recruits stood at attention beneath his cool, appraising gaze.

Darcy assisted his cousin, writing down what each man said as they answered Fitzwilliam's questions. They began with the newest arrivals to the regiment, calling them in one by one under pretense of helping the local magistrate sort out conflicting accounts of the morning in question. His questions were delivered with calm precision: "Where were you posted? Who saw you? Did you notice anyone acting strangely, either that morning or since then?"

Most of the men, unnerved by his rank and clipped manner, answered promptly. Captain Carter had been leading drills. Lieutenant Denny had been supervising several new recruits in their morning run.

A few stammered. Poor Chamberlayne could scarcely speak from nerves.

One, a soldier nearly as handsome as Wickham, attempted to lie about being asleep in his tent, though he had really been with the blacksmith's daughter.

And one tried to flirt.

The last earned him such a withering stare from Darcy that he nearly saluted the gentleman twice out of confusion.

Darcy and Fitzwilliam recorded every inconsistency, every hesitation. They asked after friendships, petty grievances, even debts. When a few men began to mention they had heard Wickham quarrel with Mr. Smithson in the weeks prior, the colonel merely raised a brow and nodded, making note—but gave no indication of whether it was new information or something long confirmed. Darcy would make a sour face at each mention of Wickham's name, helping further along any suspicions.

It was clear that the rumors Elizabeth had begun were making their way through the ranks, but the process of eliminating suspects was much slower than Darcy and Fitzwilliam would have wished. After three days of being no closer to Le Corbeau than before, they accompanied Bingley to Longbourn, discouraged.

The only one who had given Colonel Fitzwilliam any feeling of true unease had been Captain Carter. The man had greeted them with a small smirk, as if he knew of some private joke. But as the officer had been witnessed by dozens of men running drills all morning, Fitzwilliam had not choice but to cross him off the list of suspects.

Mrs. Bennet greeted them with unusual restraint—though her eyes sparkled when she mentioned the approaching ball, which was only a few days away—as the gentlemen were ushered into the drawing room. The three elder Bennet girls were sitting with their mother, each holding a piece of mending.

Elizabeth rose at once, and Darcy's heart lightened at the sight of her. She glanced meaningfully towards the window and said, "Would any of you gentlemen care for a walk? The weather is unusually fine today."

The three men accepted with alacrity, and Mrs. Bennet ushered Jane and Elizabeth out to accompany them. Mary was told to go as well, but she was obviously reluctant to go out in the cold weather. As they left the drawing room, Darcy saw Elizabeth whisper something to her middle sister, who gave her a grateful hug and dashed up the stairs.

"I told Mary she could hide in her room instead of coming out with us," Elizabeth explained as they made their way out the door and into the side garden. The chilly winter breeze tugged at her shawl, and the dying sunlight cast long shadows across the grass. "She would usually give me a lecture on honoring our parents, but she has the headache today and was grateful for the reprieve."

"It is quite in our favor," Darcy replied, "as it will allow us to speak openly."

Elizabeth tugged her shawl more tightly around her shoulders. "How are things progressing with the soldiers? Has your batman gained any usual information from any of the servants?"

"We were able to confirm that your uncle was indeed home all morning of the murder," Darcy said, "but other than that, I am afraid our efforts have yielded little fruit."

"We are running out of time," Fitzwilliam said flatly. "I have questioned nearly one hundred soldiers and officers, and I cannot swear to a single one's innocence—nor can I say which man, if any, is our target."

"Is there a deadline?" Elizabeth asked.

"I only worry that the longer it takes, the more desperate Le Corbeau will become."

"Then we need to draw him out," she replied, her voice steady.

"But how?" Darcy asked, punctuating his question with a cough.

The three fell silent for a time, then Elizabeth said at last, "Let us think on it tonight. If you will call tomorrow, perhaps we will have come up with an idea."

"Very well. We will attempt to have Bingley call with us, but we may not be able to do so. His sister has been quite overset with preparations for the ball, and as tomorrow will be the day before, he may not have the liberty to leave."

"Poor Miss Bingley," Elizabeth murmured.

"Poor *Mister* Bingley," Fitzwilliam said with a laugh. "He has my full sympathy. I would sooner face a French firing line than cross a woman in the throes of party planning."

Elizabeth smiled. "Then I pray the French do not attack before the Netherfield ball—else we may all be undone."

The colonel chuckled, but Darcy's gaze lingered on her, a faint smile tugging at the corners of his mouth. "Let us hope for a quiet night."

$$\mathchar"58$$

Elizabeth lay staring at the canopy above her bed, the moonlight casting soft shadows across the ceiling. Sleep remained elusive. Her thoughts chased each other like foxes—swift, tangled, and relentless. Somewhere across the room, Kitty snored softly, the wheeze of it punctuated by a catch in her breath that had returned with the first frost. She always coughed more in winter.

335

Elizabeth closed her eyes, willing herself to calm, to quiet her mind as the clock in the hall chimed two o'clock in the morning.

It was no use. She could not sleep. *How can we draw out Le Corbeau?*

The question haunted her, but no answer came.

The only ideas she had come up with all involved using Benjamin as some sort of bait, but she refused to even contemplate the notion. Intentionally putting *any* child in danger was nothing short of reprehensible to her.

But she could think of nothing else.

She rolled onto her side and tried to focus on something else.

Mr. Darcy's face came to mind—drawn, weary, pale beneath the early winter sunlight. He had tried to hide it, but she had seen the way his shoulders slumped slightly, the way he rubbed at his chest when he thought no one noticed.

He had coughed again that afternoon, twice during their conversation, and each time she had bitten her tongue to keep from suggesting they move indoors or offering him a warmer coat. She wanted to scold him for pushing himself, to press a hand to his brow and insist he rest.

But it was not her place.

If only it could be.

She wanted it to be.

The thought made her still. Slowly, it settled over her like a hush in a church. She did not merely admire him. It was not gratitude for his kindness, nor sympathy for his burdens, nor the thrill of his admiration that made her chest ache when he looked at her.

It was love.

Quiet, fierce, unshakable. The kind that crept in when she was not watching, that wove itself into her thoughts until she could not imagine a day without them.

I am in love with Mr. Darcy.

With that certainty came a longing so deep and burning so brightly, she had to close her eyes against it. She longed for the right to worry over him, to care for him without restraint, to share in his struggles and ease his burdens—not as a friend, not even as a confidante, but as his partner. His equal. His wife.

If she were his wife, then that afternoon she could have sent him to the fireside and demanded he stay there until his lungs were soothed and his color returned. She could have fretted over him without worrying about being too forward or unladylike.

But instead, she was left with silence and shadow and all the proper distance society required.

She sighed and pulled the covers higher, trying to settle herself.

Then she paused.

A scent.

Faint, but there— foreign and musky, not the usual sharp tang of pipe smoke from her father or the faded rose water the maids favored. It was a man's scent, and not one she recognized.

A muffled thump echoed above her, and her blood ran cold.

Benjamin!

She bolted upright, her heart hammering. Without thinking, she snatched her parasol from the corner and crept to the door, easing it open.

The hallway was quiet.

Too quiet.

She moved quickly and silently up the servants' stairs to the third floor. As she reached the landing, another soft thud made her breath catch in her throat.

Then, from within the nursery, a low rustling sound.

She flung the door open.

Moonlight spilled across the room through the open window, catching on the edge of the cradle. The maid and the nurse lay motionless on the floor, and a tall, dark-cloaked figure stood just beyond the cradle, reaching down toward it.

Something primal surged up in her chest.

She screamed—a ragged, guttural sound—and charged.

The man spun, startled, just in time to raise his arms as she swung the parasol with all her strength. The crack of wood on his forearm echoed through the room.

He stumbled back.

She struck again.

And again.

And again.

Her arm ached, her breath ragged, but she would not stop.

He caught the end of the parasol at last, and for one terrifying moment, they struggled for control. Then came the thunder of feet on the stairs and shouts echoing up the hall. The man's head whipped toward the door.

His eyes—pale blue and furious—met hers for a heartbeat.

Then he turned and dove through the open window.

"No!" Elizabeth rushed forward, reaching the sill just in time to see—

Nothing.

The yard below was empty. No body. No figure running. Nothing disturbed.

He had vanished.

She stared into the dark, wind stinging her face, her knuckles white on the windowsill.

How did he get up three stories without a ladder? How did he get down? *Where did he go?*

Behind her, a footman rushed into the room. "Miss Elizabeth?" he asked, gaping around the room from her at the window to the fallen nurses on the floor.

His voice broke through her foggy mind, and she realized that Benjamin was screaming from his bed. She rushed over to the cradle and snatched him into her arms, frantically checking him for injury.

He was fine.

Angry at be awakened so harshly in the middle of the night, but unharmed.

She let out a slow breath of relief and held him tightly to her as more servants swarmed in the room, along with her father. Mr. Bennet began barking orders for Mr. Jones to be summoned, as well as a magistrate. He then moved to his daughter's side.

"Elizabeth, what on earth is going on?"

"There was someone in the nursery," she choked out. "He tried to get to Benjamin."

Mr. Bennet's face was pale white. "Why on earth would someone do that? What in heaven's name is going on? First the Gardiners, now us…"

Elizabeth bit her lip, and Mr. Bennet's face grew severe. "Elizabeth Rose, you will tell me what you know this instant."

She hesitated. "Papa… I… I cannot. At least, not right this moment. Could… could you send a note to Netherfield for Colonel Fitzwilliam and Mr. Darcy? They can explain things better than I can."

His frown deepened. "You mean to tell me that two wealthy, single young men know more than I do of a matter that involves my household— my *daughter*—and you say that I must consult *them*?"

Elizabeth's eyes widened. She had never seen her father so angry before.

"Please, Papa," she whispered. "I cannot—"

Her voice broke, and her eyes filled with tears as the sheer magnitude of what had occurred caught up with her. His face softened, and he sighed heavily. "Very well, my dear. I will send them a message immediately, demanding their presence here as soon as it is light. But be assured that I *will* get answers, Elizabeth."

"Yes, sir."

He sighed again. "Now, you ladies all return to your beds. Mr. and Mrs. Hill can manage the servants, and I will send for Sir William."

"Are they… are they dead?" she asked, craning her head to look past her father at the nurse and maid on the ground.

"Looks like a blow to the head each," Mr. Hill said from his position on the floor, examining them. "But they are both breathing."

"Send for Mr. Jones, then," Mr. Bennet said. "Now, Lizzy, put Benjamin back in his cradle and return to your room."

She clutched the crying child tightly to her chest. "I cannot leave him! It is not safe, especially with Nurse and Sally unconscious."

He frowned. "Very well. Have Jimmy move the cradle to your room for the night. He can stay with you until we get it all sorted out. I will have Jimmy stay outside your door until your friends from Netherfield arrive."

She nodded in agreement, and Jimmy—the burly footman who had been the first to enter the room—came to her side.

"What is this?" he asked, looking inside at the bedding.

He held something up, and Elizabeth let out a horrified gasp.

It was a single black crow feather.

Chapter 24

Darcy walked beside Elizabeth through a mist-draped forest, their hands brushing now and then as they followed a well-worn path. The filtered light made her eyes seem almost golden, her laugh like birdsong in the distance. She turned to say something, her expression radiant. Her face was full of trust and something deeper, something fragile and precious.

"Darcy... Darcy...wake up..."

He shook his head. *Why is Elizabeth telling me to wake up? We are walking together.*

She grabbed him by the arm, shaking him.

"Darcy!" she shouted.

The pressure grew firmer, and suddenly she disappeared. The mist turned to smoke, and he could see the orange glow of flames licking through the trees.

"Darcy!" came the voice again—sharper now, deeper.

"Elizabeth!"

He gasped awake, the dream shattering into pieces as he sat bolt upright in bed. His eyes darted wildly, searching for her, for the forest—for any trace of the world he had just left behind.

"Elizabeth?" he repeated hoarsely, his breath coming in short, startled bursts as a familiar vise tightened around his lungs.

"Sadly no," came a droll voice, "but I am flattered by the comparison."

Darcy blinked hard, trying to shake off the fading embers of the dream. "Fitzwilliam? What are you doing in my chambers at in the middle of the night?"

"Clearly not having dreams as sweet as yours."

Darcy groaned and rubbed his eyes, allowing his cousin to come into better focus. "What time is it?"

"Shortly past two." The colonel was standing at his bedside, his features flickering in the light of the candle he held.

"That had better be the hour in the afternoon."

"Tragically, it is not," the colonel said, voice turning grim. "My batman woke me up—a message arrived from Longbourn not a quarter of an hour ago from Miss Elizabeth's father. It is addressed to you."

Darcy shot upright. "What happened? Is she—are they—?"

The colonel handed over a folded letter, its seal broken. "Read it yourself."

Darcy unfolded the page and motioned for Fitzwilliam to bring the candle closer.

Mr. Darcy,

There has been an intruder in my home. The attack occurred in the nursery during the night. Elizabeth was able to protect the child, though the two women tending him were knocked unconscious.

When questioned, my daughter informed me that you would provide that information.

It appears you and your cousin, two unmarried gentlemen, have been encouraging her to keep things from me, which has put her life in danger.

As I have now had enough of secrets, I expect you both at Longbourn the moment it is light enough to ride.

—Thomas Bennet

P.S. Elizabeth asks me to inform you that a black crow's feather was discovered in the cradle. I trust you will understand the significance of it.

Darcy read the postscript twice. His blood ran cold, and his grip tightened on the page. "Le Corbeau was in her house." His voice was murderous.

"It appears so," the colonel replied. "He sees to be getting desperate, which means time has run out for us."

"She fought him," he whispered. "She must have fought him off. Is she unharmed?"

"I am afraid I do not know any more about the situation than you do."

Darcy stood, already reaching for his coat. "We need a plan. We cannot wait any longer."

"I agree completely, but we cannot leave now—it would raise too many questions in the household. Besides, it would not be safe to ride over until there is a little light, at least. To go now would be foolish—not to mention the fact that you are still in your night shirt."

"How can you jest at a time like this?" Throwing his coat down in frustration, Darcy sat back on his bed and glared at his cousin.

The colonel shrugged. "In my line of work, you end up forming a sort of gallows humor. It prevents you from descending into madness at the evil that exists in the world."

The look in his eyes was so bleak that Darcy immediately felt ashamed. "I apologize, Fitzwilliam. I cannot imagine what you have been through these years."

"Someone has to do it," the colonel said with another shrug.

"Still, I am grateful."

"Thank you." The colonel's voice was hoarse.

"You do not *have* to do it, you know. You have your allowance from your father and the small estate from your mother's brother."

"But I did not have those things when I enlisted."

"You do now, though. Why not sell your commission? Surely there are others who can

"I have put off retirement these last few years," the colonel said, "only because I refuse to quit until I have stopped Le Corbeau. If we can catch him in Hertfordshire, then perhaps…perhaps I can at last be free."

Darcy studied his cousin in the flickering candlelight. His cousin looked tired—older than the man who had laughed his way through so many London drawing rooms, the same man who had once charmed every matron in Mayfair with a wink and a bow. This version of Colonel Fitzwilliam bore weight in his eyes that no jest could dispel.

"I will help you," Darcy said quietly. "Whatever it takes."

The colonel gave him a faint smile. "I know. That is why I brought you into this. Not just because you were close to the child, but because I knew I could trust you to do the right thing."

Silence stretched between them as the last vestiges of sleep fell away and tension tightened like wire in the small chamber.

At last, Darcy stood again, pacing a few steps before stopping near the hearth. "We tell Mr. Bennet everything. No more half-truths. He deserves to know exactly what we are facing—especially after tonight."

The colonel nodded. "I agree. If he is to protect his family, he must understand what they are up against."

"We will tell him as soon as it is light, then."

The following hours were spent attempting to read to pass the time, although Darcy spent more of it staring blankly at the same page as opposed to actually reading it. At last, the dim room grew lighter. Darcy turned towards the window and saw the sky streaked with the faintest grey-blue of coming dawn.

"It is time," he said.

Fitzwilliam pushed away from the wall and reached for his coat. "Then let us be off."

They left Netherfield in silence, their horses cutting through the frost-covered ground with urgency. As Darcy rode through the dim, mist-hung morning, the wind bit at his cheeks and the reins burned against his gloved hands—but he barely felt it. His thoughts were too loud.

The moment he had read Mr. Bennet's note, something within him had snapped tight, like a wire drawn too far. *Elizabeth fought off an assassin.*

The words replayed in his mind over and over, each time twisting the knot deeper in his chest. *She fought Le Corbeau.*

He could have lost her.

The thought of Elizabeth—alone in the dark, armed with nothing but courage, facing down a trained killer—filled him with both awe and terror.

His hands tightened on the reins. If anything had happened to her...

I cannot lose her. Not when I have just found her.

He knew not when he had first fallen in love with her—it was as if he were in the middle of it before he even realized it. But when he did know…

That knowledge had come to him like a tide at high moon—gradual, inevitable, and now all-consuming. But he had told himself to wait. She had already borne so much—the fire, the child, the revelations. He had not wanted to burden her with the weight of his feelings while she was already carrying the weight of the world.

He had imagined a peaceful day, some quiet moment after the danger had passed, when he might speak to her alone, take her hand, and offer her not just his heart, but a life of calm and certainty.

But there was no calm.

There was no certainty.

And he realized now, with piercing clarity, that waiting was *not* romantic—it was foolish. If he had lost her before he had told her—before she knew, truly knew, how entirely she had captured his heart…

I would never forgive myself.

He thought—he hoped, at least—that he saw the return of his love in her eyes. There was a softening when they spoke together, a light that seemed to flicker to life in her face when he was near.

It was not proof that she loved him in return, but it was enough.

He could not waste another day.

As Longbourn's familiar outline emerged from the silver haze of the morning fog, Darcy felt his resolve settle like steel within him. He would speak to Mr. Bennet. He would tell him everything—about the investigation, about Le Corbeau, about the dangers.

But he would also ask him for permission—permission to marry Elizabeth.

For if she would have him, he would not let another morning pass without claiming the honor of protecting and cherishing her for the rest of his life.

Upon arriving at the front door, Darcy dismounted and handed the reins to a sleepy-looking stable boy, who yawned so widely it nearly unseated his cap. The colonel followed suit, tossing a coin into the lad's palm with a murmured, "Mind those hooves, lad."

The front door opened before they could knock. Mrs. Hill stood there with her arms crossed, a shawl wrapped tightly around her shoulders. Her eyes, red-rimmed from lack of sleep, narrowed at the sight of them.

"The master has been waiting for you," she said, not bothering with a proper greeting. The tone in her voice made Darcy feel, absurdly, like a boy about to be brought before a headmaster. She turned without waiting and led them through the dim halls to Mr. Bennet's study.

She opened the door with more force than necessary. "Mr. Darcy and Colonel Fitzwilliam, sir."

Then she shut it firmly behind them.

Mr. Bennet sat behind his desk, a blanket over his shoulders and a decanter already uncorked at his elbow. He looked up slowly, his icy gaze sharp as a bayonet. The temperature in the room dropped five degrees, and Darcy shivered.

"Do you have any idea what it is like," he said, his voice low and controlled, "to be woken in the dead of night to find your daughter had been attacked in her own home?"

Neither man spoke.

"Of course you do not. Neither of you are fathers."

He rose, walking around the desk with calm that was far more ominous than shouting. "Let me tell you precisely what that is like. It is to know a horror unlike any other. It is to feel helpless. It is to imagine every second that your child—your child—is lying somewhere bleeding, or worse, because someone brought danger to your door."

He stopped before them, eyes blazing. "Then to find that she has been fraternizing—conspiring—with two men whom she has known for mere weeks, and who have, by their own actions or associations, placed her in mortal peril? Tell me, gentlemen—what would *you* do?"

Neither spoke.

"I have half a mind to challenge you both to a duel," he said coldly. "And the only reason I have not already called for pistols is because Elizabeth refuses to say anything about the situation until I have spoken to you. So, speak. Now. And do *not* lie to me."

The silence that followed was thick enough to choke on. Even the colonel, who had smiled his way through more battles and threats on his life than he could count, paled under the force of Mr. Bennet's wrath.

Clearing his throat, Darcy took a small step forward. "You are correct," he said simply. "If I were in your position, I would be infuriated. My cousin and I both have guardianship of my younger sister, Georgiana. She is twelve years my junior. I have been more father than brother to her since my father died. If she were in Elizabeth's place, I would not hesitate to string the men responsible from the nearest tree. I cannot begin to tell you how sorry we are."

"Then *why*?" Mr. Bennet snapped. "Why was this kept from me? Why my daughter? Why this house?"

Darcy looked at Colonel Fitzwilliam. *It is not my place to share matters of national security.*

Fortunately, the colonel had at last found his voice. He began to explain everything, from the moment he received the intelligence about the Bourbon heir to Denisse's rescue, the smuggling of the infant out of France, Smithson's murder, and the final confirmation that the Le Corbeau had followed them to Hertfordshire.

Mr. Bennet sat speechless throughout the entire account. When the colonel finished, he sat heavily in his chair and stared at the far wall, his face looking suddenly far older than it had at the beginning of the tale.

When he finally spoke, his voice was quiet. "I understand the need for secrecy. I do. The Home Office is not known for its transparency, and I am not known for being the most vigilant of fathers. My wife, bless her, cannot keep a teacup steady without announcing it to the county. I understand why you chose to keep this from me."

His gaze met theirs, eyes sharp again. "But that does not change the fact that my daughter and household are in grave danger. So. What are we going to do about it?"

Darcy and Fitzwilliam exchanged glances.

"We were hoping," the colonel said, "to consult with Miss Elizabeth. She is clever and perceptive, and—"

"Yes, yes, she is," Mr. Bennet interrupted with a faint, tired smile. "That girl always had the sharpest mind in the house. Very well. I shall have someone fetch her." He began to rise from his chair.

It is now or never, Darcy.

Heat rushed over him as he stepped forward. "Sir, before you do, there is something else. I... I would like your permission to marry Miss Elizabeth."

Mr. Bennet froze halfway out of his chair. Then, slowly, he sat back down.

The silence that followed was almost comic in its length. His mouth opened, closed, opened again. Thirty full seconds passed in stunned disbelief.

At last, he let out a strangled croak. "My first inclination is to deny you outright, sir. But my daughter would never forgive me if I presumed to speak on her behalf in this matter. So—yes. You have my permission to address her. But you do not have my permission to marry her. If—*and only if*—she accepts you, and *if* we survive this debacle, *then* you may ask me again."

Darcy exhaled in relief. "That is more than reasonable, sir. And perhaps more grace than I deserve."

Mr. Bennet snorted. "I do not do it for *you*, Mr. Darcy. I do it for her. If she loves you, she will say yes. And if she does not, she will say no—and do a much better job of thrashing you with words than I ever could. Which I would enjoy watching, frankly."

Darcy swallowed hard. The colonel clapped him on the back, grinning. "Cheer up, cousin. Who knows? We may all be dead within the week, in which case you will be spared the rejection."

Mr. Bennet gave him a long, deadpan stare.

The colonel cleared his throat. "Ah. My apologies, sir. That was... rather flippant."

To everyone's surprise, Mr. Bennet barked out a laugh. "I think I might begin to like you, Colonel, despite my better judgment."

He stood, going to the door. "Now. Shall we have Lizzy sent for? Unless you, too, would like to ask for one of my daughters? I am afraid only Mary remains, but she's a good enough girl."

The colonel choked. "I... that is... I assure you, sir—"

But he never finished, for the door opened to reveal Elizabeth herself standing there, a knowing arch to her brow and Benjamin cradled in her arms. Though she was dressed in a plain morning gown with a simple coiffure, Darcy had never seen anything more beautiful.

Mr. Bennet raised an eyebrow. "Well, then. No need to send for you after all."

Elizabeth stepped forward. "I heard raised voices. I assumed that meant the gentlemen had arrived." Her tone was mild, but her eyes flicked knowingly between the three of them.

Mr. Bennet's gaze softened slightly. "Indeed, they have. Come in, my dear. We have much to discuss."

※

Elizabeth stepped into the study with Benjamin in her arms. The air was thick with tension, and her father stood behind his desk, arms folded in a severe scowl. Darcy and Colonel Fitzwilliam were standing before him, both men looking grim— shoulders squared, expressions hard.

Darcy's eyes immediately found hers, dark and searching. His gaze swept over her with barely concealed worry, lingering at the slight shadows beneath her eyes, the protective way she held the child. She felt his concern as surely as if he had spoken it aloud.

She gave him a small, reassuring smile, her fingers absently stroking Benjamin's back as she said, "This conversation may take some time. I believe, Papa, we should at least offer the gentlemen a chair."

Mr. Bennet sighed. "Very well, but only one."

The two men looked blankly at one another, and Elizabeth suppressed a giggle. "Really, Papa, this is no time for your teasing. Gentlemen, you may *each* take a seat."

Elizabeth raised her brows but said nothing. The colonel quirked a brow toward Darcy, clearly deferring, and stepped back as Darcy moved toward the chair. As he passed her, his arm brushed lightly against hers— only a glancing touch, but it sent a current through her that made her breath catch.

Darcy sat down without a word, but the set of his jaw and the way his gaze flicked back to her told her he was here—for her.

Her attention was called away when Mr. Bennet said, "We need a plan—one that keeps this house, this family, and that child," he nodded at Benjamin, "safe from the man who tried to kill him."

Darcy straightened. "I will send word to London this morning to have several of my own footmen travel down—men I trust, not just for their discretion, but for their strength and loyalty."

"And I can fetch several men of my own," Colonel Fitzwilliam added. "Soldiers who once served under me, now retired or recovering from wounds. Many live in London, and they can travel with Darcy's men. They will be grateful for honest coin and clear orders."

Mr. Bennet eyed him sharply. "And none of them will be able to be bought?"

The colonel's response was immediate. "No, sir. Not these men—I would trust them with my life."

"You had better be correct," Mr. Bennet muttered, "because I will be trusting them with my family's lives."

A tense silence fell again. Elizabeth looked from one face to the next, noting the exhaustion etched into their expressions. Even the prospect of reinforcements did not seem to ease the weight in the room.

"Guards are not a permanent solution," Mr. Bennet finally said. "They cannot surround Longbourn forever."

"There may be other options," Darcy offered. "We could arrange to have Benjamin removed from the area. Smuggled to a safe location—perhaps even the palace? If it is safe enough for His Majesty—"

"No!" Elizabeth said at once, her voice sharp enough to make Benjamin stir in her arms. "He is not a parcel to be hidden away. He needs a home. He needs warmth and care and people who love him, not a tower and a set of guards."

"And even the palace would not be secure enough from Le Corbeau," Fitzwilliam added grimly. "Someone would slip. There would be whispers, spies. And harboring him openly would provoke Napoleon. Fleeing French loyalists are one thing. Housing a Bourbon in the seat of English power is another."

Mr. Bennet nodded. "What do you think we should do, then, Lizzy?"

She looked down at Benjamin in her arms, his tiny fist curled against her chest, his breath warm against her collarbone. She kissed the top of his head as he nestled into her.

"I think," she said slowly, "that we need to end this. We cannot guard every door, every window, every servant's tongue forever."

They all stared at her.

She met each of their gazes in turn—her father's stern, Fitzwilliam's calculating, and finally Darcy's, which held an emotion so raw she could barely stand to meet it.

"I think," she said again, stronger this time, "we need to draw him out. And I believe the only way to do that… is to make me the target instead."

Chapter 25

The room erupted.

"No," Darcy said sharply, rising to his feet. "Absolutely not."

"I forbid it," Mr. Bennet barked, nearly at the same moment.

Colonel Fitzwilliam swore under his breath, and had the circumstances not been so dire, Elizabeth would have laughed. Instead, she raised a hand, and the room quieted.

"Listen to me," she said firmly. "Based on what Colonel Fitzwilliam has told us about Le Corbeau, I am already a target. I have stopped him from completing his mission twice now. I daresay I could recognize him by his eyes or his scent. And since a woman was able to beat him off, I imagine his pride is now wounded, too. And surely he cannot be so fearsome if my little parasol was the means of his undoing."

Her attempt to lighten the mood failed. Her father was scowling and Darcy looked stricken. It was Colonel Fitzwilliam who spoke next. "She has a point," he said slowly, eyes narrowed. "He will want to silence her."

"What do you have in mind, Lizzy?" Mr. Bennet asked.

She drew in a breath. "The Netherfield ball is the day after tomorrow. I will begin spreading word today that I recognized him based on his features—something I could use to identify him again. Maybe we say that the attack helped me remember that I had seen him fleeing after discovering Mr. Smithson or something. I shall make it known I intend to give my account to Sir William, but only after the ball. I will claim that my mother refuses to let anything interrupt our preparations."

"She would, too," Mr. Bennet muttered, a wry expression passing over his face. "The house could burn to the ground, and she would still insist Lydia's hem must be even."

Elizabeth pressed on. "Meanwhile, you can use the militia to inspect the soldiers. If he was struck on the head, he may be bruised or favoring one side. That should narrow your search—or at least increase his desperation."

Fitzwilliam nodded. "That might work. It would certainly light a fire under him."

"How can you even be considering this?" Darcy blurted out, looking at Mr. Bennet.

"Because I see no other way forward," the older man said, his shoulders sagging. "If you have any alternatives that would be more successful, I beg you to share them now."

Shaking his head in resignation, Darcy slumped forward and put his head in his hands.

"And," Elizabeth continued, her voice steady, "you will say, for Benjamin's safety, that he is to be brought to Netherfield for the ball. There will be a nursemaid, of course, carrying a bundle."

"But the child will not be at Netherfield?" the colonel asked.

"No, he will remain here, heavily guarded."

"Go on," the colonel urged when she paused. "What else are you thinking?"

Elizabeth's hands fidgeted together as she explained. "During the ball, I could leave to go check on Benjmain. It will be a perfect moment for Le

Corbeau—there will be chaos, new servants hired just for the event, a hundred distractions. He will act."

"I do not like this," Darcy said, his voice low. "Even with guards—"

"He will not expect guards," Elizabeth said, wincing at the look that crossed Darcy's face. "I could dismiss the nurse and send the footman away on some errand. But in truth, you will have soldiers stationed— hidden. When he comes for me, you will already be waiting."

There was silence for a long moment. "I think this has potential," the colonel said slowly. "Although he may suspect something if you disappeared without a reason during the ball. Perhaps if a footman were to tell you Benjamin was ill? Then the fact that you were leaving would be more public as well."

Then Mr. Bennet sighed and ran a hand through his hair. "As much as I despise this, I cannot help but agree."

Darcy said nothing. His jaw was clenched, and Elizabeth could see the war waging in his eyes.

"Can you think of a better plan?" she asked him softly, her eyes imploring him to understand. "One that will stop him before he tries again?"

Darcy looked away, then shook his head.

At last, Mr. Bennet nodded. "Very well. I do not like it, but I do not see another option."

The colonel straightened. "I will ride into Meryton and speak with Colonel Forster. We must get things in place immediately."

"I shall begin drafting letters to send to London," Darcy said, his voice grave. "My footmen can be here within the day."

"I will speak to Hill," Mr. Bennet added. "We shall say the baby is ill and must be kept in Lizzy's room. That will explain why the cradle is not returned to the nursery."

He stood from his desk, causing the other three to rise with him. Coming around, he extended his arms to Elizabeth. "Here, I will return him upstairs, my dear. You be so good as to show our guests to the door."

Bewildered at her father's offer, Elizabeth made to protest, but then realized she might have the opportunity to speak to Darcy alone. She accepted and passed the baby to Mr. Bennet, then followed the two remaining gentlemen down the hall to the front entrance.

The colonel collected his gloves and hat, then said, "Darcy, I will meet you at Netherfield in two hours, after I speak with Colonel Forster. There is much to be done."

Darcy gave a short nod, but his gaze was fixed on Elizabeth. He was watching her with such intensity, such quiet resolve, that her heart gave a hard, painful beat.

They were alone.

Elizabeth swallowed nervously and looked down at her clasped hands, unsure of what she wanted to say. The silence stretched between them, not uncomfortable, but charged—like the breathless pause before a storm or the stillness before a violin's first note.

Before her jumbled mind could process anything, she blurted out, "I suppose you must be going as well."

"In a moment," he said softly.

Something in his tone made her glance up. His eyes met hers—dark, solemn, intense—and her heart began to pound in her chest.

"Miss Elizabeth," he said softly, and her name in his voice sent a shiver down her spine.

"Yes, Mr. Darcy?"

"I had intended to wait." He took a step closer. "To give you space, time, peace. I thought… when all this was over, when we were safe again, then I might speak. But last night changed everything. The idea that I might have lost you—that he was in your home—"

He broke off, his jaw tightening, and she saw the flicker of anguish in his eyes.

"I cannot wait, Elizabeth. I am in love with you. Hopelessly, irrevocably. I have loved you for weeks now. Perhaps longer, though I only allowed myself to name it recently. You are the bravest, cleverest, most astonishing woman I have ever met."

Her breath caught, and she knew— as surely as she knew her own name—that she loved him in return.

"If you can return my affections," he continued, "if there is even the possibility you might love me in return—then I ask you to let me offer you what I can. My name. My protection. My devotion."

He took a step forward, voice quieter now, almost reverent. "Elizabeth… will you marry me?"

A thousand thoughts raced through her mind. Of course she should not say yes—not now, not with so much still unknown. It was too soon. It was dangerous. It was madness.

And yet.

In his eyes, she saw everything she had ever longed for: truth, honor, tenderness. The fire that had burned through her since the moment she'd faced Le Corbeau in the nursery was matched now by another—one steadier, quieter, but no less fierce.

Still, her voice was trembling when she said, "You know that I am stubborn. That I speak out of turn. That I tease and laugh and sometimes question things no one else dares to."

A faint smile curved his lips. "I do."

"You also know that my family is noisy and troublesome, and that we are in the midst of a situation that would terrify most men."

"I do."

"And yet you still ask?"

"I do."

She drew in a breath, and something in her chest eased, some ache she had not fully recognized until now. "Then, yes," she whispered.

His expression changed—hope blooming into something almost disbelieving. "Yes?"

"Yes," she said again, firmer this time, and she smiled. "I will marry you, Mr. Darcy."

There was a moment of stillness between them, wonder and disbelief suspended in the air. Then—he let out a breath, like a man who had been drowning and had just found the surface.

He reached for her hand, lifting it to his lips. "You have made me the happiest man alive."

She laughed softly. "I hope you will still feel this way after the ball," she teased, "but you have made *me* the happiest of women."

"Forget the ball; I would feel this way even if the world burned around us."

She leaned in, unable to help herself, her voice a murmur. "Let us hope it does not come to that."

He smiled, a real, open smile, and gently touched her cheek. "No matter what happens, we face it together now."

She nodded, hand still in his. "Together."

And as they stood there in the quiet entryway, the morning light peeking through the windows, the world and its dangers faded into the background for one precious moment. There was only the warmth of his hands, the truth in his eyes, and the beginning of something beautiful.

Neither was ready to break the spell between them.

Elizabeth still held his hand, marveling at the quiet warmth of it, the way his fingers curved gently around hers, not possessive but protective. His presence, which had once so unnerved her, now settled into her like a balm— steady, anchoring.

She had never felt more herself.

Darcy studied her face for a long moment, then gave a faint, sheepish smile. "I ought to confess something."

"Oh?" she said lightly, her thumb brushing against his.

"I spoke to your father this morning."

Her brows rose. "You did?"

"I asked his permission to address you. He did not grant permission for marriage—not yet." A flicker of self-deprecating humor crossed his expression. "He said he would allow me to ask for your hand, but only if you accepted. If you had not, I imagine I should have been ejected from the house by now."

Elizabeth laughed softly. "That sounds very like him."

Darcy's voice gentled. "He was… protective. Rightly so. But you ought to speak with him before I address him again."

"Very well," she agreed, "but I would prefer that we do not make any formal announcement to anyone—including my mother—until after the ball."

That coaxed a grin from him. "You wish to postpone the inevitable celebration?"

"I wish," she said dryly, "to preserve what remains of our wits. The moment she finds out, she will insist on inviting half of Meryton to the wedding and will likely ask if we might be married by next Tuesday with a common license…or in six months with a special license, which she may just demand, whether or not it would even be possible."

Darcy chuckled. "You have a point. Shall we keep it our secret, then?"

"For now. Just ours. And Papa's, of course. I may wish to tell Jane, though, and I imagine you will want to tell your cousin and friend."

"I will tell the colonel, but Bingley cannot keep a secret to save his life. He is too honest and transparent."

She laughed lightly. He looked at her for a moment more, his expression unreadable and full.

Then he bowed, a slow, reverent gesture that carried far more weight than formality. "Until tomorrow, my love."

She curtsied in return, lips trembling on a smile. "Until tomorrow."

As he stepped out into the morning light, Elizabeth remained in the hallway, her fingers brushing her lips, her heart beating faster than it ever had before. The world was still full of danger, still darkened by shadows—but her heart was alight.

She had said yes.

And somehow, that changed everything.

$$\mathfrak{X}$$

Elizabeth spent the remainder of the day in a kind of golden haze, drifting through her duties as though she walked in a dream. Her heart was still light with the weight of her answer to Mr. Darcy—her Mr. Darcy—and yet, she had told no one. Even Jane remained unaware. Though she longed to share her happiness, something within her held back. It was too new, too precious. She wanted a little more time to feel it privately—to turn the word yes over in her mind like a secret jewel.

There was precious little time to dwell on it, however. With purpose and careful subtlety, Elizabeth set about the task she had agreed to—sowing rumors with the skill of a gardener anticipating spring.

To Mrs. Long, she mentioned that she had caught a glimpse of her assailant's face, and that to keep Benjamin safe, he would be moved to Netherfield for the ball.

To Lady Lucas, she added that she was almost certain it was the same man who had attacked the insurance agent, and she would most definitely recognize him again.

To Charlotte, she murmured loudly that she would be giving Sir William a full description the morning after the ball, once Benjamin was safe at Netherfield.

Each word planted with care. Each glance deliberately uncertain. Each pause filled with just enough suggestion to spark speculation. The effect was exactly what they needed. Whispers began to pass from drawing room to dining table, trailing behind her like smoke from a candle. Shock and indignation met her in equal measure from all corners of the neighborhood—particularly when it became known that someone had broken into Longbourn in the dead of night. That she and the child were both unharmed seemed only to magnify the drama.

By the time she finally reached her bed that evening, her limbs ached with exhaustion, and her throat was hoarse from so much careful conversation. Yet as she drifted into sleep, her fingers curled loosely beneath her cheek, her last thought was of a man with solemn eyes and an earnest voice, asking her to be his wife.

The next afternoon was bright and cold, the kind of winter day where every sound seemed sharper in the still air. Longbourn was a flurry of movement and barely contained chaos.

Elizabeth's room was awash in soft light as she stood before her mirror, holding her breath while Jane fastened the final clasp at the back of her gown. The dark cream fabric shimmered with a delicate sheen, and a sapphire blue ribbon complemented her dark curls and the pale glow of her skin. It was not a new gown, but with a few clever stitches and the addition of a silver sash borrowed from Jane, it looked nearly new.

"Turn," Jane said softly, and Elizabeth obeyed. Jane's fingers tugged gently at the sleeves, smoothing the seams. "It suits you, Lizzy. You will be the most beautiful woman at the ball."

"I believe the honor will fall to you, Jane," Elizabeth said. Then she smirked and added, "Though with Lydia not in attendance, I may succeed in being your second."

"Lizzy!" Jane admonished in protest, though she could not hide a slight smile. "You ought not to say such things—especially not when Lydia might be able to hear."

Too late.

From the corridor, Lydia's voice wailed, "Why should they get to go to the ball, when we must stay home like children? I am nearly sixteen!"

"I wish I could stay home," came Mary's terse voice. "Be grateful for what you have."

"But that is because you do not care about dancing," Kitty replied from behind their closed door. "You only want to read essays and talk about funerals."

"I do not! I—" Mary's voice cut off abruptly, as though she had caught herself mid-sentence.

A thump, a sniffle, and then more footsteps followed—Mrs. Bennet's, no doubt.

Elizabeth winced and glanced at Jane in the mirror. "Shall I guess how long it will be before Mama tries to reverse her own ruling?"

"She has tried twice already," Jane said with a fond sigh. "Papa has stood firm."

Down the hall, Lydia's complaints reached a new crescendo. "Elizabeth *always* gets to go! She always gets *everything*—and she is not even pretty! Just clever, and she always knows who people are by *smell*, like a dog!"

Elizabeth rolled her eyes but smiled despite herself. "Charming, is she not?"

Jane's mouth twitched. "You must admit—it is something of a gift."

"Well, let us hope it proves useful this evening." Elizabeth turned back to her reflection and reached for a silver hairpin shaped like a laurel leaf. "I do not suppose my sense of smell will help me identify a disguised murderer, but I dare say it may help me detect his strong cologne in a crowd."

Jane arched a brow as she arranged Elizabeth's curls, coaxing them into soft waves. "You speak as though you are not nervous."

"I am utterly terrified." Elizabeth gave her a smile that trembled at the edges. "But I am doing my best not to show it."

They stood in silence for a few moments as Jane finished with her hair and then turned to her own preparations. Mary passed their room once, pausing long enough to ask in a small voice, "Do you think I should wear the green ribbon or the ivory?"

Elizabeth looked up in surprise. "The green, I think. It brings out your eyes."

Mary nodded, clearly trying to conceal how much the compliment pleased her and disappeared down the hall without another word.

Before heading downstairs, Elizabeth stopped at her mother's room. Benjamin's cradle had been moved to Mrs. Bennet's changing room, which did not have any windows and could therefore be better guarded. It would also allow any crying or candlelight to be prevented by being seen from the outside, in case Le Cordeau was watching.

The lad sat on the floor with a few toys, having only recently learned to sit up on his own. She reached down and placed a soft kiss on his head. "Be brave, my dear boy. Remember that no matter what happens, you are loved."

"We will keep him safe, Miss Lizzy," said the nurse, a fierce expression on her face.

"Thank you."

By the time Elizabeth moved to the stairs, the rest of the household was in a flurry of shawls, gloves, and final instructions to the footmen. A carriage basket had been stuffed with a doll wrapped all in blankets, giving the appearance that Benjamin was going with them to Netherfield.

She paused at the top to take a steadying breath before descending. Her father stood waiting at the base of the stairs. As she approached, his expression softened into something both proud and wistful.

"My dear," he said, offering his arm, "you are a vision. Mr. Darcy will be speechless—though as I understand it, that is not saying very much."

Elizabeth flushed but smiled. "Thank you, Papa."

He leaned closer and whispered, "Though I will admit, if he does not look at you with worship in his eyes, I shall begin to suspect he is not half so clever as we have all been led to believe."

"I shall try not to notice," she whispered back.

Moments later, the family assembled for departure. Jane was radiant in a gown of soft rose with delicate embroidery at the hem, her expression a portrait of serene delight.

"Mr. Bingley has asked me for the first dance," she confided as they settled into the carriage.

Elizabeth raised a brow. "That is wonderful. I hope it is the first of many."

"Do you have a partner?"

"Mr. Darcy asked me for the first," Elizabeth murmured.

Jane turned to her, eyes wide. "Mr. Darcy? Truly? I would have thought he would ask Miss Bingley, given she is his hostess."

"That honor may fall to Colonel Fitzwilliam. As the son of an earl, he ranks above Mr. Darcy."

As the carriage rolled toward Netherfield and the fields turned silver with frost in the fading light, Elizabeth sat with her gloved hands folded in her lap, her stomach twisting with anticipation. Not only would tonight be her first evening as Mr. Darcy's intended—if secretly so—but it might also be the night Le Corbeau made his final, fateful move.

"Are you ready for the evening?" her father asked quietly.

Elizabeth turned her head, and though her pulse danced with nerves, her voice was steady when she replied, "I am."

Chapter 26

The carriage turned onto the long, winding drive that led to Netherfield Park, the wheels crunching softly over gravel rimed with frost. As the house came into view, Elizabeth's breath caught in her throat.

Netherfield Park stood bathed in bright light, every window ablaze with dozens—no, hundreds—of candles, their warm flicker making the great windows gleam like polished gold in the dark night.

A collective murmur rippled through the Bennet family.

"Oh!" Jane breathed, her hands clasped before her.

"Gracious," Mrs. Bennet whispered. "What a grand display, but I daresay he can afford the expense."

Even Mr. Bennet raised his brows in appreciation. "It appears Mr. Bingley intends to light half of Hertfordshire. Let us hope he does not frighten the livestock."

As the carriage rolled to a stop before the entrance, Elizabeth found herself unable to look away. Garlands of greenery and white winter roses twined around the columns, and footmen stood at crisp attention beneath gas lanterns. Every detail, from the polished brass fittings to the snowy steps cleared of even a single flake, gleamed with elegance.

For all her pretensions, Miss Bingley certainly does know how to plan a ball.

Elizabeth climbed down carefully, gathering her skirts and drawing her shawl close. Her nerves, which had calmed somewhat during the ride, stirred again as she looked up at the towering façade of the house, causing her heart to pound. The house looked like something from a fairy tale—

glowing and resplendent, untouched by fear or secrets. It was difficult to imagine it would be the site of a trap.

Somewhere behind those windows lies a traitor and a murderer.

They ascended the steps together, and a footman opened the door with practiced grace. Inside, the entrance hall had been transformed into a winter wonderland. Candles floated in glass globes suspended from the ceiling. Music drifted faintly from the ballroom beyond, and the scent of pine and oranges lingered in the air.

Elizabeth whispered to the nurse, who was holding the bundle with the false Benjamin, and the woman nodded and made her way towards the staircase to go up to the nursery.

Guests were already arriving, forming a tidy line to greet the hosts. The Bingleys and Hursts stood in fine array at the head of the receiving line. Mr. Bingley beamed, his face wreathed in smiles as he shook hands and welcomed his neighbors.

"Miss Bennet," Mr. Bingley said warmly to Jane. "You look lovely. I am most glad you are here."

Mrs. Hurst stood at his side with quiet elegance, and Mr. Hurst looked moderately awake. Caroline Bingley wore a vivid orange gown embroidered with gold—stunning in its extravagance and clearly chosen to dazzle. Her eyes flicked over the incoming guests with a queen's narrowed scrutiny.

Elizabeth curtsied low to the hosts, offering Miss Bingley the same polite, bland smile she had offered everyone else. The haughty woman sniffed in return and quickly turned to the next guest, leaving Elizabeth to the Hursts.

Mr. Hurst nodded absently as his wife fluttered a fan with a bored expression. But it was not until she reached the end of the receiving line that her eyes locked with Darcy's—and the world seemed to hush.

Her steps slowed ever so slightly she took in his handsome appearance. His dark coat was perfectly fitted, his cravat immaculate, and his eyes—oh, his eyes—were fixed on her as though she had just walked out of his dreams.

When she reached the end of the line, he stepped forward, bowing deeply. "Miss Elizabeth," he said, his voice low and reverent, "you are absolutely radiant this evening. I believe I may be the most fortunate man in all of England." Her blush rose immediately. "You flatter me, sir."

"I am only speaking truth." His eyes lingered on hers. "I look forward to the first dance with great anticipation."

Her heart fluttered once more, only this time, her anticipation was of a more pleasurable nature. "As do I. Although you may need to check your card again, sir; I believe I am to dance with"—her voice dropped to a whisper— "my betrothed."

His eyes gleamed. "Then I shall appeal to your generosity and hope you will not rescind the favor."

Before she could reply, Colonel Fitzwilliam stepped forward, elegant in his regimentals and very much enjoying the spectacle. "I believe I may claim the second set, Miss Elizabeth? Unless my cousin intends to steal all of your dances tonight."

Elizabeth smiled. "I would be delighted, Colonel."

Darcy, not to be outdone, added, "And the supper set, if you are not otherwise engaged."

She hesitated—just long enough to enjoy the way his hand twitched slightly at his side—before she grinned at him, her eyes twinkling. "You may, sir."

A sharp, strangled noise came from nearby.

Miss Bingley's fan snapped shut with a violent crack. Her smile, plastered on for the benefit of those behind them, wavered like a candle in a draft. A muscle twitched in her cheek as her gaze darted between Elizabeth and the two gentlemen.

"My, Miss Elizabeth," she said in a voice sharp with forced civility. "How very popular you have become. One might think *you* were the hostess."

Elizabeth opened her mouth to reply, but Fitzwilliam, ever the diplomat, swept in with a grin. "And yet no one has yet claimed your first set, Miss Bingley. What a shocking oversight." He bowed deeply. "May I have the honor?"

Miss Bingley, momentarily caught between rage and triumph, managed a tight nod. "If you insist."

"Oh, I do."

Elizabeth caught the faintest twinkle in the colonel's eyes and had to look away quickly before she laughed aloud. Miss Bingley then turned her gaze towards Darcy's, giving him a pleading expression beneath batting eyes. The colonel, however, once again provided cover as he offered Miss Bingley his arm and led her away.

Turning his attention back to Elizabeth, Darcy asked quietly, "Are you well?"

"I am," she replied. "Though my stomach feels like I have swallowed a flock of sparrows."

His expression sobered slightly. "We will keep you safe."

She nodded once, the ballroom doors opening before them to reveal a dream of light and motion.

Darcy offered his arm. "Shall we, Miss Elizabeth?"

"Yes," she said softly, placing her gloved hand atop his. "Let the evening begin."

X

Darcy could scarcely believe it.

Elizabeth was radiant.

She stood across from him at the center of the set, cheeks faintly flushed with color, eyes bright with that quick, curious spark that never failed to undo him. Her gown—a rich cream silk embroidered in gold— clung to her figure in a manner that was entirely modest and yet entirely distracting. The candlelight caught in the dark waves of her hair, pulled half up with deliberate softness, and he could not stop staring.

She was, quite simply, the most beautiful woman in the room.

And she had said *yes*.

It still stunned him to remember. The knowledge of it burned in his chest—warm and steady, like a brand seared into his heart.

He knew it was not for proposals or passion. Tonight would decide everything. Their safety, their future, Benjamin's very life.

And yet for the length of this dance, he was determined to steal one perfect moment from the edge of chaos.

The music began, and Elizabeth stepped forward, meeting him with practiced ease. Their hands met and parted again as they turned. There was silence between them for a time—only the rustle of skirts, the glide of slippers, and the swell of violins. Each time their hands touched, a jolt shot up his arm. The heated glances between them made him wish he could sweep her off her feet, carrying her away so they could be alone.

Darcy felt all eyes on them, but for once, he did not care.

Finally, Elizabeth tilted her head and said lightly, "You are very silent, Mr. Darcy. Are you consulting your mental list of eligible young ladies to whom you will next refuse a dance?"

He smiled. "Only narrowing it down to those I have not already offended beyond redemption."

"That will be a very short list indeed."

"Then I had best stay close to the only one who still tolerates me."

She arched a brow. "I tolerate you now, do I?"

"Gladly and gloriously," he said under his breath, and her eyes sparkled in return.

They stepped apart, then back together again.

"You know," she said in a musing tone, "you really ought to say something about the size of the room. Or perhaps the number of couples. That is the usual formula."

Darcy tilted his head. "Would you prefer I comment on the weather, or offer a dry remark about the price of ribbons in Meryton?"

She gave a mock gasp. "You do know how to flirt."

"Do I?"

"Barely."

He huffed a quiet laugh, then leaned a little closer. "I confess I was too overwhelmed to remember my conversational duties. You are quite— bewitching tonight."

Her eyes widened, but she only murmured, "That will do nicely for a start."

They danced in silence for a few steps more, the air between them warm and charged.

"It is quite crowded tonight. I see Mr. Bingley has invited the officers."

He nodded, sobering slightly. "He has. We may have… influenced him into inviting them in order to give certain people more access. His sister did not wish to do so, and he would have acceded to her wishes had Colonel Fitzwilliam and I not… intervened."

Elizabeth frowned. "Does he give way to his sister often?"

"I am afraid so."

She bit her lip, drawing his gaze to her mouth. "That does not bode well for my sister's future happiness. Jane is so good and giving, and if her husband does not protect her, she will allow herself to be walked all over."

He grimaced. "Perhaps several hints to him would not amiss. Colonel Fitzwilliam and I will do what we can to assist in the matter."

"Thank you. I appreciate your care over my sister."

"She is to be my sister soon, as well. I would be remiss if I did not do what I could to secure her happiness."

Elizabeth gave him a brilliant smile, and joy filled his chest. Then she asked, "Did Mr. Wickham accompany his fellow officers?"

"He did."

"Do you think he holds up well under the present scrutiny?"

Darcy's eyes flicked briefly across the room, toward the back where the officers stood talking amongst themselves. "I have not had much opportunity to speak with him—he and I are meant to behave as if we still bear a grudge. But from what I can observe, he plays his part well."

"I hope it is not too hard for him."

"Strangely," Darcy said, his voice gentling, "I believe he feels some purpose in it. And I have you to thank for helping us find a resolution. I owe you more than I can say."

Her lips parted, but she said nothing—only held his gaze for a long, quiet moment.

The music slowed.

With great reluctance, Darcy stepped back and extended his arm to escort her from the floor. As they walked, she whispered, "I am quite amazed, sir. You did not cough once during our dance."

His brow rose in amazement, and he placed his hand over hers on his arm, giving a gentle squeeze. As they approached a group of chairs, Colonel Fitzwilliam appeared, Miss Bingley clinging to his side after their own dance. He offered Darcy and Elizabeth an easy bow. "You two dance splendidly."

"Thank you," Elizabeth said, paying no attention Miss Bingley's quiet snort of disgust. "You do as well."

"It is my turn, I believe, in a few minutes," the colonel said, also ignoring the woman smoldering with resentment at his side.

"Indeed, it is," Darcy replied, though his eyes lingered on Elizabeth's face a moment longer. "Enjoy yourself, Miss Elizabeth."

"I shall try."

"I cannot imagine what possessed Charles to invite so many soldiers," Miss Bingley burst out, her ire evident. "I do so prefer gentlemen of refinement. Officers can be so... common."

Darcy frowned severely at her as Elizabeth gaped. The colonel chuckled. "My apologies, Miss Bingley. I had not thought that the second son of an earl would demean any occasion, even if I am dressed in a red coat."

Miss Bingley flushed a brilliant shade of red, which even Darcy could tell clashed horribly with her hair and dress. *What is the woman thinking, putting such colors together?* he wondered. *It is a good thing Georgiana is too young to go shopping with her. I shudder to think what she would order.*

"Oh no!" Miss Bingley gasped. "I did not mean *you*, sir. Certainly not! No one could ever mistake you for a member of the militia! No, I merely meant that I prefer to dance with men who are more refined and gentlemanly."

She batted her eyes furiously at Darcy as she said this, who did his best to not blanch and shrink away. Fortunately, the first strands of the music began, and he had an excuse to leave. He inclined his head with cool politeness. "My next partner awaits. If you will excuse me."

He did not look back to see her reaction. He did not have to. The flicker of satisfaction in Elizabeth's eyes as he turned away told him everything.

As he searched out Miss Jane Bennet, the colonel escorted Elizabeth out.

And Miss Bingley was left alone. Partnerless. And enraged.

Nearby, a commonplace officer saw her expression and smiled.

This will be all too easy.

)(

Elizabeth moved easily through the steps of the dance, grateful to have the colonel for her partner. His energy, though tempered by the room's tension, was as lighthearted and easy as ever. But she knew better than to assume he was only here for the pleasure of conversation. His eyes swept the crowd regularly, sharp and discerning beneath his pleasant smile.

"You look as though you are waiting for someone to jump out from behind the lemonade table," she said softly as they turned.

"Only the usual assassins and revolutionaries," he replied with a grin, eyes flicking to the far corner where several officers were posted. "Though the scrawny fellow by the cheese tray does look like he might collapse under the weight of his own sword."

Elizabeth laughed. "Truly, Colonel, I do not know whether I should be reassured or alarmed."

"Perhaps a bit of both. This is a ball, after all."

They separated and skipped around the couple next to them. As they came together again, she tilted her head. "If I did not know any better, I would say your observations were due to watching a young lady with her partner. So, tell me, Colonel, which of our fair Hertfordshire maidens has caught your eye?"

He blinked, clearly caught off guard. "What?"

"Oh, do not pretend," she teased. "You watched someone very closely a moment ago. It must have been for flirtation, not espionage. You blushed."

380

"I did not."

"You did." She peered at him in genuine surprise. "Well, perhaps not, but you are doing so *now*."

He coughed into his hand, clearly flustered, and Elizabeth laughed at the idea that her teasing had rung true. "I am sorry," she said softly. "You do not have to say anything."

"No," he said after a pause, the mask sliding neatly back into place. "You were not wrong. But some things are... complicated. And some people are not yet ready to hear them."

She understood. "Then I shall leave it be. For now."

"Thank you."

They moved together in companionable silence for a few moments, then Elizabeth glanced at him slyly. "So, if you will not tell me who you admire, you must at least tell me what Darcy was like growing up."

"Oh, you wish for scandal, then."

"Of course. Any stories of rebellion? Mischief? A youthful prank or two?"

Fitzwilliam chuckled. "We were not entirely without mischief. There was the time he and I climbed onto the roof of the Matlock estate to prove we could see the Irish Sea—"

"You could not."

"We could not. And we nearly broke our necks proving it. But for the most part, Darcy was not a child given to recklessness."

She frowned. "Because of his illness?"

"Because of his father," Fitzwilliam said quietly. "You know about the illness, of course. His mother had not been dead a year, and her passing took away any ounce of compassion known at Pemberley. My uncle was a rather hard man."

"I see," she murmured.

"His first Christmas home after having been at school, he played outside with Georgiana. They came inside when his lungs seized up, and he was in the foyer coughing like nothing I had ever heard—we were visiting, you see. My father was attempting to help him, and several servants hovered around. Uncle Darcy came into the room, saw the scene, and rather than being alarmed for his son, he—" Fitzwilliam paused. "He blamed him. Said it was a performance. Said he was weak. Every time Darcy coughed after that, he tried harder to hide it. To bear it in silence. It only made him worse."

Elizabeth's throat tightened. "How horrible."

Fitzwilliam appeared to not hear her; he was lost in his memories. "After that, Darcy was sent away to school, and he only returned home in the summers when it was warm. Each winter, my uncle refused to let him come home for the holidays—he did not want his malady disturbing the house—or rather, himself." Fitzwilliam's mouth tightened. "So instead, Darcy was sent to stay with us in London."

Elizabeth's heart ached. "That must have been difficult."

"It was. He would never say so, of course. But I could see how much it hurt. One afternoon, just after a walk, he had a bad fit—he went into the drawing room, thinking it was empty. But my mother was there, seated in the corner. She called his name and tried to reach him—wanted to help—but the sound of his deep, wracking attack upset her nerves too much. She has always been delicate, and... she swooned."

"Oh no," Elizabeth groaned softly.

"He was still coughing too violently to do anything. He managed to make it to the bellpull and ring for a servant. When a maid finally arrived, his body was still wracked with the coughing fit, leaving him unable to do anything but gesture towards my mother. He could barely breathe, let alone explain."

Her hand tightened slightly in his grip as the clasped hands to spin.

"My mother was mortified once she recovered. She tried to reassure him that it was not his fault—she even wrote to him afterward—but I do not think he ever really let it go. He blamed himself. He always did. I will never forget the look on Darcy's face when I joined them in that room: mortified, silent."

They danced in silence for a few steps, her heart breaking a little more with each beat.

"I never knew." She swallowed past the lump in her throat. "Thank you for telling me."

"I knew he never would himself, but as you are to be married, it is important that you know," Fitzwilliam said simply. "But it is part of him. The reason he holds the world at such a distance. The reason he does not speak unless he has something worth saying. You are one of the few to cross that wall. I am very glad he has you now."

Elizabeth swallowed hard, blinking back tears. "Then I must be very careful not to wound him."

Fitzwilliam smiled gently. "He is stronger than you think. But thank you. For loving him."

"I will take good care of his heart."

Any reply was swallowed in the gentle applause of the crowd at the end of the set. He took her arm and began to guide her towards her father. "Are you ready to do what must be done?" he asked gently.

Elizabeth nodded, though her voice trembled. "Yes. But if anything goes wrong—if this all fails—you must promise me something."

"Anything."

"Tell him I loved him. That it was not his fault. He will blame himself—I know he will—but he must not. Not for this."

Fitzwilliam's eyes softened. "Audentes Fortuna iuvat." *Fortune favors the brave.*

Elizabeth smiled, blinking quickly to keep the tears from falling. "Ave, imperator; morituri te salutant." *Hail, Emperor; those who are about to die salute you.*

He gaped at her. "You speak Latin? And have read Suetonius."

"I had a very curious childhood."

He shook his head in amazement. "You and Darcy are well matched indeed."

She was laughing as they reached Mr. Bennet, who looked at them curiously but said nothing. Darcy approached from the other direction, having left Jane to Bingley's attentive care.

"It is time," Fitzwilliam said quietly.

Elizabeth's heart beat like a drum, but she met Darcy's gaze without flinching.

"Let the games begin," she said.

And may we be the ones to win.

Chapter 27

The air in the room was thick with candle smoke and scent. Elizabeth danced two more sets—one with Mr. Bingley, who seemed positively transported as he spoke glowingly of Jane's grace, wit, and remarkable gentleness, and another with Captain Carter, whose name she nearly forgot. He was kind enough, though his conversation centered mostly on the quality of the punch and the rumor that a peer of the realm was in attendance.

Her smiles came easily, but her mind was elsewhere.

She did her best to glance now and then toward her father, Colonel Fitzwilliam, and Mr. Darcy without drawing attention, reassured by their watchful presence. Still, her thoughts remained tethered to the nursery upstairs, where the decoy lay waiting.

Her next partner was Wickham, who approached her as designed. Everyone turned to stare as he approached her, eager to see if she would identify him as the murderer.

He appeared before her with his usual charming grin, bowing with a flourish that earned him a flutter of glances from nearby young ladies. "Miss Bennet," he said with a hint of strain in his eyes, "may I have the honor?"

She gave a dramatic pause, causing everyone nearby to hold their breath. Before she could respond, a footman approached, his voice carefully loud enough to carry.

"Pardon me, Miss Elizabeth. The nurse sends word that the baby has developed a fever. She begs you come at once."

A hush seemed to ripple outward from the words. Conversations stilled. A few heads turned. Elizabeth's heart pounded, but she did not allow it to show.

She turned quickly to Wickham with a soft, apologetic smile. "Forgive me, Lieutenant. Duty calls."

"Of course," he said, stepping back with a brief bow. "I hope the child recovers swiftly."

Elizabeth inclined her head and turned, her steps measured and graceful as she crossed the floor and exited the ballroom to a chorus of gossip.

Good, everyone will soon know that I have left the room. Now all there is to do is go upstairs… and wait.

Her heart thudded in her chest, her mouth suddenly dry. Every rustle of silk, every echoing step in the marble corridor seemed too loud, too exposed.

She ascended the stairs with practiced calm, her hand steady on the banister. A few guests glanced curiously as she passed, but she met no one's eyes. Only when she reached the third-floor landing did she allow her shoulders to tighten. The nursery door creaked open beneath her hand, and she went in.

The room was dim, lit only by the low glow of the fire and a single oil lamp on the small table near the crib. The air was warm, almost stifling, filled with the scent of lavender oil and milk.

The nurse stood when she saw Elizabeth and bobbed a curtsy. "He's quieted some, miss, but he is flushed."

Elizabeth nodded and approached the cradle, peering down at the carefully swaddled bundle. The false baby—stuffed with blankets and tucked carefully beneath one of Benjamin's gowns—lay still. Elizabeth reached in and adjusted the blanket as though checking for fever.

"Would you fetch a cloth soaked in cool water?" she asked gently. "And have Samuel in the hallway go down to fetch a fresh basin. I will stay with him."

"Of course, miss."

The nurse gave her another curtsy and slipped out, the door clicking shut behind her.

Elizabeth exhaled slowly and took her seat beside the cradle.

She began to hum softly, smoothing the fabric as if calming a fretful child. Each breath came with effort now—not from fear, but from anticipation.

The trap was set.

And she was the bait.

✕

Darcy had never been so aware of the passing of time.

Each tick of his pocket watch in his coat pocket seemed to echo like a cannon blast in his ears, beating in time with his thumping heart. Though he stalked darkly along the edges of the room, watching the dancers, his mind was elsewhere—three floors up, in a quiet nursery, where Elizabeth waited alone.

His Elizabeth.

His hands were clasped tightly behind his back, every muscle in his frame straining to keep him rooted to the polished floor and not bolting up the stairs like a madman. The music, the laughter, the sparkle of chandeliers—all of it grated. It felt wrong to pretend all was well, to feign interest in flirtations and refreshments while she placed herself in danger.

He should never have let her do it.

What if something went awry? What if one of the guards hesitated? What if Le Corbeau was cleverer than they anticipated—faster, stronger, crueler? What if—

"Your expression would be terrifying, Mr. Darcy, were you not so very still."

He startled at the voice behind him and turned to see Mr. Bennet approaching, a glass of punch in hand and a raised brow.

Darcy's mask fell back into place with mechanical precision. "I was not aware I had an expression."

"Oh, you do not. Not visibly," Mr. Bennet said easily. "That's what makes it so unsettling. I would not have guessed anything at all, but the colonel sent me to fetch you. He said you were likely staring holes into the ceiling and needed someone to drag you back to earth."

Darcy's lips tightened into something approximating a smile. "Your daughter is very dear to me."

"I suspected as much." Mr. Bennet nodded sagely. "I, too, am contemplating storming the stairs and locking her in a pantry until this is all over. But I am assured there are plenty of guards stationed in and around the nursery. All seasoned men, retired or injured in service. My study is currently housing more in case someone makes an attempt there."

"But none of them are in the same room as her. Even those stationed in the nursery are hidden back in the small nurse's bedchamber behind a closed door."

"I know," Mr. Bennet said kindly. "I have the same concerns, but she was already in danger before this. At least we control the circumstances for now, as opposed to being surprised."

Darcy inclined his head. "Thank you. That does ease my mind—somewhat."

"She will be fine, Mr. Darcy." Mr. Bennet's tone turned unexpectedly gentle. "That girl may have been born in a bonnet of lace, but she came out swinging."

A small breath of laughter escaped Darcy before he could stop it.

But peace did not last long.

"Mr. Darcy!" came a sugary voice from his left. "There you are. I have been searching *everywhere* for you."

Darcy turned with reluctant politeness as Miss Bingley glided toward them, her orange gown shimmering far too aggressively in the candlelight. She stopped before him with an artful tilt of her head, opening her fan and fluttering it below her chin.

Her smile was bright, eyes alight with calculation, as she said, "I do hope the ball has met your standards. I did my best to ensure that I was giving the people of Meryton an example of what they would see amongst our circles, although I was forced to compromise in several areas."

"It is a fine evening," Darcy replied evenly, "and your efforts are evident."

"I am delighted to hear you say so," she said, tilting her head. "There are so few gentlemen who appreciate refinement properly. Most are taken in by a pretty face or a lively manner. I daresay true taste is much harder to find."

Mr. Bennet made a quiet noise of amusement beside them.

Miss Bingley leaned in a little, her tone lighter. "And now the supper dance approaches. Surely, as a gentleman of discernment, you will choose your partner with care. The hostess, for example, is a most suitable choice."

Darcy turned slightly, his brow lifting. "Do you suggest yourself, Miss Bingley?"

Her laugh was light and practiced. "Well, I would never presume. But I do happen to find myself without a partner, and you are here alone."

His eyes darted towards Mr. Bennet at his side, who did his best to hide a smirk at the woman's intentional slight.

She continued, voice soft and coaxing. "It would be such a shame for the hostess to go unpartnered at such an important moment. Do you not agree?"

He offered a polite smile. "I am sure you will find no shortage of gentlemen eager to correct the oversight."

The fan snapped closed with a quiet crack. "Oh, but I had hoped for a partner of particular refinement." Her smile strained. "One who appreciates true accomplishment in a lady."

Darcy inclined his head slightly, still not taking the bait.

Miss Bingley pressed on, her tone sweetening further. "You have often said you value women of accomplishment. I wonder—what do you consider a true accomplishment, Mr. Darcy?"

Darcy glanced briefly at Mr. Bennet, then back to Miss Bingley. "A woman of true accomplishment must possess rare qualities."

Miss Bingley beamed. "Indeed! A thorough knowledge of music, singing, drawing, dancing, and the modern languages—"

"Not merely those," Darcy interrupted gently. "I have known many women who possessed such accomplishments, but very few who possessed what I consider the true measure of refinement."

She blinked. "And what is that?"

Darcy's voice was cool but steady. "Compassion. Intelligence. Sincerity. Strength of character. The ability to laugh at oneself. Generosity of spirit. A willingness to act bravely and wisely, even when no one is watching."

Miss Bingley's mouth parted in offense, her cheeks coloring rapidly.

"And," he continued, his gaze steady, "the courage to protect the vulnerable at any cost. That, Miss Bingley, is what I find most admirable."

Mr. Bennet let out a low hum of approval beside him. "Well said," he murmured.

Miss Bingley stood stiffly, her composure barely intact. "Besides," he added, "I am afraid I am already engaged."

"To *another?*" Her eyes narrowed, incredulous. "Mr. Darcy, I must say I am surprised. You would dance with that… hoyden and her sister, but not with me?"

Darcy's voice was calm, low, and cutting. "Miss Elizabeth Bennet is a lady of intelligence, compassion, and extraordinary courage. She is the best judge of character I have ever known. She is fiercely loyal, speaks with sincerity, and possesses both wit and wisdom in equal measure. If these are not the marks of a true lady, then I should be ashamed to know one."

Miss Bingley's mouth opened and closed like a fish in a drying stream. Her jaw worked soundlessly, color high in her cheeks.

Before she could compose a retort, a sound split through the ballroom.

A scream.

Faint, distant, unmistakably female.

"Elizabeth!" Darcy cried.

)(

Elizabeth forced herself to look down at the false infant, cooing gently as though soothing a feverish child. Her hand stroked the top of the bundle, her eyes fixed on the shadowy corners of the room, ears straining for the slightest sound.

Then she smelled it. The same foreign, musky scent that she had smelled a few nights prior at Longbourn.

He's here!

Her body reacted before her mind caught up. She spun around to face the intruder, ducking low as she did so.

The glint of metal flashed as a dagger embedded itself into the wall where her head had been. Pain flared in her arm, and she gasped, clutching her sleeve where the blade had grazed her.

A figure wearing a red coat stepped forward out of the shadows, his face mostly concealed beneath the brim of a militia hat. He looked familiar.

What was his name again? Captain... Carter!

She had been briefly introduced to him at her aunt Philips's card party and danced a set with him this very evening. *He* was Le Corbeau?

But he seems so… normal.

There was no more time for thinking, processing.

He lunged at her.

Elizabeth flung herself aside, banging her hip on a rocking chair as she attempted to get away. Carter's momentum carried him into the cradle, overturning it with a violent crash. The fake baby rolled limply across the floor in his direction.

Carter snatched the bundle up, yanking back the blanket with a victorious grin that froze as soon as he saw it was empty.

"No," he gasped. "No!"

Elizabeth scrambled backward towards the door that led to the nurse's adjoining bedroom where the guards were supposed to be hidden, blood running warm down her arm. Carter rounded on her, his green eyes wild and filled with rage.

Where are they? Do not they know he's here?

Sucking in a deep breath, she screamed with all her might.

Doors exploded open—both the one behind her and the one that led to the hallway. Half a dozen men burst into the room, their movements quick and precise. Carter turned to run towards the window, and Elizabeth's heart clenched.

Not again!

"Do not let him get away!" she called. "It is him! He tried to kill me— he tried to kill the baby!"

He almost reached the window, but the nearest guard tackled him mid-stride. The others descended in a blur of motion, ropes already in hand.

Two guards wrestled Carter to his knees, binding his arms tightly. He thrashed once, but the rope held. Blood trickled from a split on his temple where he had hit the floor.

She sighed in relief.

Darcy barreled through the doorway. "Elizabeth!"

She hardly saw him before she was in his arms, her fingers gripping the lapels of his coat, her cheek pressed to his shoulder. He smelled like fresh air and warmth and safety, and she sank into the comfort of his embrace.

Mr. Bennet arrived seconds later, his cravat askew, a look of fury in his eyes. He took in the scene with a long, sweeping glance, then looked at Darcy with raised brows. "Well," he said dryly, "I see I have been replaced. Ah, the passage of time."

Elizabeth let out a choked laugh against Darcy's chest. He gave a breathless chuckle in return and tightened his hold on her.

Colonel Fitzwilliam stalked toward the bound figure. "Report."

Before they could speak, she turned her head and said indignantly, "I was nearly killed. He threw a knife at me, and if I had smelled him just a half-second later, I would have been dead."

Darcy looked down sharply and sucked in a breath. "You are bleeding."

"I am fine," she said faintly, though her arm throbbed with pain.

Mr. Bennet rounded on the colonel. "She is not fine! I thought you said she would be protected!"

"I take full responsibility," Fitzwilliam said, jaw tight. He turned and glared at one of the men, whom Elizabeth presumed to be the leader. "What happened?"

The guard straightened, his hand twitching up as if fighting back a salute. "We needed to be sure, sir. With witnesses. With evidence. We were watching from the adjoining room through a crack in the door, but he threw the knife so silently, we did not notice it until she had screamed. As soon as we heard her, we entered."

Understanding dawned as Elizabeth let out a slow, deep breath. "I see. If he had not reached for the cradle or attempted to attack me, it could have easily been explained away in court."

"That does not mean I will not wring his neck myself," Darcy growled.

Mr. Bennet stepped back, his eyes on the wound. "I will fetch Mr. Jones."

"Also, Sir William and Colonel Forster," Fitzwilliam added. "They will need to see this for themselves."

Mr. Bennet nodded and left the room. Darcy began ushering Elizabeth in the same direction. "Come, let us remove to the library, where you can be properly tended. And out of the reach of...*him*." His lip curled in disgust.

Allowing herself to be led away, Elizabeth chanced one last look back at the man who had caused so much terror in the past weeks.

She wished she had not: the burning fire of hatred in his green eyes would, she knew, haunt her nightmares for many months to come.

Ж

Several hours later, Elizabeth found herself lying in her own bed, wrapped in a cocoon of blankets, her arm cradled against her side and pulsing with a dull, persistent ache. Mr. Jones had declared it a clean wound, but the stitches tugged and throbbed with every heartbeat.

The willow bark tea she had sipped not long ago was beginning to soften the sharp edges of the pain, though not quickly enough for her liking. Laudanum had been offered—of course it had—but she had refused. It made her feel itchy and strange, as though her limbs belonged to someone else, and she could not bear the thought of being anything less than herself tonight.

As she attempted to fall into slumber, the events of the evening played out in slow, flickering scenes behind her tired eyes.

Mr. Jones had found her in the library, white-faced and tight-lipped, and tended to her arm with quiet efficiency. She had tried not to flinch under the needle. He had praised her bravery, though she thought it less bravery and more stubbornness at this point.

Her stomach had growled mid-procedure, drawing a rueful smile from Darcy, who stood behind her chair like a sentinel. He sent a servant to the kitchens, and soon she had been coaxed into nibbling on a plate of cold meats and fresh bread.

Sir William Lucas and Colonel Forster had arrived shortly after, summoned by her father to take down her statement. They had both looked exceedingly grave as she recounted every moment of the attack, from the scent in the air to the gleam of the dagger to the way the cradle had tipped.

Colonel Fitzwilliam, standing in the corner like a watchful hawk, had nodded at every point and confirmed that Captain Carter had been securely bound and transported to a holding location under the watch of soldiers he trusted. He would be transferred to London in the morning.

Mr. Bennet had returned not long after the others left. He sat beside her, looking more tired than she had ever seen him, though there was a proud light in his eyes. He informed her, with a twinkle in his eye, that while she had been recovering, she had missed the announcement of Jane's engagement and its accompanying chaos.

"Mr. Bingley proposed in the hallway after supper was concluded," he said with a smirk. "Could not wait, the poor fool. He found me directly afterward and nearly stammered himself into a stupor asking for my blessing. Of course, I granted it, and I encouraged him to make the announcement straight away. And, well, if your mother was… distracted from any inquiries as to why you were absent, that was simply icing on the cake, so to speak."

Elizabeth smiled faintly. "And Miss Bingley?"

"Ah yes," he said with great satisfaction, "her expression was something between a cat in a rain barrel and a woman who has just been told she must live in Cheapside for the rest of her life."

The moment made her laugh, though it had hurt her arm. After that, he called for the carriage and insisted she return home at once, saying he would send it back for the rest of the family later.

Darcy had led her gently down the corridor to the Netherfield foyer, one arm braced around her shoulders, his other hand careful beneath her elbow. It had not escaped anyone's notice—least of all Miss Bingley's, and the woman's face was nearly purple with apoplexy. Elizabeth had been too weary to savor the woman's outrage at the sight, but the memory brought a spark of amusement now.

She had arrived home exhausted, eager for a comfortable nightgown and warm sheets. She was not too tired, though, to give Benjamin a kiss before the nurse took him from her mother's changing room up to the nursery. "It is over," she had whispered as her lips pressed against his brow.

It is finally over. And yet…

As she stared at the ceiling above her bed, Elizabeth's smile faded. Her body sank down into her mattress under the warmth of the covers, the pain dulled enough to allow reflection, and the fear she had pushed down during the chaos came rushing in at last.

I very nearly died tonight.

She had seen the gleam of a blade inches from her face. She had flung herself across a room, she had bled, she had screamed.

At the time, she had not allowed herself to think. She had simply reacted. But now, in the stillness of her room, the truth settled over her like a cold breath: she had faced a murderer.

And not a monster with horns or hideous scars. A man. A soldier. A familiar figure from a dozen community events—Captain Carter, who had bowed politely, who had worn a neat red coat and offered small, stiff smiles. His face was ordinary. Unremarkable. Almost kind.

And yet behind that face had lurked the devil.

Her brows drew together as a sliver of unease twisted in her gut.

Something does not feel right.

As her eyes drifted shut, the memory returned. His eyes—green and sharp with fury as he lunged at her, full of venom and desperation.

But then—

Her eyes flew open.

His eyes.

The man who attacked her at Longbourn…

He had *blue* eyes. Icy blue.

She sat up sharply, the pain in her arm forgotten for a moment as her heart slammed against her ribs.

Her mind raced. Had she been mistaken? Could she have imagined it? But no—she had looked into those eyes as he tried to force open the nursery door. Pale, cold, blue.

Carter's eyes had been green. Distinctly green.

She was not wrong.

Then who attacked me at Longbourn? And who did I face tonight?

The blanket twisted in her lap as she stared into the dark. The room was quiet again, but her thoughts were anything but.

Something was wrong.

Very, very wrong.

Chapter 28

Darcy slumped into one of the deep armchairs in Bingley's study, cravat undone and waistcoat unbuttoned. His dress coat had been discarded over the back of a nearby chair, and his boots were scuffed from pacing. A glass of port rested on the table beside him, though he had not taken more than a few sips.

Across from him, Colonel Fitzwilliam looked no better—his usually impeccable regimentals had been stripped to shirtsleeves and braces, one cuff stained with something that might have been wine or blood or both.

They were both exhausted. And yet, neither of them could relax.

In the corner, Charles Bingley—still half in his evening wear, though he had at least changed his shoes—was bouncing on the balls of his feet, utterly oblivious to the tension still thick in the air.

"I still can hardly believe it!" Bingley said, beaming. "Jane said yes, and I could tell she meant it. I thought perhaps I ought to wait until the next day, but I saw her smiling at me, and I knew I would never forgive myself if I let the moment pass. And then when I found your father, Darcy, I thought he would make me write it out on paper before he gave me his blessing, but he just said—"

"You are going to be happy, Charles," Darcy interrupted gently, managing a thin smile. "We are glad for you."

Bingley's grin widened. "Thank you, old fellow. And I cannot wait for you to join me in marital bliss, eh?" He winked.

Before Darcy could muster a reply, Miss Bingley swept into the room like a thundercloud edged with tulle. She stopped in front of the hearth, her cheeks blotchy with fury and her bodice rising and falling with angry breaths.

"I suppose," she hissed at her brother, "that we are to offer congratulations for throwing yourselves away on a family so far beneath us they should be scrubbing our floors."

"Now, Caroline, I know you are disappointed, but—"

"But nothing!" she shrieked. "Although I do not know why I am surprised; I should have expected such foolishness from you. But *you,* Mr. Darcy!"

She rounded on Darcy, who had been looking at the floor, wishing she would have saved her vitriol for a private moment. His head shot upwards as she continued her diatribe. "I am completely astonished at what I saw tonight. I simply do not understand why you would want such a… a… a *trollop* like Eliza Bennet!"

Rage filled Darcy's chest, but it was not he who responded.

"Careful," Colonel Fitzwilliam said, swirling his port and not looking up, "you are starting to sound like a farmer's wife who has just found her new neighbor keeps hens in the parlor."

Caroline went rigid. "What did you say?"

"If Darcy wanted refinement," Colonel Fitzwilliam continued smoothly, "he certainly would not have looked twice at a woman who dresses like a melted pumpkin, mocks his friends, and cannot hold her tongue."

"You arrogant—!" Caroline sputtered. "Clearly your time in the army has addled your sense of propriety. I am not surprised you too have been taken in by that shameless little—"

Darcy rose to his feet, his chair scraping sharply against the floor. "Enough."

Even Colonel Fitzwilliam had stopped smiling. He looked at her now with cold disdain. "Miss Bingley," he said, voice like steel wrapped in silk, "I would caution you to mind your tongue. You are betraying your tradesman roots with every word. Do not presume that wealth alone makes a lady."

"You—how *dare* you!" she squawked. She looked around the room to her siblings. "Charles! Louisa! Will no one speak for me?"

Mrs. Hurst shifted uncomfortably in her seat next to her husband, who was dozing on the settee. "Perhaps it would be best, Caroline, if we all got some sleep. We could resume our conversation in the morning when we are rested and refreshed."

"You traitor!" Her face was a mottled purple, and Darcy began to genuinely fear she was going to suffer an apoplexy.

"I take it back," Colonel Fitzwilliam said with a sigh. "Calling you a tradesman's daughter was too generous."

She blinked.

"You are acting more like a fishwife."

The shriek Caroline let out could have shattered glass. She stormed from the room in a flurry of silk and indignation, Louisa rushing after her, attempting to calm the storm.

Hurst drained his glass and stood. "Well," he said with a sigh, "at least the evening turned out less dull than expected." He shuffled out without a backward glance.

The room fell silent. Darcy turned to Bingley and began to apologize for Colonel Fitzwilliam's remarks, but Bingley waved a hand. "Do not apologize. I am only surprised neither of you said anything sooner than tonight about her behavior. She has been unbearable ever since I asked to court Jane."

"Speaking of Miss Bennet," Darcy replied hesitantly, "I think you may need to make a decision about what to do about Miss Bingley once you are married."

"What do you mean?"

"He means that your harpy of sister will make your new bride's life— and therefore yours—quite miserable."

Bingley gaped, and Darcy hurried to explain. "What Colonel Fitzwilliam *means* to say" he gave his cousin a dirty look "is that it is doubtful Miss Bingley will be willing to graciously turn over hostess and mistress duties to Miss Bennet."

Enlightenment dawned on Bingley's face. "You mean it will become a power struggle."

"More like a child getting trampled by a runaway carriage," the colonel muttered.

"Miss Bennet is a kind, gentle lady," Darcy said hastily. "Not unlike Georgiana. I imagine she will do everything she can to prevent conflict, even at her own expense, which will cause Miss Bingley to think she can do whatever she likes. As a husband, it will be your responsibility to protect your wife, to shield her from those who would upset her."

Bingley nodded slowly, looking thoughtful. "Yes. Yes, I see. I must... be better." He murmured something like a goodnight and wandered out, deep in thought.

The door clicked closed behind him. Silence fell again, broken only by the pop of the fire.

"Good riddance," the colonel muttered, settling deeper into his chair. "Well. That was satisfying."

Darcy glanced at him. "How do you feel?"

"Triumphant, obviously. The fishwife speech? One of my better ones, I dare say."

Darcy gave him a look.

"Oh. About Le Corbeau?" The colonel leaned back, tossing one leg over his knee. "Uneasy."

"I would have thought you would feel relief. You have finally caught your nemesis."

"You would think so, would you not? But no, there is something about it all that causes me to feel...unsettled."

"Why?"

"I do not know," he admitted. "I was just so surprised that Le Corbeau turned out to be Carter. I could have sworn I had entirely eliminated him from our list of suspects. It is not like me to be so... erroneous."

"You say that like it is the first time you have ever been wrong about something," Darcy teased, trying to elicit a grin. When no smile was forthcoming, he asked, "What made you think it was not Carter?"

The colonel grimaced. "I cannot recall. There were too many blasted soldiers for me to remember them all."

He pulled a small, worn notebook from his waistcoat pocket, and began flipping pages. Darcy moved to look over his shoulder, only to frown at the bizarre markings. "That is... gibberish."

"It is my own shorthand," the colonel said absently. "I copied your notes, then burned them. Home Office habit. Assume everyone is a spy, even your own valet... or batman, in my case."

"You have trust issues."

"You try chasing the world's deadliest assassin for six years and *not* develop a few."

Just then, the door opened and Wickham stepped in, still in his red coat but looking weary and pale.

"I was just relieved from watch," he said, scrubbing a hand through his hair. "Carter—or whatever his name is—is tied like a Christmas goose and sedated. "I thought I would check in with the two of you before heading back to the barracks." He hesitated. "Something is just not sitting right with me. There is something... off."

Darcy turned sharply. "Colonel Fitzwilliam just said the same thing. You feel it, too, then?"

Wickham nodded. "Carter just does not fit."

The colonel's head snapped up. "Aha!" he shouted, jabbing a finger at a line in his notebook.

"What?"

"Carter's company was running all morning the day Smithson was killed. Thirty witnesses. I wrote it down." He held it up like a prized relic. "He *could not* have done it."

"But he attacked Elizabeth tonight," Darcy protested, chest tightening at the memory. "Half a dozen guards *saw* it."

Colonel Fitzwilliam closed the book with a sharp snap. "Then there is only one explanation."

Darcy and Wickham looked at one another, then back at the colonel expectantly.

"An accomplice."

For a beat, no one moved.

Then the three men bolted to their feet.

"We have to get to Longbourn," Darcy said, already moving.

Please, Lord, do not let us be too late.

𝄪

Elizabeth rushed down the hall towards her father's room, a sense of urgency filling her. Her dressing gown fluttered behind her as she knocked once, then flung open the door without waiting for an answer.

"Papa—wake up!" she cried, crossing to the bed. "We were wrong!"

Mr. Bennet stirred, blinking at the light she carried in her hand. "What is it? Has something happened? Is the baby—?"

"It is not Captain Carter," she said breathlessly. "The man tonight—the one who tried to kill me—he had green eyes. But the man who broke into Longbourn before had blue. I remember it. I saw his eyes. It was not the same man."

Her father sat up straight, suddenly very awake. "Are you certain?"

"Absolutely." She met his gaze, her own steady. "I thought I was going mad, but I am sure of it now. Carter is not the only one. There are *two* of them."

Mr. Bennet swung his legs out of bed. "Get Benjamin," he said grimly. "I will wake the servants. We will let the rest of the family sleep until we know exactly what we are facing."

Her heart thudded wildly as she reached the nursery. Inside, the room was still and dark. The nurse, roused by her entrance, stirred sleepily. "Miss Elizabeth?"

"There is no time," Elizabeth said quietly. "I will take Benjamin. Go wake the staff and join my father. Quickly."

The woman, startled by the urgency in her tone, obeyed without question. As she slipped out, Elizabeth turned to the cradle. Benjamin was sleeping soundly, bundled in his blankets, his soft breath even and warm.

Carefully, she scooped him into her arms, nestling him close to her chest. His warmth steadied her.

There is more than one assassin.

Dread coiled tightly in her chest. It was not logical, not truly—after all, the danger was not necessarily immediate. But something still felt *wrong*.

She stepped into the corridor, Benjamin cradled against her, and quietly shut the nursery door behind her. Quickly making her way down the steps, she hurried to her room. Her hand hovered over the knob, but something made her pause.

Then she smelled it.

That same scent.

Musky. Rich. Masculine.

Her stomach dropped.

She turned.

At the far end of the hallway, half-shrouded in shadows, stood a man in a red coat. His posture was too still. Too poised. And as he stepped forward, the light caught his face.

It was Carter.

But…it was also *not* Carter.

Peering more closely, she could see that this man's eyes were blue, and his features were slightly different. But there was no mistaking that this man was just as much a danger as Carter had been.

"Papa!" she screamed. "He's here!"

She turned and bolted into her room, shutting the door behind her with a loud slam and locking it. Benjamin stirred and gave a soft, confused wail as she backed away, arms trembling.

No one had answered.

She dashed toward the door to the changing room and stumbled into it, bolting it behind her—then rushed through to the connecting door into Jane's chamber, which was empty. *Jane must have slept with Mary tonight,* she thought.

As she bolted for the door, she tripped on something on the floor. Her foot went one way as her leg went another, twisting her ankle painfully. She attempted to stand, but the shooting pain told her she would never be able to outrun Le Corbeau.

Limping to Jane's door, she turned the lock. She then hobbled back into the changing room, locking the other door in there as well.

She was sealed in with Benjamin.

Moments later, the pounding began. *Please, Lord, let the doors hold until someone can come.*

Then a voice came low and smug through the wood. "You are clever. I admire that."

Elizabeth swallowed hard and shifted Benjamin's weight in her arms. "What do you want?" she demanded.

"The boy. That is all I have ever wanted."

"You are not Carter."

"No," the voice said. "He is my brother."

Brothers? Elizabeth blinked, her mouth going dry.

"Twins," he added, pride evident in his voice. "Indistinguishable except for the eyes. We were raised together in Paris, sons of the Revolution. Our parents spared no expense to teach us to fight against those who would look down on us because of our station."

"Then why do you sound like an Englishman?"

A laugh. "Our governess was English. She taught us your language and your ways. We were meant to be invisible."

Her mind raced. "Why tell me any of this?"

"Because you are delaying," he said, amusement curling in his voice. "But I am in a generous mood. I will make you a bargain."

"I do not make deals with murderers."

"I spared the nurse. I would spare you. Leave the boy and walk away."

"Never," she hissed.

His voice darkened. "You are beginning to irritate me." Another hard shove against the door. "*Come out.*"

Where is Papa? Where are the servants? Anyone? "Help me!" she shouted.

He laughed. "I am afraid they have been delayed... a distraction out near the stables should keep them occupied for a time."

As he spoked, she could smell the faintest whiff of smoke. "Why are you doing this?" she asked in a whisper.

"Because it is my job," he said simply. "My last job. As soon as the brat is eliminated, I retire. Some place warm—maybe Barbados. Or India. A man in my profession makes enemies. It is time to vanish."

Suddenly, his voice cut off abruptly. She heard some scuffling, and hope rose within her breast. *Perhaps someone has come.*

"Hello?" she asked tentatively.

"Still here," he said coolly, and her blood turned to ice as his new tone. "You *will* come out, one way or the other. The boy will die, one way or the other. The only decision you have to make is whether or not you will die with him."

At that moment, a wave of smoke rolled under the door from Jane's room, thick and choking.

"What have you done?" she cried.

"I told you, you will come out. Or you will die. Will you suffocate to death with the child, slowly burning as the fire I have set consumes you? Or will you come out, hand the boy over to me, and save your life?"

"You are a monster!" she screamed. *"Somebody help us!"*

"You will burn or surrender. It is your choice."

Elizabeth coughed and looked wildly around the small closet.

There was no escape. Fire through one door, an assassin on the other.

She clutched Benjamin to her chest and screamed again, as loud as she could, praying someone—*anyone*—would hear.

The wood was warm now. The smoke thicker.

She squeezed her eyes shut.

"Please," she whispered. "Please come."

)(

Darcy, Colonel Fitzwilliam, and Wickham rode hard along the road that went from Netherfield to Longbourn. They reached the Bennet estate just as the first glow of dawn began to rise behind the trees. But it was not the gentle light of morning that met them—it was fire.

A fire roared in the distance, the stables fully alight, the orange glow reflecting off the house's windows like hell's own lanterns. Shadows danced along the gravel drive as servants dashed back and forth with buckets and wet cloths, fearfully shouting to one another as they fought the growing flames.

Darcy leapt from his horse before it had fully stopped, heart pounding. At the edge of the drive, Mr. Bennet appeared, ushering Mrs. Bennet and four daughters away from the house. Mary clutched Kitty's hand, who was coughing into her sleeve. Lydia was weeping noisily, and Mrs. Bennet wailed that her nerves would never recover.

But it was not the absence of composure that struck Darcy—it was the absence of one face.

She's not here.

He ran to Mr. Bennet with Colonel Fitzwilliam and Wickham close behind. "What has happened?" he demanded. "Where is Elizabeth?"

Mr. Bennet's face was pale and grim. "She realized the man from the ball and the man in our nursery were not the same person. I told her to fetch Benjamin while I gathered some footmen. But as I woke servants, I saw the fire, so I also woke my family."

Darcy's mouth went dry. "She is not with you now."

"I believed she had already come out while I gathered the others." Mr. Bennet looked back toward the house, and for the first time, uncertainty crossed his face. "She must be here. She would not have stayed inside, would she?"

"We need to find her! She could be—" Darcy's voice broke off as the coughing fit he had been fighting back threatened to take control. *Blast this smoke and cold air!*

"But what brought you here so quickly?" Mr. Bennet asked, turning toward the others, confusion etched on his face. "It is far too soon for my messenger to have reached Netherfield."

"We reached the same conclusion she did," Colonel Fitzwilliam said, his tone tight with fury. "There is an accomplice."

Darcy had barely heard. His eyes scoured the crowd of servants and the smoke-streaked lawn again. "Where is Elizabeth?" he cried between coughs. "Where is she?"

A high-pitched scream pierced through the smoky haze.

They all turned. Smoke now billowed from one of the second-story windows, curling out like an omen. A second scream followed, louder than the first, filled with desperation. Darcy's heart stopped.

"That is Elizabeth's room!" Mr. Bennet shouted, his voice raw.

"The accomplice must be here," the colonel said, drawing his pistol. "The fire outside was a distraction."

Another scream rang out—hoarse and desperate.

Darcy did not hesitate. "Elizabeth is still in there," he said, already moving. "We have to save her!"

He ran for the door.

Behind him, he could hear Colonel Fitzwilliam shouting orders, Wickham calling for buckets, but none of it registered. He saw only the smoke. Heard only her scream.

If he lost her now—

No.

He would not lose her.

Not tonight. Not ever.

Taking a deep breath, fighting the tightness in his chest, he entered the house.

Dear Lord, let her be alive. Help me find her.

Chapter 29

Elizabeth lay on her side, her cheek pressed against the cool floorboards, the air sharp with smoke. She had placed Benjamin beside her, curled close to his tiny, heaving chest, and tried to breathe in what little clean air still came through the cracks of the far door.

She had planned to wait until someone came to find her and would distract him, then she could slip out the second door. But he had known. Somehow, he had known. While she had been focused on calming Benjamin and covering them with a blanket to hold off the smoke, he had moved.

Now he stood at the door she had meant to flee through. She could see the shape of his boots under the crack, could hear his calm, maddening voice.

"Still alive in there?" he drawled. "You have a stubborn constitution, Mademoiselle Bennet."

She coughed violently in response, unable to summon the breath to reply. Benjamin whimpered, his small frame racked with trembling sobs and rasping barks. She held him tighter.

"You know," Le Corbeau said lazily through the door, "there is a kind of poetry in it, is there not? You rescued the child from a fire, only to now be consumed by flames."

Smoke was beginning to trickle through the seams of the second door now—the one he had been blocking. She heard him curse under his breath.

"Ah. I see the flames have grown greedy." His voice was harder now. "Too late for you, I am afraid. There is no exit left, Mademoiselle. None that does not end in ashes."

Elizabeth coughed again, eyes streaming as she buried Benjamin's face in her neck. Her muscles trembled. Her throat ached. She could hardly tell if the heat on her skin was from the fire or her own rising fever of panic.

"Farewell," came the final words through the smoke. "I shall think of you fondly when I reach warm shores and kinder winds."

Then silence.

She waited.

Nothing.

Is he gone?

She stared at the door, unsure if she dared try it. But her body was shaking, her breath failing. She did not have long.

Then—her name. Shouted hoarsely, ragged with coughing.

"Elizabeth!"

Darcy.

She scrambled to her knees, the sound pulling her like a rope through the haze of pain and fear. Unlocking the latch with numb fingers, she threw open the door.

The hallway was awash in smoke and flame. A figure stood just beyond the frame—tall, staggering, one hand braced against the wall as if the mere act of standing were a trial.

"Darcy!" she screamed.

He turned at the sound of her voice, his face pale beneath soot, his lips parted with another violent cough. He took a step toward her, but his knees buckled.

She flew to him.

"I have you," she said, one arm curling around his waist as she slung his arm over her shoulder. "We are getting out of here."

Benjamin whimpered in her other arm, pressing his hot face into her collarbone.

Together they moved, step by agonizing step, through the smoke. The floor trembled beneath them. The beams groaned above their heads. Elizabeth's eyes burned, her lungs felt shredded with each breath.

They reached the stairwell—but she could barely see through the thick, rolling smoke. Her foot missed the first step.

They fell.

She screamed as gravity yanked them forward, and instinct took over. She twisted her body midair, curling protectively around Benjamin as they tumbled down the steps, over and over. Her shoulder struck the railing. Her hip slammed the edge of a stair. Her back hit another with bruising force.

Darcy fell alongside them, rolling head-over-heels until they reached the bottom. He hit the ground, the wind knocked out of his fragile lungs. He gasped for air, one hand reaching blindly toward her as she lay shielding the child with her body.

For a moment, there was only the thud of her pulse, the baby's faint cries, and the thunder of fire above them.

"Darcy," she gasped, trying to sit up, her bruised body aching everywhere. "We have to get up."

He tried. He truly did—but his body gave out beneath him, another coughing fit tearing through his lungs. "Darcy, come on! I cannot carry you both!"

"Leave me," he gasped out.

"What? No!"

He shook his head, eyes closing in pain. "Go," he rasped. "Save him. Save yourself."

"No—please—"

He opened his eyes again, the agony in them nearly undoing her. "I love you," he said between heaving coughs. "Go."

"I love you," she whispered. "I cannot—"

"You must!"

"I cannot do this—" she sobbed, trying again to lift him while still holding Benjamin. "Do not make me choose between him and you."

"Choose to *live*, Elizabeth! Go, before it is too late."

He could scarcely speak between gasps for breath, and she closed her eyes, fighting back the tears streaming down her cheeks, mingling with sooty ash.

I have to. God forgive me, but I have to go.

She rose to her knees, holding a prone Benjamin in her arms. Turning from Darcy, she began to crawl, attempting to stay down below the smoke. But then, through the haze in front of her—a figure.

Red.

A soldier.

No! How is he still here?

She turned back to Darcy, shielding Benjamin again with her body. Through the roar of the fire above, she heard a faint call.

"Darcy! Miss Elizabeth!"

It was Colonel Fitzwilliam.

Not Le Corbeau.

Another man moved beside him—Wickham.

"Oh, thank God," she sobbed.

Wickham gently took Benjamin from her arms. The colonel hauled Darcy upright with a grunt of effort.

"You are all right?" Fitzwilliam asked, his voice sharp with concern. "Can you walk."

Elizabeth nodded, too choked to speak.

"Come," he said. "This way."

And through the smoke, they went—together, alive.

Once through the door, she blinked against the bright sun just peeking over the horizon to the east. She nearly collapsed, but Wickham held her tighter. "Just a little further now. We are nearly there."

But Le Corbeau is out here. Benjamin!

"It was him," she choked out. "Le Corbeau. They are twins."

"We know," the colonel said behind her, staggering under the weight of Darcy's frame. "The fool did not anticipate that I would already be here when he left the house. Wickham and I were able to apprehend him just as he reached the edge of the garden," the colonel finished grimly, his voice hoarse with smoke and fatigue. "He will not be going anywhere now."

Elizabeth stumbled again, and Wickham adjusted his grip to keep her steady, the baby still cradled against his chest. "Easy now," he murmured, "You did it, Miss Elizabeth. You kept him safe. You kept both of them safe."

The words nearly undid her. Her knees buckled, but she forced herself upright. Benjamin whimpered softly, still buried against Wickham's shoulder, his small face blotched with soot.

Colonel Fitzwilliam lowered Darcy gently onto the dewy grass. The tall man slumped back, his eyes closed, chest heaving with shallow, labored breaths.

"Darcy," Elizabeth whispered, sinking to her knees beside him. She reached for his hand—it was warm, but his face was pale, and each wheezing inhale sent a spike of fear through her.

"I need a physician here now!" the colonel bellowed toward the cluster of servants and townsmen who were pouring water onto the smoking remains of the barn. "Where is Mr. Jones?"

"Gone to retrieve more supplies," someone shouted back.

Elizabeth pressed the back of her hand to Darcy's cheek. "You are safe," she murmured. "You are safe now, Darcy."

His eyes fluttered open, glassy and unfocused, but then they locked on hers. A faint smile tugged at the corners of his mouth. "You are all right?" he rasped.

She nodded, tears spilling freely now. "Yes. We are all right."

Colonel Fitzwilliam straightened and turned to look down at her, his face grim and smudged with ash. "Le Corbeau—the one with blue eyes—is bound and under guard near the stables. Sir William and Colonel Forster are already en route. The second twin—the one at Netherfield—is locked up as well. I never thought…" He shook his head. "Twins."

Elizabeth stared at him, still struggling to process the full weight of what had happened. "He said it was his last job. That he would disappear after it."

"He nearly succeeded." Fitzwilliam's voice was low. "But you stopped him."

"I did not," she said quietly, looking down at Benjamin's sooty curls. "We did. All of us."

From across the lawn, Mr. Bennet came running toward them, his face lined with worry. Behind him trailed Jane, her skirts muddy, and behind her—Mrs. Bennet wailing, "My poor baby, my poor Lizzy!" though she made no move to approach.

Elizabeth met her father's eyes, and his steps slowed.

"I knew you would save them," he said, voice rough with emotion as he reached her side. He dropped to his knees and pressed a kiss to her forehead. "I knew."

She closed her eyes, letting herself finally lean against him for just a moment.

Then Wickham handed her Benjamin, who whimpered and clung to her as though he might never let go. The tiny noise he made was the sweetest sound she had ever heard— evidence that he was still alive.

"It is over," she whispered hoarsely to him.

But even as she said it, she knew it was not. Not entirely.

There would still be questions. There would be aftermath. The threat had been stopped—but not without scars.

Still, the sun had risen.

And they had survived.

𝕏

Darcy stirred, the dry rasp of breath against his throat pulling him from sleep. His chest ached, his head throbbed dully, and the air in his lungs felt like it had been dragged across sandpaper. He coughed—a shallow, grating sound—and winced.

A flurry of motion came from the corner of the room.

"Oh, thank heavens, sir! You have woken!" cried Bates, his valet, bustling forward. The man's usually stiff composure had cracked with visible relief.

Bates turned and flung the chamber door open. "Tell them Mr. Darcy is awake," he barked into the hallway, then shut the door behind him with a sharp click.

Darcy's lips parted. "Eliz—" His voice broke on the first syllable, dry and cracked beyond recognition.

"Do not try to speak, sir," Bates urged, hurrying to his side. "You must be parched."

Darcy moved to sit up, but then realized he was already half-reclined on a large stack of pillows. He shifted into a better position as Bates took a glass of water from the bedside table and held it to his lips.

"Small sips," he instructed.

424

The first swallow burned. The second was only marginally better. Still, the moisture eased the burning in his throat.

"What happened?" Darcy rasped after a few moments.

"You took in a fair amount of smoke, sir, and struck your head during the fall down the stairs," Bates explained. "You were brought back to Netherfield in a cart yesterday morning and lost consciousness along the way. You have been asleep ever since, though you were coughing quite a bit in spite of not being sensible to the world."

Darcy's brow furrowed. "Elizabeth?" he managed.

"She is well, sir," Bates said quickly, anticipating the question. "She and her family are staying at Stoke Estate. The fire destroyed most of Longbourn, I regret to say."

"And the child?" Darcy asked hoarsely.

"The babe is safe as well, sir." Bates hesitated at Darcy's skeptical glance. "Well, all three of you have had rough coughs, but they are improving steadily—thanks to Miss Elizabeth's herbal blend. Mr. Jones is rather astonished at the recovery. They are being kept upright as much as possible, though, to prevent a buildup of fluid in the lungs. And though none of you should speak more than necessary, there is every reason to believe they will continue to improve."

Darcy leaned back slowly, letting the words settle over him. The ache in his ribs still pulsed with every breath, but the tight fear in his chest began to ease.

The door banged open.

"Well, well," came a familiar voice, brimming with amusement. "The great Mr. Darcy has finally deigned to wake up."

Colonel Fitzwilliam strode into the room, his coat thrown over one shoulder, his cravat askew. His face was streaked with soot that looked like it had been smudged off in a hurry, and his eyes gleamed with exhausted relief.

"You lazy dog," he continued. "Lying about like a Roman emperor. Another day or two and I might have stolen Elizabeth out from under you."

Darcy's smile was faint, but real. "You would have had to carry her over my dead body."

The colonel flopped into a nearby chair and propped his boots on a stool. "It would not have been that hard, considering you were almost a corpse yourself."

Darcy's eyes sharpened. "Is she truly safe now? All of them?"

The colonel's grin faded. "Yes. The danger is over."

Darcy narrowed his gaze. "The twins are in custody, I am assuming. What if they escape?"

"They will not."

Darcy frowned. "You sound too certain."

The colonel's expression grew grim. "They are both dead."

A sharp breath escaped Darcy's lips. "What?"

"Apparently," Colonel Fitzwilliam said, with a grimace of distaste, "each brother had a pair of vials hidden on their persons. We did a full search after capture—believe me, more thorough than I ever wanted to conduct—but they must have concealed them in places best not spoken of in polite company."

Darcy's face twisted. "I think I can imagine."

"The vials were harmless on their own," the colonel continued. "But together—when their contacts were mixed—they formed some sort of fast-acting poison. It killed them both in their cells before we could stop it."

Darcy let out a long, shuddering breath and pressed a hand to his chest. "Then it is truly over."

The colonel stood and stretched with a grunt. "It is. You can finally stop worrying."

Darcy looked skeptical.

"Come now," the colonel added with a smirk. "You have a wedding to look forward to. Once I submit my report, I suspect word will spread like fire in London. You will be more popular than ever at every soirée."

Darcy groaned softly and dropped his head back against the pillows. "Spare me."

The colonel chuckled. "Cheer up. At least you will have Elizabeth to shield you from the matchmaking horde. That woman would sooner bite than let a matron paw you."

Darcy's answering smile was slow and full of affection. "Yes," he murmured. "I believe she would."

And for the first time in many weeks, he allowed himself to rest—knowing the woman he loved was safe, the danger had passed, and the future—uncertain though it might be—belonged to them.

※

Two days later, however, Darcy was sick of resting. The light streaming through the windows felt too bright, his limbs ached, and his throat was raw from coughing. Worse still was the stifling frustration of being confined to his bed like a child with a winter cold.

"I can sit in a chair," Darcy muttered as Bates entered the room with a fresh cup of willow bark tea. "Or walk to the study. I am not an invalid."

"Of course not, sir," Bates replied neutrally as he set the cup on the table. "Shall I carry you or fetch a bath chair from the village, perhaps?"

Darcy shot him a glare.

"Forgive me," Bates added, not entirely managing to hide the amusement in his tone.

Darcy exhaled heavily and rubbed his temple. "I apologize. This confinement has made me short-tempered."

A bark of laughter came from the doorway.

"Now that sounds familiar."

Darcy turned his head. Wickham leaned against the doorframe, grinning. "You were the exact same way when you were twelve. It is a relief to see that even the impeccable Fitzwilliam Darcy has a flaw or two."

Glaring, Darcy hurled one of his dozen pillows towards his old friend. The throw was weak, and Wickham was able to easily avoid being hit.

"Now, now—is this the thanks I get for coming to cheer you up?" Wickham smirked, sauntering into the room and producing a familiar deck of cards from his coat pocket. "I am not as lovely as the fair Miss Elizabeth, I will admit—but I have been told I am moderately good-looking and quite good at cards."

Darcy gave a soft huff that could almost be called a laugh. "Your modesty remains unchecked, I see."

"Never had any use for it." Wickham pulled a chair close to the bed, sat down, and began to shuffle the cards. "And besides, I needed something to do during my liberty now that I am not playing the part of a suspect."

They played in silence for a few moments, until Darcy looked up and asked quietly, "Are people treating you any differently now?"

Wickham's eyes did not leave the cards. "Some are. Word has begun to spread that I am not a murderer after all. But most people still give me a wide berth. Reputation, once spoiled, does not wash clean with a single rinse."

Darcy nodded, absorbing that. "And what will you do now?"

Wickham shrugged. "I am not much of a soldier. I have always preferred ledgers to rifles. I miss clerical work. London, the noise of the docks—making sense of other people's chaos."

"Do you think you might go back to your old post? Have you had any word about your former employment?"

A humorless smile touched Wickham's lips. "It seems that many of the insurance companies have run out of funds. The barrister for whom I worked is no longer in business."

Darcy hesitated. Then he said, "I could hire you."

Wickham's head shot up. "What?"

"You are clever. Capable. You understand trade, and I have been ill too long. My affairs need careful tending, especially if my recovery is… prolonged."

"I do not need charity," Wickham replied. "I am hardly destitute, as you well know. I still have nearly the entirety of your father's bequest."

Darcy met Wickham's eyes evenly. "This is not charity. It is an offer."

"You would trust me? After everything?"

"You have earned it," Darcy said simply. "You protected Elizabeth and Benjamin. That cannot be repaid, but I can offer you honest work."

Wickham looked away, blinking rapidly. "I will think about it," he said gruffly. "It would be... nice. Honest work. Being useful again."

They returned to their cards, and as the morning wore on, the tension between them softened, replaced by familiar rhythms and quiet laughter.

And for the first time in years, Darcy did not hear his father's reprimands echoing in his ears.

Chapter 30

One month later…

Elizabeth drew her shawl closer around her shoulders as she climbed the last incline of Oakham Mount. The early December air stung her cheeks and bit at her fingers, despite the thick gloves she wore. Snow crunched beneath her boots, packed and slick in places, and more than once she had to pause to catch her breath.

She used to make this walk with ease. That had been before the fire—before the smoke and ash had left their mark on her lungs.

Still, she pressed on.

When she reached the top, she closed her eyes and turned her face into the wind. The sky stretched wide and pale blue above her, the last hues of dawn still clinging to the eastern horizon. The chill air filled her chest and made her eyes water—and she promptly doubled over in a fit of coughing.

"I could have told you that would happen," a familiar voice said from behind her, warm with wry affection.

She spun around.

Darcy sat atop his dark gelding, wrapped in a fine wool coat with his collar turned up against the wind. His expression was amused and altogether too handsome for so early in the morning.

"You rode," she accused, laughing breathlessly. "That is cheating."

He dismounted with easy grace, boots crunching on the snow as he walked toward her. "Well, if you want me to actually be able to make it to our wedding in a few hours, I had to." He smiled and reached for her hand. "You would not want me fainting halfway through the vows, would you?"

Elizabeth laughed again. "I suppose I must accept your excuse, weak though it is."

"Generous as ever," he murmured.

Before she could reply, he leaned in and kissed her.

Her eyes fluttered closed. The world dropped away—the cold, the snow, the tightness in her chest. All of it vanished under the warmth of his lips. His hands cupped her cheeks, gloved but firm, steady, and the kiss deepened. Her stomach flipped and fluttered, and her hands rose instinctively to grasp the front of his coat.

When they parted, he rested his forehead against hers, his breath clouding in the space between them.

"In a few hours," he said softly, "you will be my wife. And I will kiss you as often as I please."

Her heart soared.

She slipped her arms around his waist and held him tightly. He wrapped her in his embrace, and she closed her eyes again, breathing in his scent—leather, pine, and the faint trace of cloves. It grounded her. Made her feel safe. As if, for once, everything was exactly as it should be.

They stood there in silence, watching the colors of sunrise fade into full morning, but then a loud *caw* shattered the moment.

Elizabeth turned toward the sound, where a large black bird glared at them from a snow-laden tree. "I suppose that is our cue," she sighed. "If I do not return soon, my mother will send out a search party."

"Georgiana will worry, as well," Darcy said with a smile. "She was most put out when snow delayed her arrival. I believe she intends to make up for lost time."

"I am very glad she arrived safely," Elizabeth said warmly. "And I look forward to being her sister."

Darcy offered his hand. "Ride back with me?"

Elizabeth tilted her head playfully. "Are you offering from chivalry or because you fear the wrath of Mrs. Bennet?"

"Both," he said solemnly.

"Then I accept."

His touch nearly burned her as he put his hands on her waist to lift her onto the horse in front of the saddle. He swung up behind her with ease, then pulled her towards him until she was practically in his lap.

The warmth of him at her back, the pressure of his arm anchoring her, sent a delicious shiver through her. She leaned into him slightly, allowing herself to savor the feeling.

As the horse picked its careful way down the snowy trail, Darcy bent his head to murmur near her ear, his breath warm against her chilled skin.

"Did you sleep well last night, my love?" he asked softly. "No nightmares?"

Elizabeth smiled and tipped her head back slightly against his shoulder. "No," she said truthfully. "They have been easing. It grows better every day."

He pressed a tender kiss to her temple, and she closed her eyes, letting herself bask in the simple comfort of being in his arms.

For a few moments, they rode in easy silence, the cold air brisk against their faces, the sound of the horse's hooves muffled by the snow. Elizabeth watched the sunrise fade, the last pink and gold streaks melting into a pale winter blue.

"I cannot tell you how proud I am of you, Elizabeth," Darcy said at last. His voice was low, but rich with emotion. "What you endured, what you survived. I am in awe of you."

She turned slightly in the saddle to look up at him, her heart full. "We endured it together. I was never alone."

He gave a slight, disbelieving shake of his head, his eyes fierce with feeling. "You have no idea how often you have been my strength."

Elizabeth smiled and reached up to touch his cheek lightly with her gloved fingers. "Then let us agree that we are stronger together."

He caught her hand and pressed a reverent kiss to her knuckles. "Always."

At the bottom of the mount, they came to a fork—left toward Longbourn, right toward Stoke Estate. They turned right, and Elizabeth looked wistfully in the opposite direction as they rode towards the Gardiner's home.

It still felt strange to her, even a month later. Left had always meant home. Now it led only to a burned shell of a house. Longbourn had not been insured. There were no funds to rebuild, and no word yet from the investigators about whether a new heir would be found.

The past, it seemed, had been claimed by fire.

But the future rode with her now— solid and steady behind her.

When they reached Stoke House, Darcy pulled the horse to a gentle stop at the edge of the estate gardens. Elizabeth reluctantly slid down from the saddle, and he dismounted beside her.

She began to walk towards the house, but he caught her hand and pulled her into his arms for a slow, lingering kiss.

This time, there was nothing restrained or hurried about it. His lips met hers with a hunger that stole her breath, yet with a tenderness that made her heart ache.

The world melted away—the cold, the snow, the trials of the past months. There was only the feel of his mouth on hers, the taste of him, the heat of his body against the chill of the morning.

Her arms crept up around his neck, pulling him closer, and he groaned low in his throat as his arms wrapped tightly around her in return, lifting her slightly off the ground.

Elizabeth's stomach swooped in the most delightful way, and she felt as though she were flying. Her fingers curled into his thick hair, savoring the solidness, the reality of him.

When they finally broke apart, they were both breathing heavily, and her cheeks were pink from more than just the cold.

Darcy rested his forehead against hers, his voice rough. "That is the last time I shall kiss you as Miss Elizabeth Bennet."

She gave a breathless laugh. "Then I hope you will not waste much time once I am Mrs. Darcy."

He chuckled, a sound so warm and rich it sent a fresh wave of butterflies through her chest. "No, my love. I intend to make up for every moment we have lost."

He pulled her close again, and for a few moments they simply stood there, hearts beating in rhythm, sharing the quiet wonder of all that lay ahead. Then, reluctantly, she pulled away. "It would not do to be late to my own wedding, else we shall have to wait until tomorrow. I had best go upstairs and prepare."

Darcy mounted his horse and looked down at her with a tender expression. "I will see you at the church, then, Mrs. Darcy."

"Not yet," she teased. "A few hours more."

He smiled and watched as she slipped inside through the kitchen entrance, snagging a muffin to eat on her way up to the stairs. Once there, she opened the door to the small bedchamber she shared with Jane. Her wedding gown hung from the wardrobe, the ivory silk glimmering faintly in the morning light.

On the bed, Jane stirred beneath a heavy quilt and blinked awake.

"We are getting married today," she whispered, her face breaking into a radiant smile.

Elizabeth laughed and climbed onto the bed beside her sister, her whole body tingling with joy. "Yes, dearest Jane. We are."

For a moment, they simply sat together in the soft morning light, two sisters on the cusp of a new life. Elizabeth let her head rest against Jane's shoulder, both of them smiling like schoolgirls with a shared secret.

Below stairs, she could hear the faint sounds of bustle—footsteps hurrying across the flagstones, the clatter of pots, the hurried voices of servants preparing the breakfast and assembling trunks for the afternoon departure.

Today, they would be married.

Today, they would leave the past—the ruins of Longbourn, the terror of smoke and fire—and step into the future.

Elizabeth looked up at Jane and whispered, half in wonder, "Can you believe it?"

Jane's blue eyes shone. "I can. You deserve it all, Lizzy. Happiness, love, a true home."

Her throat tightened. "And so do you."

They sat for a moment longer, wrapped in the quiet, breathless magic of the morning.

Then a loud, impatient knock sounded at the door.

"Come along, girls!" called Mrs. Bennet's voice, bustling and imperious. "We have not a moment to lose if you wish to be beautiful brides!"

Elizabeth and Jane laughed, springing to their feet. The room soon became a flurry of cheerful activity as Mrs. Gardiner and a pair of maids came in, bustling about with ribbons, pins, and flower sprays. Elizabeth allowed herself to be led to the dressing table, where Jane was already seated.

Mrs. Gardiner helped brush out Elizabeth's hair, smoothing the dark curls with a loving hand. "I never thought someone I knew would marry the master of Pemberley," Mrs. Gardiner said, her eyes misting. "You will be greatly missed, my dear."

Elizabeth smiled warmly at her aunt in the mirror. "You have always been like a mother to me. I will miss you, too."

"No, once you get your first look at the beautiful grounds at Pemberley, you will forget all of us entirely!"

The room filled with giggles as the maids began weaving fresh winter roses and myrtle into their hair. Once their coiffures were completed, Elizabeth and Jane stepped into their dresses, and the maids stood back in admiration.

"You look like angels," Mrs. Gardiner said, dabbing at her eyes with a handkerchief.

There was a knock at the door. Mr. Bennet's voice, dry and affectionate, drifted in.

"Are my daughters ready to ruin two perfectly good gentlemen's lives?"

Elizabeth laughed and hurried to open the door. Mr. Bennet stood there, looking rather fine himself in his best coat, though his cravat was slightly askew. His eyes softened as he looked at her.

"You are beautiful, Lizzy," he said quietly, his voice rough with emotion. "Darcy is a lucky man indeed."

Elizabeth blinked back tears and pressed a kiss to his cheek. "Thank you, Papa."

He gave a similar compliment to Jane and then offered his arms to his daughters. "Shall we?"

Arm in arm, they made their way down the sweeping staircase to the front hall, where the carriages waited to take them to the little church just down the road.

As Elizabeth stepped outside into the crisp December air, snowflakes began to fall lightly around them, dusting the ground in a soft, sparkling white.

Jane laughed in delight. "A Christmas snow! What could be more perfect?"

Elizabeth lifted her face to the sky, letting a few flakes land on her cheeks. A new beginning. A new life.

In the carriage, she and Jane clutched each other's hands, whispering last-minute reassurances.

"I am not nervous," Jane said with a laugh that belied her trembling fingers.

Elizabeth squeezed her hand. "Neither am I."

But her heart was pounding so hard she was sure the others could hear it.

When they arrived at the little stone church, it was already filled with family and friends. Mrs. Bennet was crying loudly into her handkerchief, flanked by Mrs. Gardiner and Mrs. Hurst. Lydia and Kitty sat giggling in the back pews, while Mary sat primly beside them with a prayer book clutched in her hands.

Colonel Fitzwilliam, resplendent in his dress uniform, stood with Darcy and Bingley at the front. Wickham sat nearby with the militia officers, looking rather proud of himself.

Elizabeth's breath caught when she saw Darcy turn toward her.

He looked devastatingly handsome in his dark coat and crisp white cravat, his eyes never leaving hers as she made her way up the aisle on her father's arm.

As she drew nearer, she could see it in his face—love, devotion, and awe. Her knees wobbled slightly, but she smiled and held his gaze.

Bingley, beaming from ear to ear, looked every inch the man in love as Jane approached him.

The vicar smiled warmly at them all, and the ceremony began.

Elizabeth scarcely heard the words—it was all a blur of vows and promises and tender glances. But when Darcy took her hand in his, she felt the weight of it, the certainty, the deep rightness of it.

When he said, "I do," his voice was rich and steady, and she thought her heart would burst with happiness.

When it was her turn, she managed a clear, confident, "I do," though her voice trembled slightly with joy.

And then it was done. They were husband and wife.

Mr. Bennet wiped his eyes discreetly as the congregation erupted in cheers and applause.

As they stepped out into the snowy morning together, Darcy pulled her close, wrapping his arms around her, and whispered against her ear:

"My wife…now I can kiss you whenever I like."

She laughed through tears of happiness. "I hope you intend to start now."

He did not need any further encouragement. Right there on the steps of the church, with snowflakes clinging to her lashes and the morning sun gleaming off the fresh white drifts, he kissed her thoroughly—slowly, reverently, and with a passion so deep it made the world spin away. Elizabeth clung to him, feeling as though her very soul had found its home.

Around them, the crowd laughed and cheered again, but she barely heard it.

The snow swirled around them in a sparkling dance, and Elizabeth knew that whatever fires may burn in the future, she would face them all— so long as she faced them with him. Arm in arm, they made their way to the waiting carriage, Darcy's hand resting over hers with tender protectiveness.

If they arrived at Stoke House with swollen lips and hair slightly mussed, Darcy's cravat a touch askew and Elizabeth's cheeks glowing far more than the brisk weather warranted, no one dared comment. The laughter and glances were fond rather than mocking.

And as they stepped into the warm, welcoming brightness of the Gardiners' ballroom, Elizabeth gasped. It had been transformed into a beautiful celebration of light and warmth. A roaring fire blazed in the hearth, wreaths of holly and ivy decked the walls, and a long table groaned under the weight of meats, pastries, jellies, fruits, and pies. Crystal glasses sparkled in the light from the chandeliers, and the air was filled with the scents of cinnamon, roasted meats, and sweet wine.

Elizabeth scarcely knew how she got to her seat. The room swirled with smiling faces, well-wishers, and excited chatter. Mrs. Bennet, resplendent in a new gown of lavender silk, was already telling anyone who would listen about "her two married daughters," while Mr. Bennet stood at the sideboard, calmly surveying the chaos with a glass of claret in hand.

Darcy guided Elizabeth to the head of the table with a hand at the small of her back, a touch so light and yet so grounding that her heart fluttered anew. He pulled out her chair for her, bowing slightly as she took her seat, and then seated himself beside her.

Jane and Bingley sat across from them, their heads bent close together, whispering and laughing so sweetly that Elizabeth could hardly look at them without smiling herself.

Colonel Fitzwilliam, seated nearby, raised his glass in a silent toast to her and Darcy. His eyes twinkled with mischief as he mouthed, *Finally* across the table, making Elizabeth chuckle under her breath.

Wickham, sitting further down with several of the militia officers, gave her an exaggerated wink when he caught her looking, then feigned swooning against his neighbor's shoulder, causing the nearby footman to nearly drop a plate.

Elizabeth felt as though she floated above it all, light and buoyant with happiness. Yet every time she glanced sideways and caught Darcy's gaze—so steady, so full of fierce, quiet joy—she was brought back down to earth, grounded in the miracle of the present moment.

As the meal continued, laughter and clinking glasses filled the room. Bingley rose to make a short, effusive speech about happiness and blessings, and the health of his lovely new wife. Darcy stood afterward, a little stiffer, but his voice was rich and steady.

"I have no great talent for speeches," he began, his dark eyes locking with Elizabeth's, "but I can say with full certainty that this is the happiest day of my life. I am blessed beyond anything I ever deserved."

Elizabeth's cheeks warmed as everyone raised their glasses in a hearty cheer.

When he sat back down, he leaned close, his breath tickling her ear. "I am tempted to steal you away this instant," he murmured. "I doubt anyone would dare stop me."

She smiled, her hand finding his under the table and squeezing it tightly.

"I might not let you bring me back," she whispered.

He kissed her knuckles reverently, the gesture hidden from the crowd by the table linen.

Desserts were brought out—fruit tarts, gingerbread, marzipan—and after the final toasts, people began to rise and wander the room, forming little laughing groups near the fire and windows.

Elizabeth found herself momentarily separated from Darcy, surrounded by a cluster of well-meaning neighbors offering advice on married life. She laughed and nodded, accepting their suggestions without really listening; but her eyes sought him across the room instinctively.

He stood near the window, speaking with Colonel Fitzwilliam and Mr. Bennet, but even from that distance, she could feel it: the magnetic pull between them. As if he sensed her gaze, he turned—and smiled.

A small, private smile meant for her alone.

Her heart caught in her throat, and a flame began to burn warmly deep within her. In that moment, Elizabeth understood—this was what life was meant to be.

Not without hardships, no. They had faced danger and terror, loss and fear, walking through the fire. They had stared death in the face and fought to survive, watching as the world crumbled to ashes around them.

But as Elizabeth crossed the room to take her husband's hand, she knew with perfect certainty: whatever storms might come, they would face them together—with courage, with hope, and with a heart full of gratitude for all they had been given.

They had been tested by fire, but from the ashes, they had found something that even flames could not consume: trust, truth, and a love that endured.

From ashes, they had forged understanding.

And in understanding, they had found forever.

Epilogue

One year later…

Elizabeth sat in the small, sunlit parlor of their London townhouse, her needle tracing a delicate rosebud onto the hem of a tiny christening gown. Her work lay in her lap, and she paused for a moment to rest her hand atop the gentle swell of her stomach. A smile curved her lips as she thought of the latest letter from her Aunt Gardiner.

My Dear Mrs. Darcy

I cannot stop myself from addressing you that way, my dear Lizzy. Now that you have seen Pemberley for yourself, I imagine you can understand why.

Things are going well here in Hertfordshire. Your mother is adjusting better than we dared hope to life at the dower house, though she is not without her fits of temper. She sometimes forgets herself and issues commands to my housekeeper, which causes no little amusement to the children. Your father bears it with his usual dry humour and spends many a happy hour in the library, pretending not to hear her scolding.

Mary continues to grow into a young woman of sense and feeling. Her courtship with Mr. Welles, the new curate, is progressing with great solemnity; they read Fordyce's Sermons to each other during their walks, which I find both tedious and oddly touching. She has grown gentler with the children, and Benjamin adores her most particularly.

Speaking of Benjamin—he is a handful! He has discovered a passion for climbing, and no table, chair, or unattended footman is safe. But he has the sweetest nature, running to embrace whomever he fancies with sticky fingers and a shining smile. You will scarcely recognize him for the stout, laughing boy he has become.

Jane and Charles are blissfully happy at Netherfield. Charles has at last learned to stand firm against Caroline's interference, and your mother's visits have become far less frequent, which is a blessing to all parties.

As for Kitty and Lydia, the school you and Mr. Darcy chose for them has wrought near-miracles. Their letters home are neatly written and full of sensible observations, though I cannot promise it will last once they return for the holidays! Still, hope springs eternal.

We miss you dearly, Lizzy. Christmas will not be complete without seeing you, though we rejoice in the happiness you have found. Give Mr. Darcy our warmest regards—and I trust you will give him a great many of your own as well.

With all my love,

Your affectionate aunt,

Madeline Gardiner

Elizabeth smiled as she folded the letter carefully and set it aside. It warmed her heart to think of Stoke bustling with life and laughter again, even if she sometimes missed the crumbling, creaking halls of Longbourn.

Her reverie was interrupted by the sudden thunder of boots down the hallway. She looked up just as Darcy, Wickham, and Colonel Fitzwilliam came flying into the room, all of them slightly disheveled, their faces unusually intense.

Elizabeth raised an eyebrow in mock alarm. "Well," she said archly, "should I be glad that you gentlemen left your childhoods behind at last?"

Darcy, coughing a little from exertion, crossed the room in three long strides and grasped her hand. "Dearest," he said, his voice low and urgent, "I need you to be sitting down for this news."

She blinked in confusion. "I *am* sitting," she pointed out dryly.

His lips did not even twitch at her jest, causing her to become genuinely concerned. She looked at his two companions to see if they would appreciate the situation, but Wickham and Fitzwilliam hovered just behind him, pale and tense.

Elizabeth's stomach tightened in sudden fear.

"Darcy, what has happened?" she asked anxiously.

He squeezed her hand. "It is all right—nothing is wrong. At least, not precisely. But we have been summoned." He drew a breath. "By the Prince Regent."

Her mouth fell open. "The Prince?" she gasped.

He nodded grimly. "A carriage is waiting. We are to go at once."

"But—but I cannot! I must change—I must—" She looked down helplessly at her simple blue gown, her hair only half-pinned for comfort.

"You look perfect," he said firmly. "There is no time."

The colonel muttered under his breath, "Probably for the best. If you looked any more beautiful, Darcy would end up fighting a duel with his Royal Highness, and I would hate to have to be his second... being tried for treason was not in my plans after catching Le Corbeau."

The absurdity of it made her laugh—a high, nervous sound—but it did help steady her nerves. They hurried out together to the waiting carriage, Elizabeth clenching Darcy's hand tightly as they rattled through the London streets.

They waited for what seemed an eternity in a grand antechamber at Carlton House, until at last, a liveried servant bowed them into a formal audience room. Elizabeth's heart hammered painfully as she sank into a low curtsy before the Prince Regent.

447

The corpulent, richly dressed prince regarded them with an expression of bored indulgence. "We have read the full account of your…adventures," he said, waving a jeweled hand languidly. "It appears England owes you a debt."

One by one, the Prince dispensed rewards with the carelessness of a man tossing coins into a crowd: Darcy was granted a knighthood. Colonel Fitzwilliam received twenty thousand pounds for his service. Wickham, who looked ready to swoon with disbelief, was awarded a modest estate in Derbyshire.

When he turned his gaze to Elizabeth, it was with a leer that made her skin crawl—until his eyes caught the slight swell of her belly. He grimaced as if he had bitten into a sour lemon.

"We understand," he said in a pained voice, "that your family's estate at Longbourn has been lost. Such tragedy must not go unrewarded. Therefore, we shall see the house rebuilt."

He looked her up and down, then added, "And as you, as a woman, are not capable of managing the estate, we will grant it to your father to be held free and clear. After his death, he may leave it to whomever he wishes."

Elizabeth curtsied again, biting her tongue at his dismissive mention of women's inability to manage property. It was a struggle not to retort, but she reminded herself of where she was—and that there were greater victories to savor today.

Before any of them could even open their mouths to express their gratitude, the Prince lifted his hand once again, waving it with an air of lazy dismissal.

"You are excused," he said.

Bowing and curtsying backward, careful never to turn their backs, they withdrew from the room in silence.

Did that just really happen? Elizabeth asked herself in amazement.

Only once they were safe in the entrance hall did Wickham exhale sharply and mutter, "Well. That was...unexpected."

"No one would believe it if we told them," the colonel added, his voice still faint with disbelief. "Somebody should pinch me."

Wickham reached over, causing the colonel to swat his hand away. "None of that, now. I will thank you to save your fingers for wooing ladies."

Darcy said nothing. He only reached for Elizabeth's hand once more and pressed it tightly to his heart. As they rode home in the carriage, silently processing everything that had just occurred, Elizabeth stared out the window. She took in all of the signs of rebuilding—the repaired streets, the rising scaffolds, the city stirring itself back to life.

So it is with us. With change comes growth. Fire brings devastation, but also renewal. And in the ashes, we find understanding.

She leaned against her husband with a sigh, feeling the steady beat of his heart against her ear. The chill air slipped through the carriage windows, but Elizabeth felt only warmth. The world beyond the carriage was still uncertain, still imperfect.

But she knew that in the end, they had found what mattered most: a love that burned brighter than any flame ever could.

And that was a reward worth more than anything the Prince could give them.

THE END

About the Author

Tiffany Thomas is a chocoholic former math teacher with Crohn's Disease and homeschooling mom of four kids. She and her husband Phillip (who is an engineer) work together on the blog Saving Talents. They enjoy spending time with their family, geeking out over sci-fi together, and saving money.

Tiffany discovered Pride & Prejudice as a teenager, and even made poor Phillip watch the six-hour version with her on their honeymoon when they got snowed in. After reading fan fiction for over a decade, she finally broke out into writing some herself, with the support of her husband.

You might also enjoy reading Tiffany's other works:

A Look Behind the Mask

The Sins of Their Fathers

When Summer Never Came

A Most Beloved Sister

Fine Eyes & Beastly Pride

A Dear, Sweet Girl

Pride, Prejudice, & Permutations

www.ingramcontent.com/pod-product-compliance
Lightning Source LLC
Chambersburg PA
CBHW072017020726
47501CB00006B/1850